MASQUERADE IN EGYPT

MASQUERADE IN EGYPT

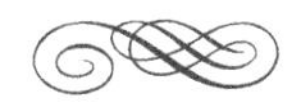

LUCY MONROE

Lucy Monroe LLC

Copyright

MASQUERADE IN EGYPT
by Lucy Monroe
1st Printing May 2023

ISBN 978-1-961214-00-2

Dedication

For Tom because no matter where my dreams take me, you are always there, cheering me on. You are my soulmate, my best friend, my dearest love. There is a part of you in every hero I write because you are the best man I know. After decades together you still give me joy each day just by being part of my life. Thank you! I love you. Happy Anniversary!

Note: For anyone not familiar with the layout of Egypt. Upper Egypt is in the South and Lower Egypt (including Cairo) is in the North. The upper and lower indications are in regard to topography not direction.

Contents

I

Los Angeles

Early September, 1923

"Let me in, Frankie!" *Pound. Pound. Pound.*

Frances Edwina Somers dropped the book she'd been reading by electric lamp in the front parlor. Rushing into the hall, she could not miss the increasingly loud demands for entrance.

What on earth had gotten into her brother?

The door shook with the vibration from his fist as she hurried to open it before her twin, Edwin Francis Clarke, discombobulated her lodger with his antics.

Good lodgers weren't so easy to come by.

"Frankie!" Muffled by the door, Edwin ' shout was still loud.

Frankie winced. Was her brother corked?

He liked his hooch as much as the next fella, but it wasn't like him to imbibe too deeply.

She swung the door wide, stepping back fast in case Edwin, in his agitation, was still trying to knock. She'd no interest in getting a facer for her troubles.

But Edwin dropped his hand to his side. "Oh, there you are."

"Here I am, brother mine. Are you blotto, or something? What is all the ruckus?"

"I haven't had a drop! It's Pater. He's gone around the bend." Edwin stepped inside, moving past Frankie only to spin around and face her. "Absolutely crackers."

Her brother's posture was tense, and his usually dapper hair a mess from fingers running through it. He wore no hat, despite having traveled from the family home in Beverly Hills, near Billionaire's Row. His eyes, the same dark brown as her own, were wild.

But Frankie would have known the level of Edwin' upset without seeing him in this state, simply by his use of the term *crackers*.

He was careful not to use anything that might refer to insanity or mental illness around Frankie. After spending six months in a sanitorium against her will, she was admittedly a smidge sensitive on that subject.

Frankie reached out and laid her hand on her brother's arm. "Calm down. I'm here for you, whatever you need."

"I knew I could rely on you, though honestly..." Edwin let his voice trail off. Then he just drooped, all the manic energy draining away like it had never been. "I don't know if anyone *can* help."

Her brother might enjoy acting, but he wasn't prone to drama in his personal life, and Frankie felt a frisson of worry go through her.

She shut the door and then tugged the sleeve of his grey worsted silk suit jacket. Imported from London, it had a looser fit than American suits. The four buttons of the jacket were usually closed, but Edwin' were open, revealing his waistcoat and the chain of his pocket watch.

This dishabille, especially outside the house, was so unlike him, Frankie felt another jolt of worry. "Come on. We can talk privately in my study."

Showing more restraint than she expected, considering his state, Edwin said nothing as she led him down the hall to the room near the kitchen she'd commandeered as her own private space since she started taking in lodgers. The tiny room was intended as a sewing room for the lady of the house.

Frankie gave a mental eyeroll. No thank you. She was a modern woman of the 1920s. Sewing was not how she chose to spend her evenings. She much preferred her studies and attending lectures.

Once in a while, she even put her glad rags on and went with her brother to a Speakeasy.

Frankie did not sew. And with the readymade clothes available through catalogues, that even a woman in her straightened circumstances could afford, Frankie did not have to.

She kept two bedrooms for lodgers in the bungalow she'd inherited from her husband upon his death in The Great War.

And the lodgers kept Frankie from having to sell the house, which meant a level of independence she would never relinquish again. Her job as a bookkeeper paid a low wage, but enough to maintain her frugal lifestyle otherwise.

Edwin plopped down onto the settee without any of his usual young-man-about-the-town airs.

"Would you like something to drink?" she asked.

"No noodle juice, but I'll take a tipple."

She didn't argue. From his behavior, she agreed he might need stronger fortification than tea.

Prohibition might reign, but Frankie was no more willing to teetotal than the next modern woman. She kept a small supply of rather good, bootlegged giggle water hidden in the sewing machine cabinet, where the machine would have gone.

She made her brother a cocktail and decided she might need bracing herself, for the coming discussion, so made a second one.

Edwin drank his down like water on a hot day.

"Hey, that hooch cost as much as last month's groceries," she chided him. "Slow down."

Edwin frowned. "I'm sorry, sis. I forget you live like a miser."

"Yes, well. You don't." Was that the problem? Edwin' attitude seemed extreme for having overspent his allowance again.

Unless. "Is father threatening to cut you off?"

Edwin had a job at their father's company, but the income was not sufficient for her twin's more lavish lifestyle. He was reliant on the monthly allowance their parent provided to keep his motorcar running and buying suits. While Frankie was content to get her clothes from a catalogue, Edwin special ordered from the fashion houses in London and Paris.

Father had offered her an allowance as well, after her husband John's death. If she sold her home and moved back to the family mansion.

Frankie had turned the old man down. And she hadn't been diplomatic about it. Which was no doubt why neither had ever broached the subject again.

She wasn't budging on moving back "home" and her father's dignity had been offended. He wouldn't offer her an allowance without an apology.

Something she was in no way offering him. Ever.

"Cut me off! Fire me *and* throw me out!" Edwin said in high dudgeon.

"He never." Father and Edwin didn't argue.

The only time the two men had in her memory, had been over her. She and her brother might have shared a womb, but her twin was charming where Frankie leaned toward bluntness. Her humor, such that it was, often got her into trouble when her plain speaking didn't.

According to her father, she was also too quiet on social occasions, a shortcoming she was too stubborn to overcome. He could be right about that one. Frankie was in no way shy. It wasn't that she found it *difficult* to talk to people, but that she did not *want* to talk to most of them.

Her friends in in the female adventurer's club, *Et Audaces in Mulieriebus*, were the exception, but then they did not bullishly try to order her life. Or question her intelligence simply by the dint of her being female, as so many of the male persuasion were wont to do.

"He did," Edwin assured Frankie. "They might as well measure me for a Chicago overcoat now."

"Stop trying to sound like a hoodlum. You're not going to need a coffin."

Edwin sighed, his head dropping forward so she could not see his expression, the picture of defeat. "He heard about the movie."

"I shouldn't think that would upset him enough to threaten such things."

Edwin had requested time away from work in order to make a

movie. Of course, he'd told their father and older brother he was taking the train to visit friends back East.

The friends were actually Hollywood film producers who specialized in avant-garde films, and the train was the Eastbound streetcar on Beverly Boulevard. It had dropped him in Tinseltown, not Allentown.

Even if their father had discovered the deception, why would that cause such a ruckus?

Yes, Father had made it clear no son of his was becoming an actor, most especially his *favorite* son, but this movie had been a lark. A one off, and not exactly a life changing role for her brother. Edwin had played a bit part in the film, mostly helping with production.

"I can't believe anyone even knew you were in it," she said to Edwin. "You barely got any screen time."

He had lamented about that often enough to her. She couldn't believe his kisser had been on screen long enough to be recognized. Especially with the exaggerated makeup actors wore for the silver screen.

"Someone saw it who recognized me all right and they told Pater."

"Surely, that didn't send him into such a tizzy he threatened to throw you out." None of this made any sense.

"You haven't seen the movie."

"You told me it wouldn't be in a theater around here."

"I lied."

"Apparently." Her brother didn't often lie to her and only ever to spare her. "Why?"

"I played myself, well not actually Edwin Francis Clark, but *me*."

"What does that mean?" she asked, afraid she knew, foreboding skating up her spine.

"A homosexual man."

Frankie was careful to keep her expression neutral. Concern could too easily be taken for condemnation. Worry for her brother's choice in exposing his true self to strangers didn't explain their father's reaction. "But Father knows you aren't attracted to women."

It wasn't spoken about at home, but Edwin had not hidden his lack of desire to find a suitable woman to marry when they were younger.

And one night during a family dinner when everyone but her was getting in on the matchmaking act, he'd told them all he intended to be a lifelong bachelor.

Since only the hopelessly unsophisticated wouldn't know what that meant, and no one could accuse her father of that, she knew George Clarke was well aware of where her brother's interests lay.

Even if it was never spoken about, the matchmaking had stopped. Their father had never treated Edwin any differently either.

It was one of the reasons Frankie still had an active relationship with the old man, after his refusal to help her when *she* needed it most.

"I kissed another man on screen," Edwin said with an air of defiance.

Frankie gasped. He could get arrested for that! "But you said you were barely on screen!"

"I was! I was a background actor in a Speakeasy scene."

"A Pansy Club?"

"No."

"But you kissed a man."

"Yes."

"All right," she said carefully. "And this upset father?"

"Upset is not the word. My world is ending." Edwin said the dramatic words with too much dispassion for Frankie to ignore how deeply he had to feel them. "He's said if I don't do as he says, he'll completely disown me."

Frankie drank her own cocktail in two gulps, the moonshine burning and making her eyes water. "What is he saying you have to do?" Was their father going to try to force Edwin into marriage?

She could not imagine it.

As much as she absolutely would not support such a plan, Frankie understood where it might come from though. Regardless how antiquated some of her father and older brother's beliefs were, none of them wanted to see Edwin in jail.

It might be 1923, but homosexual acts were still illegal, which was ridiculous, but in a country that outlawed drinking spirits and still allowed husbands legal sovereignty over their wives, what could one expect?

"You could be arrested for kissing another man on screen," she said a second time, in case he'd ignored the first go round. Frankie got up and mixed them both a second cocktail. "You're going to have the blue-haired brigade after you."

Edwin took his drink, sipping it this time. "I know, but it's not the Dark Ages anymore, Frankie. There are scads of openly homosexuals and bisexuals in Hollywood."

"Piffle. Some maybe, not scads."

"Anyway, I'm not going to have to go on the lam. Well, maybe from Pater."

Frankie wasn't nearly so confident. "You're the son of a business scion, not a Tinseltown star. I don't think it's as safe for you as them anyway."

Their father's business rivals could go after Edwin to get at the powerful mine owner, George Clarke. There were plenty of men in Los Angeles that would stoop that low to get their hands on shares in her father's many mines and other business concerns.

"You might be right." Edwin looked at her with wounded eyes. "But it's not fair."

"Neither was my husband having the right to have me locked up in an asylum because I didn't want sex after my miscarriage." She hadn't particularly enjoyed sex before losing the baby, but she'd hated being touched at all after. "We deal with the life we are given."

"Well, I'm not going to some bloody dig in Egypt to make father happy."

"He wants you to go on an archeological dig? In Egypt?" Frankie could barely get breath in her lungs at the very thought of such a thing. This was her brother's idea of his world *ending*?

Most of the artwork in her home were Frankie's own drawings of Egyptian hieroglyphs and antiquities she'd done as a result of her studies. Studies she'd had to sacrifice and fight for because of her gender and straightened circumstances.

Studies her brother had almost no interest in, except in relation to the Egyptomania that inspired popular clothing and home décor styles.

"How?" Archeological digs were planned at least a year in advance and the members of the team selected well before the digging season, which could start as early as the following month in Egypt.

This year's digs would be particularly difficult to get on, coming as they did after the most amazing find in a century of Egyptian archeology. The discovery of the tomb of the Pharaoh Tutankhamun.

"The company is a major underwriter on one of Pater's alma mater's sponsored expeditions. He's got the strings to pull and says he's going to tug them all right."

"But how is that a punishment?" Frankie asked, unable to stifle her jealousy at her brother's good fortune completely.

"*He* doesn't think it is." Edwin' tone left no doubt her twin considered it punishment all right. "Pater just thinks he's getting me away from temptation."

"To kiss on screen again?" She was confused.

"Something like that. And he thinks the whole thing will blow over before I get back."

So, Father wasn't a monster intent on rejecting his son. Good to know, though Frankie really hadn't thought that. Irrespective of his opinions on not interfering between a man and his wife, even when that wife was the man's own daughter.

"So?" she prompted. "If I had the opportunity to go on a dig, I'd jump with both feet."

"Yes, *you* would. You're the reason I asked Pater to get us a tutor in ancient histories."

"And you're the reason I begged for a drama instructor." Though now she regretted that just a bit.

Even at twenty-eight, her brother could still be impetuous.

"Because I enjoy acting."

"And you are good at it," she offered without hesitation despite the dangerous actions his love of acting had led him to.

"Thank you, but Frankie, I am not you. I don't consider a trip to the backwaters of the world adventure. I hated studying ancient histories and I'm not spending months wasting away in the hot desert sun."

"Stop being so dramatic. There are no cameras here to film your perfectly horrified expression." She wasn't being fair, she knew it.

Edwin really *was* horrified.

"I don't understand how we can be so alike and so different," he lamented.

He was right. Though their personalities and interests diverged greatly, they shared very similar physical features. They weren't identical twins, obviously, but looked enough alike no one ever doubted they were related.

Tall for a woman, Frankie's five-feet-seven-inches was only one shy of matching Edwin for height. The square jaw that looked so handsome on Edwin made for a rather plain woman, but Frankie didn't mind.

She wasn't seeking male attention. Not after the disaster of her marriage.

They shared the same red hair, even a similar build.

"Why are you looking at me like that?" Edwin put his now empty cocktail glass down on the small table beside the sofa.

Frankie drained hers. Thinking. What if? No, it was impossible. Wasn't it?

Could they possibly get away with it?

"You've got that look."

"What look?" she tried for innocence.

Edwin' expression said she'd failed. "That look, the one that says you're plotting."

"I'm not plotting." Was she?

"I came hoping you'd let me move in here if Pater kicks me out."

No use even asking their older brother Charles; his views aligned too closely with their father's. And Doris, their younger sister, still lived at the Clarke Mansion just as Edwin did. Without a job, Doris was reliant entirely on her monthly *hush money*, what she and her flapper friends called their allowance.

"Of course. I will always have room for you in my home." Even if it meant Frankie putting him on the Chesterfield in the front room, though that would not be necessary at the moment. "However, I may have a better solution."

Edwin sat up with an air of expectancy, color coming into his cheeks, hope lighting his eyes. "I knew you were plotting!"

"Remember when we were younger?"

"We're only twenty-eight, not exactly in our dotage yet, sister-mine."

"Yes, well, remember how I sometimes masqueraded as you so I could attend the lectures with our tutor?"

"We were teenagers then! You didn't have your women's bits."

"I can bind them now. Lots of women do."

"Our voices are different."

"Not so different I can't mimic yours," she said casting her tone lower.

Excitement began to glimmer in his brown gaze. "It would be easier now in some ways. Your hair is shorter and you don't have to try to hide it under a cap."

She didn't wear it in the straight, sleek bob her younger sister did, but Frankie's curls had been trimmed chin length. "I could cut it even shorter and wear it pomaded with a part down the middle."

Edwin grimaced. He preferred a dashing style, longer on the top of his head and parted to the side.

Frankie rolled her eyes. "Don't be vain. If I wore it just like you the differences in our appearance would be more noticeable for anyone checking passports."

"And what am I supposed to do while you are off in Egypt? Pretend to be you here? I'm pretty sure your lodger would peg the truth before strangers in another country would begin to suspect your masquerade."

"No, of course not. I'll come up with an excuse. Say I'm going on a trip. You can stay with friends, or something." Which, come to think of it, might not be the smartest thing for her brother to do right that minute.

He needed to be out of Los Angeles, maybe even out of America for a bit. Her father was right about that anyway.

"Can you afford to travel?" Edwin asked flippantly.

Frankie sat down in her own armchair with a plop, deflated that quickly. "No." Even if her father was paying for the trip to Egypt, she could not afford to take the time off her bookkeeping job for two months.

Going to Egypt might be the deepest, longest held dream of her heart, but it could not compare to her absolute need to retain control of her own life. And that meant keeping her job and maintaining her independent household.

Besides, while their father might have chosen the least likely destination to appeal to Edwin, the old man was right about one thing. Her brother did need to get out of Los Angeles until the potential scandal blew over.

It wasn't just sad wives, grieving the loss of the baby they hadn't thought they wanted, who could get locked up in the Looney Bin.

2

"Frankie, Father would be paying. I was being a Smart Alec."

"I know, but you know I can't take the time off of work."

"I could pay your wages for two months."

Hope tried to unfurl in her chest. She tamped it down. "I would lose my job."

"Get another job."

"I like my job. I don't have to talk to annoying people."

"This is your dream, Frances Edwina Somers. Are you going to give it up for a *bookkeeping* job?" he demanded.

"How did we go from the end of your world to me having a new one?" she asked, trying to ignore the hope and pure longing coursing through her.

"It was your idea."

"But it's not practical."

"Isn't it?"

"You really think I could do it?" she asked, already knowing the answer.

Her ability to imitate her brother was not in question. Just as her brother had gotten top marks in ancient history despite not liking it, Frankie had done very well in drama as well.

For a woman who despised deceit and was really awfully bad at telling lies, she excelled at playing a part.

"Yes."

"But you'll be seen. Someone you know will see you wherever you are staying and tell father or Charles."

"Chuck isn't as much of an old stick as you think he is, but it doesn't matter. I'll be in Berlin."

"Berlin? What? Why?"

"My friends that made the movie that's got Pater in an uproar are hot for the film scene in Berlin." Edwin's voice now rang with excitement. "They're making groundbreaking stuff over there."

"I thought they were still recovering from the war."

"What does that have to do with making movies?"

"Nothing?"

"Right."

"So, you want to go to Germany."

"Not all of it. I'm not interested in sightseeing. I want to go to Berlin and make a movie that matters."

"Another movie where you' kiss a man onscreen?" she asked, not sure if she was appalled or in awe of her brother's courage.

"Another movie that doesn't ignore the existence of homosexuality. If it will put your mind at rest, I've discovered I like it behind the camera rather than in front of it more."

"You do?" That surprised her.

"Yes." He nodded, looking just a little loopy.

The moonshine wasn't bad hooch, but it packed a punch.

She stood up, feeling a bit woozy herself. "Come on. You can have the second spare room. No lodger in there right now. If this idea still seems sane in the morning, we'll work out the mechanics of it."

Even zozzled, Frankie found it difficult to fall asleep.

To be able to work on a dig in Egypt. For crying out loud! It was a dream so fantastic, she'd never even dreamed it. A possibility absolutely outside the realm of reality.

Frankie had been fascinated by ancient history since she was school aged, and her most passionate love, like so many others, was Egypt.

There were women on digs, though not very many, and they were almost always married to one of the men on the archeological team.

There was Gertrude Bell of course, but for a young widow like Frankie to get approved as a member of an archeological team?

What were the chances?

Nil, and she knew it.

She knew she and Edwin were different, but for him to not *want* to go, to see the time spent on an Egyptian archeological dig as a *punishment*. That boggled Frankie's mind.

Could she really be thinking about seizing the opportunity herself though?

Was it worth giving up her job and risking her reputation to pretend to be her brother?

Applesauce! Had her life changed her so much she was even asking that question?

Absolutely, pos-i-lutely, it was worth it!

"You're going to do it?" Edwin sat at the small kitchen table, nursing his cup of Joe, the eggs on his plate untouched.

Frankie had eaten already and was dressed for work. "I am." She could barely believe her own temerity, but she wasn't a member of *Et Audaces in Mulieriebus* for nothing.

"You won't regret this, Frankie. I know you won't."

"As long as we're not found out, I won't."

"No chance of that. I'll be in Berlin. You'll be in Egypt."

On her own. In Africa. Pretending to be her brother. The idea was enough to make her feel zozzled all over again.

Edwin drained the last of his coffee. "So, I'll see you at the house for dinner Sunday night."

"What? I wasn't coming for dinner." She attended the Sunday family dinner once a month, less if she could help it.

She had just been two weeks past and wasn't expected again until the middle of next month.

"Um. I was supposed to tell you about it yesterday." Edwin had the grace to look abashed.

"You mean when you came over without a hat and looking like your world was ending?" she razzed him.

"I wondered why I couldn't find my hat. I wasn't wearing one?"

She shook her head in the negative. "I think we should be grateful you didn't crash your motorcar on the way over."

"I very nearly did."

Her heart contracted. Edwin took entirely too many risks behind the wheel of his Duesenberg. "Well, you won't be crashing when you take me to work."

"Why am I taking you to work?"

"Because it's on the way to your own place of employment and will save me taking the streetcar."

"You like riding the streetcar. It infuriates Pater."

There was that. She didn't bother denying that her father's annoyance at the idea of his daughter riding public transportation wasn't one of the reasons she did it, but the other was that Frankie simply could not afford to buy, much less keep up a motorcar.

She could have bought a Ford on credit like so many people were doing now. But Frankie did nothing that could put her at the mercy of someone else. Not even a loan that could be called in early.

Others might say that wasn't possible so long as she made her payments on time, but she'd seen the ruthlessness of businessmen her whole life. She knew better. She also knew there was no way to guarantee those payments would always be made on time.

Unexpected things happened in life, and she refused to be at the whim of them. So, she was saving for her own Model T and wouldn't buy it until she had enough to do so outright, as well as enough set aside to cover repair expenses as they came up.

Which they inevitably did. Even on an automobile as nice as Edwin's.

"Well, today you are driving me to work, brother-mine."

"Happy to sis, happy to. And I assume by me driving you, you actually mean you driving my Duesy until we reach your place of employment."

"Naturally."

Frankie closed the front door on the last member of *Et Audaces in Mulieriebus* and locked it for good measure.

While the secret women's adventure club was hardly illegal, membership could get some of the ladies present in trouble with their families and/or places of employment if they were found out.

She and a group of friends had formed the club of lady adventurers when they were all in finishing school. They now had small clandestine chapters in three cities, as they had all recruited others from their own localities after returning to their respective homes.

The original five kept in touch by letters, though some actually lived in the same cities, like her and Winnie.

"Where is your boarder tonight?" Winnie asked, picking up a plate of sandwiches before sitting down beside one of their younger members who was planning a journey to South America.

Her father was a surveyor and often took his family with him when traveling to distant locales.

Lucky young woman.

Frankie's father had sent her to Finishing School in Europe because it was the thing to do. Rather an old stick when it came to modern ideas, he had categorically refused to allow her to travel even as far as Mexico when she had been a teen, though Edwin had made the sojourn across the border several times with friends.

Since becoming a widow, Frankie had traveled to Mexico twice. Her father was unaware of both trips. Just as he had no idea that Frankie could shoot a pistol with supreme accuracy.

There had been a time Frankie had trusted her father with her confidences, but now she lived an entire life that he knew nothing about.

Frankie got her own plate of sandwiches, though she was so excited she wasn't sure she'd be able to eat and sat in the armchair closest to Winnie. "My boarder has a dinner with her beau tonight."

Frankie and Winnie become fast friends after learning how close their names were their first week together of Finishing School. Frances Edwina Clarke, who had been called Winnie by her own mother, and no one else, and Winnifred Clark (no e), called Winnie by all.

It was Winnie who had first called Frances, *Frankie*. Their band of friends had quickly followed suit.

Frankie liked the nickname so well that she used it with everyone. Well, everyone but her father and older brother who insisted on continuing to refer to her as Frances.

"Will you be needing a replacement boarder?" Dr. Julia Parton asked from where she leaned on the fireplace, her bob slicked close to her head, her trouser suit on the edge of acceptable fashion.

"As to that, I already do," Frankie lamented. "My second bedroom has been empty for two weeks already."

"You cannot rent to just anyone." Winnie sighed, looking wistful. "I wish I could take the spare room."

Winnie's meager income from her salesclerk position at a downtown department store went to helping her family without enough left over to sustain her living in even a rented room.

"One day, maybe." Frankie patted her friend's arm consolingly.

Julia sighed. "My landlady has taken into her head to start matchmaking."

"Are you looking for new rooms?" Frankie asked hopefully.

Having another member of the society living in her home would make the monthly meetings that much easier to organize.

"I am, but I'm used to having my own sitting room."

Frankie bit her lip in thought. While the bedrooms in her bungalow were not pokey, none of them boasted an attached sitting room, much less an *en suite*. Everyone in the house shared the single bathroom. Julia's current rooms were in a house nearly the size of the Clarke Mansion and had both.

"I suppose I should buy my own house," Julia lamented.

Left unsaid was the truth that while a male doctor would have no trouble doing so, a female doctor's income was nowhere equivalent. Nor would every bank provide a mortgage to a woman without a male signatory.

Julia would never stand for having a male relation have legal claim to her hard-earned property.

"How soon will your current boarder be taking up residence

elsewhere?" Julia asked, her disdain for the institution of marriage a long standing opinion of which they were all familiar.

"Three months."

"Would you allow me to take over the rent of that room as well and turn it into my private sitting room?"

Julia's question filled Frankie with hope, but she hesitated to answer. What would happen if Julia moved out? Then Frankie would be looking for two boarders at the same time.

"I will give you two month's notice, or rent in lieu of once I am able to purchase my own home."

"Oh, Frankie, say yes! It would be just ducky," Winnie said with enthusiasm. "Julia will be able to save the money to buy her own home faster if she's renting here, and you'll have someone from *Et Audaces in Mulieriebus* sharing your space."

"And how," Frankie agreed. She smiled warmly at Julia. "That would be swell. When do you want to move in?"

"Next week?"

That could work really well for Frankie on more than one level.

The group engaged in idle chatter for a while longer, until it came time to sharing their plans for adventure. Some had far more thrilling adventures planned and experiences to discuss than others, but even living vicariously was bee's knees compared to not experiencing any sort of adventure at all.

When Frankie's turn came, she brought up the renewed excavating planned for the newly discovered tomb of the Pharaoh Tutankhamun.

"It's so thrilling," one of their quieter members said, her eyes lit with a fire Frankie understood well. "To be able to go on a dig like that."

"As to that, I might actually have the opportunity." Frankie's announcement was met with shocked exclamations and flat out disbelief.

"It would require me pretending to be Edwin for the full two months." Saying it out loud to someone besides her brother brought home how ridiculous the idea was.

How had she convinced herself otherwise?

"You could do it, I'm sure of it," Winnie said immediately and without the slightest doubt in her tone.

Julia rubbed her chin, her expression thoughtful. "You are a terrible liar, and you do not enjoy acting, I know."

"You're right," Frankie agreed glumly.

Winnie opened her mouth, her expression saying clearly she intended to hotly dispute both Julia's honest assessment and Frankie's agreement with it.

Julia raised her hand, as if to forestall Winne's words. "Hear me out." She fixed her pragmatic doctor's gaze on Frankie. "However, I think Winnie is correct. Because as much as you may not be the passionate thespian your brother is, you *are* very good at it. When you are playing a role, you embody it entirely. You don't stumble over your words, or blush like a schoolgirl like you do when you tell a fib."

There was something to be said for having two of her oldest friends being part of the *Et Audaces in Mulieriebus*. Frankie had met Winnie at Finishing School, but she'd known Julia since they were both small girls. Julia had gone to university and then medical school rather than finishing school, but they had remained close in adulthood. And the other woman had been keen to join the women's adventurer society.

Not one member of the society believed it was a problem for Frankie to take Edwin's place. Several made comments like, "I would do it if I had the chance."

Winnie was most vocal of all, telling Frankie she couldn't give up this one chance she had to follow her passions. "Imagine, you on a dig. You've got more education about Ancient Egypt than most male university graduates," she said stalwartly.

"And the experience would be lost entirely on Edwin," Julia said, without the least rancor toward Frankie's twin. "If he was filming the experience, it might be different."

Frankie couldn't argue. "He thinks it's a punishment."

"Travel! A punishment!" Winnie shook her head. "I would give almost anything for the chance to travel again."

And that was how Frankie decided that she had to at least try. She owed it to her fellow adventurers. Winnie might never get to travel because of life's circumstances, but Frankie could bring back stories to share.

She could live her own life as an adventurer.

In this instance at least, she could throw the blanket of fear off that kept her life so boxed in and small.

Frankie dressed carefully for the family dinner that evening. Her dark blue silk charmeuse was from last year's catalogue, but still stylish. She tied the belt around her hips, giving it the popular drop waisted look. The handkerchief hemline stopped daringly above her ankles.

Despite the raised hemline, it was perfectly modest, even with her new corset (a gift from Edwin) that had no boning.

She hadn't seen anything like the undergarment in her catalogues, but he'd gotten it from one his favorite Parisian design houses. Embroidery in a darker shade of blue leant the quarter length sleeved dress and air of elegance her father would approve of.

While Frankie did not particularly care for their father's regard, not like Edwin, she was careful to cultivate an air of respectability George Clarke could not question.

Yes, she had her little rebellions, but nothing anyone could ever point to again and say, "Look, that poor woman needs to be in a sanatorium for her own good."

Most especially not her father.

Now that her husband was dead, Frankie's father was the only man who posed a real threat to her continued freedom, simply by the dint of being her father and a very wealthy, powerful man.

She pulled on black stockings, rolling them over her garters just below her knees in silent, hidden defiance of the modest mores of the day.

Her black pumps had three straps across the top and boasted a French heel. They were also from the previous year's catalogue and Frankie planned on them lasting for several years to come.

She wore no jewelry, having taken her wedding ring off long ago with no intention of ever putting it back on and not inclined to the multistrands of pearls or stacks of bracelets up one arm that were so popular. Even if that popularity was born of an attempt to emulate Ancient Egyptian styles.

The stacked bracelets always felt too clunky to her, though her younger sister wore them with perfect elan.

Frankie appraised her image in the mirror and critically considered whether she needed earrings, but decided not. She wasn't going to a Speakeasy, but dinner at her father's mansion.

A much more reserved affair.

And if she didn't hurry, she was going to miss her streetcar.

Clutching her handbag lightly and wishing she'd taken Edwin up on his offer of a lift, Frankie rushed down the sidewalk toward her father's home in Beverly Hills.

Frankie's forward momentum was abruptly halted by a wall that hadn't been there the last time she visited her father.

"Oof." The wall spoke and shifted just a little.

Frankie's head jerked up and she found herself staring at the back of a vaguely familiar masculine head, though she could not have said where she'd seen it before.

Being five-foot-seven inches when the average height for a woman was five-foot-two, Frankie didn't look up to a lot of men, but this man was definitely taller than her. The gentleman with light brown hair and wearing an evening suit, was easily six feet.

He turned around, revealing grey eyes under furrowed brown brows, intensifying her sense of familiarity but she still could not think from where.

"I ran into you," Frankie said, finding that circumstance a little difficult to believe, and so stating the obvious.

"You did."

His blunt agreement startled Frankie. He was dressed like a gentleman, standing in front of her father's house. But he made none of the superficial attempts to politely save her feelings she expected.

"I am sorry," she offered.

He inclined his head. "I suppose you were in a hurry."

"I am expected for dinner," she agreed.

"Then, I will not keep you." The man stepped back, so she could pass.

Had he neglected to introduce himself because he was old fashioned and considered a self-introduction gauche, or had he simply not wanted to?

The fact she was even wondering nearly startled Frankie into immobility again. But she *was* late and she had no time to stop and ponder what even such a passing interest in the male of the species might mean.

3

"It appears we are going to the same place." That now familiar deep voice stated as Frankie stepped through the wrought iron gate for personal entry beside the main gate used to keep out unwanted vehicles.

Frankie stopped and spun around. "But you're not driving a car."

"Is that required?" he asked with remote curiosity. "I rode the streetcar."

Like her, but he hadn't been on her car. She would have noticed him. And that truth was unsettling.

"The closest stop is blocks away," she pointed out. "Wealthy men don't *ankle* that far in their dinner suits." And any man dressed for dinner with her father wasn't going to be poor.

Was he? No. The suit was well tailored and of good quality wool, his bowtie done with perfect symmetry, his shoes shiny, his dark overcoat distinctly not from a catalogue.

"And yet here, I stand." The expression in his eyes said he found her observation humorous, but there was no evidence of that humor on the rest of his features.

He hadn't denied being wealthy either, but he didn't have the usual air of arrogance men like her father and older brother had perfected.

"I do seem to be making a habit of stating the obvious," Frankie offered with self-deprecating humor.

There was a barely there tilt to his lips, gone almost as quickly as it arrived. "It is often in ignoring the obvious we are caught unprepared."

Silently agreeing, Frankie put out her hand. "Frances Somers, daughter of George Clarke."

Something came over the professor's features at the mention of her father's name and it wasn't sweetness and light. Now that she thought of it, she'd run into him because he had been standing and looking at her father's house, not moving forward to be in time for dinner.

Not in a hurry to eat with a powerful, wealthy man?

That intrigued Frankie in a way she had no intention of admitting to.

"Dr. Henry Thomas." He shook her hand with formal, but perfunctory politeness.

Again, he didn't offer the polite banalities she was used to. No, *pleasure to meet you.*

Frankie liked the bluntness. She found most people hid behind a surface veneer of manners that did little to reveal their true natures.

And it was the true nature that interested her. She didn't trust people. Not anymore. And she particularly didn't trust the polite gentleman, not after being married to one, who was a very different man than what he presented to the world.

Though he would never have said so. John had considered himself the epitome of modern man.

Frankie held a very different view of the man she'd married.

Shaking off the memories, she realized suddenly why the man in front of her looked familiar.

"You spoke about your dig in Egypt last summer at the Ladies Aid Society." Frankie maintained her membership for reasons that had nothing to do with social climbing.

"I did."

But he'd had a beard then and had dressed in brown tweed, looking very much like a rather rumpled professor.

"It was a fascinating talk."

"And yet, you asked no questions."

The implication he would have remembered her doing so wasn't lost on Frankie. She liked knowing he thought she was memorable right up until the moment it occurred to her why he was here.

"You're the head archeologist on the dig my father wants my brother to join next month." She tried very hard to keep the horror from her voice.

Her masquerade as Edwin hinged on the people she would be working with being unfamiliar with both of them. Sharing dinner with this man could very well scupper any hopes they had of pulling off the switch.

"I am." He didn't look a lot older than her, maybe a few years, but Dr. Henry Thomas had a stuffy air that he managed to imbue even into his short answers.

He didn't use a bit of modern vernacular.

"Shall we finish our walk up the drive together?" she asked, her brain spinning with thoughts of how to fix this awful happenstance.

Could she fake a headache and cry off dinner?

"If you like, Ms. Somers."

Irrespective of her inner panic, Frankie liked he hadn't automatically called her Mrs., despite her having a different last name to her father. Though it was the proper form of address for her, Frankie preferred Ms. She was no longer John Somers wife and didn't plan to be anyone's *Mrs.* Ever again.

Frankie wasn't surprised when Dr. Thomas did not put his arm out for her to take, but was unpleasantly shocked by her own disappointment.

They walked side by side toward the mansion she had called home once upon a time.

The three-story brick exterior was impressive without being overly ostentatious. She would give her father that. He knew how to display his wealth without tipping over into the vulgar.

He'd purchased the house for her mother when Frankie was a wee girl. Although her mother had never fully recovered from childbed after giving birth to her and Edwin, Frankie had wonderful memories of her childhood while the loving, gentle woman lived.

Mother had become even more fragile after giving birth to Doris and been taken by the influenza only a few years later. Even after her death,

Frankie's childhood had been a good one. Her father might have been a business tycoon, but he'd always shown affection for his four children.

No matter how many happy memories the house had for her, Frankie would never willingly live there again.

As soon as they were ushered inside by the butler, Frankie excused herself and went in hurried search of her brother, hoping against hope that Edwin was not already in the drawing room for pre-dinner drinks.

Not of the alcoholic variety.

Her father never served illegal spirits at family gatherings, even though all his children were adults. No, he made the pretense of following the law, though she doubted very much he did so when his children were not there to see.

Frankie blew out an air of relief when she caught her brother coming down the stairs. "Edwin, we have to talk."

"Now? You know Pater doesn't like it when we're late for dinner."

"The gong hasn't gone yet. Come on." Frankie grabbed Edwin's arm and unceremoniously dragged him into a private nook they'd been using since childhood.

"What's the matter? You're not having second thoughts, are you?"

"Second and third thoughts, but that's not the worst of it."

"Are you going to tell me what is?" Edwin asked with some impatience.

Frankie glared up at him. "He's here."

"Who is here? Pater? Of course he is."

"No. Dr. Henry Thomas. The head archeologist on your dig."

"Don't you mean your dig?" Edwin teased.

"Not if he gets to know us both so well he'll be able to tell I'm not you when I show up in Egypt." She had another horrifying thought. "What if he expects to travel together?"

"You just take on the guise of being me that much sooner. Calm down, Frankie. Our tutor knew us for two years and never once did he cotton on when you dressed as me to attend a lecture with him."

"But that was more than ten years ago."

"What difference does it make? We still share the same jaw line, hair color, eye color. Darken your brows a bit and you'll look exactly like me. As you pointed out, your feminine bits aren't that imposing."

"What about mannerisms?"

Her brother rolled his eyes. "You know mine well enough to emulate them. You're a good actor, Frankie, even if you have no interest in pursuing it."

"Father would send me right back to the sanitorium if I did."

"No." Edwin's entire countenance changed to something far more serious. "Pater would never do that to you."

"Wouldn't he?" He'd certainly left her trapped in the one John had put her in.

"Of course not. He didn't want to interfere in your marriage but that's not the same thing as being willing to do the same thing."

"Says you. I'm not convinced."

Edwin's sigh was sad, but Frankie ignored it. He and their father were close. Always had been. He could never understand how Father's refusal to help her so completely obliterated Frankie's ability to trust.

But then she'd never shared all that she'd endured while in the sanitorium. She never would. Her past was her own.

Frankie had reason to respect her brother's acting abilities as dinner wore on. Rather than acting like himself, he took on a more serious mien, one he knew Frankie would find more natural to maintain for her two-month masquerade.

It wasn't just her brother that sparked increased admiration in Frankie as the dinner progressed either. Dr. Henry Thomas had an air of competency about him she found intriguing because it wasn't coupled with her father's arrogance, or her eldest brother's certainty he knew best.

Dr. Thomas was an expert in Ancient Egypt and had been in charge of his university's dig for the past three years, but had been doing field work in Egypt since his teens. He'd taken time off to serve in the war, but refused to talk about that time in his life.

Doris, Frankie's younger sister, who shared all of her curiosity and none of her hard-earned reticence, had asked.

There could be no question Dr. Thomas had full confidence in his own abilities as a historian and archeologist. However, he left the discussion of business to her father and brothers, not even attempting to pretend an interest.

Frankie was mesmerized by such an attitude. Even Edwin did a fair job of playing serious businessman for the sake of their father and brother's approval.

"You must enjoy travel," Doris said to Dr. Thomas, her brown eyes lit with excitement. "Going to Egypt every year is the bee's knees."

The professor frowned. "I do not think it is a matter of enjoying travel, but rather that travel is necessary to pursue my life's work."

"Oh, but surely the journey by steamer across the Atlantic is thrilling." Doris looked dreamy for a moment. "I remember my one and only trip to Europe for finishing school. I loved every bit of it. The train ride across country. The luxury liner to England."

Frankie remembered the same journey of her naïve eighteen-year-old self with fondness.

"Maybe not the airplane ride to Paris." Doris wrinkled her pert nose, in a face so like their beautiful mother's it sometimes made Frankie ache with memories.

Unlike Frankie, Doris had blond hair like their mother as well and the same pixie face and diminutive stature so approved of by men. Frankie's younger sister was a *bright young thing*, who dressed like a flapper and teased their father with her *outrageous* views.

Also, unlike Frankie, she had *not* married right out of Finishing School.

"I spend both the train ride and the ocean crossing in my studies," Dr. Thomas answered repressively.

"Oh." Doris looked quite taken aback.

Frankie gave her sister a reassuring smile, though privately impressed by how unaffected the archeologist was by the charms of a *bright young thing*. "I'm sure Dr. Thomas reserves his enthusiasm for his work in Egypt."

"As he should. As he should," their father butted in. "I wouldn't like to think I had donated so much money to my alma mater for a dig the head archeologist took lightly."

The warning in her father's tone sent Frankie's instincts on alert. Was the professor being strong armed into accepting her brother's presence on the dig?

"That's hardly going to be the case, Father," Frankie offered. "Dr. Thomas is the preeminent expert on Ancient Egypt at the university, but is also well respected in academic circles."

His reputation locally rivaled his counterpart at Harvard, but because his university was smaller and lesser known, he was less well known nationally and internationally. Somehow, she doubted that mattered much to the professor.

"How would you know that?" George Clarke demanded, his tone arrogant and combative as it so often was with her since she refused to move home.

"I read, father. The same as everyone else."

"But not the same things, I'll wager. You've got yourself hidden away in that dinky house, doing nothing but reading musty old tomes and drawing."

Naturally, he did not mention the job he would much prefer she did not keep. And the house that he'd praised to John as a wonderful starter home was now considered dinky. Typical.

"Both perfectly acceptable pastimes for a lady," her sister defended Frankie.

Frankie smiled her gratitude to Doris, but shook her head slightly. She didn't want her younger sister, or anyone else, getting on the wrong side of their father on Frankie's behalf.

"Well, it's past time you stopped moldering away, Frances." Father set his gimlet gaze on Frankie.

"You know I prefer Frankie."

"That's a boy's name," the Clarke patriarch harrumphed.

Doris made a scoffing sound and rolled her eyes at Frankie.

"That will be enough out of you, missy." But the look their father gave her younger sister was indulgent rather than angry.

Doris looked too much like his beloved dead wife to ever be the recipient of Father's wrath in any true sense. Or so Frankie hoped.

Not that Father had ever been genuinely furious toward her either, but she doubted very much he would have left her sister trapped in a sanitorium on the flimsy say so of her husband.

"It is funny you should bring that up." Frankie managed to keep a straight countenance telling that fib, as if one thing could be counted on it would be her father lamenting her living in her dinky house and moldering away.

Though he never suggested she come home to live, the implication was always there.

Not going to happen.

"I thought I might take a journey," she said now. "Spend some time in a new location for a couple of months."

Frankie thought keeping as close to the truth as possible the smartest tactic if she had any hope of pulling off this subterfuge with her brother. So, she didn't embellish, or prevaricate about a visit with friends.

Everyone at the table, except their dinner guest, showed some sign of shock at that announcement. Edwin's startlement was wholly believable, showcasing his stellar acting skills.

"Well, that's fine to hear," Father said robustly. "Fine to hear, indeed. You have grieved John's death long enough."

Frankie's mouth opened, then shut with a snap. She had grieved the loss of John's life for the sake of those who loved him, but not herself.

Their marriage had not been what she had expected, but the death knell on any feelings she had for him had fallen when he had her put in the sanitorium.

Silence reigned at the table for a long minute. Frankie refused to respond to her father's comment. Him pretending that she had been grieving her dead husband wasn't doing their relationship any favors.

But then if he cared about being close to his older daughter, he would not have ignored her pleas for help.

In her mind, George Clarke's refusal to act made him complicit with John Somers leaving his wife helplessly imprisoned in the sanitorium, forced to take pharmaceuticals that left her feeling disconnected from reality and unable to even track the days as they passed.

Frankie very purposefully pushed away, uglier, darker memories from that time.

"Yes, well, I believe the plans I have made will be welcome."

Foreboding made Frankie's shoulders tense.

"Your plans to send Edwin to Egypt?" she asked, knowing it could not be that simple.

"I decided to take advantage of his time in Egypt to provide you and your sister with a tour of Europe. He will accompany you both to England, and go on to Africa after seeing you safely in the care of my cousin."

More like second cousin, twice removed, or something like that. Father liked to hark on his family ties in England, but they were remote.

"I did say I had plans of my own," Frankie said mildly.

Well, mildly for the fury coursing through her. Here was Father trying to dictate her life again and she wasn't the young ingenue that trusted him to do that for her any longer.

But they had a dinner guest and Frankie wasn't showing her anger in front of a stranger. No doubt her father was banking on that. He'd had these plans in mind all along and that was why she'd been invited to this command performance dinner.

"I am sure you can postpone your plans for the opportunity of a tour of Europe."

If she were going in order to take in the reopened museums and intellectual culture after the war, Frankie might have agreed. But she was no fool.

This was a husband finding mission and their "cousin" would have strict instructions to introduce Frankie and Doris to eligible men. Though why her father thought their chances were better in Europe, when they had tragically lost millions to the Great War and millions more to the Spanish Flu.

The United States had suffered less than a million deaths combined. Enough for great grief to wash over their nation, but there could be no question that the pool of eligible bachelors was bigger here than abroad.

Not that she was interested in either.

Frankie frowned at her father. "Perhaps, I do not wish to change my plans."

"And disappoint your sister?"

Frankie looked at Doris and sure enough her expression was a cross between sheer joy and trepidation.

"Why would me going have any impact on Doris going?"

Before her father got a chance to answer, Frankie felt a sharp pain in her ankle. She jerked, but kept her countenance.

Her gaze shifted to Edwin even as their father blustered on about her keeping an eye on Doris for his good conscience, or something like that.

Edwin made an infinitesimal shake of his head.

Frankie's brows drew together. He wanted her to accept their father's *largesse*?

Sure enough, Edwin tilted his head toward their father, like encouraging Frankie to listen to him.

"We can discuss this later," Frankie offered, as far as she was willing to go toward acquiescence.

The rest of dinner was uneventful. Her father quizzed Dr. Thomas on his plans for the dig, showing how widely read he was even if he wasn't as approving of Frankie's self-education.

As the evening went on, Frankie found it difficult not to ask all the questions she wanted to of the archeologist. However, she could not ignore the prospect that the more interaction they had, the harder it would be for her to convince him that she was Edwin when she got to Egypt.

She was storing all her questions for then.

She wanted to corner Edwin for a private talk after dinner, but their father suggested that Edwin give both her and Dr. Thomas a lift home in his motorcar.

4

Frankie felt like screaming with frustration when Edwin slid into the back with a jaunty salute. "My sister prefers to drive."

To his credit, Dr. Thomas said nothing in response to that, simply taking his place in the front seat.

"You don't mind a woman driver?" she asked him as the roadster's engine roared to life.

"Not if you're competent and I have no reason to believe you will be any less so than your brother."

"That's a refreshing attitude," Frankie couldn't help saying as she expertly shifted gears and took the corner at the end of her father's street onto the main thoroughfare of Beverly Boulevard.

"Is it?"

"I'd say. Father won't ride if Frankie is driving," Edwin piped from the cheap seats.

"Does your father object to your driving? It seems perfectly acceptable to me."

Stuffy. Definitely stuffy. Why was Franking finding that charming rather than annoying?

She didn't find men charming. She tried not to find them anything at all. The whole sexual freedom the flappers spoke about with such savoir faire at the Speakeasy was lost on Frankie. Risking pregnancy, and thereby her prized freedom, for the minimal pleasure sex offered seemed rather silly to her.

But then she'd experienced a side to married life women rarely spoke about. The very real problem of having another human being with legal rights over her and able to dictate her medical care.

Even with the vote, and the other freedoms women enjoyed now the War to End All Wars was over, a woman's husband had rights over her that were not at all reciprocated.

"Oh, Frankie is a much better driver than I am, but Father's a dear old stick." Edwin's more serious character was slipping and his own way of speaking and seeing the world was slipping through. Frankie frowned as she slowed to get past a bicycle.

"See, that right there? I don't slow for bicycles. Frankie always does."

"I've never caused someone to fall off their bike either," Frankie reminded her brother repressively.

"I've never caused major damage either."

She wanted to say, "Not the same thing." But just focused on her driving.

"I do not think that is quite the same thing," Dr. Thomas said.

Edwin just laughed, not surprising Frankie at all. Last night had been an anomaly. Her brother's sunny nature was up to most things life had to offer.

"Do you want to go on the dig?" Dr. Thomas asked.

Panic washed over Frankie. Was he talking to her?

She just managed to stop herself answering from her subconscious with a resounding *yes* as logic prevailed.

Of course, the professor was talking to Edwin.

"What makes you ask that, Dr. Thomas?" her brother asked instead of answering.

"You have asked very little about the dig, or what you might expect there."

"Naturally, I am curious, but I felt you were being sufficiently quizzed at dinner."

"This is all very sudden," the older man said, not sounding happy about that at all.

"It is rather, but when father gets a bee in his bonnet, the rest of us buzz."

"And this bee? What is it?"

"That I should use the education given me."

"You studied ancient history at university?"

"As to that, I did take a course or two." So he could pass the materials on to Frankie, who was married before he finished studying for his bachelors.

Edwin had always been the best of brothers.

"And these random classes are the ones your father does not want you to waste?" Dr. Thomas did not sound convinced.

"He also employed an ancient history tutor for two years."

"I see. Do you have any concept of life on a dig?"

"As to that, no. But I don't imagine you did the first time you went on one either."

"My father was an amateur archeologist. Once I was old enough to travel, he took my mother and I on his excavations every year before we lost him."

"I am sorry for your loss," Frankie and Edwin said together, both with as much sincerity as politeness. They understood the loss of a parent.

"Do you do that often?"

"Speak at the same time?" they asked together and then laughed.

Dr. Thomas didn't join in their merriment. "Yes."

"Sometimes." The only reason they didn't speak at the same time again was because Frankie bit her lip to stop blurting her first thought.

She and Edwin could get into a cycle that was hard to break out of and as amusing as it could be on occasion, it could also be equally frustrating.

"You wanted to say the same thing," Dr. Thomas opined.

Frankie nodded. "How did you know?"

"I saw you literally swallow the word."

"Yes, well, it can become a near unbreakable pattern."

"I see."

Did he? Frankie wasn't sure she understood herself how close she and Edwin were considering they were not identical twins.

Dr. Thomas subsided into silence, but Frankie realized her brother needed to be asking him questions.

"I'm sure Edwin would appreciate any insights on gear and the like he should make sure to have for his time in the Egyptian desert."

"Serviceable clothing of course. You'll want your own trowel and brush." Dr. Thomas continued more volubly than he had been all evening, listing everything from oils to keep the bugs away to headache powders.

Frankie took mental note of everything he said.

"I assume your French is more than passable?" he asked Edwin when he was finished listing everything the other man should pack for the dig.

"I thought Egypt was under English rule?" Edwin asked.

"Technically, the country is sovereign to itself, since the revolution, but is de facto still run like a British colony in many ways. However, there are many who speak French and even more who converse in Arabic." His tone said he was sure the latter was beyond Edwin's skills.

He would be right, but Frankie actually had a moderately working knowledge of Arabic, the written word anyway. It had become necessary to decipher some of the writings she'd worked so hard to get her hands on.

"My French is excellent," her brother boasted truthfully.

He had a wonderful ear for languages. It was one of the many abilities they had in common, despite the fact their life's passions were so very different. But like many things, even in their alikeness, they differed. Edwin tended to pick up the spoken word more easily and Frankie found the written word easier to understand.

"And you, Ms. Somers, do you speak French?"

For a terrible moment Frankie worried he'd figured out their plan, but then she scolded herself internally. Of course, he hadn't. The man was just making conversation.

"She speaks it beautifully, but is even more fluent in the written word," her brother slotted in as Frankie gathered her scattered thoughts.

Deception was not her forte. It never had been, their trading of places as teens notwithstanding. But as Julia had said, *that* had been Frankie playing the role of Edwin, not lying about her plans.

If she'd been better at dissembling, she might not have ended up a prisoner in the sanitorium. But that was a thought for another day.

Or never.

As much as she wanted to converse with the professor, she knew she mustn't just yet. Besides driving this winding road with a steep cliff on one side was taking all of Frankie's concentration.

The sudden lurch of the roadster caught her by surprise. Had a tire blown? Had they been hit?

"What the hell?" her brother yelled. "They hit us!"

The roadster started spinning and Frankie reacted with instinct. Tightening her grip on the steering wheel, she accelerated, guiding the Duesenberg into a controlled skid before bringing it to a full stop, facing the other direction and in the other lane.

Frankie immediately shifted down and then quickly pulled the automobile across the lane onto the side of the road, away from the cliff they had very nearly gone over.

She looked over her shoulder catching only the backend of a black Model T speeding away.

Frankie laid on the horn, knowing it was probably useless as a protest to the reckless driver of the Model T.

"The devil?" Edwin shouted again from the backseat.

Dr. Thomas laid his hand on the steering wheel beside Frankie's gloved one. "Are you all right?"

"Yes. That was close. They didn't even slow down."

"They came out of nowhere," Edwin said, furious. "They've scratched my paint, I'll bet. A person who drives like that has no business owning an automobile."

Frankie did not reply to her brother's high dudgeon. It was her experience that there were plenty young swells who drove with little regard for the safety of others. She'd never had such a close call before, but she'd had plenty of opportunity to exercise her defensive driving skills the many times her brother had let her drive his car.

"It makes one think the efforts to require a license for driving are necessary," Dr. Thomas said mildly.

"Do you want me to drive?" her brother asked.

Frankie gave him a look and guided the roadster back onto the street going the direction they'd initially been headed. "I'm fine."

"You've got pluck, sister-mine. I'll give you that." Edwin whooped. "Don't you agree Henry?"

Frankie cringed. She was fairly sure the professor/archeologist had not given her bother leave to use his first name.

However, Dr. Thomas didn't take umbrage, not aloud anyway. He merely reacted to Edwin comment with a noncommittal grunt.

Edwin reengaged Dr. Thomas in conversation, using the more familiar address, and maintained it until Frankie pulled the roadster to a stop where Dr. Thomas indicated. In a different part of town, the large three-story building was no less impressive than her father's mansion.

"This is where you live?" Frankie blurted. He was a professor and archeologist, for goodness' sake.

"It is my grandfather's home. I live with him."

"Oh."

"I suppose he pulls your purse strings like Pater pulls mine," Edwin said in a bald moment of total candidness.

Dr. Thomas grimaced, the first fully realized emotional expressions Frankie had seen on his face all night. "You could say that. He's the bulk financier behind my digs."

"I thought Father's company was?" Frankie blurted and then wished she'd remained quiet. The less interaction between her and the older man, the better.

Not least of which because the more time she spent in his company, the more fascinated by the gruff archeologist she was.

"They do supply needed funds, but without grandfather's patronage, I would be hard pressed to make up the difference. And I hate drumming up funds." The man shuddered.

Frankie had no difficulty believing that. A stuffy, somewhat grumpy professor? Would not be the cat's meow as a salesman.

"It's a good thing they're both so supportive then," she said a little more bracingly than she'd meant.

However, it was fast becoming obvious to her that Dr. Thomas had been strong armed into taking her brother on the dig. That didn't bode well for her comfortability around him masquerading as Edwin in Egypt.

Dr. Thomas frowned, gave her brother a baleful look, and then nodded morosely.

It would have made Frankie smile if she weren't sure her own experience was going to be influenced by the attitude.

Oh, well, she'd survived worse. And for her dream of being on a dig in Egypt? She would suffer more than an unwelcome demeanor from her "boss".

They said their goodbyes to the professor and Edwin settled into the front seat beside Frankie.

"Why didn't you let me turn Father down flat about the trip to Europe?" she asked him as she pulled the Duesenberg away from the curb. "I don't know if it has escaped your notice, but if I'm in Europe with Doris, I can't be in Egypt pretending to be you with Dr. Thomas."

"Jeepers! Can you believe Father had him over for dinner? It's a damn good thing I pretended to lose my passport. We'll be a week behind him."

She didn't bother asking why her brother had pretended to lose his passport. She could guess. He wanted her to have her own copy to travel with once they reached Europe.

Edwin might be impulsive, but that didn't make him any less canny than she was. And she was grateful for it.

Still, he seemed to be overlooking one very important issue. "Again, *you'll* be a week behind him getting to Egypt and I'll be in Europe if Father has his way."

"Pater wants to mend fences. You need to let him."

"Why must I let him?"

"He loves you, Frankie. You know he does."

"And I love him."

Edwin made a frustrated sound. "I know Pater let you down, but we're a family, sis."

"You were the only family that visited me in the sanitorium, the only family that argued with John for my release."

"Yes, well, we're twins. We have to look out for each other."

And because being close to the rest of the family was so important to Edwin, he thought he was looking out for Frankie trying to get her to make up with their father.

"Not to belabor the point but if I'm in Europe letting Father make it up to me," she let her sarcasm show on that aspect. "I am not in Egypt pretending to be you."

"We'll have to bring Doris in on the scam."

"We can't. She'll tell Father."

"You don't know her very well, do you?"

"I know her as well as you do."

"You really don't. Doris is a Flapper who believes in the independent womanhood."

"So independent she's going to Europe looking for a husband at his behest."

"She's going for the travel. She has no plans of getting married any time soon, if ever."

"She never says so."

"Because she's better at hiding her motives than you are doesn't mean she falls in with Pater's plans any more docilely."

"Still, you think we can trust her?" They would both be facing serious consequences if Doris betrayed them.

"Yes."

Frankie spent several silent seconds taking in her brother's certainty. Contrary to what he believed, she *did* know Doris, if not as well as he did, living with their sister fulltime. The younger woman wasn't entirely under their father's thumb and Frankie knew that.

But could she trust her very freedom to Doris's sense of filial loyalty and discretion?

"You are certain?" she asked Edwin.

"For crying out loud, Frankie, you're all wet if you think our sister is some kind of Dumb Dora. She won't rat us out to Pater." The genuine anger in Edwin's tone soothed Frankie more than his vociferous protestations of Doris's trustworthiness.

"Okay," Frankie agreed with a smidge of continued reluctance. "We tell Doris what we are doing. She still needs a companion on her tour. Father's distant relation is expecting us both."

"We'll write her a letter from Father saying you've come down ill and couldn't travel at the last minute."

That wasn't a bad idea, helped along by the fact that Edwin's handwriting was very much like their father's script already.

"Then who will watch out for Doris?" Frankie demanded.

"Ho ho, your chauvinism is showing!"

"How so? I didn't suggest a man do it." Her brother and his ideas!

"But you never asked who would look out for me when I went East to University." That their father hadn't insisted Edwin go to his alma mater had been down to his own snobbery. Edwin had gotten into Yale, after all. Besides, Edwin always got his way around Father. With few exceptions.

Apparently kissing a man, while being filmed on celluloid, was one of them.

"If you will remember, I started at my French Finishing School the same time you began university." And what any of this had to do with Doris traveling Europe without Frankie to watch out for her, she did not know.

"Yes, but you never questioned me being on my own."

It was all Frankie could do not to roll her eyes, but she wasn't taking any chances on being blindsided by another dangerous driver. "You weren't though, were you? You joined one of those crazy fraternities and lived in a house with your *brothers*."

"And Doris will be with family."

"Family we don't know any better than we know the man on the moon."

"There is no man on the moon. It's cheese, I tell you."

"No nonsensical arguments right now, Edwin. This is serious. Doris may have the sensibilities of a Flapper, but she hasn't the experience of one. I know what it's like to live in Father's house."

And Frankie wasn't going to Egypt to follow her own dreams at the expense of her younger sister's safety. Doris might think the risks of sex were worth it.

Prepared to talk to her sister about the Birds and the Bees when she'd never expected to have to do any such thing, Frankie was still determined Doris would not go to England without someone there to look out for her best interests.

It wasn't chauvinistic, as Edwin suggested, but hard-won wisdom Frankie wished she'd had at a more tender age. Certainly, before agreeing to marry her first beau.

"What do you suggest? I suppose I could take *your* place and make it a proper swap."

"Not dressed as me." Frankie was pretty sure he couldn't carry that off.

"No, as me. We'll say in the letter that my plans for Egypt have had to be postponed so I could accompany Doris."

But Edwin really wanted to go to Berlin. Frankie wasn't even sure if he hadn't been plotting how to make that happen *before* Father's ultimatum.

"I have a friend," she said now, thoughtfully.

"You have several despite your antisocial ways."

"I am not antisocial."

"You are, but that is not the point. This friend?"

"She has a passing resemblance to me." In fact, Winnie and Julia were the only women of Frankie's personal acquaintance who matched her for height.

Frankie slowed down to take a right turn. "She's wanted to travel since finishing school."

Unlike Frankie, Winnie had not married right out of Finishing School but that was more to do with the scandal of her father losing his fortune and dying soon after than anything else.

Well, maybe not anything. To Frankie's knowledge, Winnie had never *wanted* to marry either. She'd had a much more cynical view of the institution of marriage than Frankie had while they were in Finishing School together.

"And this is pertinent why?" Edwin asked.

"Winnie can take my place with Doris. She won't have to do much dissembling. Her name is close enough to mine that calling her Winnie won't raise any eyebrows. As you've pointed out, I'm not particularly close to Doris, so they won't interact much differently than we would. Winnie is a dear friend and knows as much about my history as anyone."

"If I didn't know for a fact you just thought this up, I'd believe you'd been planning this for days. You've got a devious mind, Frankie."

"No really, I don't, but I have always been good at solving problems." If only John had let Frankie find her own solution to the sadness and grief she'd been experiencing after the loss of their baby.

"True."

"You will have to spring for her passage and compensate her for wages lost, as well as getting her the necessary papers for travel." Frankie bit her lip.

This was getting more and more complicated.

But maybe something good could come of it for her friend as well as herself. Wasn't that worth a little complication?

"You trust her."

"More than I trust Doris."

"Because you probably know her better."

Frankie sighed. "Yes, you are no doubt right, brother-mine. Feel better?"

"I always like being told I am right."

"I know."

"If you ask Father, he will pay for her passage as a companion to you."

"I'm never asking him for anything, ever again." In letter after letter, she'd begged George Clarke to get her out of the sanitorium.

He had always refused to interfere between a husband and a wife.

Their bond of trust had been irrevocably broken.

"I don't think he would make the same decision now, Frankie."

"I know you would like to believe that, Edwin. I would too. I wish I could, truly. I just can't."

It was Edwin's turn to sigh. "Okay, so I pay for Winnie's passage, we figure out a wardrobe for her and she goes with Doris. I think Doris is going to be mightily offended."

"If she's the person you think she is, she'll want to provide this opportunity to Winnie as much as we do."

"We?" Edwin asked with some emphasis. "She's your friend."

"And a good one at that."

"All right. All right." Edwin put his hand up in surrender. "*We* want to see she gets to travel with Doris."

Frankie's heart filled with a real sense of hope they could pull this thing off.

5

The next weeks were fraught with preparations for the trip abroad for the three siblings. Edwin's gambit at putting off their departure by pretending to lose his passport had not worked. Their father had used his considerable influence to swiftly replace his son's passport as well as one for Frankie.

Frankie and Edwin had been hard pressed to get Winnie's traveling papers pushed through in time, but they'd managed it.

George Clarke insisted on providing the necessary funds to compensate Frankie for her lost wages while she was traveling with Doris. Which quite frankly shocked Frankie until Edwin fessed up that it had been his idea. *That* did not surprise her.

He also insisted on providing a new wardrobe for the visit with his English relatives and chaperoned tour of Europe, with a generous clothing allowance for purchasing necessary items once they arrived in England.

Since refusing her father would have caused a kerfuffle when they could least afford one, she agreed. Besides, Frankie also considered it more her father helping Edwin out than *her* since Edwin had already agreed to pay her lost wages.

That left her brother flush to offer Winnifred Clark the same thing.

Knowing that Winnie would have access to the clothing and sundry allowance while in England also put Frankie's mind at rest that her friend's straitened circumstances would not impact her enjoyment of this rare opportunity to travel.

Winnie took some convincing to participate in the scheme, but her deep desire to travel finally won. Especially after Edwin promised her a position in the Clarke Mining & Concerns offices when they all returned. The wages weren't much better than what she earned as a salesclerk at Hamburger's department store, but the hours were much better.

None of them made what they had working in the factories during the war, Frankie acknowledged sadly.

Her independence would have been so much easier to continue to finance on the wages she'd made in the factory once the United States had entered the war officially. Not that her father had approved of Frankie working, but she'd argued John was doing his bit in The Lafayette Flying Corps, and had been since 1916. She needed to do hers as well.

John lasted longer than most fighter pilots, but had been shot down in 1919, only a month before armistice.

Frankie and her fellow female workers had lost their jobs a few months later as the men returning from the War also returned to their old positions in the factories and farms. She'd found a job as a bookkeeper and stuck with it ever since.

Letting go of that tie to security was hard for her, but the prospect of being on an actual dig in Egypt more than made up for it.

Which she kept telling herself on the long train ride across country to New York and right up until they walked up the gangplank of the Olympic class ocean liner her father had insisted booking their Atlantic crossing. Slower than the famed Mauritania, it had more amenities for the voyage and offered more privacy.

Frankie had to admit that the huge ship was both smart and imposing with its fresh white and grey paint. The captain greeted all the first-class passengers personally and Frankie gave him her most charming smile, which probably didn't compare to her brother's practiced glad handing, but it got her past the ship crew and onto the deck.

Clanging and thumping sounded both from their own ship and

those around them in the busy port, the sea air a mix of salty brine and smoke from the stacks on the ships and the surrounding buildings.

"Isn't this just the bee's knees?" Doris demanded breathlessly.

Frankie turned to her sister with a smile. "It is impressive."

"I wonder what our rooms are like?" Winnie said, clasping the valise with her notebooks and travel guides she'd refused to relinquish to the porters.

"Shall we find out?" Frankie asked.

"Definitely." This from Edwin, who waited with an expectant air for her to lead the way.

Everyone was waiting on Frankie, though she couldn't have said why.

Not one to wait on any sort of ceremony herself, she turned smartly and headed the direction the purser had indicated when they boarded.

The ship was huge, but had been built on a mathematical grid and Frankie found navigating it quite straight forward once she figured out which deck she'd started on and which one they were headed to.

Their staterooms were lovely, though not overly large. She was nevertheless glad that it had been decided Doris and Winnie would share the more luxurious first-class stateroom with a portal booked by George Clarke for his daughters. They could continue getting to know each other, in order to better perpetuate the masquerade of Winnie being Doris' older sister.

Which meant that Frankie had the smaller inside cabin across the hall, booked by her brother for Doris, to herself. She closed the door on all the hullabaloo in the hallway and relaxed onto the bed, not at all surprised her luggage was already sitting neatly in a pile against the wall.

She had packed rather lightly, having already transferred most of the clothing her father had purchased for *her* sojourn in Europe to Winnie. Frankie had a few dresses for her travel across country and the ocean crossing, but her trunk had the clothing Dr. Thomas had suggested Edwin pack for his time in Egypt as well as a set of archeological tools Edwin had bought her as a gift.

Winnie had promised to cut Frankie's hair on the last day of their voyage, so she could style it in a masculine part down the middle with pomade keeping it sleek to her head.

Frankie was a little worried about how the pomade would stand up to Egypt's heat and sand kicked up by the wind, but men had been dealing with such, no doubt she could too.

The sound of her brother's voice in the hall raised in surprise had Frankie popping up from the bed and throwing her cabin door open.

No. It could not be.

But it was!

Dr. Henry Thomas stood, his back to Frankie, in front of a door right beside her brother's cabin. "I was led to believe you would be two weeks behind me in arriving in Egypt."

His deep tones did something unexpected to Frankie's insides which she did her best to ignore.

This was a disaster! After a week together aboard ship how was she supposed to perpetuate the masquerade of being her brother in Egypt?

Frankie stepped back quickly, shutting her door so only a crack to see and hear through remained.

"As to that, I'm sure I will be," Edwin replied. "A week anyway. I have to accompany my sisters to London and see them safely to my father's cousin before continuing on to Egypt."

Frankie lamented that single dinner and drive because if it had not happened, they could introduce Winnie as Edwin's sister and Frankie could have spent the voyage avoiding the professor.

She would still have to spend the voyage avoiding him, but how would Edwin do the same? Dr. Thomas would expect her brother to be prepared to discuss their upcoming dig.

"I suppose I should not be surprised. I missed my train out of Chicago and therefore missed my planned sailing as well."

"I say, you look like someone's given you a facer. Are you all right?" Edwin asked.

Frankie sucked in her breath. Someone had punched Dr. Thomas?

"I was accosted by miscreants on the train platform in Chicago. That is why I missed my train. I believe they thought to mug me."

Edwin looked at the professor consideringly. Oh, Frankie wished she could see Dr. Thomas' face. "Other than that bruise on your cheek, you don't look any worse for wear."

"My attackers were not expecting me to fight back."

"But you did?"

"I sent them packing." Dr. Thomas sounded pleased by that.

As he should. Apparently his training in Judo had come in handy.

"You are lucky none of them had weapons," Edwin opined.

"Two had knives." Dr. Thomas sounded so pragmatic saying that.

While Frankie felt her knees weaken in concern. He could have been killed!

Her brother said exactly that.

But Dr. Thomas shook his head. "They were untrained ruffians."

Once again charmed by his formal way of speaking, Frankie found herself smiling where no one could see her.

"And you are trained, in fighting?" Edwin asked with equal parts disbelief and curiosity. "You're a professor."

"And archeologist," Dr. Thomas added.

"So, I should have taken boxing or something?" Edwin demanded, his expression growing worried as he cast glances in the direction of Frankie's door.

"Not at all. Nothing to worry about on my excavation site."

"Yet, you are a trained fighter."

"Judo. The focus is on defense."

Edwin looked ready to engage the archeologist in a discussion on Judo.

"I have notes and a book, or two, you can study on the voyage," Dr. Thomas offered before Edwin could say anything else.

While Edwin looked anything but keen, the professor's words sent hope coursing through Frankie.

That was right. The Dr. Thomas had said he spent his time traveling on study and research.

Maybe all was not lost.

"That would be much appreciated," Edwin said, rallying and evincing all the enthusiasm Frankie felt at the prospect.

Her brother really was a swell actor.

"Wait a moment and I will get the book I finished on the train journey."

"Funny we weren't on the same train."

"Hmm." The noncommittal sound held no interest in speculation.

Frankie didn't think it odd though. Just because Dr. Thomas had missed his first train didn't mean that he hadn't been in New York a couple of days longer than they had.

Still, Dr. Thomas really wasn't the most personable of men.

So why did Frankie find him so interesting?

Not only interesting, but alluring. It had taken a great deal of will power to stay behind the crack in her door and not burst into the corridor to inspect Dr. Thomas' injuries.

Not wanting to be caught when the older man turned to find his own cabin and the promised book, Frankie shut her door.

She didn't have to wait long before a brisk knock sounded on it.

Expecting her brother, she still said cautiously, "Who is it?"

"Edwin. Open the door, Frankie."

She did, just enough to let him inside her cabin. He shoved a book at her. "You'll have to give me summary talking points so we aren't caught out."

She grabbed the annotated diaries of a 19th century Egyptian archeologist and explorer and hugged it to her chest. "I will. Oh, Edwin, can we still make this work? What if he sees me?"

"He's going to see you, it can't be avoided. But he's a boring old stick and will spend most of his time in his cabin reading. You heard him."

"Not all of it, though. Maybe I should fake illness and eat my meals in my cabin."

"And miss out on the bathing pool when you know he won't be there."

"But..."

"You can't spend your life under the shadow of fear, Frankie."

She knew her brother was talking about more than getting away with their subterfuge.

"That's easy for you to say."

"Is it? Frankie, I could be sent to prison for being who I am, a lover of men. I have to work every day not to give into fear and despair."

"You don't act like it."

"Then I'm winning."

"I'm not," she admitted and plopped on the end of her bed. "I have nightmares about that place, the things that happened there."

"You've never told me—"

"And I never will," she interrupted fiercely. "That's my past and I won't live through it again."

"It sounds like you already do, in your dreams."

She couldn't deny it, but that didn't change how unwilling she was to talk about her time in the sanitorium. She had seen horrors she never wanted to witness again. She had experienced a sense of helplessness she wasn't sure she would ever be fully rid of.

Henry set his notes aside, unexpectedly restless.

Edwin Clarke was here on the ship. Did that mean that his altogether too intriguing sister accompanied him?

That had certainly been the elder Clarke's intention. Henry had gotten the distinct impression Mr. Clarke's widowed daughter wasn't keen to take her father up on his offer of a trip abroad.

Unusual enough was this level of interest in the woman, when usually his interest in the fairer sex was confined to just that. Sex. However, the effort he had expended to find out about Frances "Frankie" Somers was completely baffling to Henry.

He'd learned she was a war widow with no children. His grandfather had also said that there were rumors she'd been committed to a sanitorium for six months before her husband had joined the Lafayette Flying Corps a full year before the United States entered the war.

Grandfather had not known why she might have been committed. Certainly nothing in her life since had been remarkable. Yes, she eccentrically insisted on keeping her own home rather than moving back into the family mansion, but that was no indication of mental instability.

Henry would keep his own rooms, if living with his grandfather was not a requirement of him receiving the funds necessary to finance his yearly archeological digs in Egypt.

Grandfather was not a mean man, was in fact rather generous, but he liked to control his world. Much like George Clarke.

Henry did not usually care. His studies were all that mattered.

Until his grandfather and Mr. Clarke's need to control their world had resulted in Henry being saddled with Edwin Clarke as member of his dig team.

The young man was not objectionable, but neither was he shaping up to be an asset to the team.

He'd shown only perfunctory interest in the upcoming dig season.

Henry sighed. Only time would tell.

His sister, on the other hand, didn't talk much, but her lovely brown eyes lit with interest when Henry talked about Ancient Egyptian history.

Henry shook off the fanciful thought. Lovely indeed. Since when did he notice the loveliness of a woman's eyes?

Having no interest in marriage, Henry had kept his liaisons with women to the practical and the very, very private.

Older and more experienced women who had no desire for marriage themselves. It was not as if he needed sex all that often.

A couple of times a year seemed to keep his temperament balanced. The rest of the time, his hand did just fine.

When he'd been younger, he'd wondered if he'd shared his father's particular predilection, but had realized after having sex with a woman for the first time, that it was not the case.

The female form excited his libido whereas the male form did not.

Henry had never been ashamed of his father's differences, but he'd grieved the loss of a man who had been Henry's dearest and closest friend since his birth. He'd adored the man who had taken his own life rather than subject his family to a very different kind of scandal.

Confident that Dr. Thomas was holed up in his cabin reading, Frankie accompanied the others on their explorations of the ship.

There was a bathing pool, just as Edwin had claimed. Even though it looked like an ancient Romance bath and had Winnie and Doris making immediate plans for taking a dip, Frankie was more interested in the ship's library. It boasted glass doored bookcases filled with fiction and nonfiction alike.

Newspapers from both London and New York hung over wooden dowels, keeping their pages crisp for whoever might wish to read them.

Frankie's fingers itched to grab the London Times and settle down for a good read, but her companions wanted to continue exploring.

Making a promise to herself to return to the library at the first possible moment, she acquiesced.

Chairs intended for catching the fresh sea air in comfort neatly lined the promenade deck. The large formal dining room looked more like a palace ballroom than someplace to eat, but both Winnie and Doris went into raptures over the décor so Frankie kept her thoughts to herself.

Watching her younger sister interact with the friend she'd known for more than a decade, Frankie thought Doris and Winnie would have no trouble pulling off their part of the masquerade.

Both were avid travelers wanting to experience every new thing along the journey. They had spent hours together on the observation platform of the train from California to New York. Frankie had no doubt they would be equally inseparable on the ocean liner.

She wasn't jealous of their time together, but rather relieved she could spend as much time as she liked studying the material provided by Dr. Thomas. Without guilt.

Edwin would find a group of swells to occupy his time as he always did, and Frankie would revel in her freedom to sketch and study without being interrupted.

Early the next morning, she was ensconced in the library, reading the ship's latest copy of the London Times when a masculine throat clearing brought her head upward, her mind still focused on the article she'd been reading on the Mummy's Curse.

"Would it be possible to have that when you are finished with it?" Then before she could answer. Dr. Thomas said, "Ms. Somers isn't it?"

"Yes." Oh, gosh. What in the world was she supposed to do? "I, yes, of course you can have the paper when I'm finished."

He nodded and turned to go without another word.

Frankie knew she should not prolong the conversation, but the opportunity to discuss her passion with someone else was too much to resist.

"There's an excellent article on the Mummy's Curse," she said.

He stopped and turned back, the fading bruise on his cheek adding to his grim expression. "There is no such thing."

He didn't look like he'd taken on more than a single would be mugger, but he'd used the plural when referring to them. She had to bite back a sigh of pure feminine appreciation in the man's prowess, when she never felt appreciation for such things.

"You don't think so?" she asked, not convinced either way herself, and doing her best to focus on the discussion at hand, not thoughts of this man fighting multiple assailants at once. "Mrs. Corelli's suppositions seemed rather compelling to me."

"I am sure she is a brilliant novelist, but she is not a scholar."

"She quoted the ancient text from *An Egyptian History of the Pyramids*."

"A compilation of fairytales," he said dismissively.

Frankie frowned. "Is that how you see the hieroglyphs on the walls of the tombs?"

"Naturally not. They represent the ancient religious beliefs of the Egyptian people."

Surprised by his respectful response, not always reflected in archeologists, she nodded. "I agree."

"So, you wonder why I dismiss *An Egyptian History of the Pyramids* so easily?"

"Yes, actually."

"Because the author made much of it up."

"I didn't know that," Frankie said musingly. "But Lord Carnarvon *is* dead," she couldn't help pointing out.

"People die every day. That is hardly proof of some curse. Howard Carter is *not* dead. And the claim there was some kind of warning curse in the hieroglyphs is false."

"How do you know?"

"Carter denied it."

"And you believe him?"

"Naturally. He is a testy man with a temper, not a dishonest one."

"Everyone thinks Mrs. Carelli predicted Lord Carnarvon's death."

"Marie Carelli is a novelist, not a clairvoyant." Dr. Thomas gave Frankie a look that seemed at odds with their conversation.

It made her feel hot and tingly in ways she'd never done with her deceased husband. What in the world was going on with her?

"Does being a novelist preclude her being both a scholar and a clairvoyant?" Frankie asked, doing her best to ignore the reaction of her body to the archeologist's presence.

Dr. Thomas looked taken aback. "Naturally not."

"So, then how are you so certain she is neither scholar, nor psychic?"

"Her education is not a scholarly one," he said practically and maybe even a little dismissively, but without an attitude of *overt* superiority.

"You might be surprised what kind of education a woman avails herself of given the opportunities to do so."

"Hm..." He was silent for a moment and then nodded. "I see, yes. I suppose that is possible."

"As for being psychic..." Frankie let her voice trail off.

"I do not believe in the occult."

It was her turn to say, "I see. So, naturally that means you don't believe anyone is able to see the future."

"Precisely."

"Isn't that a bit stifling of an outlook?"

"Truth is not stifling. It simply is."

"But what if you are wrong?"

"I am not." He didn't sound arrogant, just matter of fact.

It was a strange juxtaposition for Frankie. A man who believed he was right, but clearly didn't need her to agree with him. In fact, seemed not at all bothered that she might not. And yet...yet, he also didn't seem like he was judging her for not agreeing with him.

Unique indeed.

"I'm open to the possibility," Frankie said. "I don't think we can dismiss the timing so easily."

He nodded and turned to leave again.

Frankie forced herself not to call the archeologist back. She had to avoid him this week, or the masquerade would never work.

But you deceived your tutor and he knew you very well indeed, a small insidious voice in her head insisted.

Henry sat down in one of the library's reading chairs as far from the tempting Ms. Somers as he could get. He'd meant to leave the library entirely, but had remembered at the last moment that he'd asked to read the newspaper when she was done with it.

If he'd gone, he should have looked a right fool.

He felt a bit of a fool around Frankie Somers. Her beauty was not conventional, not with her red hair, brown eyes, square jaw and smattering of freckles across her nose and cheeks. If she were going to Egypt, the baking sun would soon double those adorable little cinnamon specks.

She was tall for a woman, but as he was rather tall himself, he liked that. He liked her forthright way of speaking when she did speak. He liked the soft, almost husky tone of her voice.

Why had he simply walked away? He should have asked her to join him for a turn on the deck, but he didn't do things like that. Oh, he had had more than one tryst while traveling to and from Egypt, but he wanted to *talk* to Frankie.

She was off limits for bedroom games. A widow yes, but too young not to have expectations of post intimacy commitment.

Still young enough to have children and the daughter of a very conservative man, he did not think she would have the necessary knowledge of contraceptives against pregnancy to make a sexual liaison anything but a badly taken risk.

"I'm finished, if you would like the paper now." The woman's husky voice interrupted his thoughts.

Henry felt heat crawl up his neck. He'd been thinking about sex with her. Of course, she could not know that.

But he did.

6

He reached for the broadsheets folded neatly in half. "Thank you."

"There is a fascinating article on the opening of a new exhibit of antiquities in Paris."

"Perhaps you will get to see it."

She jerked, like his words surprised her, but she nodded. "Perhaps." Frankie bit her lip. "That is something to look forward to."

She sounded more like she was regretting it than looking toward it, but it was not his place to say so.

"Have you read the accounts of the Carter tomb?" he asked, when he was sure he'd meant to tell her goodbye and bury himself in the paper.

"Oh, yes. It was so thrilling. I thought I would expire when I realized the rumors were true and Mr. Carter and Lord Carnarvon had actually found an intact tomb in the Valley of the Kings."

"It was the find of a lifetime," he agreed, though his own aspirations were less grand. Henry was interested in everyday life in Ancient Egypt. Not a popular topic in the general public, or even among his own peers.

His concession was for a dig site in Upper Egypt, at least a day's journey south of the Valley of the Kings.

"What is it like?"

"I'm sorry?"

"Being the first person to see something ancient in hundreds if not thousands of years. What does that feel like?" Her brown gaze glowed with the light of a zealot.

He understood that light, the warmth that passion gave to a man's insides. Apparently to a woman's as well. He never remembered his mother being nearly as excited by the actual work as his father had been, though she'd seemed happy enough to be on what she called an adventure with her husband and son.

"There is a sense of being part of time." Someone who mattered. Someone who could not disappear even with the power of a pistol's bullet.

"It must be the most wonderful feeling imaginable."

"I have always thought so." It was the curse of the archeologist, to find life's meaning in discovering the past.

It did not always leave time for relationships in the present.

As both his grandfather and mother often lamented.

"What is the most exciting find you have ever had?" she asked.

He considered answering that question the way he would have if he were standing before the Ladies Aid society, or even a classroom full of students and then decided he would be honest. "Last summer, I found a roughly hewn amulet of Horus in a modest grave."

"Oh, yes?" she didn't sound disappointed. "What was so significant about that amulet?"

"It would indicate that either the person who had been buried worshipped Horus, or the Pharaoh who considered himself the embodiment of Horus."

Frankie's expression was filled with earnest interest and delightful intelligence. "And it was significant because you found it in a modest grave. It would indicate that the people of Egypt did in fact worship their king as a god."

"It could indicate that, yes."

"I thought that was an accepted belief."

"Temples to a god king are not proof that god king is worshipped as a full deity."

"But being buried with talismans to him might be."

She was very insightful. "Yes."

And lovely. And interested.

It was a potent combination, to which the tightening condition of his trousers could attest.

Glad for the covering of the newspaper over his lap, Henry cleared his throat. "At the very least, it confirmed the Horus cult was active among the greater Egyptian population during that period."

"Did you write a paper about it?"

"I did." It had gotten very little interest in any but the most scholarly circles. As Frankie had said, it was an accepted belief that the Pharaohs were worshipped as gods. "Howard Carter's discovery is more interesting to the general public."

Henry had no doubt he would spend more time answering questions about the newly discovered tombs than any of his own discoveries in the coming years. It was a pity that his own interest didn't lie with the Pharaohs, but the people who lived during their reigns.

"It is thrilling," Frankie said with feeling. "But there is so much more to Ancient Egypt than a single pharaoh's tomb."

"You are one of the few people to think so."

"But you do, or you would be digging near Luxor, or even Alexandria."

"Your brother told you where my dig is?" he asked. Perhaps Edwin had paid closer attention than Henry had thought.

Frankie blushed, pinkened skin disappearing into the neckline of her midi blouse in a most intriguing way. "Um, yes, he did."

"Perhaps he has more interest than I thought."

"I am sure my brother will be a congenial companion, but will also endeavor to be a most useful participant on the dig."

As to that, Henry would withhold his judgement, but he appreciated Frankie's loyalty to her sibling. Many of his own cousins, the closest thing he had to siblings, were not nearly as certain of his value, or usefulness in the family, and were rather vocal about saying so.

His mother's family were more supportive, but Henry's lack of interest in building the coffers of the family fortune had never gone over well with his father's brother, or his children.

The fact Henry, as his father's only child, stood to inherit a substantial portion of those holdings upon his grandfather's death, only made the thorn of his existence within their family sharper.

Remembering his manners, Henry indicated a nearby chair. "Would you like to sit down?"

Fully expecting the lovely Ms. Somers to decline and leave the library, she surprised him by settling gracefully into the proffered seat. Unsure what to say, Henry did what he usually did. He remained silent.

"When I was little, my mother used to say my face would set like that if I weren't careful," Frankie said, her tone implying she was amused by him.

"What do you mean?"

"You look less than happy."

"Am I supposed to smile all of the time?" he asked.

She looked like she was hiding her own smile. "Well, no, but I sort of assumed when you asked me to sit down that you actually wanted my company. Perhaps you were simply being polite?"

How was he supposed to answer that? He had been motivated by polite behavior, but he *did* want her company. Not something he should acknowledge.

Her laughter startled him. "I hope that cards are not one of your vices."

"Why do you say that?"

"Your every expression shows on your features."

Horrified at the very idea, he scowled. "I do not think so."

"Perhaps only the negative ones?" she asked, clearly humoring him. "Or is it that you are a naturally grumpy person?"

"You do not sound like the prospect upsets you much." He'd been called a cranky sod by more than one acquaintance or colleague.

Stick in the mud was another favorite.

Henry could not help it if he preferred his own company to that of others. Only this woman was different. He *liked* talking to her.

Very strange.

"Now you look perplexed."

"Is there any point in me talking at all? You seem to enjoy drawing your own conclusions as to my thoughts." Okay, so he sounded annoyed.

Her smile was too damn charming and had a decided effect on his sex.

"Why are you smiling?" he asked. People usually frowned at him.

She shrugged. "Why are you frowning?"

"You confuse me."

"Do I?" She didn't sound bothered.

"You are very forthright."

"Does that bother you?"

"No." Confound him? Yes. Bother him? No.

"Good. I do not believe in the feminine ideal of perpetual charm and masking one's opinions and feelings with polite civility."

"Why?" Her father did not strike Henry as the type of man to raise his daughter to be so dismissive of societal conventions.

"Because I prefer honesty."

He wasn't sure she was ready for the honesty that she turned him on like no one else had in a very long time. It had been his experience that women did not like that much honesty, even those prepared for no strings liaisons.

"I do want your company."

"But you would prefer you didn't?" she asked, her brows drawn together in question.

"I am too busy with my work to be intrigued by a woman." Damn that had been blunt. Did he have no sense of decorum?

The answer was as it always had been.

No.

But rather than take offense, she smiled. "Tell me about your dig and what you hope to find there."

So, he did.

That conversation was the first of many and while Henry enjoyed the intellectual stimulation of Frankie Somers' company, his desire for her grew more intense with each encounter.

Sometimes, he thought she was avoiding him, but when he engaged her, she would let go of her reticence and spiritedly discuss his work, Howard Carter's discovery, and dynastic theories, that few even in his department of antiquities at the university were aware of.

"What's going on in that noggin of yours, Frankie? You haven't heard a word we've said." Edwin gave Frankie a worried frown across the dinner table. "Are you nervous about the masquerade? You've spent a lot more time with Dr. Thomas than I thought you would."

The low hum of clattering cutlery and dozens of conversations in the large ballroom style dining room gave the opposite impression than it should. Despite being in a sea of diners, it felt private and yet, her brother's mention of the masquerade had Frankie's head jerking up.

She glared at him. "Edwin!"

That was all she said, but he got her meaning quick enough, looking chagrined at his own slip.

"I'm pretty sure that's exactly who she's thinking about," Doris said with a knowing look beyond her years and no apparent awareness of Frankie's concern for privacy. "He's seems like a drab old stick to me, but Frankie finds him dreamy."

"I never said that," Frankie said with a huff.

"You're not denying it." Edwin's concerned demeanor deepened. "Are you attracted to him?"

Frankie didn't answer, refusing to lie.

"You are." This from Winnie. "I remember that look. You had it when John was courting you."

Cold chills went down Frankie's spine. "I am not falling for him."

Attracted yes, but she'd learned her lesson about entrusting her heart to a man. The power dynamic between the sexes was too out of balance for a woman to safely give her heart.

"I think you might be," Edwin said. "We need to reconsider this plan."

"Nonsense. This is *my* dream Edwin, just as going to Germany and making another film *that matters* is yours."

"And I will give up that dream to protect you."

"I don't need protecting. What do you think is going to happen while I'm in Egypt pretending to be you?"

"You hate lying."

"This has just occurred to you?"

"You aren't going to be able to keep up the subterfuge for the whole digging season."

"Of course I will." Only the idea she would merely be playing a part and not actually being called on to lie didn't hold up when she actually knew one of the people she would be deceiving. "Needs must."

"No, Frankie..." Edwin went silent for several long seconds and then shook his head, his expression nothing like his usual sunny countenance. "What was I thinking?"

"We were thinking that this is my chance to participate in an archeological dig. I'm not giving it up." No matter how attracted she was to the professor in charge of the dig.

"Don't give me that stubborn look, Frankie. I only want to protect you."

"John said the same thing."

Silence descended on the table, Edwin's expression going from worried to wounded in a heartbeat.

Frankie sighed. "I know you did not mean it the same way, but Edwin if you respect me, then you will allow me to make my own choices about my life."

"How can I do any less for you than you do for me?" He reached out to squeeze her hand. "You are the best sister."

"What about me?" Doris said in an obvious bid to lighten the mood.

"You are in a class all your own," Edwin said.

Doris narrowed her eyes at their brother. "What is that supposed to mean?"

The younger woman had not batted an eyelid at the masquerade plan when Frankie and Edwin presented it to her. She'd been all for both of them pursuing the deepest dreams of their hearts and had not put up a single objection.

A wealth of emotion washed over Frankie. "You are our baby sister and could not be dearer to either of us."

Doris blinked, the flapper countenance dropping for a moment to reveal a young woman deeply touched by simple words. "Well, that is good to know."

"I wish I was as close to my brothers as you all are," Winnie said wistfully.

"You've become our honorary sister, hadn't you realized?" Doris asked with sincerity ringing in her tones.

Frankie agreed. "You have been one of my closest friends since finishing school, but after this adventure, how can we be anything but sisters?"

Winnie blinked away suspicious moisture. "You too."

"Excuse me, but I consider you my sister too," Edwin said with teasing humor laced with sincerity.

"I'm not sure I want to claim *you*!" Winnie winked, making it clear she was joking. "You're a trouble magnet."

Edwin put his hand over his heart. "I am wounded. How could you say such a thing?"

"So, it was not you that the purser threatened to ban from the bathing pool?"

"When was this?" Frankie asked, having no trouble believing it.

"I just thought a rousing game of water polo would entertain."

"The blue haired brigade taking their afternoon constitutional in the bathing pool were not impressed."

Edwin tried to look innocent, but Frankie wasn't fooled for a second. "What did they say?" she asked, knowing there had to be more to it.

"One of them made a pointed comment about the moral character of young women today."

"So?"

"It was clearly directed at Doris."

"Oh. I'm surprised you didn't dunk them."

"He did, or as good as." Winnie giggled. "The game got them so wet they would have no option but to wash and redo their hair."

"Those of us with short hair don't have those concerns," Doris said smugly. "And that's not immoral, it's practical."

The bright moon reflected on the dark expanse of water as Henry stood at the rail after dinner.

He should be in his stateroom, reading the Harvard publications on last year's dig he'd managed to get his hands on only the day before boarding his train East. He'd left it for reading aboard ship, having other things already scheduled for study on the train ride.

He had not expected any sort of distraction aboard ship.

Nothing like Frankie Somers, sister to the man who was supposed to join his own dig in the Cobra province.

Henry wanted her to the point it interfered with his concentration on his studies.

The past three nights he'd woken from erotic dreams about her, his sex aching with arousal. And on one memorable occasion to his seed spending as he woke, coating the sheets with his ejaculate.

She'd eaten with her family tonight, as she seemed to do every night. They talked and laughed in a way that revealed affection and closeness.

He'd never wanted to join in such a scene before, but he had tonight.

His own desultory conversation with table companions who had been strangers three days before had centered as he'd expected it to, around Howard Carter's discovery in the Valley of the Kings.

The other diners had expected Henry to be expert as he himself was a Professor of Antiquities and one of the few American archeologists heading his own dig in Egypt now that the Great War was over.

The War to End all Wars had certainly ended archaeological endeavors in Egypt and the Middle East.

But he and other dig teams were doing their best to make up for lost time, some with far less concern for preservations of the *in situ* discoveries than him and his team, who followed Reisner's methodology of meticulous documentation.

That lost time meant he had little to spare thinking about women.

Or rather, one woman.

An intriguing, independent minded female whose grasp of Ancient Egyptian history rivaled his own.

He could wish that it were she who was joining his dig this Season. If he wasn't so intensely attracted to her.

"You look lost in thought." The sound of Frankie's soft tones broke into his thoughts.

And sent blood rushing to his penis in a near painful surge.

What was it about this woman that affected him so strongly? He had never been a man governed by his lust.

But it would take very little for him to forget his certainties and follow that lust to powerful completion.

"I should be working," he replied, forcing himself not to turn and look at her.

"But the moon called you?"

"I am not a quixotic man."

"Is it romantic to be drawn into thought under the moon and stars?" she asked, her tone tinged with teasing as it was so often when she spoke to him. "I would think it was what engaged those thoughts that might be termed dreamy, or not."

If only she knew. "You find me humorous."

"I find you interesting."

He turned his head then, to see her expression. Because there had been something in her tone. Something he could not define.

Her eyes were fixed on him, not the moon or the glorious array of stars to complement it.

"You find me interesting," he remarked.

"I do."

Something in her expression matched that odd tone in her voice.

"You are not happy about that," he opined. No more happy than him. Another thing they had in common.

"No."

He glared off into the distance. "I find you interesting as well."

"I do not think that makes you any more pleased than my interest in you does me." Her acuity did not surprise him.

"It does not."

"Why?" she asked.

"You distract me."

"And you would rather work with nothing to divert your thoughts?"

"I *should* want to work undistracted." He was quite sure of that.

"But you don't?"

"I do not."

"What do you want then?" she asked, no humor in in her breathless tone now.

They were closer than they had been though he could not say which of them had moved, or if indeed they both had done.

"You."

Her lovely brown eyes widened, her mouth parting on a small gust of air. "Oh."

"Does that offend you?"

"No."

"Shouldn't it?"

"I want you too." And she sounded confused by that, if not a little chagrined.

"You were married."

"I was."

"Didn't you want your husband?"

A shadow passed over her gaze. "At first, but the act of copulation is not for a woman's pleasure, but a man's."

"You believe that?"

"Shouldn't I?"

"It is an outdated notion."

"You think so?" Cynicism dripped from her voice.

"A woman can find as much, or more pleasure from the act, as a man." He wanted to show her that pleasure.

More than he wanted to take his next breath.

More than he wanted to read the Harvard journal.

7

"As a man, I am sure you would say so."

"So do the flappers."

She grimaced. "I know. It worries me."

"Because of your younger sister."

"Yes."

"What exactly worries you?"

"That she will risk pregnancy for an act that is all build up and no pay off." This woman's honesty was refreshing, even if her beliefs were misguided.

"Is that how it was in your marriage?" he could not help asking.

She tilted her head, her red hair dark in the moonlight. "Isn't that a very personal question?"

"Isn't this a very personal conversation?" he countered.

She was silent for several long seconds, but he did not press. Was not sure he wanted her to answer. The more he knew about her, the more he wanted her.

It was that simple.

And that damnably complicated.

"I enjoyed the closeness of marital congress but it always held the stress of potential pregnancy."

"You did not engage in any form of contraceptive." As he'd thought, she was too innocent to be knowledgeable about such things.

"I wanted to. John was horrified when I brought up the suggestion on our wedding night."

Oh. That put a different picture on things. "He refused to use contraception?" Not all men were willing to wear a condom and indeed it was still illegal in many places to purchase them, but there were other options for the married woman whose husband agreed to them.

"He wouldn't even consider it. He was furious I knew about such things and had I not been a virgin on our wedding night, would no doubt have accused me of all sorts."

"He was an old-fashioned man."

"He considered himself a Modern Man. When we first married, I certainly believed he was different than my father."

"But he was not?"

"His use of modern slang and the fact he encouraged me to have opinions about politics, books and the like deceived me into believing that he valued those opinions." She sounded sad, having clearly been disappointed in her belief.

"He expected you to think as he did."

It was a common enough conceit among married men.

"You just assume that. And you're right. I was naïve. I thought he wanted a wife with opinions."

"I'm sure he did."

"But only if those opinions agreed with his. He refused to consider waiting to have children. Waiting for anything."

Something about the way she said it bothered Henry. A great deal.

"He forced you."

She shook her head. "He pressured me."

Men were taught that was their right. Henry had never believed that to be true. Perhaps it was having a father who had societally unacceptable desires. Perhaps it was simply that he was too pragmatic to believe that any human being had agency over another.

"You don't have children."

"No." There was no mistaking the shadow in her eyes now.

Henry would not pry. He hated when nosy people pried into his past, poking at the wounds of loss that would never heal completely.

Not the loss of his father.

Not the loss of other soldiers he had called friends in the war.

Not the loss of innocence he had experience seeing the ugly death and carnage in the trenches.

She had lost too. What or who, he did not know, other than the husband who had not respected her mind, or rights to her own body.

Henry could not regret that man's death. And if that made him a bad person, he would accept it. He would never countenance the mistreatment of one human being by another, even when society said that mistreatment was in fact their *right*.

His own father had been respectful and caring toward his mother, treating her as an equal, regardless of societal norms.

She'd never remarried, saying she would never find a man like that again.

Henry privately agreed.

His father had been unique. In both acceptable and unacceptable ways by the standard of society.

"My father taught me to love the study of ancient civilizations," Henry offered as a change of subject, but also as personal information he did not often share with others. "He was convinced they had much to teach us."

"I'm sure he was right."

"He was a gentle man."

"I'm sorry you lost him."

"I am too."

She stepped back from the rail. "I should find my cabin."

He nodded.

"Good night then." She turned and headed toward the stairs that would take her down the lower deck.

"Good night," he replied. "Your husband was inept."

He did not know where the words came from or even why he said them. They'd navigated the shoals of the rocky personal conversation without crashing into them.

But leaving her believing sex wasn't good for women as well as men? He couldn't do it.

She stopped, turned and stared.

Silence stretched between them.

"What do you mean?" she finally asked before stepping nearer, as if drawn by the same invisible force that pulled his attention to her with irrevocable power.

"Your body is made for pleasure."

"Are you a ladies' man?" she asked, her brows drawn together. "Only I wouldn't have thought so. You're so staid."

"I enjoy sex on occasion, but when I do, I make sure my partner enjoys it as much, or more than I do."

"You think so?" she scoffed, so very clearly unconvinced.

"I do." A woman could fake an orgasm.

Other men talked.

But Henry had always approached sex as he did everything else. With the curiosity and the mind of a scientist.

Slick moisture in the vaginal channel. The rictus of climax that drew every muscle taut before shudders of satiation. The involuntary cries, the expression a woman's face made when she climaxed, how her pupils dilated, and her nipples grew turgid and red during arousal.

They were all responses he had carefully catalogued and then sought to elicit during sex.

"You're so confident."

He shrugged.

Henry didn't do things he had no aptitude for. He did not play football, but he did study Judo, and had the black belt to prove it. He had taken a single course in literature, and then never again. Because he found the emotions and motivations of other people too confusing to dissect.

He engaged in sex, therefore he was good at sex.

He thought with this woman, he might be spectacular.

Frankie could not believe that she was having this discussion with this man, or any man. Certainly, sex was an open topic of discussion among the lady adventurers. The single women particularly were keen to know what their mothers had never told them.

Frankie and Julia had shared information on contraceptives and Frankie had been candid in her assessment of the sexual act.

But she had never discussed such things with a man. Not since her unsuccessful efforts with her deceased husband. John's disgust and condemnation on their wedding night had shocked and hurt her.

But still, she'd tried one more time to broach the topic of contraception, believing that her concern over getting pregnant could be why she found so little satisfaction in the sexual act. John's vitriolic reaction that time had left Frankie shaken and unwilling to broach any sort of intimate topic again.

He'd made it clear that, like any other man, he expected his wife to provide children. She hadn't disagreed with the idea of having children, only of the when, but he'd refused to hear her. Further, he'd said only a slut worried about enjoying herself physically in marital coitus. That Frankie's satisfaction should come from doing her duty and providing *him* with pleasure.

She hadn't agreed and even told him that she thought that was a selfish attitude for him to take.

That's when things got really ugly.

He hadn't hit her, but she hadn't been sure he wouldn't. And that knowledge had been intensely demoralizing.

Edwin thought the first time Frankie had asked for intervention from their father had been when John had her committed to the sanitorium. It wasn't.

She'd gone to her father the day after that awful fight, and told him she wanted to move back into the family home and divorce her husband.

George Clarke had refused her sanctuary and informed Frankie he expected her to work things out with John. He'd told her that he and her mother had their fair share of dustups until they learned how to live together in harmony.

Frankie had read the message behind the words. *She* had to learn to compromise. *She* had to make things works and accommodate.

There had been no room for discussion of her deep feelings of sadness and failure after her miscarriage, or most particularly her physical reaction to John after Frankie lost the baby.

For his part, her husband had been mightily offended by the way she shied from even the most innocuous of touches.

And yet, here she stood, talking about the most intimate of acts with a man she barely knew.

"What are your thoughts on contraception?" she asked, disbelief at her own temerity warring with curiosity.

"That unless you are planning to have a child, it should be used."

Frankie gasped, shocked despite herself. "That is a very modern way of looking at it."

"Pragmatic more like. I have no desire to marry. If I were not willing to use contraceptives, then I should have to practice abstinence like they preached at us during the War. It was not effective then and I've no desire to follow those tenants now."

"And even if you were married, what would you think?" she pressed.

"That my wife and I would have to be in accord in not using it."

But that implied... "You think she should have final say."

"It is a moot point for a man who has no intention of marrying, but yes."

He was implying his stance was an easy one to take because he had no plans to have to actually take it. But even in the abstract, it was not a common attitude.

The movement for birth control in previous decades centered around a woman's right to her own body had been circumvented recently by the medical establishment.

Doctors now touted contraception for the sake of health but in a way that made it clear it was up to a woman's husband whether or not it was to be used. And any single woman who wanted to take advantage of the medical advances was *no better than she should be.*

"So, you use condoms?" she asked, breathless for reasons she was not inclined to examine.

"I do, though if my partner is not using her own contraceptive, I also pull out."

"You are so frank." And how could she be finding discussion of this topic so arousing as well as enthralling? Surely it was no more than scientific curiosity on her part.

Only it wasn't and perhaps a woman who was so poor at lying ought not to try to lie to herself.

"Would you rather I was not?" he asked.

"No."

"Frankie, Miz Somers, I mean, I believe we should say goodnight before I say or do something that might offend you."

"You may call me Frankie." She liked that he did not use Frances, her given name, but the one she'd said *she* preferred.

With his brain, she had no doubt he remembered her saying so at the dinner at her father's house.

"And you may call me Henry, but I will still say goodnight."

"I..." She wasn't sure what she wanted to say. She did not want him to go, but asking him to stay was beyond her.

He turned to leave, and she saw the way his trousers tented in front, his arousal obvious.

"Oh!" she exclaimed on a gasp.

He stopped. He made a sound like a growl and turned back to her.

"You really do want me." And the evidence of that desire was mesmerizing.

She could not look away, though there was nothing even remotely acceptable about staring at that part of a man's body.

A sound between a laugh and a groan came from him. "Was that in question?"

"I do not know." He'd said it. She'd told him the same, but this? This showed that his desire for her was acute.

She could not remember a time that John had gotten an erection outside of the bedroom. He must have done. It was entirely natural, or so she had read. But she'd never been aware of it.

"Yes, I want you, Frankie, but as intelligent and well read as you are, you are not a woman of the world."

"Only because I have never wanted to be," she assured him.

If she had wanted to take lovers after her husband's death, she would have done so. Maybe.

Okay, fear might very well have won out, even if she thought sex was more exciting than it really was. Fear of another man refusing to use contraception. Fear of being found out and scolded, or worse, locked up again, for her own good of course. By her father this time.

Two of the women who had been in the sanitorium with her had been placed there by their fathers. Both because they had been sexually active while not married, and their fathers considered that behavior aberrant enough to justify clinical treatment.

Her own father was far away right now.

And this intriguing man who Frankie could admit, if only to herself, was the real cat's pajamas, was right here.

"But the fact remains, you are not."

"Are you saying the only women you have sex with have a certain level of experience?" she asked, disbelievingly, her own shock shifting her gaze from his tented trousers to his face as she tried to read the level of sincerity there.

"Yes." Bald and spoken without inflection.

But nothing in his expression gave lie to his claim either. He met her gaze, his own eyes dark and unmistakably determined.

Frankie still took the affirmation as an insult. "You think because I don't enjoy sex like a man does, that I am not capable of being a good sexual partner?"

John hadn't had any trouble finding pleasure in her body even if he had made little effort to reciprocate it. "John thought only whores enjoy sex."

Henry's jaw hardened. "I am afraid I would have had very little use for your deceased husband."

"He was a war hero."

"Good for him."

"You fought as well, didn't you?"

"Yes." Henry's expression turned wary.

"Thank you."

He looked startled. "It was my duty, but I will never say it was my pleasure."

"Good. There is nothing pleasant about war."

"No there is not."

"My former in-laws still grieve the loss of their son. As do so many others."

"And you? Do you grieve his loss?"

More comfortable talking about sex, Frankie thought about how to answer. Finally, she said. "Perhaps I grieved what could have been, but I cannot claim to grieve the loss of a man I was happy to never see again."

"You have your reasons for feeling that way, I am sure."

"I am equally certain few in our society would agree that any reason would justify my attitude."

"Our society breeds hypocrisy, not honesty."

She could not disagree. The very politicians who publicly supported prohibition could be found in the speakeasies and had their own well stocked liquor cabinets masquerading as innocuous study décor, like globes and bookcases.

"John used to say it was his job to protect me. Society claims to agree, but in the name of that protection, he engineered my worst memories." Why had she said that? To a near stranger, no less.

"Society would have called my father depraved, but he was the best man I have ever known." Henry looked no less startled by his own admission.

Perhaps because her brother was a homosexual, perhaps because that word was bandied about so often as a label for women and men who loved their own sex, but Frankie immediately wondered if Henry's father had been like Edwin.

She and Henry stood in silence for several long seconds, their words hanging between them, but not only words. Desire thrummed in the air, an invisible pulse between them.

He had said he wanted her. She wanted him.

He was a proponent of birth control.

"I do not agree with society's stance on sex outside of marriage." Not on the immorality of it, or that sex itself had one goal: procreation.

If she could agree with the male dominated medical profession on one thing, it would be that population control was necessary for the good of that population and the world it inhabited.

"Nor do I."

"I gathered."

Henry smiled, his lips tilting ever so slightly. The heat in his eyes held no humor though. It was pure sexual want.

Frankie took a step closer to him. He shifted his own body, so a mere breath was between them. He tilted his head down.

She tilted hers up, feeling strange doing so.

John had been the same height as Frankie.

"May I kiss you?" Henry asked in a deep rasp.

"Yes." She just stopped herself saying please, but Frankie would never plead for anything from another man.

Nor did she want this moment relegated to societal politeness.

It was too real. Too primal.

Henry looked at her for another second, or two, and then he nodded. Like he'd settled something in his mind.

She hoped it was the notion that Frankie was in charge of her own body and knew best what she wanted and what was good for her.

He cupped her face. "Your eyes shine with curiosity."

She was curious. How far she would allow the curiosity to take her, she was not certain.

But she wanted his kiss.

When it came, their mouths pressing together was unlike anything she had experienced before. Henry showed no tentativeness, none of the lack of finesse found in his social skills.

His lips moved over hers with pleasure giving mastery, sending zings of delight along her nerve endings. She felt like a lightbulb, turned on to glowing brightness by the electric connection of their mouths.

Henry's arms came around her, pulling her body flush to his.

Frankie pressed harder against him, reveling in the sensation of her nipples rubbing against the fabric of her corset. She pressed her legs together, sending sparks of pleasure to her feminine core.

Without conscious thought, she tunneled her hands inside his formal dinner jacket, letting her fingers map the contours of musculature. She felt the fur of chest hair through the fine lawn of his shirt and the thin fabric of his undershirt, something that had been rather sparse on John.

Banishing any further thought of her deceased husband, Frankie continued her touch exploration of Henry's impressive chest.

Something else felt impressive. The length of hard male sex pressing into her stomach. She wanted to reach down and feel its dimensions, but was not sure if she was ready for where that might lead.

Tonight she would have a kiss. Tomorrow was soon enough for further explorations. If she chose to pursue them.

No matter how her body clamored for an as yet unknown fulfillment at the hands of another.

She'd once thought that fulfillment would come from copulating. She knew better now and wasn't giving into her body's urgings without careful thought.

Henry ran the tip of his tongue along the seem of her lips. Frankie gasped in surprise, having never experienced anything like that.

He slipped his tongue inside her mouth, playing with hers, inviting her to respond. Desire whooshed through Frankie like a spark set to dry tinder.

Unbelievably to Frankie, the kiss grew more and more intense. That sensation between her legs had become a steady throb, a need to be filled and yet, she maintained enough presence of mind not to just ruck up her dress and offer that very thing.

The fact she wanted to? Made her feel half seas over and she hadn't had a drop of alcohol since this voyage had started.

Henry's hands shifted down to cup her backside and he lifted her enough so that his hardness pressed against the apex of her thighs. There were layers of cloth between them that might as well not have been there at all for how intense were the sensations coursing through her.

Their bodies shifted, but she paid little attention to where he was moving them, opening her eyes only when he broke the kiss.

It was dark where they were and she realized he'd pulled her back behind a lifeboat where no prying eyes could see them.

Noting that situation with a certain amount of gratitude, she leaned up to press her lips to his again. She craved his taste, the feel of their mouths joined.

This time she was the aggressor in the kiss, rubbing her body against his with abandon.

When he once again broke the kiss, she made a sound of disgruntlement.

His husky laughter did *not* endear him to her. "Do you trust me?" he asked.

"In what way?" She could not help the clarification.

Trust was not a currency Frankie traded in with very many.

"To give you pleasure."

"You were doing just fine," she said crankily. He must have known that.

"I would like to do better," he said, his tone husky and alluring.

8

Still not sure she trusted him, she asked, "What do you mean?"

"I want to touch you."

"You are touching me."

"More intimately."

"How?"

"Let me show you."

Frankie considered it. Could she trust him to do it? Looking around at the privacy he'd thought to provide them despite how lost they had both been in the kiss, she thought maybe he'd earned at least a certain level of trust on her part.

She nodded her agreement.

His smile had actual teeth this time and elicited one of her own.

"Turn around."

She did not ask why, too curious to see what came next.

Strong but gentle hands pulled Frankie back against Henry's hard body. Then those hands brushed up her body to cup the small mounds behind her corset.

"No boning," he said in an approving tone.

He squeezed her breasts through the fabric and pleasure arrowed directly to her core.

Needing something to keep her steady, Frankie reached behind herself and locked her hands behind his neck, anchoring her body to his.

"That's right." His approving rumble went through her like another caress.

Frankie wished she was wearing a different sort of gown, something that would allow him to dip inside her cleavage and touch skin to skin.

But she'd only brought two evening gowns for the formal dinners on the ship and both were classic designs that hid more than they revealed of Frankie's body. Bought when the last things on her mind was attracting the attention of men who could endanger her independence.

Henry didn't seem bothered. He caressed her body as his hands traveled downward, stopping at her hips. Then he started the process of rucking up the soft chiffon of her long skirt, a little at a time.

The agonizing slowness of revealing her legs to the night air was an enticement all on its own.

"Stay just like this, Frankie," Henry instructed, his words a whisper in her ear that sent shivers of pleasure down her spine.

"Not moving," she vowed, the promise of pleasure too enticing to do anything to circumvent it.

His lips moved on her neck, and he nibbled on her earlobe, as her skirt rose inch by silky inch up her legs.

Cool air caressed her legs through her sheer stockings. Even though he was not in a position to take full advantage of the sight of her body as it was revealed, Frankie felt deliciously exposed.

That sensation intensified tenfold when he deftly sent her skirt drawers sliding down her legs to pool around her ankles.

He cupped her, his big hand covering her most intimate flesh entirely, and rumbled in approval. "So hot, *ma belle*."

At another time, Frankie would have objected to being called beauty. She was no feminine ideal, but she was hot. On fire, in fact.

"Do something," she urged.

One finger slid between the tender folds of her sex to dip into her swollen channel. He brought moisture up to rub slickly over her clitoris, that nub of flesh so few mothers told their daughters about.

Her entire body went taut with pleasure as he rubbed and circled, dipping into her wetness time and again to keep the entire area slick for his ministrations.

Frankie had touched herself, but it had never occurred to her that a man would do the same, or to such effect.

It was not the same when she could not anticipate what touch came next, or how much pressure would be applied.

To have this happening on the deck, even as tucked away as they were, added an illicitness that drove her excitement higher.

She turned her head into his, pressing her lips where she could reach, needing a connection beyond the feel of his hand on her most intimate flesh.

His head turned too and then they were kissing, open mouthed, tongues entangled.

Pleasure built inside Frankie, and she canted her hips back and forth, desperate for more stimulation, intent on reaching the pinnacle she had only ever achieved with her own hand.

When it came, she cried out and his mouth pressed immediately over hers completely, sealing the sound between them.

He did not stop touching her until he had wrung the last bit of pleasure from Frankie's body. She hung limply against him, her hands having dropped by her side at some point. Only his arm around her waist and hand still cupping her intimately kept her upright.

He let her stay exactly as she was, showing no hurry to move, though she could feel his hardness against her backside.

"That was unexpected." Her voice was wispy to her own ears.

He kissed her sweaty temple. "You are amazingly responsive."

"Am I?" Her own response certainly had amazed her.

Was it possible that with an attentive lover, even coitus could be as pleasurable?

"You are. Your passion could become addictive."

"You don't sound worried."

"I might be, if we weren't going our separate ways after this sea voyage."

When Frankie was a child, Edwin used to taunt her into jumping into the river from the diving rock in the summertime. The feel of water colder than an icehouse enveloping her body in one shocking moment had felt exactly like this moment.

What was she thinking? Had she lost the plot entirely?

She had gone from a woman who thought of sex as blah, to being governed by sensual impulses that could destroy her one chance at realizing her dream to study Ancient Egypt in situ.

Frankie tried to jump away only to nearly trip on the drawers now acting as bonds around her ankles. Henry steadied her and then doing the unexpected, knelt down to pull her drawers up her thighs.

"Thank you," she choked out. "We should not have done that."

He did not reply, but helped her straighten the skirt of her dinner dress before standing.

"I am sorry you feel that way." His face was cast in shadows, his expression hidden from her.

Henry's tone gave no indication of his feelings, whether he was angry or disappointed by her words. He did not sound surprised, but perhaps resigned?

"I just..." What could she say?

They were *not* going their separate ways once they reached England. She was following him to Egypt and they would spend the next two and a half months together.

Frankie was furious with herself for giving in to her fascination with the professor at all. What was wrong with her?

She knew time spent in his company risked her success at the role of her brother. *This* only compounded that risk.

Frankie stepped backward. "I do not think we should converse further."

"I see. It is as I thought." Henry gave her a slight bow. "Have a good life, Ms. Somers."

It was only as he walked away that Frankie realized what Henry thought he saw. He'd said she wasn't a woman of the world and thought she was too naïve for a sexual liaison.

He now believed he was right.

Why wouldn't he? It was only after he'd mentioned not seeing her after the voyage that she'd raised a ruckus.

She wanted to chase after him and deny his conclusions, but she had no better explanation to give.

Henry undressed with measured movements, refusing to allow his anger to manifest itself. He wasn't mad at Frankie, but himself.

He'd known the intriguing woman was an innocent despite her status as a widow.

He had allowed his own libido and her irresistible curiosity get the best of him.

Henry had no one to blame for that state of affairs than himself.

And yet, he could not regret touching her.

Her silky warmth had been near unbearably enticing. Her response to his touch would fuel his own masturbatory fantasies for many nights to come.

"I cannot believe how much you look like Edwin." Doris' tone reflected her words. "It's uncanny." She smiled at Winnie. "You really are the bee's knees at cutting hair."

Winnie grinned. "I've been trimming my family's hair since I got home from finishing school."

Frankie looked at herself in the cabin's small mirror and had to agree with her sister's assessment. She'd put on the fake mustache Edwin had gotten her from one of his friends that worked makeup and wardrobe on the film lot.

She really did look like her brother. "It's perfect, Winnie."

"I wonder how long it will take to grow out," Edwin lamented.

He'd been growing a mustache since their train ride, which he informed any of them that listened he was shaving off at the first opportunity. But two nights before, he had allowed Winnie to cut his hair into the parted down the middle slicked back style that Frankie now sported as well.

Edwin had made a point of greeting Henry and had dined with the other man the night before.

Frankie and the other two women had not joined them. She was intent on not making any more bad decisions where the lead archeologist was concerned.

She'd managed to avoid him almost entirely for the remaining four days aboard ship, helped by the fact it was obvious he was avoiding her too.

Which should not hurt her feelings.

At all.

What the man thought of her did not matter.

If she laid awake at night trying *not* to think about that very thing, that was her business and no one else's.

"Okay, back to yourself for the next couple of days," Winnie said briskly, handing Frankie a cloth with cream to remove the small dots of spirit gum used to hold the mustache in place temporarily.

They would travel to London together, Frankie as herself. There, she would take on Edwin's persona before boarding the train for Dover, where she would cross the channel to Calais and catch another train south, followed by another sailing across the Mediterranean to Cairo.

It would take her about a week to reach Cairo, all of it traveling as her brother.

Good practice for when she reached Egypt.

Only after they arrived in London, Edwin informed her that he had booked her a flight to Paris and a second flight from Paris to Cairo, with a refueling stop in Italy.

"But I thought I was doing the overland route. You've already given me the money to book my passages."

"Keep the money, but I'll feel better if you fly." He handed her tickets he must have procured that very morning. "You'll spend the night in Paris before catching your next flight the next morning."

Frankie had never flown before, but she had always wanted to. "I can't believe you took on this extra expense."

"I want you to meet Thomas in Cairo and travel with him."

"You would have travelled alone."

Edwin shook his head. "Says the sister who insisted on a second masquerade, so our younger sister wasn't alone in Europe."

"What?" Doris piped up. "I'm going to be with family."

"Distant relations none of us have met," Frankie said dismissively, consigning her brother's poorly timed revelation to purgatory.

"And you thought I couldn't watch out for myself? I thought Winnie was coming to give her a chance to travel."

"I am pretty sure that played as heavily in your sister's mind as the chance to have me around to watch over you."

"I'll be watching over you too," Doris replied staunchly.

"That's what sisters do," Frankie agreed. "We watch out for each other however we can."

"Brothers do the same, which is why you are flying to Cairo and not spending a week alone on a train and ferries."

Frankie wasn't happy but she couldn't exactly blast Edwin for being overprotective if she didn't want the same response from Doris.

"Frankie is keen to watch out for others, but she's intent on protecting herself alone." Winnie didn't sound judgmental, more resigned. "It's a trust thing."

"What? I trust you." Frankie looked between her brother, her sister and back to Winnie. "All of you."

"Good. I want a letter with all the details on Cairo," Doris instructed.

"I want to hear all about the flight," Winnie added.

Doris made a moue of distaste. "I've flown. It's more blah than the bee's knees. Trust me."

"A first-class train carriage is a great deal more comfortable," Edwin agreed. "But planes take hours to travel the same distance the train takes days."

"And there is no chance of Frankie being importuned on a plane." Doris sounded like she was far more worldly than Frankie knew her sister to be.

Frankie frowned. "I'm going to be traveling as Edwin. No one is going to importune me."

"Don't you believe it," Edwin said with feeling. "And it will not go well if a man feels you up expecting to get something between your legs that isn't there."

"Men do that?" Winnie demanded, sounding a lot more curious than alarmed at the prospect.

"Yes."

Frankie just shook her head. "I wouldn't be flirting like you might with said gentlemen."

"I'm not sure the man described would be considered a gentleman," Winnie teased.

Edwin raised his brow, like that was in question.

Frankie just shook her head. "I'm actually quite keen to fly."

"I cannot imagine why," Doris said.

"It's not all about creature comfort. You are up in the air, like the birds. That is amazing."

"Not if you get airsick, it's not," Doris muttered.

Frankie grinned. "We will all hope I don't suffer that malady since I'll be spending the better part of two days in flight."

But she'd never gotten seasick, so she wasn't worried.

The flight turned out to be every bit as uncomfortable as Doris had predicted. And loud. But Frankie did not care. She spent most of her time in the air looking out the window. Watching the ground get further and further away so that even the London and Parisian city buildings looked smaller was amazing.

But being in the clouds was no less so. To think she was above the earth as surely no human was intended to be filled her with elation and a sense of her adventure beginning.

She might even send Edwin a letter thanking him for the opportunity, even if it had been born of unnecessary overprotectiveness. Unlike Doris, Frankie was nearly thirty and a widow to boot.

She would have been fine on the train alone, her trusty books an adequate barrier to being approached by even innocent friendly fellow travelers bent on conversation.

As much as she enjoyed the flights for the unique experience they offered, by the time she landed in Cairo, Frankie was exhausted and ready for the peace of her hotel room.

Edwin had booked her into the same hotel Henry was staying while he finished putting together the provisions for their dig.

She hoped she did not see him until tomorrow, when she was feeling fresh and ready to play the part of her brother with the other man.

Her hopes were dashed when she walked into the lobby.

Henry stood at the front desk talking rapidly in Arabic to the man behind it.

Frankie waited until they were finished speaking before approaching the desk. Another man materialized from behind a screen and greeted her in French.

Frankie cleared her throat, cast her pitch low and returned the greeting.

Henry turned quickly and stared at her. "You weren't supposed to be here for another week, I believe?"

"I flew."

"I believe that was the plan, but not until after you saw your sisters safely with your other family."

Frankie shrugged, a move common to her brother. "They met us in London." The lie fairly stuck in her throat.

Henry's eyes narrowed. He stared at her for several tense seconds and then the most thunderous expression came over his face before he spun on his heel and marched off across the lobby without another word.

Was he angry she (or rather Edwin) was early? But why should he be? It made no difference to Henry. Did it?

Frankie was too tired to worry excessively at what had gotten into Henry. She checked into the hotel as her brother and asked if there were any messages or parcels delivered there for Edwin Clarke.

The friendly clerk seemed to have no question that Frankie was who she claimed. No more than any of the people on the planes or at the hotel she'd stayed at in Paris.

Each day she pulled off the subterfuge built her confidence she could maintain it. If only she knew what had Henry so angry.

Frankie got the key to her room and went up the grand staircase to the second floor, or was it considered the first floor, like in Europe? She would have to ask Henry.

She could ask him anything she liked now. In her guise as Edwin.

Frankie slid the key into the lock of her room.

"What the blasted hell do you think you are doing?" Henry's furious whisper sounded behind her.

Frankie jumped, her entire body reacting to the shock of his presence and apparent anger with her. Her heart sped up, her breath exhaling on a gasp.

She spun around, nearly losing her hat as she did so. "Henry! I mean, Dr. Thomas. This is my room, I assure you."

"It is Edwin Clarke's room," he said from between gritted teeth.

"I am Edwin Clarke, therefore it is *my* room." Frankie did her best to sound confident, but this wasn't playing the part of her brother, it was lying.

A distinction she'd already realized would be a problem for her.

"I do not know what you think you are playing at, Frankie, but no Dime Store mustache and masquerade in your brother's suit is going to fool me."

Nonplused, Frankie stared at Henry for long seconds, taking in his near incandescent rage and the certainty of his opinions burning in his grey gaze.

Needing a moment to gather her thoughts, she turned back to the door and opened it. "You'd better come inside so we can discuss this odd notion of yours."

Henry did not reply but he followed her into her room, shutting the door firmly behind him. He crossed the room to the window, open to allow a slight breeze and shut it too and then yanked the curtains closed, casting the room into an afternoon gloom.

Frankie hung her hat on the hook provided, but did not remove her suit jacket, as much as she might have liked to.

This morning she had been confident she had managed a masculine profile under her shirt, but now she could not risk the telltale bump of even her smallish breasts giving her away.

"Take off your jacket. It's stifling in here," Henry said gruffly. "You aren't going to convince me you are your brother and if you waste time trying, you will only make me angrier."

Frankie wasn't a weakling. And she wasn't giving up her dream without a fight. "I say, old man, I'm not sure what bee is buzzing in your bonnet, but I'm here as I said I would be and ready to do my best on your dig."

"Damnation, Frankie. Why are you doing this? You're putting my dig at risk, my reputation, not to mention your own. That vaunted independence you are so keen to keep goes the way of the dodo if you are caught out by someone else and how you think that won't happen is beyond me." As he spoke, Henry's anger seemed to turn to something like disbelieving consternation.

Frankie had a choice. She could keep trying to convince Henry he was wrong, or she could start work on convincing him to go along.

The fact she hated bald faced lying played a part in her decision, but so did the fact that she didn't want to lie to *this* man.

"I do not know how you are so certain I am not Edwin, but I assure you, no one else has any such suspicions." There. It was not another lie, but it was not an admission either.

"Your features are similar, I will give you that. But your brother has no effect on my libido. Even angry, my body craves yours." He gestured to the erection now tenting the front of his trousers.

Frankie gasped and then tried to laugh it off. "I am flattered, but I have that effect on more men than you."

Henry's growl was really quite animalistic. "Stop it, Frankie. I spent a week onboard ship with you and your brother. I was in his company more than I was in yours and not once did I ever get aroused."

Unsure what to say to that assurance, Frankie removed her suitcoat. Henry was right. If he was indeed convinced she was herself and not her brother, doing so wasn't going to make any difference. Conversely, if she couldn't convince him of that with it off, she was going to be miserable for the two and a half months she planned to spend in Egypt.

She already found men's clothing far more confining and warm than her own made from lighter weight fabrics. Women's jodhpur trousers had more room as well, not fitting so snuggly to her curves.

"Where is Edwin?" Henry asked. "Whatever harebrained scheme you two have cooked up, you need to stop."

"I am Edwin."

"If you are Edwin, you will not mind me doing this." Henry was suddenly right there, in front of her.

He put his big hands on her shoulders and pulled her forward, bowing his head. "Will you?" he asked.

She stared up at him. Henry wanted to kiss her.

Again.

How he thought that would prove she wasn't Edwin, she did not know. He was right. Edwin wouldn't mind kissing Henry.

Her brother had told her he thought the professor was attractive for a fuddy duddy too old for his years.

"I...no...but—"

Her words were cut off by Henry's lips. The kiss was fueled by anger, but there was passion there too.

Frankie found herself responding to all of it. She returned the kiss, but refused to give into the urge to press her body against his.

He nipped her bottom lip and she gasped in surprise, though it had not hurt. His tongue swept inside her mouth, the kiss taking on a carnal quality she found extremely invigorating.

His hand dipped between her legs, rubbing her through the fabric of her trousers and the masculine drawers she wore under them.

It took her several seconds of pleasure to realize what he was feeling, or not feeling. He had to know without doubt he was right, but Henry made no move to stop their kiss or remove his hand.

Frankie could not be so sanguine. She broke her mouth away from his and panted, trying to catch her breath, before saying, "So, now you know."

Henry stepped back and met her gaze, his own serious. "I knew in the lobby downstairs."

9

"How?" she asked, closer to tears than she had been in years.

Frankie did not cry. She could not afford to show weakness. She'd learned that lesson too well to ever forget it.

"You look very much like your brother, especially with your hair cut in that fashion." He shook his head. "And the mustache is actually very good, but Frankie, anyone who has seen you two together would know the difference."

"Our tutor never did."

"You've done this before? You think this is some kind of youthful prank you can keep playing?" he demanded, his anger coming back, if not as hot as before, still very much there.

"It is *not* a youthful prank. It never was. We tricked our tutor because I wanted to learn about ancient civilizations, but Father thought drama a more fitting pastime for a lady."

"So, you got the drama instructor, and he got the ancient history tutor?" Henry looked confused. "How did that help either of you?"

"Our tutors taught us both. Father thought he was getting more for his money." She frowned. "However, when it came to attending lectures or going to exhibits, Henry was expected to accompany our history tutor."

"You went instead."

"I did."

"And you think the tutor never noticed?"

"I *know* he never noticed. He talked to me like I was Edwin, like I was male."

"What does that mean? Like you were male."

"He might have been instructed to tutor us both, but he treated me like a woman with no thought of anything but fashion and finding a husband."

"And he treated Edwin differently?"

"Yes. Also, *he* was attracted to Edwin. And he never seemed to realize I wasn't Edwin when he flirted with me." Frankie had taken her cue from her brother and kept the tutor at arm's length.

Edwin probably would have pursued something with the older man if it would not have put Frankie in a bad position, or made it impossible for her to attend the lectures pretending to be him.

"And you thought I would not notice the difference?"

"I still don't understand how you did." And so quickly. Had she said more than five words to Henry in the lobby?

She did not think so.

"I do not understand how he did not."

"Oh."

"Frankie, tell me why?"

"Why the subterfuge?"

He jerked his head in a nod, his choler still obviously up.

"How can you not know? What Edwin saw as a punishment, I saw as the fulfillment of dreams I thought I could never even have."

"To participate in the dig."

"Yes."

"At the risk of my dig? My reputation? Did you think of nothing but what you wanted?"

"I didn't think there was any risk to you. Do you honestly think I would have done this if I thought there was even a remote possibility of being found out?"

The look he gave her showed no appreciation for her impassioned declaration. "You are not the cautious woman you see yourself as."

"You are wrong. I *am* very cautious and I have reason to be. I discussed this with Edwin, with some very close friends and everyone agreed that I could pull it off."

"But you did not."

"Not with you." And still she really did not understand why. But that was not the issue at stake here. "You must see that anyone else would be fooled."

"I do not see that. I see the risk to my dig." He stood immobile, his regard so intense, it felt like a physical touch. "If you are found out, then we would be forced to marry to avoid a massive scandal. Is that what you want?"

"You know it isn't."

"No, I do not know. You have lied to me once, why should I believe anything else you have said?" The derision in his tone stung.

"I don't know," she admitted, taking no offence at his words, though they had hurt. "I hate lying and I hate being lied to. I can only assure you that the one thing I have ever lied to you about is me being Edwin."

Henry did not reply. He just stood there glowering.

"You must see that the person most at risk is myself," she implored him. "I *do not* want to marry again, but you are right, if I am caught out, my father will insist on a quick marriage with someone, if not something worse."

"What worse?" The meticulous archeologist missed nothing.

Frankie had no desire to spill her secrets. Perhaps Henry would agree with John's actions and her father's inaction. She realized that rational, or not, if Henry did, she would be devastated.

He had far too much influence over her emotions for her wellbeing. Especially after such a short acquaintance.

And yet, she sensed that only full disclosure would convince this man of her earnestness and lack of desire to compromise his dig or reputation.

Henry was a forward thinking man, but not one prone to compromise.

"I spent six months in a sanitorium at my husband's behest," she admitted baldly. "My father refused to get me out. You must believe I would *never* willingly risk going back there."

"You think if your father discovered this charade that he would put you back in the sanitorium? You are a widow, not an unmarried daughter living in under his roof."

"With a man as powerful as George Clarke, my status as a widow would be of little consequence if he decided to act on my behalf as my father."

"And yet you are willing to risk it."

"That is my point. I am *not* willing to risk it. I am no Fakeloo artist, but I would not have embarked on this adventure if I had not believed with a certainty that I could carry it off in the guise of my brother." Nevertheless, she could not ignore the potential outcome if she were caught.

Henry stared at her in silence for long seconds and then shook his head.

She did not know what that headshake meant.

"You said Edwin saw this dig as punishment," Henry said finally. "For what?"

Frankie wouldn't have told Henry, but Edwin's actions had been on the silver screen, for anyone to see. Besides, perhaps both her and her brother owed the professor full disclosure after trying to deceive him. "Edwin took a bit part in an *avant garde* film."

"And?"

"And he kissed another man on screen."

"Surely he knew the terrible consequences that could lead to?" Henry asked, his tone filled once again with what she thought this time was unreasoning fury.

"He's impetuous."

Henry glared. "I would say it is a family trait."

Offended, Frankie said, "I don't—"

"Your younger sister is in on this masquerade, is she not?" the archeologist interrupted her.

Frankie wished she could deny it. "Yes."

"Impetuous." He shook his head again. "And your friend, the one that was traveling with you?"

"She is playing the role of myself as Doris' chaperone."

"And if she is caught out?"

"There is no chance of that. The family Doris and I are supposed to be staying with are distant relations who have never met either of us."

"And your father never sent them pictures? They don't read the society pages?"

"The only time I made it into the society pages with a picture was for my wedding ten years ago."

"It is still a risk."

"A minimal one."

"It seems a lot of people are taking a terrible gamble with their own reputations so you can go on this dig."

Put like that, she sounded like the most selfish of beings, but it wasn't like that.

"It's not all about me," Frankie said, stung. "Everyone gets something out of it. We all took the *exceedingly small* risk of being found out because the potential benefit was worth it."

"Considering the fact you have already been found out, that risk can hardly be termed anything but robust."

"I believe you are an exception."

He sighed and shocked her by admitting, "You may be right. Tell me about the benefits to the others."

Was he considering going along with the subterfuge? Did she have a chance to convince him?

"Winnie has always wanted to travel, but since her father lost his fortune, she has been stuck working to help provide for their family."

Henry nodded as if he wanted her to continue and took a seat in the armchair.

Frankie was going to sit on the end of the bed, but a knock sounded on her door.

She opened it to the porter, who had her things. She let him into the room, her face hot at being discovered alone in a hotel room with a man.

She managed to tip the porter and thank him without incident though.

After locking the door, she turned only to find Henry watching her intently.

"You are going to have to stop blushing when you are caught alone with me," Henry mused. "Your brother would have no reason to be embarrassed."

"Does that mean you aren't going to send me packing?"

"Tell me what is in this subterfuge for the others."

"Oh, well, Doris is also a keen traveler and the truth is I probably would have refused to go as her chaperone if I did not have the dig as incentive."

"Why?"

"I had to quit my job."

"Surely your father would have compensated you for lost wages."

"He did as Edwin has done for Winnie, but getting another job upon my return won't be easy."

"You could work for your father."

"No, I could not."

"I see."

"I doubt it."

Henry waved that away. "So, Winnie and Doris get to travel and search for husbands."

"Travel yes. Neither are any keener to marry than I am." Though their reasons for that disinterest in the married state were more philosophical than personal as hers were.

"And Edwin?" Henry asked, without commenting on the marriage issue again.

This was where things got tricky. How much candor did she (or her brother) owe Henry about Edwin's future plans? She could reveal some, while keeping vague the details of the type of movie Edwin wanted to make.

"He's going to Berlin to make another movie."

"Will he be starring in it opposite another man?" Henry asked, his tone clear what he thought of that idea. And it was not good.

"No." While she doubted she and Henry's opinions came from the same source, hers was from concern for her brother, she did agree Edwin needed to be circumspect. "He'll be behind the camera."

"That is a modicum safer, I suppose."

"I did not realize you were so averse to homosexuality." Henry had acknowledged her brother's proclivities earlier without any animosity.

"I am not. I am against Henry putting himself in a position where he will do harm to himself or others because of his impetuosity."

"He isn't going to hurt anyone else."

"The other man in the film he was with? Do you think he has the wherewithal to leave the country?"

"He made his own choice about doing the scene." Edwin certainly hadn't been party to convincing the other man to play the role he'd played.

She thought. Assumed.

But honestly, Frankie did not know.

"No doubt, but not all choices are good ones." Henry's tone was mild for the amount of fury he had exhibited earlier.

Still, she felt compelled to champion her brother's cause. "It should not be such a problem. And honestly, things are not as bad as all that."

"Aren't they? What if someone decides to blackmail your brother, or your father with the kiss? Film, or no film, homosexual acts are illegal."

"It was a kiss, not sex."

"But your brother does engage in sex and if someone got it into their mind to follow him and catch him out, both he and your family would be vulnerable."

Frankie had never considered that. "It's not fair. He should be able to love who he loves."

"I agree."

"You do?" She plopped down onto the bed in shock.

"Yes. More than you can imagine, but that is *not* the way it is. Even the most circumspect gentlemen or lady engaged in same sex coitus is at risk for blackmail."

Was that true? Henry sounded like he knew what he was talking about. Only she was fairly certain he was not attracted to his own sex. Not only because the passion he exhibited to her, but his admission he did not find Edwin sexually attractive.

Frankie sighed. "I hate that Edwin has to face that sort of thing."

"But he does have to face it." Henry shrugged out of his own jacket and laid it over the back of his chair. "He must learn caution."

"He's not going to be in another film. He says he likes working behind the camera better." Though she wasn't sure her father would be any more impressed with that as a pastime for her brother.

Henry removed pulled his tie out of his vest and loosened it. "If your father is as canny as I believe, George is making sure the original footage of that film has been destroyed."

Frankie considered that and thought Henry was probably right. "He wanted Edwin out of country." And now she realized it might have been more to keep Edwin distant while her father took care of the film, than to keep him out of the local public eye.

"Edwin is going to be furious," she said, thinking out loud.

"Edwin is lucky to have a man as powerful as your father on his side."

"I suppose." She would have been happy if that power had been turned in support of her at one time.

"Even the son of a powerful man can lose everything with one bad decision."

"You sound like you know what you are talking about."

"I do." Henry unbuttoned his waistcoat.

"You have never been in a scandal." She would have known. Her interest in the professor had been a bit obsessive over past weeks.

"No, but my father killed himself to avoid one."

The stark words hung there between them.

But even they could not hold her entire attention as she watched Henry remove his tie and then his waistcoat, with methodical movements.

"I am very sorry about your father," she said, her eyes fixed on the patch of chest hair revealed as Henry unbuttoned the top fastener of his shirt. "What are you doing?"

"Am I right in guessing that you backed out of having sex with me because you were afraid I would get to know you too well?" Henry asked, rather than answer.

She nodded, her throat suddenly too dry for her to speak.

"Maybe one day I will tell you about my father, but today is not that day. I have other things on my mind."

"You mean sex," she croaked out.

"I mean sex."

A sudden thought brought her up short. "Do you expect me to have sex with you in exchange for your silence?"

"I do not yet know if I am going to offer my silence, much less my complicity in your scheme. I am hoping you are going to have sex with me because you want me as much as I want you."

She did want him. And with each article of clothing he removed, Frankie wanted Henry more.

His thin undershirt fit snugly enough she could see that his chest was covered in dark whorls of hair, and his small male nipples were pebbled. It could hardly be from the cold. It was far too warm.

Was that a sign of male arousal, as it was on a woman?

She wanted to ask, but what came out of her mouth was an admission, not a question. "I want..." Frankie cleared her throat. "I want you," she said with more force than finesse.

"Good."

He slipped off his braces and then the shirt under them, revealing the rest of his masculine torso in all its glory. His thin white undershirt clinging to somewhat surprisingly thick muscle for a professor. Even one who spent his winters as the lead archeologist on a dig in Egypt.

This was no man who spent all of his time in books, no matter how important he found his studies. "You are very fit."

"Judo."

"That is some kind of Eastern fighting technique, isn't it?"

"It is."

"And you practice it?"

"I practice five days a week when I am not in Egypt."

Henry toed off his shoes and then his socks, laying them neatly across the shoes as if his erection wasn't jutting obscenely from his body, insistently tenting his trousers.

He removed his trousers with no evidence of embarrassment at being nearly naked in front of Frankie while she was still fully clothed. She was glad because she was too intent on seeing him for the first time to do a thing about her own clothing.

Without the slightest hesitation, he took off his undershirt and drawers, laying them on the chair before standing proudly nude in front of her, his sex flushed dark with blood and nearly hitting his navel in its tumescence.

"You've left your undressing to me." He approached Frankie where she sat in still wonder on the bed. "Good."

"You want to undress me?" Her voice squeaked in a most embarrassing way.

His smile said he noticed, but the heat in his gaze said he didn't find it gauche. "I very much do."

"Okay."

"I like that word."

"Me too." One relic of the war that she didn't mind having.

"It will be a new experience for me."

"Undressing a woman?" She didn't believe it.

"Undressing a woman dressed as a man, though I think it is something I may grow expert at."

That implied he meant to keep her around. Frankie wanted to rejoice in the message of his words, but she was too busy trying to breathe. It wasn't so easy with all the masculine beauty on display for her.

Henry tugged her tie out of Frankie's waistcoat as he'd done his own, but somehow it felt even more sensual from this side of things. She'd thought of wearing a bowtie that morning, but had settled on the more traditional cravat style.

Now, she was glad. The very act of sliding the fabric up her chest had aroused her.

His fingers brushed her chest as he undid the buttons on her waistcoat. "You would be cooler traveling as a woman," he said conversationally. Like he wasn't undressing her. "But I find I like all these layers to unwrap."

"Oh."

He leaned down and kissed her, his lips familiar against her own now. Then he lifted his head just enough so their eyes met. "Yes, oh."

He proceeded to unwrap her methodically and sensually, caressing her through each new layer so Frankie got to the point where she just wanted to tear her own clothes off and be done with it.

But Henry would not be rushed.

Henry slid Frankie's braces over her shoulders, letting them hang as he began work on the buttons of her shirt.

He neatly folded each garment as it came off her. He *unwrapped* her with a care that she thought was wholly unwarranted, but he seemed to be enjoying.

Her breath was coming in short gasps, her body hot with excitement.

"Why is it so different with you?" she asked, not expecting an answer.

But Henry stopped what he was doing and smiled. "Because it is."

"That's not a very scientific answer."

He shrugged and went back to undressing her. "You are beautiful, Frankie."

She laughed. Beautiful? She was ordinary, and right now she had a mustache.

Oh, for crying out loud. She had a mustache!

She reached up to peel it off, not sure it would be an improvement to have the red upper lip that persisted after she removed it for sleep.

He stayed her hand. "You do not know if you will need to answer the door again, and there is dinner later."

"But..."

"Frankie, I know you are a woman."

"But it must be strange to kiss."

His smile was devilish. "It is that."

She reached for it again.

He shook his head at her. "No. For now, you keep it on."

"For now?"

"You may have to consider *shaving it* as I do not think you will want to sleep in it and there is too much risk you being seen at night."

She hadn't considered that. So far her nights had been spent in hotel rooms with their own bathrooms. Edwin had seen to that.

But in the desert, she would be sleeping in a tent. Any nighttime sojourns to relieve herself would require leaving that tent. There was also the risk that others could enter her tent for any number of reasons while she slept or before she had a chance to affix her mustache in the morning.

"Then why not now?"

"Because it is safer. The bellman and clerk have already seen you with it. That you might shave it off midafternoon could cause speculation." He gave her that devilish smile again. "And I do not want to wait for you to get the spirit gum off of your lip."

He swallowed her breathless laughter with a kiss.

10

Henry had removed her final clothing right down to the cotton she had wrapped around her breasts to flatten them before she even realized what was happening, she was so lost in the kiss.

But he broke his mouth from hers, moving so there was enough distance between them so he could see her body as he unwound the gauze. "This cannot be comfortable."

"It is better than a whalebone corset," she said dismissively.

Cut right, and worn without a tight lacing, a corset did not have to be uncomfortable, but she had no doubt such a thing would have been much too hot in the desert climate of Egypt.

Not that *she* would have worn one, even had Frankie been traveling as a woman. Ever since Edwin had bought her the unboned corset, that was all Frankie had worn, when she wore a corset at all.

How often she went without was not something she would ever admit to. But the looser fitting garments in fashion did not require corsets like the styles popular a decade past.

When she wore a women's suit jacket over her midi blouse to work, she saw no reason for the extra layer of a corset as well. She thought Henry might appreciate that practice, rather than condemn it as other men would do.

He certainly seemed taken with the sight of her modest curves as he revealed them.

Her nipples were a raspberry pink and as firm as early spring berries.

Henry blew on one and then the other, sending chills of sensation along her nerve endings.

"You are so responsive."

"You said that before. On the ship."

"I like it."

He hadn't said that, but she'd taken it as given. Though she enjoyed hearing it now.

She had never been this responsive with anyone else. If she had, she did not think she would have been so sanguine about celibacy since John's death.

Henry cupped her small breasts with both hands, sliding his thumbs over her nipples.

She moaned, arching toward his touch. She felt every brush over her nipples to the very core of her, making her move restlessly.

"You like that, don't you, sweetheart?"

Endearments? The man used endearments.

"Yes." Frankie saw no reason to deny it.

This was why the flappers said they wanted sexual freedom. This feeling was worth going through the black market to get ahold of contraceptives.

Frankie gasped and stilled. "You have contraception?"

"I do," he promised gruffly.

"But..."

"I stopped at my room before coming here."

He'd planned to have sex with her? Even though he'd been furious with her?

Rather than offend her, knowing he wanted her that badly, increased Frankie's own ardor.

She pressed her thighs together, trying to assuage the ache and excitations in her most intimate flesh. It did not help.

She moaned again. "Do something," she demanded.

He took her drawers off, leaving her completely naked to his gaze and more importantly, completely accessible to his touch.

"I will, but you cannot make too much noise. This hotel's walls are thicker than some, but we cannot give rise to speculation."

For more reasons than the protection of her subterfuge.

Frankie nodded her rapid agreement, biting her lip to stop the sounds that wanted to come out of her mouth.

The hotel believed she was man and if someone heard them, she and Henry could end up in jail before they knew what was happening.

She shuddered at the thought of what could happen to her there once they discovered she was actually a woman pretending to be a man.

Even those thoughts could not dampen her desire. There was also a frisson of excitement enhanced by her need to keep her moans low.

Still, she was grateful for a plaster covered, brick built building that gave far more privacy than most hotels she had stayed in.

Henry slid down her body.

He looked up at her from between her legs. "Remember, quiet."

She nodded.

Then he leaned down and his mouth was on her. *Right there.*

Frankie had heard about cunnilingus, but never thought to experience it.

In some places there were laws against it just like sexual acts between people of the same sex. Even where it was not expressly forbidden, many considered it taboo.

Henry clearly did not have that viewpoint.

He slid one thick finger inside her, pressing upward on a spot she had never found herself that sent ecstasy cascading through her. All the while he licked her tender flesh.

When he found that spot of intense pleasure, he laved it with his tongue.

Frankie bit her fist, trying to keep her cries inside, her hips canting upward seeking more sensation.

Henry nipped gently on her clitoris and then he sucked on it. Frankie saw sparks behind her closed eyelids, the pleasure so great she had no hope of controlling it.

One finger became two and Henry set a steady rhythm like the pistons on a well-oiled engine.

Frankie jerked her hips to meet his finger thrusts and somehow, he managed to keep his mouth on the bud of her pleasure.

Her climax hit Frankie without warning as her entire body went rigid in ecstasy. She screamed into her fist, bowing upward for long seconds filled with a wholly consuming physical joy.

He seemed to sense the moment his touch was too much and withdrew his fingers and mouth with a final lick.

Frankie shuddered and settled boneless onto the bed, watching Henry from slitted eyes.

His expression was intent, no indication he was finished with her.

But then he turned.

Her eyes flew wide. "Where are you going?" She forgot to keep her voice down.

He pressed his finger to his lips. "Shh. Remember?" he whispered, his tone anything but chastising.

"Where are you going?" she repeated in a low whisper, not at all satisfied.

He fiddled with his clothes and then he turned to face her as he donned a condom.

Frankie relaxed and watched avidly as he slid the rubber guard down his erection.

"I could come from the way you watch me alone," he told her, his tone whisper low, but heated all the same.

"I...it's...I've never seen someone use one before."

"Curiosity is not the only thing I see in your lovely brown eyes."

"I still want you," she said, a little surprised at herself. She would have thought after reaching that pinnacle of pleasure that her interest in what came next would be from the perspective of giving pleasure only.

It wasn't. She wanted to feel him inside her. Craved it. And despite the relaxation of her body, it buzzed with a current of need that could have lit a ballroom given enough time.

"I want you too." He didn't take her right away, though.

Instead, Henry began touching her all over again, this time putting his mouth on her nipples, suckling until she was whimpering with pleasure all over again.

She went to bite her fist again, but he stayed her. "Leave that poor hand be. You've already got bite marks."

"I need something," she told him.

He nodded and then went to the stand with the water pitcher and basin. He grabbed a linen towel and tied a knot in the middle of it before handing it back to her. "Use this."

She stared at the knot that would work as a gag and that frisson of excitement skated along her spine like the sharp blades across a frozen over pond.

She put the knot in her mouth and bit down on it, comforted that she would not accidentally give them away. She would ask Henry how he managed his own sounds so thoroughly. Later.

He lifted her legs, sliding his thick forearms under her knees, spreading her thighs indecently wide. This was not the barely acknowledged penetration she had experienced before.

Henry pressed the head of his erection against her opening. "All right?" he asked, the stress of stopping clear in the tight lines of his face and strained tones of his voice.

She nodded, not trusting herself to take that makeshift gag out of her mouth even to answer.

Henry took her at her nod and slowly pushed forward with inexorable intent, his rock-hard penis pressing against her sensitive vaginal walls. Her body accommodated him, stretching for his generous proportions.

It took long seconds for him to gain full penetration and yet he allowed her body to adjust to each inch of penetration before increasing the depth of his egress into her body.

He pulled back, pleasure sparking anew along her intimate flesh, but leaving her feeling empty.

That sensation lasted only until he surged forward again. He went a little faster this time, but still showed impressive self-control. They continued this horizontal dance for several more thrusts, his pace increasing with each one until he was pounding into her with the power of a locomotive.

Incredibly, renewed pleasure built inside her, tightening until she felt like a spring wound too tight and yet, not tight enough.

Her moans were constant behind the knotted towel.

He grunted, his teeth gritted against his own sounds of pleasure.

Then his movements increased, and he did some kind of swivel with his hips on every downward thrust. Frankie could feel the pinnacle close and she grabbed at his chest, her nails digging in.

He gave her a feral expression that would have fit well on a Saracen, she had no doubts.

Then he dropped one of her legs and pressed his thumb against her clitoris.

Frankie came apart, pleasure rolling over her in waves.

He made a guttural sound, his body going rigid above her and she knew he was finding his completion as well.

Henry's head dropped forward, sweat dropping from his temples to her chest and the bedspread.

Suddenly he pulled out and jumped backward, staring at her with a look of consternation.

"What is it?" she mumbled and realized her words were unintelligible.

She spit the towel out of her mouth and then cleared her throat. "What? What is wrong?"

"I did not pull out."

"But the condom held, did it not?" She had heard they could break.

"It held."

"I don't understand."

"I always pull out unless the woman I am having sex with has her own contraception as well."

She remembered he'd said that. And she lauded his care, but surely it was nothing to cause such a high level of consternation? The rubber had held after all.

"There is no leaking around the edge?" she asked, trying to understand his source of concern and determine how worried *she* should be.

"No. It held as it should."

"Okay."

"You don't understand."

"No."

"I *never* forget."

He was upset because his self-control had been compromised. She understood *that* just fine.

Frankie was feeling a little vulnerable herself.

"Sex like that could be addictive," she admitted in a tone that let him know she did not see that as a good thing.

Henry followed Frankie into the hotel dining room. It shocked him that no one seemed to question her male persona. Frankie had received no odd looks, or double takes on the way from her room to here.

The maître d' had called her Mr. Clarke without the slightest hesitation.

Frankie was a good actress, Henry would give her that.

She had her brother's mannerisms down and walked with the gait of a man. Which wasn't something Henry had ever really considered before.

That men and women carried their bodies differently when they walked.

Her movements were still smooth and her face was still lovely, even with the realistic looking mustache. She shared her brother's squared jaw, but on Frankie it looked more delicate. More feminine.

Though Henry seemed to be the only one who thought so.

Her hair was slicked to her head with a middle part in a masculine style that Henry thought looked anything but manly on her. Others appeared to find nothing amiss, however.

He stifled a sigh.

That was not a style that was going to work well in the desert. Sand would stick in the pomade, though if she kept a hat on at all times, it would be better.

And why was he thinking of ways to make her male disguise work?

Was he considering helping her maintain her subterfuge? Henry nearly snorted.

Who was he kidding?

Henry had been contemplating it since she first looked at him with those big brown eyes and passionately said how much she wanted to go on the dig.

He had sympathy for her brother as well, more than many would expect, Henry's background being what it was. But that was exactly why he sympathized with Edwin. No man should be forced to spend a lifetime in pretense of being something he was not.

Even so, Henry worried Edwin would end up hurting Frankie with his lack of forethought.

The younger Clarke did not understand what a precarious life he led. If he did, he never would have kissed another man onscreen.

Henry had lost his father, who had by all accounts been the word in discreet about his liaisons with men.

At some point that discretion had let him down.

Henry did not know who had tried to blackmail his father. He did not know who was responsible for driving Andrew Thomas to despair so deep he had taken his own life at the age of forty.

The not knowing of which was no doubt for the best.

Henry had a slow burning temper, but when ignited, it burned hot and deep. If he ever discovered who had driven his father to suicide, he would return the harm.

Some way. Some how.

Edwin was putting his life, and that of his family, at unnecessary risk.

When the dig was over, Henry thought he would have a talk with the younger man. As much as Henry was loathe to embroil himself in the personal lives of others, the young thespian deserved to know how careful he must be, what the consequences of one wrong choice could be.

The terrible cost those who loved him might pay, those like his loyal sister.

If after he counted the cost with serious thought, Edwin still believed the risks he took worth it, then so be it. But the younger man deserved to know the truth of the risk he took.

As much for his own sake as for that of his loyal sister.

"You look very pensive," Frankie said, her voice cast in a slightly lower register than normal.

Would she be able to maintain that for two months in the desert?

"I am."

"Are you considering..." She let her voice trail off, clearly cautious about discussing particulars in the public venue of the dining room.

"I am."

"Oh." She smiled. "That is good."

"I imagine you think so."

"After this afternoon, I am more worried than I was before," she said with rueful candor. "Not that I will be caught out, but what two months in the desert with you could lead to."

Although surprised by it, Henry appreciated her honesty. She'd said sex between them could be addictive. And she hadn't liked that possibility.

He understood.

"You prefer an entirely independent life." So did he.

"Don't you?" she asked with uncanny accuracy.

He saw no point in denying it. "Yes."

And yet, the idea of being addicted to her body did not bother him as much as it should. Their sexual compatibility far exceeded anything he had known with another woman.

The fact that Frankie made it very clear she did *not* want another husband took the danger to his independence out of that scenario. Her reasons for wanting to remain a widow were well founded in his opinion.

His own views matched hers, if for different reasons. And yet, he felt that marriage to *this* woman might not be the tragedy he had always considered that state.

Not that he had any plans to court her in earnest. Even if Frankie might make some man a fine companion, that man would not be Henry Thomas.

Could not be him.

He would never allow another's wellbeing to be reliant on him.

His father had taught him many lessons, that one most certain of all.

"Are you all right?" Frankie asked, her brow furrowed.

"Of course. Why do you ask?"

She snapped her napkin before tucking it into her collar as a man might do, rather than her lap as was customary for a woman. "You had a strange expression on your face."

"Cousin Henry!"

Henry jolted, utter shock coursing through him. That voice had no place here in his Cairo hotel.

Turning his head, he watched in disbelief as his cousin's sixteen-year-old son waved and walked with the exuberance of youth across the hotel's dining room.

His father, Randall, followed far more sedately.

The maître d', an Arabic man who spoke flawless English, accompanied them, making hand gestures to others which resulted in two new place settings being added to the table.

Henry stood, and Frankie followed suit without pause.

After they had all taken their seats, Henry demanded, "What are you two doing here?"

"Hello, Henry. I am doing well, how are you?" Randall mocked with false politeness.

Henry just frowned. This was too much of a coincidence. Even if his cousin had business in Cairo, as he was sure had to be the case.

Foreboding deepened Henry's displeasure at being interrupted in his dinner with Frankie.

"Don't look so put out, Cousin Henry." Joseph smiled. "It won't be so bad. I'll be a good worker."

What the hell was the boy talking about?

Before Henry could ask, Randall put his hand out toward Frankie. "Randall Kingston, and this is my oldest son, Joseph."

"Edwin Clarke, Mr. Kingston. It is a pleasure to meet you." Frankie shook the other man's hand. She nodded at Joseph. "You as well, Joseph."

"Joey, if you don't mind."

Frankie inclined her head while Randall shook his. "The informality of youth today."

"Come off it, Pops, everyone calls me Joey except you."

Something flickered on Frankie's face, but she smiled. "My father has always refused to call me by my nickname as well."

"Eddie?" Joseph guessed.

"Frankie," Henry slotted in smoothly. If he was going to abet her in this crazy masquerade, he wasn't setting himself up for failure by trying to learn to call her by a different name.

"My middle name is Francis," Frankie explained quickly.

"My son will call you Mr. Clarke." Randall's tone and expression brooked no argument on that point of polite behavior.

Joseph grinned. "Course I will, Pops. I know my manners. I'm no hayseed."

"Yes, well, I have read that life on a dig can be less formal. I expect you to remember your place, regardless of the behavior of others."

Randall could be a bit of a prig.

The rest of what his cousin had said sank in and Henry frowned, that foreboding growing ever deeper. "What do you mean life on a dig? Did you and Joseph plan to visit us in Upper Egypt? We won't be setting up camp for another week."

The rest of his team did not arrive for five more days. Henry had planned to spend his time in Cairo procuring necessary supplies and hiring his Qifti. He had already had some trouble with supplies and the original *rais*, or foreman, from Qift he had planned to have back at his dig for the fourth year in a row had suddenly decided against returning.

Henry had no time to visit with family.

"Oh, I won't be accompanying him. I have to fly to Paris tomorrow."

"And you're leaving Joseph—"

"Joey!" his younger cousin said, interrupting.

He gave the teen a look. "Joey then." Henry turned his gaze back on Randall and waited for his cousin to reply to his question.

He could hardly believe the man would leave the boy alone in Egypt. Sixteen wasn't a child any longer, but it wasn't a fully grown adult either.

"Did you not get the telegram from your department head?" Randall asked, his brows drawn together.

"I did not get a communique from him, no." Nor had Henry expected one.

He and his department head communicated sparingly via letter when Henry was in Egypt. He'd never once gone to the expense of sending a wire telegram.

"He was supposed to wire you." Randall let out an impatient breath. "Never mind, I have a letter from him explaining more fully regardless."

"Explaining what more fully?"

Joey grinned. "I'm going on your dig, Cousin Henry."

Frankie gasped, her expression showing offense on Henry's behalf. "When was this decided and why wasn't Dr. Thomas informed earlier?"

"Who are you exactly?" Randall asked rather than answering.

"Mr. Clarke will be my personal secretary on the dig as well as a valuable member of the expedition."

He ignored the light of joy that lit Frankie's eyes, too furious to focus on anything by his cousin's words. "The only students allowed on my digs are university age and studying history."

"Your department head made an exception for Joseph since he is your relation."

"He cannot make that exception," Henry informed Randall frostily. "Only I can approve members of my expedition."

"You would not deny Joseph this opportunity."

"I most certainly would."

"But Cousin Henry..."

Henry ignored the young man's pleading tones and glared at Randall. "It is impossible. I will be far too busy to watch over him."

"I don't need watching over," Joey assured the table at large indignantly. "I am sixteen, not six. I've brought my own spade and brush along, and everything."

The look Randall gave his son was not a friendly one. "There was a bit of trouble back in Los Angeles. Joseph will benefit from the distance and opportunity to work for a couple of months."

"Don't worry, Cousin Henry," Joey said earnestly. "Father assures me I can return home for Christmas."

Henry hadn't been in California for Christmas for years. He always maximized his time on the dig and that meant staying until mid January.

However, he had to be back at the university before the second semester started, to teach his courses.

"What kind of trouble?" Henry asked Joey, ignoring his promise to be gone before Christmas.

"He—" Randall started to say.

But Henry wasn't looking for his cousin's interpretation of events. "Let the boy answer," Henry interrupted.

Joey lost some of his bonhomie. "My friends and I borrowed Judge Parson's Packard."

"Did you have permission to borrow it?" Frankie asked.

Joey cast her a sidelong glance. "Not exactly."

"You stole it." Henry wanted to curse.

"Henry!" Randall admonished.

But Henry ignored him, keeping his eyes fixed firmly on the sixteen-year-old.

Joey fidgeted under his regard. "Not exactly."

"How not exactly?" Henry asked, his tone hard.

Joey's shoulders slumped. "His son was with us."

"Did his son have permission?"

"No."

"Did he lie and say he did?"

"No."

"So, you stole the car."

"I guess."

"A man owns up to his mistakes," Henry instructed.

Joey sat up straighter. "Okay, we stole it, but we didn't mean any harm. We sure didn't mean to total it."

"You were in an accident." Oh, this just kept getting better.

"Yeah."

"Yes," his father corrected.

Joey gave Randall that look teens seemed to reserve for their parents and then sighed. "Yes." He drew the word out so it had at least three syllables.

Henry might have been amused under other circumstances. "Was anyone hurt?"

"Bantry broke his leg." Joey's expression finally showed remorse at that admission.

Randall added, "That is the judge's son."

"Anyone else?" Henry pressed.

"No." Joey crossed his heart. "I promise. We ran into the side of a hill. It did a job on the fender and the front of the car, but those Packards, they're sturdy cars. Go fast too."

Frankie made a sound. Like amusement.

Henry wasn't laughing. "My dig is not a refuge for wayward boys."

Frankie's amusement dried up and she glared at him, catching on immediately that Henry was not talking only about his cousin.

Miraculously, she said nothing however. Which considering the daggers her eyes were casting, was pretty impressive.

11

"I never said it was." Randall's entire body was stiff with offense. "However, Henry, if you were a father yourself, you would understand. I won't have my son turning into a hooligan."

"I'm not a hooligan, Pops," Joey said with affront.

Henry wasn't impressed with either of his cousins' words. "I never married because I never *wanted* the responsibility of children."

"That is hardly the attitude of a mature man. Even your father managed to have a son."

Henry knew exactly what that dig was supposed to mean. His father's homosexuality was something neither side of his family spoke about, but everyone his generation and older knew about.

Frankie watched with mounting worry as Henry went completely still. He did that when he was very upset.

As she'd learned to her own detriment.

Henry's jaw ticked. "My father has nothing to do with this."

Frankie wanted to soothe the archeologist but knew she could do nothing in her guise as Edwin.

"Let's keep it that way, shall we?" There could be no mistaking the threat in Randall Kingston's too polite tone.

Though Joey seemed oblivious, remarking loudly that he was hungry and couldn't they get some food?

Frankie interjected quickly to wave a waiter over and do just that, knowing that the conversation could not be allowed to escalate.

She was furious on Henry's behalf, that his own cousin would threaten him with his dead father's reputation. However, this was neither the time, nor the place, to hash that out.

If John sending her to a sanitorium had taught Frankie one thing, it was when to keep her mouth shut. No matter how she felt.

If Henry had not yet learned that, she would help him. It was the least she could do.

"Are you interested in history?" she asked Joey as everyone tucked into their dinners.

Joey, who had clearly responded to the tension at the table, brightened. "I am dead keen on it. I think that's why Pops cottoned onto this idea for getting me out of sight of Judge Parson's wrath."

He didn't seem like the scholarly sort, but looks could be deceiving. Frankie knew that firsthand. Right now, her looks were that of a 28-year-old man.

"What is your favorite area of history?"

"Ancient history. It has to be. It's so fascinating to think how people lived thousands of years ago."

"Don't you start spouting that evolutionary nonsense again, young man," Randall said severely. "Thousands of years indeed."

"Even Biblical and Koran scholars acknowledge the earth is at least four to five thousand years old," Henry said pointedly.

Frankie hid her smile in taking a bite of the savory and aromatic rice on her plate. Spices she had never tasted before mixed with others that were more familiar.

Delicious.

"You certainly seem to be enjoying your food, Mr. Clarke," Mr. Kingston said sourly.

Frankie tried very hard not to blush.

"Some people do not limit themselves to the familiar," Henry said with a reproving glower at Randall's plain roast and potatoes.

"I wish you'd have let me get the Koshari, Pops." Joey looked morosely at his roast, clearly uninspired by the plain meat and potatoes. "Trying new things is good for you."

"Trying new things is what got you in this mess," Randall replied.

"You'll have all the time in the world to eat local cooking on the dig, I'm sure."

Frankie quickly asked Joey another question about his interest in history before the conversation could devolve again.

It turned out that while his knowledge of Egypt was limited, he did know an impressive amount about the Spartans of Greece and the Persian Empire. Which could be helpful in his work on the dig, she had to admit.

The last of the Pharaonic lines had been Macedonian, a region in Mesopotamia, and Persia had occupied Egypt for centuries.

After dinner, Henry and Randall agreed to meet for port in the bar.

Frankie begged off and offered to walk with Joey to the suite of rooms he shared with his father.

"I don't need a babysitter."

"I wasn't aware I was offering to be one," Frankie said in her best imitation of her brother's masculine sarcasm.

With little more grumbling she saw the young man to his room, which she was glad to see was on a different floor than hers, and hopefully than Henry's as well.

Frankie woke to an insistent soft tap on her door sometime later.

She got up from her bed and padded across the floor in her pajamas. Cut for Edwin's male physic they stretched tautly across her own backside, but she'd decided to stick with male pajamas so that if she were seen at night, for any reason, her choice in sleepwear would not give her away.

Besides, the best way to stay in character was to do so at all times.

Yawning, she opened the door.

Henry glowered at her. "You didn't ask who it was," he hissed.

Rolling her eyes, she stepped back and let him in. She waited for him to shut the door before replying. "Who else would be knocking on my door at this hour?"

"Thieves. Cutthroats. It could have been anyone."

"Really? Thieves or cutthroats. We aren't living inside of a Dime Store novel."

"Aren't we? I was just blackmailed by a gangster that calls himself my cousin."

"What?" She needed more sleep. Henry's words made no sense.

"Randall. He didn't come right out and say it, but he implied my past would be brought to the attention of my department if I didn't take Joey on the dig."

"What past? You're a straight arrow." Surely he wasn't talking about the women Henry had bedded before. The man was as discreet as they came.

"My father. How he died. Why he died."

Suddenly Frankie was wide awake. "But that's terrible!"

"Keep your voice down."

"Sorry," she whispered back, still furious. "Wouldn't that come back to reflect on him?"

"He's the son of my mother's brother, not my father."

"Still, his aunt was married to the man."

"I know," Henry practically growled. "We used to be friends. There was a time I considered him like a brother."

Frankie would have taken offense, but she knew the anger wasn't directed at her, and it did not mask the pain of that admission.

"You agreed to take Joey on." He must have.

And he would be infuriated at being forced to do so. Henry hadn't been happy about taking Edwin, or rather Frankie, on. He'd had an opportunity to voice his objections though. And it wasn't his department head and family who had brought pressure to bear, but Frankie's father.

Someone who had no power to hurt Henry emotionally.

"I did, with some stipulations."

"Oh." She wasn't sure what else to say.

What would the presence of his young cousin mean to Frankie?

She had to admit it had not occurred to her to worry about running into people she had met on the dig back in California. However, Joey's arrival made that feel like a stronger possibility.

Was that because she hoped to continue her friendship with Henry when they returned to the States?

"Frankie." The not so patient tone of Henry's voice said that wasn't the first time he'd tried to get her attention.

"I beg your pardon. I'm still half asleep."

His teeth flashed white in the dim room, lit only by moonlight coming in through the open window. "I was saying that Joey will be sleeping with the other members of my team from my university."

"I thought Edwin said he would have his own tent?" If Frankie didn't have her own tent, there was no way for her to keep up her masquerade as her brother.

"Change in plans. You will be sharing my tent as my private secretary."

"But..."

"We will have to be very careful as we cannot afford anything to be taken wrong, especially now."

"Surely I should have my own tent then."

"Frankie, I have decided to allow you on the dig, but only if you agree to *my* terms." Was this about Henry taking back the control he felt he'd lost, or something else?

She gripped the lapels of his lightweight suit jacket. "How can I agree to something that will put you further at risk?"

"You have no choice. Not if you want to go on the dig."

"But I will be perfectly fine in my own tent."

"No."

"What do you mean, no?" she demanded in a furious whisper. "You cannot just say no and expect that to be the end of it."

"No," he said again, his tone taunting.

She stared up at him, trying to make out his shadowed expression, trying to understand why he was pushing so hard on this one point. "But why?"

"You are a woman." His hands were suddenly warm against the skin of her waist, under her pajama shirt, his big body closer than he had been a moment before. "That does not make you less in any way, but damnation Frankie, it does make you more vulnerable. You will *not* be staying in a tent alone."

Preoccupied by the feelings coursing through her from his fingers against her skin, she had to force herself to concentrate on what he was saying. "I could stay with your cousin."

"No. The risk of you being caught out with anyone else but me is too great."

She wanted to deny it, but he was right. She had counted on having her own sleeping quarters as Edwin would have done. "It is not fair that you think just because I am a woman, I cannot have my own tent."

"If you will notice, I have taken away private tent privileges from everyone in the party."

"You have?"

"I have."

"But why?"

"That is something we can discuss tomorrow, but right now I have other things that interest me far more."

"What?"

He answered with a kiss. Frankie responded immediately, her body swaying toward his, already familiar with the ecstasy found in his arms.

They did not talk this time, they could not.

Her window was still open. They undressed each other silently in the near dark, touching each other in silence.

There was something unutterably sensual about their need for quiet. It made everything sharper and more intense. Wanting to taste him as he had tasted her earlier, Frankie dropped to her knees.

She pushed back the foreskin on his generous erection and flicked her tongue out to taste the drop of fluid on the tip. A little salty, different than anything she had tasted before.

Having never done this before, Frankie went with her instincts to explore. She circled the thick shaft with her hand and licked all around the bulbous head. His big body shuddered, but he kept his groan low, nearly subvocal.

She smiled to herself.

This was what she wanted. To see how she could affect him. To know she was the orchestrator of *his* pleasure as he so very deftly orchestrated hers.

She pulled him into her mouth, sucking and laving with her tongue, thrilling in how his thickly muscled thighs trembled.

Suddenly, his hands landed on her shoulders, pushing her away.

Wondering what she'd done wrong, she stood.

He pulled her close and whispered into her ear. "Too close, little siren."

"Get your rubber," she told him, eager to feel him inside of her. Frankie was so excited she did not need, or want, any more touching before they joined their bodies.

She wanted him now.

Henry did not question her certainty, but did as she'd instructed and joined her on the bed immediately.

However, he maneuvered them so he was on his back and she was on top.

It was a new position for her, but she saw the potential benefits of it immediately. Frankie could set the pace and the depth of penetration. Which she did, to great effect. Less concerned about his pleasure, now that her own was in play, she hoped what she was doing was as satisfying for him as it was for her.

Frankie took Henry into her body, stopping for several seconds to just revel in how it felt. So full. So intense.

She exulted in her sensual power.

Henry did not try to get her moving, but he wasn't passive either, touching her body in ways that sent pleasure zinging through her.

Frankie began to move, sliding up and down, shifting this way and that until she found the rhythm and the exact position that steadily tightened that coil of ecstatic tension inside her. When it sprang, she threw her head back and shouted, but his hand was there, muffling the sound without constricting her breathing.

She did not care how much illicit sexual experience he must have to be so aware. Frankie was just glad that her climax had not been marred by regret or fear of being caught out.

Henry thrust upward. Once. Twice. Three times and then his body went rigid and he grunted, low and long.

She fell forward and whispered. "You did not pull out again."

"No, I did not." He did not sound angry about that fact, more resigned.

As much as she liked knowing she wreaked havoc with his control, she knew they had to figure out a secondary form of contraception, if they wanted to ensure she did not become pregnant.

Henry did not jump from the bed immediately after sex this time. Though he did take a moment to tie off his rubber and set it aside.

Cuddled against his side, Frankie was almost asleep when he spoke.

"My *rais* who has been with my dig for the past three years has decided not to return."

"*Rais*?" Frankie asked, her voice slurred with tiredness.

She had been exhausted when she'd arrived after all that travel. Then they'd had sex and the drama at dinner. She had gotten very little sleep before he came knocking on her door. Then they had made love again and she was ready for sleep. More than.

"Foreman. My head Qifti."

"Oh." She nuzzled into him, enjoying his masculine scent as she fitted the pronunciation of the word with the one she had learned in her reading. "Why?"

"That stupid mummy's curse. He says he cannot risk digging up the dead."

She patted him consolingly. "Have to find a new foreman. 'M sure they want to work with you."

He chuckled. "You are barely awake."

"Mmm."

She felt a soft kiss to the top of her head. "Go to sleep, Frankie. We will talk tomorrow."

When she woke up, he was gone and the Egyptian sun lit her room brightly. Which did not actually mean it was late in the morning. Her window faced the east.

Frankie felt surprisingly refreshed, with a sense of wellbeing pervading her.

A rat-a-tat-tat on her door had her quickly sitting up. She was naked.

"Who..." she cleared her throat and dropped her tone. "Who is it?"

There was no answer.

Frankie jumped from the bed and threw on her pajamas and robe, hurriedly smoothing down her hair before rushing to the door.

She opened it and peeked out, but no one was there. However, one of the porters was knocking on doors as he went down the corridor, saying the time in English, French and Arabic.

Frankie shut her door and set about readying for the day.

When she reached the hotel dining room, she found Henry and his cousins already at a table, drinking coffee.

She smiled at the table at large. "Good morning."

"You've shaved off your mustache!" Joey exclaimed.

"Joseph!" his father reproved him. "Making such a personal observation is in bad taste."

"But why would you?" Joey demanded of Frankie, undaunted by his parent's censure. "If I could grow a mustache like that, I wouldn't shave it."

"I thought it might be cooler," Frankie said, wondering if she'd made a mistake.

"But Cousin Henry has a beard and a mustache."

"Leave off, Joey," Henry instructed. "Mr. Clarke's personal grooming habits are his own business."

"If you say so."

He really was an irrepressible young man, Frankie thought. She liked him. She smiled at Joey to let him know his comments had not offended her.

"What are your plans for the day?" she asked Henry.

"*Our* plans are to travel to Qift and find a new foreman for the dig."

"Will I be going with you?" Joey asked excitedly.

"No. You will stay here in the hotel and make an inventory of deliveries that arrive for the dig. The management have instructions on where our supplies are to be stored. I want a meticulous accounting of what arrives compared to what is expected."

"How will I know what is expected?" Joey asked.

Henry took a sip of his tea, his steady grey eyes fixed on his young cousin. "I will leave my supply journal with you. It details everything I have ordered and who it has been ordered from to this point."

"I won't let you down, Cousin Henry."

Henry nodded. "I am sure you will not."

"Isn't that usually your foreman's job?" Randall asked, proving he was not entirely ignorant of what his cousin's work entailed.

Henry frowned. "Yes, but since we now have to get a new foreman, needs must."

"What happened to the foreman you had arranged?" Randall asked.

"He has been scared off by the Mummy's Curse." The derision in Henry's tone was unmistakable.

"But I thought that was just for the tomb of King Tutankhamun," Joey said with interest.

"There is no Mummy's Curse, but a big part of the work being done in the Wadjet Province is excavating ancient graves."

"You mean mummies?" Joey's eyes were round.

"Some have been mummified, some have mummified as a result of being buried in the desert."

Joey leaned forward, his curiosity clearly piqued. "What's the difference?"

Henry explained while Frankie made sure breakfast was on its way and ordered juice to go with their coffee.

"You will be a good assistant for my absent-minded cousin, I think," Randall Kingston said with approval.

His attitude toward Henry had been much friendlier today, but the same could not be said for the latter. Henry had not forgiven his cousin using threats to get his way and his stiff demeanor toward Mr. Kingston implied that wasn't likely to happen any time soon either.

Frankie gave an Edwin like shrug. "Dr. Thomas has enough to worry about, being in charge of an entire dig, without concerning himself with the mundane."

"He's a brilliant man."

Frankie could only nod her agreement, when what she wanted to do was ask if Mr. Kingston admired his cousin so much, how could he have threatened him?

"Both your son and I are very lucky to have the opportunity to be on his excavation."

"I am aware." The older man sounded sincere.

The look Henry gave him indicated he'd heard the exchange and he was not impressed with his cousin's sincerity.

Mr. Kingston frowned, but he did not comment.

Too excited about the upcoming trip to Qift to continue thinking about the now strained relationship between the two men, Frankie wondered when they would be leaving on their journey.

All the best excavators were supposed to come from Qift. Some families passed down the career from one generation to the next, fathers bringing their sons to digs with them when they got old enough to learn the trade.

She was surprised that Henry wanted her to accompany him rather than Joey. Frankie might have been the more natural choice to oversee deliveries and inventory supplies in her role as his assistant.

Which Randall pointed out over their food a few minutes later.

"Mr. Clarke is being trained for future archeological endeavors. He will benefit by a visit to Qift." Henry's tone did not invite further discussion.

"Surely Joseph would benefit just as much."

"Oh, do you plan for your son to go into archeology rather than banking?" Henry asked.

The scoffing sound Joey made said that was not likely. "Pops expects me to make my mark in the business world."

"And what do you want to do?" Frankie asked the young man.

"I don't know. I want to go to university, but I want to study history, not business. At least I think I do. I like numbers almost as much."

Randall gave his son a surprisingly understanding look. "The next few weeks should help you make up your mind."

So, unlike her own father, whose intention in sending Edwin to Egypt was simply to get him out of California, Randall Kingston had not chosen the dig to merely get Joey out of sight of the judge.

He wanted his son to test out his passion for history and see how deep it really ran.

The difficulties and hard work of life on a dig should do that nicely. Though nothing said that every historian had to become an archeologist.

In fact, most didn't.

The hotel manager found a driver with his own car willing to take them the Qift and stay with them as transport for the duration and return to Cairo.

He drove an old Model T in such a manner that Frankie was quickly wishing they had opted for the train, or even camel transport.

"He has no sense of fear at all," she gasped to Henry after yet another near miss.

Henry's grey eyes twinkled with humor. "None whatsoever. You will get used to it."

"If I survive the drive."

Henry's chuckle was not as reassuring as he probably thought it was.

"You don't think it wouldn't be better to have the new foreman do the inventory?" she asked, trying to focus on something other than their imminent death in a fiery crash.

"Supplies that were supposed to arrive have not. I want to know just how much damage control needs to be done as soon as we return to Cairo."

"Is that normal?" she wondered out loud.

"There is always a certain number of disappointing results when handling communications via letter and across oceans and continents,"

Henry acknowledged. "However, I have never had as many problems with workers and supplies as I have this year."

"You think it's the Mummy's Curse?" she asked.

"You know I don't—"

"Not the curse itself," she hurried to add. "But that workers, and even suppliers, are concerned about participating in excavations related to tombs, cemeteries and the like, right now."

"Before arriving in Cairo I would have said that the Mummy's Curse was more talked about by European and American newspapers than anyone in Egypt."

"But now?"

"I do not know. My former *rais* was not a man easily given to superstition."

She was sure that was one of the reasons Henry had liked working with the man. "I'm surprised he gave up his position so easily. Isn't it a matter of pride?"

"I would have said so, but he seemed quite adamant he could not work with me again this year."

Henry had a strange look on his face.

"What aren't you telling me?"

"It is nothing."

"It is something if you are thinking about it."

"He left a note for me with the hotel manager. I found that very odd."

"Why?"

"He is a man who I would have always said would come to me directly. The note felt like..."

"Like an evasion of responsibility, and he is not that type of man?"

"I wouldn't have thought so, no."

"Did you try to contact him?"

"Once we reach Qift, his house is the first we will visit."

"Good."

"I am glad you approve," Henry said with some humor.

"I wouldn't like to think that you are a man who does not listen to his own instincts."

Henry nodded. "You decided to go with the clean-shaven look."

It was such a change of subject it took Frankie a moment to answer. "Oh, yes. I knew I didn't want to sleep with the spirit gum on my face. It can become quite irritating after prolonged wear."

"You did not consider this before coming."

"To be fair, it is my first foray into the guise of masculinity."

The taxi hit something in the road and Frankie was jounced up into the air. She landed half on top of Henry.

The driver yelled invective, shaking his fist at the road behind him as if he took the poor conditions as a personal affront.

Henry held Frankie against him for a long moment before winking and setting her back on the seat.

Breathless, she laughed. "We'll be lucky if we reach Qift without two flat tires."

"Shh, do not tempt fate."

"From a man who does not believe in curses?"

Henry's laughter warmed her better than the Egyptian sun.

They stopped for lunch and to fill the motorcar with petrol from the gas cans strapped to the back around two.

There was only sand and scrub for as far as they eye could see. "We should have taken the train," Frankie mused.

"Still bothered by our driver's prowess?"

"Or lack thereof."

"If there had been time, I would have bought a car for the trip, but that will have to wait for our return to Cairo."

"You plan to buy a car?"

"Two of them. Having two automobiles dedicated to the dig will improve our transportation logistics."

"I see, but you didn't want to wait to travel to Qift to find them."

"No. My *rais* could take a position with another excavation."

She didn't comment on his certainty he would convince the foreman to return to the dig. "Still, why not the train?"

"I considered it, but then we would have had no privacy to converse."

"We have privacy with the driver?" she asked.

"He does not speak any English."

"Oh. I did not realize." But come to think of it, all the discussion between Henry and the driver had been in Arabic.

"This way, we do not have to worry about being overheard or if you slip in your persona as Edwin."

"I see. I thought I was doing well."

"You are, but there is no need to maintain the strain of doing so every minute when it is not necessary."

"You're a thoughtful man." Especially considering his misgivings about helping her with her subterfuge.

12

They arrived in Qift late that night. Their driver found them accommodations in a small hotel.

Grateful the modicum of anonymity afforded over staying in a rented room in a family's house, Frankie grabbed her things from the Model T and followed Henry into the building. She let him do all the talking with the night manager, and most likely proprietor.

Even if she had spoken Arabic fluently as Henry did, Frankie was too tired to talk.

She was so exhausted, even her bones ached with it. That could also be due to spending the day jouncing in the Model T.

Their bedroom was on the third floor. There was a bathroom at the end of the narrow hall for use by the occupants of the four rooms along the hall, the porter explained as he led them toward the door furthest from the stairs.

Henry repeated the information in English for Frankie before thanking the porter, who had clearly been woken from his bed to show them to their room.

The porter smiled sleepily and said something before stepping back.

Henry went into the room. Frankie followed him silently, sending the porter a muted smile of thanks.

An oil lamp cast a warm glow over the room with two twin sized beds. It looked clean and that was all that mattered to Frankie.

She plopped down on one of the beds. "I may just sleep in my clothes."

"Tired?" Henry grabbed his shaving kit.

"Exhausted."

"Then you should use the facilities first."

"Thank you." She forced herself to stand. "I wish we could go for a walk."

As tired as she was, Frankie wanted to stretch her legs after all day in the car.

"We'll get plenty of walking in tomorrow."

Frankie sighed, but nodded. Grabbing her own *shaving* kit, she made her way to the small room where she could perform her evening ablutions.

She was in her pajamas and in bed by the time Henry returned. He undressed and sat down on the side of his bed, fully naked.

Frankie's mouth went dry. "Aren't you going to put on pajamas?"

"No."

"Why not?"

"I don't use them."

"Even on the dig?" she asked.

"Too hot."

"But..."

"Frankie, you've seen me naked."

They were talking quietly, their voices unlikely to carry, but still she looked around like someone was going to pop out of the woodwork to overhear them. "Hush."

His smile was devilish.

There was no other word for it.

"You can't...it's not..." She'd never known a man who did not wear nightclothes to bed.

Her father did. Her brothers did. Her husband had.

Henry did not.

Proving he was not joking, he leaned over and extinguished the lamp and casting the room into stygian darkness, before the sound of rustling bedding attested he was getting comfortable for sleep.

Frankie laid there in the dark, sure she would nod off immediately.

She did not. No matter how she tried to relax, she could not sleep. She flipped from one side to the other, then onto her back and then onto her stomach. And then onto her back again.

Fabric rustled and then the soft sound of footfalls on the worn floorboards.

She shifted toward the wall just before Henry sat down beside her.

"What are you doing?" she whispered furiously.

This was no hotel built with thick stucco covered brick walls like the one they were using in Cairo.

"I know how to help you sleep."

She had no doubt. "We can't. Not here."

Someone would hear them, and she would not put him at risk like that. No matter how much her body longed for his touch.

His hand touched hers and then she felt a cloth. A cloth with a knot.

A throb of desire pulsed in her sex. He'd knotted his handkerchief for her to use as a gag again. Like the first time.

Only he had to have done it while either she, or he, was using the facilities because she hadn't seen him.

Which meant he'd planned for this.

He wanted her as much as she wanted him.

"Kiss first," she whispered fiercely.

She could feel his body moving closer, but could see nothing in the inky blackness of the room.

Then his lips pressed against hers as his body settled along hers on the narrow bed.

He unbuttoned her pajama top as they kissed, his big hand cupping her breasts, playing with her nipple. She arched toward him, reaching down to curl her hand around his hard prick.

She squeezed and he swallowed back most of a groan.

Satisfaction coursed through her. She loved having that kind of effect on him.

He pinched her nipple and the kiss muffled her own reaction.

He reached down and tugged her hand up, breaking the kiss. "Put it in."

She nodded, but realized he couldn't see her. "Okay," she whispered.

She put the knotted handkerchief in her mouth. He put his mouth on her breast, suckling on her nipple while his hand travelled down her body. He untied the drawstring on her pajama bottoms and slipped his hand inside, his finger pressing between the slick folds of her labia.

Her own hand convulsed on his rigid flesh and he pressed toward her.

They pleasured each other with their hands, his mouth sending thrills of ecstasy from her nipple straight to her core.

Her climax caught her unaware, and Frankie bowed up, trying not to cry out, biting down on the gag.

He didn't stop touching her but skillfully brought her to another pinnacle pleasure that did not reach the same height but felt like it went on and on with burst of renewed pleasure until finally she fell limp into the bed.

His hand covered hers and he guided it up and down on his big sex until he came in hot streams of ejaculate over their hands.

They panted together in silence, the dark around them absolute.

Finally, he reached for the handkerchief, unknotting it and using it to clean both their hands.

"Think you can sleep now?" he asked.

She didn't bother to answer, just allowed her body to settle into peaceful slumber.

Henry woke before Frankie and moved to his own bed lest he be caught in hers.

Last night had been hot and oh so satisfying and he would like nothing more than to spend the day in bed with his new lover. However, they had far too much to do this day to indulge, even if they could.

And of course. They could not.

Frankie was the most dangerous lover he had ever taken. Not only was she a woman who society would demand he marry if they were caught *in flagrante delicto*, but in her current guise as a man, the consequences could be devastating. Or even deadly.

Fully dressed, his morning lavation completed, he returned to the room and opened the shutters. He was glad the hotel did not send staff into the rooms to waken guests as they did in some places.

Sunlight streamed into the room and Frankie's nose wrinkled. He smiled, watching her come awake. After another moment, her eyes fluttered and then opened.

Warmth filled their lovely brown depths as she smiled. "Good morning."

"Good morning, Frankie."

She sat up, her blanket slipping to her waist, her raspberry tipped breasts framed by her open pajama top.

Their eyes met and her expression grew sultry.

"We have to go down for breakfast."

"We have a lot to do today," she agreed.

She did not make it out of the room for another thirty minutes and he had to wash up a second time.

After a breakfast of *ful* and boiled eggs, Henry had their driver take them to the home of his former *rais*.

It was near the market and the area where workmen looking for opportunities on the archeological digs congregated this time of the season.

Remembering his promise to Frankie that they would get plenty of walking in, Henry dismissed the driver.

He knocked on the door of the foreman's house, unsurprised when the man's wife answered. He asked after her health and that of their children before asking if her husband was home.

She informed Henry that Anum was at the market, looking for work.

Henry thanked her and offered a blessing for their house before she shut the door.

He turned and relayed the conversation to Frankie.

"I should have spent more time learning spoken Arabic, rather than French."

"Oh, have you studied it?"

"A little. I'm much better on the written word, but I understood only maybe one out of five words she spoke."

"That's a start."

Frankie nodded. They walked toward the market, her gaze flitting from one building to the next. She watched the people too, though more circumspectly. "It's all so amazing. I can barely believe I'm here."

"In Qift?"

"In Egypt, but yes, in Qift too. I never expected to see anything beyond Cairo and the dig site."

"You will see plenty on our journey south on the Nile, to Upper Egypt."

Her brown gaze shone. "I can't wait."

"If we are successful buying the two automobiles, some of the workers will drive them to the Cobra Province. However, you and I will take a boat up the Nile," he offered, deciding in that moment that he would arrange special passage for them and feeling more talkative than usual.

He found that in her company, he was not nearly as taciturn. Odd, but acceptable.

"You do not wish to drive?" she asked, doing such a consistent job of modulating her voice to emulate her brother's Henry couldn't help but be impressed.

He shook his head. He wanted to give Frankie a more luxurious and relaxing trip. She'd been exhausted last night after the long trip in the Model T. "Not all the workers and archeologists will fit in the motorcars and it is better to split up the camp so some can get working, even if the automobiles are delayed."

He kept to himself the fact he wanted to give her a rest from automobile travel.

"Bad roads?"

"In places." Not that that would stop most drivers in Egypt, even a lack of roads all together was often seen as more a challenge than a stumbling block. "However, lack of reliability is the real issue."

"You mean breaking down?"

"Engine troubles are a concern, yes, but so are flat tires, running out of petrol. There are a lot of motorcars here, but the further south we go, the less easily serviced and fueled they are."

"I see." She smiled. "I'm a better mechanic than Edwin."

"You are?"

"Oh, yes. I can't take apart an engine like a friend of mine, but if the trouble is something basic, I'm handy at fixing it."

"Well, that's good to know."

She gazed longingly at some camels tethered near the market. "I think I wouldn't mind traveling by camel though."

"You say that only because you have not done so."

She stopped and looked up at him, her expression earnest. "What do you mean?"

"If you think a Model T jars your bones, try spending an entire day traveling on the back of a dromedary."

She waved that away and started walking again. "But it would be an adventure."

"I suppose." He got the feeling that most things in life could be made into an adventure by this woman.

"Oh, come, you cannot tell me you have no adventurous spirit. If that were true, you would be content to do all your learning second hand and in the library."

Henry had never considered that. He'd simply known that to learn what he wanted, he had to travel to Egypt and spend time in the sand.

They reached the market, and Henry spied the man he was looking for drinking coffee with a group of other men. "There is Anum Ibrahim."

Frankie looked to where Henry had indicated.

The man Henry had pointed to was much darker than his wife, with strong, handsome Egyptian features and a dignified air, though his age was hard to tell.

"I suppose I won't understand a word he says either," she said with no small amount of disappointment.

All of her work on learning to read the language was going to do her very little good, now she was in this country with so many Arabic *speaking* people.

"My foreman is fluent in French and speaks some English."

"Listen to you. *My foreman.* You talk like you're confident you can convince him to come back to work for you." Though knowing the other man spoke French fluently delighted Frankie.

She would not tax his limited English vocabulary if she could help it.

While Frankie would do her best to learn Arabic, being able to communicate with Anum Ibrahim would be a real boon.

"Some call me stubborn."

"Since I am one of them, I have no doubt others have noticed that trait about you as well." Frankie grinned at him.

Desire flared hot and fast in Henry's gaze, but was banked just as quickly. The Qift market was no place for thoughts of that nature.

Henry became silent beside her, but Frankie did not mind.

The market was far too interesting. She did her best not to gawk at all the new things she heard and saw in the colorful, busy place.

It was so different from the department stores in downtown Los Angeles. She'd never seen anything like it, not back home, or during her time at finishing school in Europe.

Unfamiliar fruits and vegetables filled large baskets. Tables were stacked high with cloths in all sorts of colors, from the natural linens to ruby red silks.

One stall had nothing but prayer beads. Another displayed intricately cast brass cups and tall, elegant teapots. Incense and spices perfumed the air. Motorcars and animals competed for space in the narrow streets around the periphery.

The noise was overwhelming at first, sellers extolling the virtues of their wares, people in conversations, camels braying. The driver of a motorcar honking impatiently for a man pushing a cart to get out of his way.

It was a rich patina of life, different from anything Frankie had ever known.

This moment alone would have been worth all the effort of her masquerade as Edwin.

And they had not even made it to the dig yet.

Perhaps Frankie had more of the travel bug than she had realized.

Doris was not the only Clarke daughter who wanted to see new places and experience different cultures. Though the fact that Frankie was experiencing the modern land of the place of antiquity she most enjoyed studying?

That made it all so much *more* interesting.

Frankie wanted adventure too, she had to admit. More than merely hearing about it from her friends in the ladies' adventurer society. Or studying topics she was told were not meant for the mind of a woman. They were two decades into a new century, but some antiquated attitudes seemed like they would never change.

A flapper could insist on what amounted to sexual freedom, but she could not attend courses at the vast majority of the universities in both Europe and America. There *were* all women's colleges, though not many of them.

So much of Frankie's self-education had been clandestine, but it was not enough.

She wanted to experience life. Different cultures. See different places.

Her fear of ending up back in the sanitorium had dominated her life for so long, determining her choices, and curbing her natural enthusiasm for trying new things.

She'd stuck with what was safe.

For the first time in years, Frankie felt free. She inhaled, reveling in the scents of spices, animals, and humanity.

"Come, you can look at the stalls later." Henry said from beside her. "We need to speak to Anum."

Unsurprised Henry had opted for the most direct path through the market, Frankie looked again at Anum, this time taking in his companions as well. The group of men all wore robes in different shades of tan, their heads covered in tight turbans, most of their faces sporting dark beards.

They sat around a small round table, sipping at tiny cups of coffee, talking and paying little attention to the market around them.

That changed when one of them noticed her and Henry's approach.

He said something and suddenly four sets of eyes were on Henry and Frankie.

"It is a good thing you are in the guise of Edwin right now. It would not be proper for you to speak to these men otherwise," Henry said in a low tone.

Frankie did not ask why. She knew that as an unmarried woman, even a widow, she would have had a lot more restrictions on her social interaction here in Egypt than she would pretending to be her brother.

Even in this modern era, there were so many limits put on a woman's behavior, and not only here in Africa.

Henry stopped beside the table and greeted the men in Arabic.

One of the men stood and spoke rapidly to Henry. Henry replied. They went back and forth for several minutes before the other man's face creased in a big smile and he started nodding.

The men around the table nodded their approval and Frankie had to wonder what was going on, but was not going to rudely interject and ask. She understood that this conversation should take place in the foreman's native tongue. As a sign of respect, if nothing else.

Henry turned to her. "It is the strangest thing."

"What?"

"He says he received a letter from my department dismissing his services for this year's dig. He claims he never sent the letter to me at the hotel, that he had no intention of leaving the dig on his own. He entirely rejects any concept of a Mummy's Curse and says that telling the stories of the dead is important."

But then where had the note come from?

"So, he does not mind excavating them?" Frankie confirmed, just to be sure.

"No, though he prefers to do so on my dig as we rebury our dead after doing our sketches and taking our notes."

"You do?"

"Naturally, I have to bring some artifacts back to the university, but I keep it to a minimum. Once we've dug them up, the workers will come back for them if we do not divvy them between the university's museum and Egypt's Department of Antiquities."

"To sell on the black market?" she asked.

"Most likely, yes."

"Oh."

"It is their livelihood and their homeland. Those who do the grave robbing, see nothing wrong with it." And Henry's tone revealed nothing of his own thoughts.

Frankie had to ask, "What do you think?"

"That it is not my job to make sure that an Egyptian man follows his own country's laws when he is no longer in my employ."

"But..."

"Anum would not do this thing. He is a man with a great respect for history. It is one of the reasons I do not want to lose him on my dig. I value him more than the other American archeologists my university saddles me with each year."

That surprised Frankie, but she said nothing. They could discuss his opinions of his fellow university professors later.

Right now, Henry needed to get his workmen hired since Mr. Ibrahim had not done so in advance as he would have done had he believed he was still working for Henry's dig.

The rest of the day was spent talking to workmen and putting out the word that Henry's dig wanted at least eight men for the next three months, but would hire as many as a dozen. His pay was competitive, but arranging transport for the men was trickier.

It was agreed that those who did not join Anum and the other professors in the motorcars, would have their boat passage paid, and transport across the desert by camel.

"Wouldn't it be less expensive, not to mention easier, to hire more local workers?" she asked him on the walk back to their small hotel.

"Anum will hire more men locally once we arrive in Wadjet, mostly for the dirt removal. We need experienced diggers he can trust on all of the crews if we want my rules for excavation followed."

Frankie was relieved to see the familiar street for the hotel. As much as she had enjoyed their day, her dogs were tired.

She was ready to get off them and sit down somewhere quiet. "Are your rules so different from other digs?"

"Some so called archeologists have no care for the layers they dig through, if those layers are not of interest for their area, or era of study. Some leave the corpses piled in the desert after they've stripped them of any artifacts."

"That is awful."

Henry gave her an odd look. "It is far too easy to develop a certain level of callous disregard for the fact that an ancient corpse was in fact a living breathing human being at one time."

"But how?" she asked, unable to imagine being that inured to such a thing.

"When one is excavating in a cemetery, the bones can become like the sand."

Frankie shivered. "I do not want to ever see it that way."

"Then, you will not."

"Do you?"

"No."

Frankie could no more hold back her smile of approval than she could withstand her next breath.

"Don't look at me like that," Henry growled and stomped away.

Frankie could have taken his irritability personally, but she didn't.

Her archeologist was a grump, but she remembered the effect her smile had on him. And it wasn't one for public consumption.

As they entered the relative quiet and cool interior of the hotel, Frankie had to acknowledge Henry had kept his promise.

They had gotten *plenty* of walking in.

Even more than to sit down, she wanted a long, hot bath, but that was not an option. Not here in the small hotel where morning and evening ablutions were accomplished with a pitcher of water and a bowl.

Dinner was delicious, local fair, but their conversation was desultory.

Frankie was too tired to keep up her end with any enthusiasm and Henry seemed preoccupied.

"What are you thinking about?" she finally asked, feeling somewhat revived by the after-dinner mint tea.

"Someone went to a great deal of trouble to put my dig off its schedule."

She'd been thinking about that very thing on and off all day, unable to understand *why*. No matter the angle she looked at the problem from.

"They had to realize once you talked to Mr. Ibrahim that you would get it sorted."

"What if I hadn't spoken to him though?" Henry asked, his features set in a scowl. "What if I had sought a new foreman in Cairo in an attempt to regain the lost days?"

"Would you have?" she wondered.

"Clearly not."

"Who would *not* know that?" she asked, thinking that might help illuminate who would have sent the letters to both him and his foreman.

"What?" Henry asked.

"That you are too stubborn and thorough to settle for less than the best."

He looked at her, his expression grim. "I do not know. More to the point, *why* would someone try to sabotage my dig?"

"Is that what you think this is?"

"What else?"

Frankie had no answer for him. The problem had been too easily fixed for the intention to be clear. Yes, a couple of days had been lost, but not really. While it would have been better had Henry been in Cairo collecting supplies and seeing to any last-minute paperwork, he still was not scheduled to leave for Upper Egypt for a few more days.

Of course, if Joey had not been available to accept supplies and inventory them, that could have put things back further on the schedule, she had to acknowledge.

She said so.

Henry nodded. "Exactly. No one else was expected to join me from America until the end of the week. My foreman *was* supposed to meet me in Cairo when I arrived. That he was not there to take care of the things he usually does would have been more than a mere annoyance had neither you, nor Joey showed up when you did."

Frankie felt a warm glow at Henry's acknowledgement of her benefit to him.

"We can discuss this more tomorrow," Henry said with a significant look around the small dining room.

They couldn't know who spoke English and might be eavesdropping, though it was unlikely anyone did.

13

They were up before dawn the next morning and on the road as light broke on the horizon.

With minimal stops, they reached Cairo by afternoon. Henry and Frankie had spent much of the drive going over all the things that needed doing before their own boat trip down the Nile.

Frankie was delighted Henry was delegating responsibilities to her, even if he did so in a rather highhanded manner.

He wasn't treating her like she had less ability and intellect because she was a woman.

And no amount of bitten out commands could annoy her when he ended with, "I am glad it is you and not your brother coming on this dig. I trust you to follow through on these tasks and help me keep our schedule."

Warmed, Frankie smiled. "I'm not sure why it's so important not to get behind by even a day, but I'm certainly happy to help."

Perhaps if she understood then she would have some idea of who might have tried to sabotage Henry's efforts.

"You have read the journals. I know you have," Henry said, somewhat impatiently. "You read about the discovery of the tomb of Tutankhamun."

Understanding dawned. "Some of the most important discoveries have happened on the last day of digging."

"Even a single day less on the site could mean the difference between a breakthrough and an unproductive season."

"Who would benefit from that?" she asked.

"What do you mean?" Henry clearly wasn't thinking the who, but the what of the sabotage.

"I'm trying to think of who would benefit from your dig not going well. Not your university department. Your dig brings them prestige."

"The other two archeologists on the dig specialize in different ancient civilizations. They would be very happy if my university chose to pull our resources from Egypt and place them elsewhere."

"Oh." She thought about how the situation with the foreman had been handled, via letter. "They could have managed it, I suppose."

"Not without local help. The note from Anum, left here at the hotel for me, had no American postage on it."

"You saved the envelope?"

"I did not." Henry looked a bit chagrined. "I crumpled it all up and tossed it. It was not until later, I began to wonder if it were genuine."

That he had considered the question at all showed how much he trusted the other man's judgment. Henry had not believed Anum would be influenced by the Mummy's Curse and he had been right.

"You were angry," she said with understanding.

"I was, but allowing my temper to get the best of me is no way to run a dig."

"You expect a lot from yourself."

"One must control one's emotions when others rely on you."

She had to agree. Though as true as the sentiment was, Frankie also knew that it was not reasonable to think it could hold every moment of every day, no matter how hard she, or even Henry, might try.

"You noticed it was not American postage on the envelope though?" she probed.

"I did. I found the note so unbelievable at first, I thought it was a joke."

"Not a joke, but not genuine either."

"Exactly."

And not sent from America, but that didn't mean it didn't originate there with one of his colleagues. "You don't think your cousin has anything to do with it, do you?" she asked.

"Joseph? Certainly not."

"He does come off as genuinely interested in the dig, but I was thinking more about his father."

"To what end?" Henry asked.

"You said your grandfather financially supports the dig."

"He does, but he is from the other side of my family. My father's father. Randall might benefit from my death, but not my professional embarrassment."

"Why your death?"

"In two years, I come into a trust fund left to me by my mother's father. If I die before taking possession of the money, the fund will be split up amongst the living beneficiaries of his will."

Henry had been thinking hard about this. Frankie should not be surprised. Though as he said, the only benefit would be if Henry died, not got inconvenienced on his dig.

"It's rather easy for me to see Randall in the role of villain," she admitted. "Regardless of the logic of it."

Amusement flashed in Henry's gaze. "That side of my family have always been more supportive of my archeological work. As reprehensible as his tactics in getting my agreement, the fact that Randall saw my dig as a good place to send his son shows as much."

It was true. Mr. Kingston obviously cared about his son and Frankie had a difficult time imagining him sending Joey to spend several weeks with someone he didn't trust, much less wanted to undermine.

Unless Joey was in on this, but that seemed ludicrously unlikely.

"And the other half of your family?" she asked.

"The same. When my father died, my grandfather put me in the will to inherit his portion, but Grandfather Thomas is hale and hearty, so even my death would not benefit them for many years." Henry's expression shifted, like he'd just thought of something.

"What is it?" she asked.

"My uncle and his family resent that I will inherit because I am not a businessman, adding to the family fortunes." Henry frowned. "Uncle Louis resents that grandfather funded my father's excavations and is such a significant contributor to my own even more though."

That sounded like motive for the kind of prank that had been pulled, but Frankie found it hard to think a businessman of her father's age and stature would stoop to such a petty trick. Especially as a delayed dig wasn't likely to curb Henry's grandfather's support.

"Hmm," she said thoughtfully. "What about your colleagues. How jealous are they of you?"

"I did not say they were jealous."

Not in so many words. "But they would rather have digs funded in their areas of expertise."

"Undoubtedly, but how much money would be available is in question as Grandfather Thomas funds a good portion of the digs expenses."

"My father's contribution?" Frankie wished sometimes she wasn't so curious, but could not stop inappropriate questions popping out.

None of this was any of her business and yet, she kept digging.

Henry did not appear to mind. "He offered enough money to this year's dig to make saying no to Edwin's involvement foolhardy."

Frankie nodded. "That sounds like him. When Father wants something, he knows how to get it."

Henry's brows rose. "And yet three of his children have outwitted him and pursued their own agendas despite his carefully laid plans."

"I guess we all have a little of his stubbornness in us."

"Little?" Henry chided.

Frankie laughed. "Maybe more than a smidge."

"I should say so. You are, after all, prepared to live in the guise of a man for the next two and a half months. That is more than a little anything."

He sounded too admiring to be criticizing her and Frankie found herself smiling, rather than frowning at the observation.

Joey met them with notes and enthusiasm when they arrived at the hotel in Cairo. They hadn't even checked for messages before he was leading them to some chairs in the lobby where tea had been laid out on a small table.

"Most of our supplies have arrived as expected, Cousin Henry." Joey handed Henry the inventory journal. "I've put notes beside those that were short, or did not arrive at all."

This young man was working too earnestly and enthusiastically to be any part of undermining the dig he so clearly couldn't wait to participate in. Frankie recognized his passionate zeal because it was so like her own.

Henry took the notebook from his young cousin and began reading.

Joey turned to Frankie, a small sandwich in one hand. "Was it a smashing adventure in Qift?"

"It was an adventure," she acknowledged.

"Some gent has been hanging around, hoping to talk to Cousin Henry. Said he's a qualified foreman, but I thought Cousin Henry went to Qift to hire one?" Joey took a bite of his sandwich before pouring himself some tea.

Frankie followed suit, very happy to drink even tepid tea after the long automobile ride. "He and his old foreman worked out the misunderstanding. Mr. Ibrahim will be joining us on the dig."

Joey finished his sandwich and patted his stomach. "That's good news then."

Stifling a smile at the unselfconscious exuberance of youth, Frankie agreed.

However, less pleasant was the fact that clearly someone had tried to undermine Henry's success on his dig.

Joey's expression turned pained. "Here comes that gent. He's persistent."

Frankie turned and watched as a man approached, his robes similar to those she'd seen on the men in Qift.

When the man spied Frankie and Henry with Joey, he smiled, his dark eyes lit with satisfaction.

He stopped before them. "Good day," he said in slightly accented English, extending his hand toward Henry.

Henry did not respond, still focused on the notes from Joey.

Covering the faux pas, Frankie offered her own hand to shake. "Edwin Clarke," she said without giving herself away with hesitation.

The man introduced himself with a wide smile and said, "I believe you are looking for a foreman."

How could he have known that? "Where did you hear that?"

Knowing that the lack of foreman had been engineered by someone quite deliberately made Frankie more than a little suspicious of this man's knowledge.

"It is no secret, I am sure." The man shrugged, like the where was of little importance.

Frankie looked at Joey and asked a question with her eyes.

"I didn't say a word," the young man assured her. "Not a single one to anyone. I only said Cousin Henry wasn't available but left me in charge of checking the supplies as they arrived."

Which circumspection showed him to be not only enthusiastic but shrewd as well.

Frankie turned her regard to the hopeful foreman. "Surely you heard from someone specific that Dr. Thomas was looking for a foreman."

"Yes. Tell us where you heard that," Henry said, proving that despite evidence to the contrary, he'd been paying attention.

"I should not like to get anyone in trouble for speaking out of turn." The would be foreman smiled at Henry. "Dr. Thomas, it is a pleasure to meet you." Once again he offered his hand in greeting.

This time Henry gave it a perfunctory shake. "I must insist you tell where you heard it."

As affable as the man appeared, he stubbornly refused to divulge his source, though he begged a thousand pardons.

Unimpressed, Henry simply stared the man into silence. "I don't need a foreman. Wherever you heard that rumor, it is mistaken."

"You have hired someone new?" the man pressed. "But I have very good references. I speak English very well," he said.

Did he know that Henry's current foreman spoke little English? Not that Henry cared as he was happy to communicate in either Arabic or French.

Henry did not answer, but stood and turned to go without another word. The man's people skills were not well developed. That was for certain.

Joey gave the Egyptian man an apologetic look, but quickly followed his cousin.

Frankie stifled a sigh at being left to deal with the persistent man. With a longing look at the sandwiches still left on the plate, she stood. "As Dr. Thomas said, we have no need of a foreman. I am sorry."

Just then a porter came up and said something to Frankie. The only words she understood were Thomas *Sahib*. She looked back at the porter blankly.

"He is telling you that Dr. Thomas has messages and letters at the front desk."

"Thank you."

"Perhaps you need an interpreter?" the man asked. "And Dr. Henry will see what a benefit having a man such as I on the dig might be."

"Dr. Henry has no need of an interpreter." But Frankie could not deny that she would find it a lot easier to get the things done he wanted her to if she had one.

Only she couldn't be sure this particular interpreter could be trusted.

If he had learned that Henry's foreman had "quit" from hotel staff, that was fine.

But what if he'd learned from whoever had engineered the bogus communications to begin with? Then he would be invested in whatever, or whoever, was behind undermining Henry's dig.

Frankie would not give the would-be foreman access to any information that might be used in such a way.

"But *you* do not speak Arabic," the mand said knowingly.

"I am not in a position to hire anyone," Frankie said truthfully. "That is entirely Dr. Henry's bailiwick."

"What is bailiwick?"

"Purview."

"Ah, I see, but perhaps you can speak to him on my behalf."

"I am sorry, but no." She turned to go.

"But Mr. Clarke..." he said.

Frankie did not have Henry's abrupt nature, but right now she was sorely tempted to pretend she did. She turned back. "I must go, sir. I have a great deal to do."

"And I could help."

"Mr. Clarke!" Joey tugged on Frankie's sleeve. "Cousin Henry sent me after you. He's getting impatient."

Frankie did not mind the interruption. "I'm coming." She nodded toward the man who was pushing so hard to get onto their dig team. "Good day."

The man followed and Frankie did not know why she was surprised. She did her best to pretend she had not noticed. Maybe he would go away.

When they reached Henry on the landing, she told him what the Porter had told her, and he started back down the stairs.

The Egyptian man began speaking to Henry in rapid Arabic and suddenly Henry stopped. "Did you tell him you wanted to hire him as your interpreter?" he asked Frankie.

Outraged the man would lie about her like that, she glared at him before replying to Henry. "No, I did not."

"But you do need an interpreter," the man insisted. As if that was the same as her wanting him to be her guide.

"If you are looking for a position, try the Harvard group," Henry said his tone impatient. "They have a much bigger team."

"But it is your dig that I wish to work with." The man smiled. "I have heard great things about you, Dr. Thomas."

The look Henry gave him said he didn't believe a word of it. Not bothering to respond, he continued on his way to the front desk.

Henry asked for his messages and to speak to the manager.

A sheaf of papers were handed over and a moment later the manager approached at a brisk pace. "Is there something I can do for you Dr. Thomas?"

"I do not need a foreman. I have a foreman. Let it be known."

"Yes, of course, Dr. Thomas."

Without another word, and the barest of nods to the manager, Henry was off again. Frankie did her best not to roll her eyes. But the man had abrupt down to a science.

"Thank you," she said to the manager. "Goodbye," she said to the would-be foreman-slash-interpreter. "Let's go," she said to Joey. "Before he leaves us behind."

The manager engaged the other Egyptian man, wanting to know if he was bothering the guests and a mild argument ensued while Frankie and Joey made their escape.

"Told you, that gent is per-sis-tant," Joey said, drawing the last word out like it was its's own sentence.

"He is that, but to tell Henry I *asked* to hire him. That took some nerve."

"Calculated risk," Joey said, sounding older than his years for once.

"Well, he calculated wrongly."

"He did," Henry said when they reached him. "Though he wasn't wrong about having an interpreter making things easier for you. Joey was able to get hotel staff to interpret when he needed. I'll want you two together when you leave the hotel, but you'll still need someone to interpret for you."

"Why not hire him then?" Joey asked.

"He's angling for my foreman's position and that's taken. Besides, he's already proven he's willing to use to the language barrier for his own ends."

"Oh, I see. You're a smart man, Cousin Henry."

Frankie could only agree.

The next two days went by in a whirl of activity, preparing for the dig. Henry hired an interpreter for Frankie and Joey through the hotel. The interpreter also turned out to be the cat's pajamas as a guide and saved a lot of time getting to and from places Henry needed her and Joey to go.

The three of them made use of both taxis and the streetcar system in Cairo to run errands for Henry. Frankie thoroughly enjoyed her glimpses of the busy city as she and Joey chased down supplies for the dig and delivered letters in lieu of Henry's attendance on certain lower-level officials.

The head archeologist met with the higher officials, confirmed all their permits and concessions were in order and made final travel arrangements, including the purchase of two motorcars.

It was all thrilling and little overwhelming.

Frankie had never realized how much behind the scenes planning went into a short two and a half months in the desert.

Henry explained that even more had to be arranged in advance because of how far south his dig was. No easy access to Cairo for supplies and more workers.

The nights were filled with illicit passion that Frankie knew would be hard to give up once they left the relative anonymity of the hotel.

Sharing a tent in the desert without being able to touch each other was going to be a colossal challenge to her self-control. Something she would never have anticipated in the realm of sensual pleasure, a part of life she'd been happy to go without for the years since becoming a widow.

From the way Henry responded to her touch and reveled in touching her, she was certain it would be the same for him.

And that frightened her as much as it delighted her.

Frankie would never put Henry at risk, but neither did she want to be caught out in her subterfuge, or worse...thought to be engaging in illegal acts in a foreign country.

And yet, when he knocked on her door, oh so softly, in the night, she always opened it.

Anum Ibrahim was there for tea the day the other archeologists from Henry's university arrived.

"I did not realize he was coming," Frankie said in an aside to Henry.

Thus far, Mr. Ibrahim had been quite busy seeing to preparations and Frankie had only seen him once since his arrival in Cairo.

Henry smiled, the expression rather predatory for a professor. "I wanted to see if either of my esteemed colleagues was surprised by his presence."

It was a good idea, but neither of the other two academics showed any kind of discomfort at seeing the foreman there to greet them along with her and Henry when they arrived at the hotel.

Which left three possibilities, if one of the professors was involved. One, he was as good an actor as Edwin. Two, he had been given the news ahead of time that the plan had failed. Three, neither professor was in on it at all.

Which is what she told Henry later that night when he once again knocked quietly on her door.

Henry shrugged his big shoulders. "It was worth a try. I am still trying to figure out what someone hoped to gain by the prank."

"More than a prank surely."

"What would you call it?"

"Sabotage."

He reached for her. "You are good with words, but you are even better with other ways of communication."

After, as they lay sated and sweaty, holding each other in the relative dark, Frankie said, "I think I should bunk with Joey when we get to the dig."

After all their time together, the youth showed no signs of cottoning on the fact that Frankie was not actually her brother. He spoke to and treated her just like an older man, not as respectfully as he did Henry, but definitely as he would treat a man, rather than a woman.

"No." There was no give in Henry's tone.

"I'll be careful. He'll never know I am not Edwin."

"He already knows you as Frankie."

"That is not the point. He thinks Frankie *is* my brother."

"You are staying with me."

She leaned up, trying to read Henry's expression in the shadows. "Listen to me, Professor Stubborn. We can barely keep our hands off each other in private, but sound carries too easily through tent walls."

"We will both have to show restraint," he said, like that was such a simple thing.

She would have agreed with him back in California, but Frankie knew better now. "Do you honestly believe we can refrain from touching each other?"

Because if he did, perhaps Henry was not as addicted to her as she was to him. And Frankie did not like considering that possibility. Not at all.

"You will have to trust me. I will not allow you to risk yourself or the reputation of my dig."

The reminder that he was still worried about his dig's reputation should not have bothered her. It only made sense. And it was not as if they were in love or something.

This sexual liaison was entirely without emotional strings.

Only something in the vicinity of her heart was telling Frankie she was lying to herself, no matter what feelings Henry might, or might not, have.

"Neither one of us has shown much restraint thus far," she said more acerbically than she intended.

"We have taken necessary precautions and will continue to do so."

She grabbed his hand and placed it over her breast. "So, you won't be tempted to do this in the middle of the night?"

His hand squeezed her tender mound, as if it was an automatic response. Her nipple peaked, seeking the stimulation she'd come to expect at his touch.

"We will be cautious," he promised her, his mouth close to her ear, his breath sending sensation shivering through her.

"Cautious is not the same as celibate," she said, her tone breathless.

"No, sweetheart, it is not."

It was the second time he'd used the endearment with her. Something caught in Frankie's heart, something she did not want to acknowledge or name.

She reached for his sex, seeking oblivion in the response of their bodies.

And for a while, she found it.

The ship intended to take them on their journey up the Nile was a lot fancier than Frankie had expected.

It had two levels above deck and the passengers were the wealthy travelers she might expect to encounter on holiday, not a professor traveling to his archeological dig for the season.

"Where is everyone else?" she asked, seeing none of the other members of their archeological team.

"My fellow archeologists, along with some of the men will be traveling in the Studebaker and Model T Anum helped me procure. My *rais* and rest of his men are traveling by passenger barge along with the camels."

"I thought you were buying the camels when we reached the Wadjet Provence."

Not transporting them along with the workers from Cairo.

Henry led her along the deck toward the staterooms. "I thought it best not to leave anything to chance, considering what happened with the supplies and Anum."

"What do you mean the supplies?" She knew that not all the supplies had been waiting in Cairo as arrangements had been made for.

But having read the journals of past archeological digs in Egypt and several in the Middle East, Frankie knew that was not a rare occurrence. And Henry had seemed unfazed by the need to procure more.

"Some of my orders were cancelled, though it was impossible to tell if that was simply in error or if someone had arranged it. Some supplies were short on what was ordered. I do not know how much was merely the usual error to which one must become accustomed and what, if any, were deliberate ploys to undermine the dig."

"So, you decided you could not risk getting to Wadjet and not having access to good camels?"

"Exactly. It has increased the expense of this Season's dig to transport the camels, but I believe the extra expense will be worth it. When we finish our excavations for the season, we will find storage for the cars until next year."

"And the camels?"

"I am still undecided if I will sell, or board them. Most likely I will have Anum sell them."

Another layer of complication. She wondered if that bothered Henry. He seemed to be taking it in his stride.

"I guess it is a good thing, Father increased his funding this year."

"Yes, though I'd hoped to use some of it to hire more workers, but needs must. The concession purchased by my university is only good for two more seasons. After that, we have to renegotiate the concession with the ministry office."

Which left the potential of losing it. She wondered if Henry intended to move onto another concession regardless. Some archeologist dug in the same area for their entire careers, others moved from spot to spot.

"What about this?" She waved her hand around the ship with its gleaming polished wood paneling in the formal dining room and drawing room they were just passing.

The sumptuous rooms could be seen through large glass windows looking out on the main deck.

"This was a personal expense I decided to indulge in. It is our last opportunity for any semblance of privacy before we reach Wadjet."

Warmth spread through Frankie, though she reminded herself he was no doubt motivated by his libido, not his emotions.

Henry had been very clear on one point. Sex between them was just that. Sex. Not an emotional connection. Not something that would lead to anything more.

Which was exactly how she wanted it.

The very idea of marrying again gave her the heebee jeebies.

So, where all this *feeling* was coming from, she did not know.

She liked Henry, but Frankie was never giving into the weakness and danger of romantic love again.

"Are we sharing a cabin?" she asked.

"We are."

She smiled. "I suppose we will have to come out of it occasionally, so we are not remarked upon."

"I suppose we will, but our mutual love of study and need to prepare for and discuss the dig will give us good reason not to spend too much time on deck."

"Or playing Bridge with the other passengers."

He shuddered. Clearly *not* a Bridge player.

"You don't like cards, or is it only Bridge?" she asked.

"I do not like any games in which you must play with a partner."

"That does not surprise me."

"You do not think I would make a good partner?"

"Honestly? For some you would make an excellent partner, but you would have no patience with someone playing on instinct rather than reason."

"Exactly."

She smiled, pleased she knew him that well.

"Let us find our cabin."

The cabin had its own bathroom, two twin beds, each with a small nightstand, and a single desk and chair.

It was a nicely appointed room, but not lavish. "You paid for this yourself?" she asked.

"It would not have been right to put such an expense on the dig."

"Because it is a luxury."

"Yes."

"I'm glad you did."

His smile was dark and sensual, in the way she'd come to accept was another surprising facet of this academic man's personality. "Me too."

He was no mild-mannered professor.

They settled in and then she was surprised to discover, he actually did want to discuss some things he'd found time to read in the past couple of days about other digs in the Wadjet Province.

"There are very few funerary items in these graves compared to the tombs found in and near the Valley of the Kings."

"So, you think these are the graves of the regular people?"

"To an extent, yes. One must wonder if there was a class of people who had no means for funerary rituals at all, and therefore did not survive to be excavated."

"Did the ancient Egyptians have a class system like that?"

"We do not know. There could have been a class of workers that were too poor for any sort of mummification. But that is making assumptions based on our times, where we have those in poverty, those who can live moderately and of course those who can and do live quite lavishly."

"With all the ensuing political and economic power," Frankie mused.

The United States was supposed to be a country in which all men were created equal, but their history did not support such a stance. It had not been quite sixty years since the end of the Civil War and slavery. It was 1870 before the 15th Amendment that was supposed to guarantee all men the right to vote, regardless of race or former bondage.

Considering how many women, now that they had the vote, were forced to mark their ballots as their fathers or husbands dictated, Frankie could not help thinking they had a long way to go toward true equality.

It was something she and the women in her adventurer's society discussed at length. Frankie wondered what Henry's views on the matter might be.

"Assuming Ancient Egypt had a class of people who had no economic resources presupposes a capitalist view of the world that we cannot be sure existed," he said, interrupting her thoughts.

Frankie thought that over and realized it was a good point. "It is easy to assume things have always been as they are."

"Too easy."

She brought up her views on voting and he agreed. Edwin was the only man she knew who didn't think women needed coaching in their voting.

Henry mentioned his concern about the growth of fascism in the United States. Perhaps it was his job as an archeologist with his reverence for Ancient Egypt and its people, but he was adamant that race was no indicator of natural intelligence or aptitude.

Henry appeared to be one of those rare men that truly believed that all men *and* women were created equal.

Frankie loved the intellectual discussions she had with Henry, maybe even as much as she enjoyed the pleasure their bodies found in each other. And that was really quite dangerous to her.

Emotions she had been sure were permanently dormant wanted to come out to play.

It scared her to death and yet she could not build any kind of barrier between herself and this surprising man.

14

Henry should not have been surprised by how easily Frankie played the part of a man, but he was.

While he found her sexually enticing beyond all bounds of self-control, the other passengers on their river cruise passenger ship reacted to her as if she were exactly what she pretended to be. A single man in his late twenties with a wealthy father and an interest in Egyptology.

Henry could not miss the way her brown eyes glowed with the same interest and keen obsession he himself felt when she talked about the history of the ancient culture, others seemed to miss it entirely. He thought the curve of her neck the most enticingly feminine thing he had ever seen and yet, not one other gentleman on board reacted to Frankie like she was a woman.

For her part, she was very good at staying in character and engaging in the social norms of a young single man, rather than a relatively young widow.

Perhaps, she found some of those social norms freeing.

He asked her that night, after dinner when they were alone in their cabin, his voice low as their window and door was open to allow air to circulate before they went to bed.

Lounging on her bed, one leg up the other dangling over the side, her back against the wall, she epitomized the picture of casual male unconcern.

"Some, yes. Even in this modern era, men have so many more

freedoms than women." She frowned. "It is enough to send me searching for the giggle water."

He smiled at her reference to alcohol. "It is much easier to find here than back home in California."

"Don't kid yourself. I only had to look as far as my fake sewing table."

Henry's laughter took him by surprise. "Your father would be appalled."

"No doubt. Are you?" she asked.

Henry shook his head. "I haven't seen much good come out of prohibition."

"I bet that's not the line your university expects you to take."

"The same university that has only started allowing female students in the last two years? You would be right."

"Were you in favor?"

"I wish I could say I argued in favor, but I rarely get embroiled in discussions of that nature."

"About women's rights?"

"About any issues one might consider political."

"And yet you have very definite views."

"Which I state, but I have little patience for debate."

She had no trouble believing that.

"Until I met you, I never gave much thought to how very different life is for a man and a woman in our society. Watching you in this guise as your brother has given me a great deal of food for thought."

"Are you studying me, or our culture, professor?" she asked in her own lighter tone, her voice teasing.

He got up and closed first the window and then their door, turning the key to lock it. "You are more interesting than any other area of study."

Her laugh was low, but so damn tempting. "Even more interesting than ancient history?"

"Right now? Without a doubt."

"That is good to know." Her smile was all feminine enticement.

How did anyone mistake this woman for a man?

She tugged her bowtie until the ends dangled and then went to work on the buttons of her waistcoat. "You know what I don't enjoy?"

His throat dry in anticipation of what he'd be seeing any moment now, he could do nothing but shake his head. No, he did not know.

"Men's clothing. It is so much more restricting."

That pulled him up short and he stared at her in disbelief. "You cannot be serious."

"Very much so. If I was traveling as myself right now, I would have a dress and a pair of drawers to slip out of." She tugged her tie away from the collar of her shirt and dropped it on the floor. "But I've got a suit coat."

"You already..." he had to clear his throat to get his voice to work. "You already took that off."

"So I did. But I still have this vest." She slipped it off, then slid her braces down her arms, leaving them to dangle over her hips. "And these."

She shrugged out of her shirt, leaving her upper torso bare but for the gauze she wore wound around her breasts. She'd skipped the undershirt most men wore to protect their shirts from sweat and provide a better opaqueness than a single shirt layer could do.

"Then there is this." She waved her hand indicating the fabric he wanted gone so badly he could taste the need.

"Not so different from a corset, surely?"

She shrugged and then started unwrapping, her small breasts coming into view as the gauze disappeared layer by layer. "I'll tell you a secret. I don't always wear a corset."

He was not surprised. Intrigued? Yes. Surprised, no.

"You're an independent minded woman."

"You don't seem to mind."

"I like it."

"You're a special man, Henry."

It was his turn to shrug.

She stopped, her breasts on display, her gorgeous nipples already showing her arousal, the soft mounds calling for his touch, his mouth.

"No, you really are. I..." She shook her head. "Without your cooperation, I couldn't even hope to live this dream of mine. Thank you."

"Do not thank me. You have already proven yourself an invaluable help."

She gave him a come hither look. "And perhaps something more, hmmm?"

She teased him as she removed the trousers and drawers, going slowly and revealing the dark copper curls that covered her mons. She stood there in nothing but her socks and the garters holding them up.

Undeniably masculine apparel on an even more undeniably feminine woman. She turned around and lifted one foot onto the bed, bending over with overt provocation to undo the garter and slide the sock down her calf and off her foot.

How she managed to make something so prosaic appear enticingly sexual, he had no idea. Henry was sure it would not be the same at all if he were the one taking off his socks in such a manner.

But the gentle curve of her backside called to him, the crease between her buttocks, leading his eye to her most intimate flesh. Pink lips, an already moist and gleaming orifice he wanted to taste as much as he wanted to bury himself inside.

Frankie shifted, lifting her other foot to the bed and removing her final article of clothing. Nothing had changed about his view. Not really and yet Henry's need had just grown to unbearable levels.

Without being aware of giving his body permission to move, he crossed the ship cabin until he could lay his hands on that perfect backside.

She gave a low sound of approval. "I love your hands on me, Henry."

"Your skin is so soft. Like silk." He caressed over the globes of her backside and down the backs of legs, loving the sounds that simple touch elicited.

He had never had a lover who was so free with her response. Frankie made no effort to hide how he affected her physically. She did not play sexual games.

Her sensual honesty was one of the many things Henry found so irresistible about the woman.

And she thought he could let her share a tent with anyone but himself? They might both have to wear gags, but he would not spend the next two and a half months not touching her.

He could not do it.

He pressed his hard cock against her backside, rutting because he could not help himself.

"You need to remove your own trousers for that to work, Henry." The laughter in her tone was tempered by breathlessness.

She wanted him too.

He reached down and pressed one finger into her wet heat. They had not touched, but she was ready for penetration.

Slick and hot, tender tissues swollen and ready for him.

He reached down with his other hand and fumbled the fly of his trousers open, pulling his erection out without worrying about getting them off. One thing he could not forget though, no matter how much he wanted this woman.

The rubber.

He got it on faster than he'd ever accomplished before and then pressed against her slick opening. Frankie had not moved from her provocative position with one foot up on her bed. Like she was just waiting for him to be inside her.

He stilled with his hands on her hips. "Okay?"

"More than. Put it in, Henry." Her whisper was demanding and curt.

She wanted this as much as he did.

He pressed inside, the rubber barely dulling the intensity of pleasure. Henry rocked forward and back until he was fully seated, her hot vaginal walls clasping him like a silky fist.

"Yes," she hissed. "That's so good. You were made to fill me."

"You were made to take me."

It was just sex talk. It didn't mean anything, but it turned him on beyond anything he'd ever experienced. If he wasn't careful, he was going to blow on the first full stroke.

Concentrating on not doing exactly that, Henry slid one hand around to touch her clitoris, only to find Frankie's hand already there. Their fingers tangled and they pleasured her together.

It was damn sexy.

Her other hand snaked up to hook around the back of his neck to hold herself upright. "Touch my nipples," she ordered.

Without hesitating he slid the hand still holding her hip up to her breast, squeezing the soft mound and then playing with first one nipple and then the other while she moaned quietly in the still air of the ship cabin.

He pulled out of her until only his head was clasped in her wet heat and then surged back inside. They touched her clitoris more urgently as he moved in and out of her, hitting a sweet spot inside her that turned her breathing ragged and her moans into a litany of pleasure.

Henry could not tell which of them climaxed first. Their bodies were so in tune, maybe they went over that precipice together.

But as he came back to himself, he realized that their hands were entwined at the apex of her thighs while she shuddered and they both gasped for breath.

They slept entwined in one of the small twin beds that night, waking to make love not once, but twice again before dawn.

Their cruise lasted three days because the ship only sailed for a few hours each night and stayed over in two ports along the way from Lower to Upper Egypt.

Frankie was surprised by how very different the disembarking port was from Cairo. The further south they had come, the fewer peddlers met the cruise ship to tempt passengers with their wares.

Knowing the motorcar meant to meet them should be there soon, if not already waiting, she and Henry disembarked midday. They'd spent the morning making love and had packed hastily, leaving their private retreat with regret.

At least on Frankie's part. She had no doubt Henry was eager to reach the dig.

As the midday sun greeted them, Frankie could do nothing but be grateful that they did not excavate in the height of summer.

She'd spent time in the Mojave Desert, so she thought she knew what to expect. But this was different. People went about their business in this heat, working, unloading cargo, moving goods.

It was a small riverside port and she didn't think the town it was attached to had a huge population, but the people who lived there were not hiding in their homes from the heat. They were out and about.

This was their life.

As expected, a driver and a motorcar waited for them, along with one of the professors from Henry's university. It was the assistant professor, Daniel Adams.

"At your service." The tall blond man, who looked to be Frankie's age or younger, put out his hand to shake briskly. "Everyone else has headed out to the dig," he informed Henry. "Professor Miller left me to ride in with you."

It suddenly occurred to Frankie that not only had Henry personally paid for their more decadent and infinitely more private cruise along the Nile, but he had given up precious time to make it possible.

The cargo and passenger ferry had arrived two days before and most likely so had this man and his colleagues, as the drive could have been made easily in one day. Barring complication.

Henry would be the last to arrive to his own excavation site.

Something cracked inside her. She was very much afraid that it was another of the walls she'd built up around her heart.

Ignoring the inconvenient emotion, Frankie said with as much Edwin inspired bon homme as she could muster, "Good to see you again, Professor Adams."

"Call me Daniel," the assistant professor said jovially. "No need to stand on ceremony. You aren't one of my students."

"My friends call me Frankie," she responded in kind.

"Adams here will call you Mr. Clarke." Henry's tone was unbending, his expression forbidding.

The assistant professor looked surprised, but then shrugged. "If you like. Afraid of offending his rich father?"

But Henry simply ignored the taunt and said, "Let's get going."

Frankie wasn't sure what that was all about, but she thought Henry was right to encourage a certain formal distance between Frankie and the others. Less chance of being caught out after the fact if she ran into either of them back in California. No matter how unlikely that might be.

Daniel Adams waited until Henry had walked ahead to give Frankie a look and whisper. "He's a crank, but the old man knows what he's doing on a dig."

About to argue that Henry wasn't that old, Frankie remembered that her brother often called other men, even those the exact same age as him, old man.

She'd let herself become too complacent on the ship, forgetting how she needed to remain in her brother's persona twenty-four-seven. Men used slang with and about each other that women were not prone too.

She could not afford to come this far and get tripped up by her feelings.

She gave Professor Adams a conspiratorial wink and said, "So, I've heard."

"If you two are quite done gossiping."

Henry wanted word about how the trip had gone, if there had been any trouble upon arrival. Daniel Adamas seemed only too happy to fill Henry in while Frankie reveled in the knowledge that her grumpy archeologist had given up some of his control of the dig for the sake of time alone with her.

That was not just sex.

No man could be so enamored of sex he would do something like that. At least no man with Henry's fortitude. He'd wanted time *with her*.

But he wasn't in a great mood about the results of what getting that time had cost him.

Well, Henry wouldn't be Henry if he wasn't just a little cantankerous. Though she was very careful not to say so.

Professor Adams naturally assumed he would ride in the back of the four seater Studebaker with Henry, to continue the update, while Frankie drove. However, Henry directed Frankie into the backseat and joined her there, leaving the younger man to do the driving. With a long ride of turning to speak over his shoulder as he answered the lead archeologist's questions.

It did not sound like they had run into any more mishaps on the trip to the Wadjet Province, and all the supplies were unloaded at the port without incident.

It had taken two days to get everything transported to the site, so maybe Henry hadn't given up so much time after all.

Frankie was still glad he'd chosen the three day pleasure cruise for travel.

Henry was pleased with Daniel's replies to his questions.

Although Daniel had to shout some to make himself heard over the wind and engine noise, he did a fair job bringing Henry up to date on how things had gone on the journey south. As expected, Anum had taken charge of the workmen and supplies, making sure everyone and everything was delivered safely to the dig.

"He's busy hiring the extra workers," Daniel told Henry. "He'll travel with them to the dig and should be there tomorrow or the day after."

Henry was not worried.

Once the confusion has been sorted over him working for the expedition again this year, Anum had brought along his second in command like previous ones. A transplant resident of Qift, Peter had more than enough experience to see to setup as he'd done in year's past.

Though Henry himself had never been behind the others traveling and was usually there to direct.

"How was that swank cruise down the Nile?" Daniel asked with all the youthful enthusiasm of a young assistant professor, and perhaps a bit of envy.

"Productive."

"You never seemed to need that kind of ritzy travel means for productivity before," Daniel said pointedly. "But then maybe you had to make some concessions on your austere travel plans to get the older Mr. Clarke's investment in this year's undertaking."

Frankie had been listening to them with rapt attention, but had not attempted to join the conversation. She shifted now, like she wasn't sure what to say.

But Henry did not care if his colleagues saw his out of character behavior as a concession to a wealthy benefactor. "Quite."

Frankie jolted, like she was surprised by his agreement.

"It was a smashing trip," she said with fervor, her voice tipped low for her Edwin persona. "Though I'm sure our views were the same."

"They were probably a lot more picturesque from your decks than our crowded ones."

"The number of people around you does not change what you are looking at," Henry said.

"That is not what you say when you are telling the rest of us to get the hell of out of the way when you want to look at something in the ground."

Henry cast a quick glance at Frankie, offended by his colleague's use of profanity in front of her and realizing there was nothing he could do to change it without drawing attention to the fact she was not actually a man.

"Watching the scenery go by and trying to determine if something is a broken rock or piece of pottery are not the same thing." Henry made no effort to hide his exasperation with that attitude at least.

The assistant professor was definitely envious. Things like that usually went right over his head, but Henry could hardly miss the second dig at him in as many minutes.

"Well, I don't see why Dr. Miller and I could not have traveled with you and Mr. Clarke."

"Unlike you and Dr. Miller, Mr. Clarke has a genuine interest in Ancient Egypt. He and I were able to discuss theory and my approach to this year's dig in relative peace."

"You never found those last minute discussions necessary with us."

"I was led to believe your specialty is Viking lore and culture and

Dr. Miller's is Ancient Mesopotamia," Frankie said, pitching her voice loud enough to be heard, before Henry could respond with the choler building up in him.

Daniel jerked his head in ascent. "Yes, that is true."

"The only thing we need to discuss before the dig is generalized approach to history and dig protocols, which we did quite adequately back in California."

"You got me there. Still, it doesn't hurt that the amateur Egyptologist came with a big infusion of cash this year, does it?" Daniel's sneering tone was definitely the result of jealousy.

"We paid for our own passage," Henry said. The fact that by *we* he meant himself he did not feel the need to share. "Had you and Dr. Miller wanted to travel via river cruise rather than passenger/cargo ship, you could have done so."

"We don't all have wealthy family with deep pockets behind us, or supporting our academic endeavors."

That was true and not something Henry felt the need to apologize for. "We would not have been able to buy this motorcar, or the other one, if I didn't," Henry said with his usual bluntness.

He did not hide the finances of dig.

It infuriated Dr. Miller when he saw how much Henry's grandfather underwrote because he knew that even if the department were inclined to support a dig in Mesopotamia, it wouldn't be financially feasible without another angel backer.

Even so, Daniel had complained loudly the year before about not having their own automobile they could rely on implicitly for transport. He should be grateful.

"Yes, well. I suppose I should be grateful." Daniel did not sound thankful. "And I can't claim there was much in the way of conversation we needed on the river trip. Dr. Miller and I are well versed on your dig protocols by now."

"Hopefully, they are protocols you will take with you to your own endeavors in the future."

Daniel frowned. "Like that's ever going to happen."

"You never know. Look at the Harvard people. It only took the interest of one wealthy woman."

"And where am I going to meet a wealthy benefactor?"

About to say that was not his responsibility, they didn't even teach in the same subject, Henry felt a hand squeezing his leg, a clear request for silence.

He turned his head toward Frankie. "What?"

She didn't look at him, but had her pretty brown eyes fixed on Daniel. "I'll make sure you receive invites to a couple of my father's sponsored events next year."

Henry glared at her. How would that be safe for her?

"I attend few of them myself, but I'm sure you can make your own friends," Frankie continued blithely.

Henry still didn't like it, but now that he thought about it, he had never met Edwin at any of the events his own grandfather insisted Henry attend.

"That would be the duck's quack, Mr. Clarke. Thanks!"

Henry frowned. Daniel talked more like a man about the town than a professor. He sounded like Henry's younger cousin with his slang.

Both Frankie and Daniel burst into laughter.

"What?" Henry demanded, irritated.

"The look on your face, Dr. Thomas. We don't have to talk like someone from the last century to be professors." Daniel's accurate assessment of what Henry was thinking only annoyed him further.

"I don't talk like an antiquarian."

"No, not at all." Frankie would sound more convincing if she were not still laughing.

Henry wanted to kiss her so badly he glared even harder.

She didn't take umbrage, just grinned in response.

Surprisingly, she and Daniel carried most of the conversation for the rest of the journey. Henry didn't remember her being that friendly on the voyage to Europe from America, or in Cairo.

But Frankie asked Daniel a lot of questions and listened intently to his answers. She could have asked Henry about any of the topics she raised, but she hadn't.

Was she interested in the younger man? Daniel was closer in age to her than Henry was.

Daniel brought up the Mummy's Curse and mentioned that there had been talk among the workers that it was plaguing their expedition already.

"The Mummy's So-Called Curse is nothing but a bunch of bunkum," Henry said, annoyed.

"Are you so sure?" Daniel asked. "Lord Carnarvon *is* dead."

"And that is proof of what? That men with precarious health actually die at some point?" Henry asked scathingly, not at all happy that one of his archeologists was giving credence to such gibberish.

"You cannot deny the dig this year has been plagued with bad luck."

More like a saboteur, but Henry didn't say that. He just gave Frankie a significant look before turning an expression on Daniel that let him know what he thought of an archeologist who adhered to such bunkum.

"The Mummy's Curse has nothing to do with bad luck. If indeed one were to believe in it, which I categorically do not, one would be concerned about dying."

Frankie nodded her agreement and added, "Besides which, the Mummy's Curse is associated with the tomb of Tutankhamun, not every archeological dig in Egypt."

"We dig up the dead," Daniel said triumphantly. "Who is to say they didn't have similar curses put on their graves?"

"There is no curse on the Tutankhamun tomb," Henry said with annoyance. "Howard Carter has denied it."

"And of course he would never lie."

"He is not only a fellow archeologist, but he is a man known for his integrity. I suggest you not impugn it with nothing but feather brained ideas to back you up."

"Just because I am not the lead archeologist does not mean my ideas are meritless."

"Of course it doesn't," Frankie said quickly, before Henry could blast the other man again. "But don't you think it would be better not to spread those kinds of rumors around the dig?"

"They're already spread. The workmen were talking about the Mummy's Curse on the boat. Anum tried his best to squelch that kind of talk—"

"But with my own archeologists feeding it, he had no luck, I'm sure," Henry said, butting in.

"I didn't start the talk," Daniel said, his tone offended. "It was in all the papers back home. You know it was."

"About Henry Carter's dig, not ours. That you have given even a modicum of credence to it is beneath you as a scholar and a scientist." Henry was furious and made no effort to hide it. "If you are so concerned about curses, maybe you should return to California."

Daniel frowned. "I didn't say I didn't want to be here. I'm not afraid of the curse," he said, like that made him brave. "I just don't dismiss it as a fairytale. That's all."

Henry was in no way impressed with his defiance.

"You damn well better if you want to stay on my dig," he instructed the other man. "If I hear you've been feeding the rumor, I'll send you back to California and you won't be getting any kind of recommendation from me for any future archeology in the field, and sure as hell not on my digs."

Daniel paled, his expression worried.

He should be worried. Henry would not allow Daniel, or anyone else, to undermine his dig. Not with sabotage. Not with ridiculous rumors about curses.

He looked sideways at Frankie and noticed she was looking worried as well. Though he could not think why. So, he asked.

"I can't help thinking that these Mummy's Curse rumors are linked to the sabotage." She spoke low and toward Henry.

With the noise of the automobile, it was unlikely Daniel had heard her.

Henry loved how facile her brain was. He nodded his agreement. "It is very possible."

To what end, he still did not know, but it made too much sense to dismiss just because he didn't understand the why.

"I think it would be a good idea to find out who started them," she added.

"That is easier said than done." Gossip was difficult to trace to the source in the best of circumstances.

With someone who was purposefully using it to undermine the dig? They would have been careful to cover their tracks, or bring up the topic without seeming to have done so.

Henry tuned out the conversation between Frankie, Daniel and the driver as he considered who might want to get his dig cancelled.

Daniel had certainly exhibited more thwarted ambition and jealousy than Henry had been aware of before. Was Dr. Rudolph Miller equally as frustrated by being forced to participate in archeology not related to his preferred field of study?

If so, it only stood to reason that one, or both, of them were behind the sabotage as well as the rumors. Daniel had admitted already that he'd fed the gossip about the Mummy's Curse.

That kind of stupidity was hard for Henry to abide. Even if one believed in the Mummy's Curse, it was supposed to be attached to the newly discovered royal tomb in the Valley of the Kings. It had nothing to do with other tombs, and certainly didn't relate to the excavation of less affluent gravesites they were engaging in the Wadjet Provence.

15

Peter, the assistant foreman, ran to the motorcar as the driver pulled to a stop, calling out a greeting to Henry.

Suppressing his natural inclination to help Frankie from the car, as he would hardly have done so for her brother, Henry alighted and grasped Peter's hand warmly. Here was a man every bit as level headed as Anum.

English, with a passion for archeology, but no formal schooling, Peter had come to Egypt at a young age. He spoke Arabic fluently now, as well as a smattering of French. Peter had started as a dirt carrier on a dig before moving to Qift and living among the other workers.

He'd been on three other dig sites as a workman before Anum hired him to work on Henry's. He'd been promoted to assistant foreman by the second season when the other assistant foreman moved on to his own lead position.

A solid worker, Peter wouldn't be spreading rumors about curses and the like.

"How are you, Peter? Is the camp set up to your liking?" Henry asked.

The other man grinned. "All is in order, to *your* liking, *Sahib*."

His tendency to speak and act like his fellow Egyptian workers made him a favorite among them, but it had always struck Henry oddly.

"It's a good thing. He's in a bad enough mood as it is." Daniel's mutterings were loud enough for Henry to hear.

Since those sorts of comments were often made about him, he always chose to ignore them, but with his suspicions fresh in his mind, not to mention his frustration with the younger man, this time Henry decided to take issue.

"Professor Adams!" he barked toward the man walking away at a brisk pace.

Daniel stopped and turned, with a surprised expression. "Yes?"

Considering Henry had ignored all such muttering in the past, the man had a right to be startled. But he didn't have a right to undermine Henry's dig.

"If you are unhappy with me as your lead archeologist, I will repeat my suggestion of earlier."

Daniel's eyes rounded even further. "I didn't mean anything by it."

"Didn't you?" Henry asked, not appeased in the least.

Daniel shook his head vehemently. "I am sorry if I gave offense. You don't usually pay attention to that sort of thing. To be honest, I had started to wonder if you were a bit deaf."

"I am not."

"So I see."

"Well?"

"I do humbly apologize. My remark was disrespectful. Whatever my thoughts, I should keep such things to myself."

Henry almost smiled. He liked that Daniel wasn't cowed entirely, but he did not like what was happening with his dig.

"I meant what I said about perpetrating unfounded and ridiculous rumors."

"I believe you."

"And?"

"I will do my best to squelch any such rumors that come to my attention."

Henry felt a measure of relief, his shoulders dropping from their tense position. "I am glad to hear that. I have always thought that despite your area of study being entirely unrelated to Ancient Egypt, you were a benefit to the dig."

"I..." Daniel looked nonplussed. "Thank you."

Henry jerked his head in acknowledgement of the gratitude and turned back to find Frankie watching the interaction with her usual expression of interest.

"Come, Mr. Clarke, I will show you to our tent."

"This way, *sahib*," Peter said as he took the lead.

"What was that all about?" Frankie asked him as they walked across the sand toward the largest tent placed center to and back from the rest.

Even without the delectable Frankie sharing his bed, Henry had always preferred some privacy. He achieved it by having his tent located several yards back from the other tents and having his living quarters behind the open area where they examined their finds.

They walked through the currently empty room of the tent where artifacts would be stored as the Season wore on to a flap which was currently tied up to allow them to enter the living quarters of the tent. There was another flap in the back wall which would allow them to leave and enter the living quarters directly to use the outhouses and access the back of the camp.

Not for the first time, Henry considered doing as some other archeologists had done and building a house for use during the Season.

If he was certain he would remain in the Wadjet Provence for several more years of digging, he would do it without hesitation.

He was pleased to see that the space was set up as he liked it, with a table to work at, another small one, but taller with a pitcher and basin for washing. Shelves for his books and papers stood to the side of the worktable.

The only difference from last year was the extra cot on the other side of the packing box that stood use as a bedside table next to his cot.

"Which cot should I use?" Frankie asked.

"The one on the right," Peter offered before Henry got a chance. "The *sahib's* cot has been made up with his personal linens and blankets on the left."

She found his use of the term *sahib* curious since he was clearly English, though he dressed and acted like the Egyptians he worked with. "Thank you, Mr. ..."

"It is just Peter, sir."

Frankie nodded. "I am Mr. Clarke. I'm afraid Dr. Thomas would be cross if I asked you call me Frankie."

Peter smiled at Frankie and offered his hand. "It is a pleasure to meet you, Mr. Clarke."

Frankie shook hands with the assistant foreman. "It is an even bigger pleasure to meet you, for now I know who to come to if I do not know something about the camp."

Henry had to bite back the demand she come to him and him alone.

He had never experienced this feeling of possessiveness toward another woman. It was unsettling. Worse, if Frankie knew of his instincts, she would quash them without mercy.

She was a fully independent woman, and he would do well not to forget that fact.

Peter finished updating Henry on the condition of the camp.

"You are ready for the workers Anum will be bringing tomorrow?"

"We are ready, yes. We will show them all the best way to dig. The Thomas *sahib* way to dig."

Feeling better, knowing he could rely on his Egyptian workers and Peter, Henry thanked the assistant foreman. Then he asked, "Peter, have you heard any of these curse rumors?"

Peter's mouth twisted with distaste. "I have heard them, yes. I tell the men if they believe in ghosts like children, they can leave."

"Have any gone?"

"No. Your pay is good. You require fewer hours of work and make sure your workers take time to drink water, to eat. You are a good leader, *sahib*. They would be fools to leave this important dig and seek work elsewhere."

"Why would they go somewhere else?" Frankie asked. "Wouldn't they be worried about the curse on any dig?"

"Some are saying the curse has already touched Thomas *sahib's* dig. That there are bad things happening."

"The only bad things happening are at the hands of men, not some millennia old mummy," Henry said with renewed frustration.

"Naturally, but for the superstitious, they seek other answers."

"You're a wise man, Peter," Frankie praised the assistant foreman.

Henry asked, "Are there any men I need to speak to?"

"You have already had words with one."

Henry knew it. "I don't understand how a scholar and a scientist got so caught up in something so..."

"Unscientific?" Frankie prompted.

"Exactly."

"He wouldn't be the only one. The newspapers have quoted all sorts of scholars and scientist in their articles about the Mummy's Curse."

"A curse mistakenly said to have been written on the lintel of the tomb of Tutankhamun. Even if it did exist, it would not apply to my dig."

"Well, yes, that would be the logical conclusion, but as Peter has pointed out, not all men are always governed by logic. If we are honest, none of us can make that claim."

Henry opened his mouth to deny it, to say he never acted without rational thought, but the reality was that he had behaved out of character and on the spur of desire with Frankie more than once.

Peter took his leave. Henry and Frankie both started unpacking their things. He was not surprised Frankie would do so. She'd shown she liked her things ordered and stowed neatly in their cabin on the ship.

Still, he was reminded to be grateful she was not a slob, since they would be sharing their space for the rest of the dig Season.

Frankie finished placing everything but her clothes in the places Henry indicated were for her use. She kept her clothes in her case and put the closed case on a shelf well above the ground. Henry nodded approvingly. "You don't want critters getting into your clothes. Even taking those precautions, never put on something you haven't first shaken out."

Frankie smiled, warmed by his concern, though she was sure he would offer the same advice to any other roommate. "Thank you."

Though she was the only roommate he'd had on a dig, or so, he'd said.

And she believed him. Henry wouldn't be an easy companion for many.

"You seemed to enjoy talking to Adams on the way here," Henry said, his tone neutral.

Which in and of itself, put Frankie on alert. Henry wasn't a neutral man. He did cranky well. Bored. Approving. And oh so passionate. But a studied neutral was as good as saying he had feelings he didn't want to express.

And since he rarely seemed shy about expressing his feelings, she had to wonder what they were.

"I did. Professor Adams is friendly and knowledgeable."

"You won't find anyone more knowledgeable than me on this dig." Henry almost sounded offended.

But surely he couldn't be.

"No, of course not, though humility might have prompted you not to point that out."

"I prefer honesty to false humility."

"When it comes to it, so do I." She smiled. "You are a very honest man."

"I'm lying to everyone on this dig about who you are. What does that say about my honesty? I have had sex with you numerous times, though I know you aren't what one might term a Merry Widow. What does that say about my honor?"

Frankie paused in straightening the blankets on her cot. They'd wrinkled form having her case and box set on top of them.

"I am sorry, Henry. I had no intention of bringing you into my deception. The burden of that dishonesty should be mine alone." It could not be changed now, but she still felt badly.

"However, as to the other," she continued. "I am an adult, capable of making my own choices. You are not taking advantage of me. If anything, I am using you shamelessly. I knew so little about truly passionate sex, I am afraid I wanted as much of it as I could get before it was no longer on offer."

"I do not remember you being so friendly with other people in Cairo," he said, in what she considered a non sequitur. "Or even on the ship."

"I was avoiding you on the ship. How would you know?"

"You were no better at your attempts to do so than I was. Besides, I watched you."

"I wanted to watch you," she admitted.

"Sometimes you did."

"Sometimes I did." Honesty was not always comfortable, she had to admit to herself.

Excited to see the rest of the camp, Frankie asked if they could do so now they had unpacked.

Henry shook his head. "Not yet."

"What? Why not?"

He stepped into her personal space. "Because out there I cannot do this." Henry cupped her neck and leant down to kiss her.

It was not a passionate kiss, but a gentle press of his lips to hers.

Even so, she felt things inside her stirring. Desire. Pleasure. Feelings that only this man had ever elicited.

Frankie laid her hand over his wrist and just held on. Somewhere in the back of her mind, she knew this was not the safest activity to be engaging in at the moment, but she could not make herself step back.

She had come to Egypt seeking adventure and knowledge. She would never have believed that what she'd discovered with Henry would be one of her greatest adventures and knowledge of her own body and its responses that had been hidden from her until now.

The sounds of camp outside the tent finally penetrated Frankie's senses and she stepped back from the man who could make her lose all sense with something as simple as a tender kiss. "We cannot do this now."

He frowned. "I know. I cannot even tell you why I felt the need to kiss you."

Frankie thought maybe she could, but telling him she thought Henry had been jealous of Professor Adams would go over about as well as when her brother had first told Frankie women had no business driving.

In other words, not at all.

Frankie looked down that the two narrow cots. "I do not think we will be engaging in any lovemaking here."

"There is always a blanket on the floor."

The reply came too quickly. He'd thought about it.

"You said you would not allow us to risk either of our reputations or my chance to stay on the dig."

"And so I will not. A floor has no squeaky ropes, or bedsprings."

He'd really thought about it, hadn't he?

"That is good to know." She smiled. "However, I think we should explore camp right now. I'm sure Dr. Miller is hoping to talk to you."

"We are lucky he did not show up already." Henry didn't seem too worried about the possibility.

She saw why when they found Dr. Miller in his tent reading a book about Ancient Macedonia.

"Ah, Dr. Thomas, and the amateur archeologist joining us this year." He didn't greet her by name.

Undaunted, Frankie stepped forward and offered her hand. "Good to see you again, Dr. Miller."

Dr. Miller shook hands with her, his focus still on the book in his hand. "Same."

The older professor was very different from Henry. Though it was obvious he was interested in field archeology, or he wouldn't be there, he fit the absentminded professor archetype uncannily.

"He's what I think of when I think of professors," she said in a low voice as they walked away from the tent.

"You do not know?"

"I've only ever seen professors giving public lectures. I did not go to university, but finishing school." She made no effort to hide her regret at that. "I thought you were absent minded. Now, I know better. You weren't interested in the ladies of the society."

"I find acting as if I don't hear or remember most things ladies say to me keeps them from pestering me."

Frankie grinned. "You are so refreshingly honest."

"Your father did not want to send you to university?" Henry asked.

"No daughter of his was going to fill her mind with unnecessary clutter," Frankie quoted her father, doing a fair imitation of his gruff voice.

"You would have been an ideal student."

"Until I argued with my professors."

"Would you have? I did not notice you arguing much with your father."

"Before marriage. Before that time," she said, bleakly referring to her time incarcerated in the sanitorium. "I was opinionated and rather outspoken. I am still opinionated, but I keep my thoughts to myself unless I know it is safe to voice them."

"I do not notice you holding your words with me."

"No, I don't."

He smiled, seeming pleased by her agreement.

It was an admission of sorts. She'd acknowledged she trusted him as she didn't any other man but Edwin.

Frankie would trust her twin with her life.

Henry made a complete inspection of the camp and gave Frankie a tour in the process.

Dr. Miller and the younger Professor Adams shared a tent with Henry's cousin, Joey. If anyone thought it odd that Henry had opted to share his tent with a benefactor's *son*, no one remarked on it.

Anum Ibrahim and Peter shared another tent, while the workers filled two larger tents on site. There was another tent for the cook with a canvas awning set up in front of it with one table. It had one chair.

"We bring our chairs from our own tents when we eat together," Henry explained.

"Some digs have permanent homes for the archeologists nearby."

"I had considered it, but I do not know how long I will be in Wadjet."

"Why?"

"My university wants me to dig nearer the Valley of the Kings, or at the very least in the vicinity of the Sakkara Temple complex."

"More glory for the university if you excavate temples and tombs left behind by the pharaohs and their priests, rather than the average person, I suppose."

"Exactly," Henry agreed grumpily.

"But doesn't your grandfather underwrite the dig?"

"Yes. He agrees with the university."

"Oh."

"He is a keen student of history, but as he gets older, his interest in leaving behind an impressive legacy grows."

"It is the curse of the wealthy man." She'd noticed the same inclination in her father.

"Perhaps."

"I suppose it makes sense. Once they've amassed a certain amount of wealth, they have to wonder what else they are leaving behind, besides a big bank balance."

"If his remaining son had shown the acumen to grow the business, he would not be so keen for me to make a name for myself in the academic world. But while my uncle likes living the lifestyle my grandfather has provided, he's not as dedicated to working for it. It infuriates him and his family that I don't participate in the business at all, but remain a beneficiary of my grandfather's wealth."

"They resent having to work?" she asked, not surprised as she'd met men like them in her father's circles.

"Yes."

"And yet you no doubt put in longer hours than any of them." Of that she was certain.

Between his studies, his teaching and his archeology, Frankie could not doubt that Henry spent a great deal more time working than his uncle. She wouldn't be surprised if he put in more hours in his field than even *her* father did in his business.

The camp was full of excitement when Mr. Ibrahim showed up with the additional local workers later that night, rather than the next day.

"We will begin digging tomorrow, *sahib*," he said to Henry. "One day can make the difference. You have said this to me often."

Henry's delight at his foreman's attitude overcame even his usual cranky countenance and there was a festive feeling as everyone found their tents early in expectation of the long day ahead.

It was still dark outside when Frankie heard Henry stir. She'd been awake, buzzing with anticipation for some time. They had not made love the night before, but he had kissed her quite thoroughly before gently pushing her toward her own cot.

She could not help thinking what it would be like to married to such a man and accompany him on his digs as Mrs. Thomas had accompanied his father.

Frankie was certain that Henry would not expect to leave his wife at home in America when he came to Egypt. He wasn't like that.

He had such a respect for her brain, but it wasn't because they were lovers. It was just the way he was. Not charming. Not debonair. But honestly respectful of a woman's intelligence.

He expected as much from Frankie as he would from her brother, Edwin. Probably more so because he knew that Frankie had actually studied ancient Egypt with enthusiasm.

Reading about the painstaking process of removing the layers of sand and dirt from the dig site was a lot different than actually doing it, Frankie realized very quickly. Henry had been patient showing her the technique, but he expected her to get it so he could move on to his own pursuits.

She was probably overly cautious, but she didn't want to make a mistake.

Frankie used her trowel to dig up the sand and shook it on a pan as he'd shown her, watching for the smallest sherd of pottery, a bead, or the like. It was unlikely she would find a grave. As a new member of the archeology team, she was training on the least likely area of the dig.

She understood the need to do this and was still excited to be out here in Egypt, trying to uncover the secrets of the past.

That excitement had waned a bit a couple of hours later, when it was time for breakfast. She put her trowel and brush down with relief she did her best to hid.

"The first day, it is always the hardest," Mr. Ibrahim said consolingly from above her. "Look at the new workers who are training with my Qifti. They are tired as well."

He wasn't exaggerating. There were smiles and jostling among the men, but the workers brought in from the local area were clearly no more used to the meticulous digging than she was. While she didn't understand their Arabic, the way they rubbed their own backs and shook out their hands was a universal language.

Though she'd taken water breaks like everyone else over the last couple of hours, Frankie relished her cup of water as much as the food. Never had bread tasted quite so satisfying, or aged cheese been so flavorful. She craved the olives served with it and had to stop herself eating more than her share.

There were even boiled eggs. She only ate one, realizing if she got too full, she'd find it difficult to return to her labors.

"Are you enjoying yourself?" Professor Adams asked. "I remember my first day on a dig, I was so excited to learn how to do all the things properly and I was sure I would find something significant in the first hour."

"Did you?" she asked with a smile.

"Not likely. Not even in the first week. But that first time I did? It made all the hard work worth it. Didn't matter that it was an Egyptian artifact when I'd rather be finding those of the Vikings. I held a little piece of history in my hand, that *I* had found."

"That must have been amazing."

"You're not as likely to find anything where you are excavating," Dr. Miller said repressively. "Don't get your hopes up."

And people called Henry grumpy.

Henry, for his part, wasn't paying any sort of attention to their table talk. He was eating and by the look in his eyes, thinking about ancient Egyptians and what they buried with their dead, when they *weren't* royalty or priests.

Frankie knew that Henry worked the same hours as everyone else on the dig, but that didn't mean those hours were short.

16

By the time Frankie was allowed to retreat to her tent to wash her hands and face before dinner, she was exhausted. And she knew she wasn't the only one.

Joey had offered up how tired he was, but hadn't made a complaint out of it, which made her like the teenager all the more. Frankie wasn't sure she would have been so hard working at the age of sixteen.

He wasn't training on the digging just yet, but was doing all sorts of dogsbody chores. He'd brought water to the workers, dumped baskets of dirt and ran messages for Henry.

While Frankie was truly excited to be learning the art of archeology, she couldn't help being a little envious of the teenager's ability to spend the entire day in Henry's company. Even if it was as something of a personal gopher.

For his part, Joey didn't seem to mind that part of his job. He got the benefit of a professor, who actually enjoyed teaching, sharing his knowledge of not only ancient Egypt, but the process of archeology.

"Good, you have washed. Dinner will be served momentarily." Henry set about washing his own face and combing out his beard before doing the same to his hair.

"You look awfully dapper for an archeologist after a day spent digging."

"I do more supervising than digging these days," Henry said.

From his tone, she couldn't tell how he felt about that. "And teaching. Joey is lucky to have a cousin like you."

"You think so?"

"Yes. I wished more than once I was close enough to hear what you were telling him."

Henry stopped what he was doing and turned to face her. "Really?"

"I think you know by now that with one very big exception, I am not at all keen on dishonesty."

"Playing a role is not the same as lying."

"You've changed your tune on that."

Henry frowned. "I find myself changing all sorts of thinking around you."

"Does that bother you?"

He shrugged. "A man who cannot change his thinking might as well stop studying."

That was a non-answer if she'd ever heard one, but Frankie did not press. "You put in a long day on the dig."

"With so few weeks to excavate, every hour is precious."

Frankie covered her mouth as she yawned. "No doubt."

"You are tired."

She nodded. "It is harder work than I imagined."

"You need not continue digging this late in the day. Miller and Adams were in their tents two hours ago."

"You weren't."

"It is my dig."

"Joey is a hard worker."

"He is. He does his parents proud."

"Considering he was raised with the same privilege we were, he really does."

"Yes. My mother's family do not resent the work necessary to maintain their wealth like my uncle and cousins on my father's side."

"Do you think your cousin will really accept it if Joey decides to study history rather than business?"

"I do."

"Wow. Edwin would be a lot happier if my father had that kind of enlightened thinking."

"I do not know if my cousin would be any more amenable to the film industry than your father," Henry offered.

"My father was adamant that Edwin come into the company along with our older brother, Charles. I have no idea if Charles dreamed of other pursuits. He was never given the chance of going after them."

"Both of your brothers had choices. They chose to fall in with your father's plans, whether out of obligation or desire."

"Father controls the purse strings."

"No doubt. And yet, *you* did not move back into his mansion after your husband's death. *You* did not choose to remarry as your father no doubt expected you to. *You* got a job and supported yourself in a far less lavish lifestyle."

Warmed by what was clearly seen as praise by him, Frankie said, "Less lavish, but with a great deal more freedom."

"Freedom you fight for every day."

"I..." She didn't know what she wanted to say. Frankie was touched to her very core by Henry's assessment of her life.

She *had* fought hard for her freedom. She had turned away from the wealthy lifestyle she'd been raised in so that *she* could choose where she lived, who her friends were and how she spent her time.

"Come, let us get some dinner. Perhaps food will revive you." The heated look he gave her left no doubt why he was hoping her energy was revived.

Dinner was flavorful and filling, made up entirely of native dishes.

"I do not know why we cannot request some more traditional food," Dr. Miller grumbled.

Professor Adams gave the older man a chiding look. "This *is* traditional food. Here in Egypt."

"When I have my own dig, we will have a proper American cook," Miller harrumphed.

Henry didn't seem to be paying either the least attention.

"I like this," Joey piped up. "What is it called?"

Professor Adams answered. "It is called Mulukhiya. The cook makes it with different meats, but this one made with fish is my favorite."

He tore off a piece of his pita bread and dipped it into the stew before taking a hearty bite, a blissful expression breaking over his features, proving he spoke the truth.

Dr. Miller shook his head. "Stew."

That he could imbue so much disgust in one word impressed Frankie, though she did not share his lack of enthusiasm at all.

"It's the bee's knees, if you ask me," she said, her tone in Edwin's register. She appreciated that she could eat with an enthusiasm that would have been remarked unfavorably upon if they knew she was female.

Joey gave her a tired grin. "I concur."

Henry finished the notes he'd been writing and closed his journal. "As do I." He gave Dr. Miller a significant look. "And because I am lead archeologist on *this* dig, it is my opinion that counts. When you are subsisting on rations our workers show gratitude for, you can complain."

"They provide their own food?" Frankie asked.

Henry nodded. "Traditionally workers bring a week or two's worth of flour for bread and perhaps some other foodstuffs, as well as dried leaves for their tea."

"When the rations are used up, the workers will return home. Some return to the dig after, some do not," Dr. Miller added.

The younger Professor Adams gave Henry an inscrutable look. "However, Dr. Thomas has his workers turn their rations into his cooks and those cooks then provide three meals each day for all the workers with a great deal more protein and vegetables than they would have otherwise."

Frankie could not tell if the other man approved, or questioned, the wisdom of Henry's implied largesse.

Henry scowled. "A well-fed worker can pay closer attention to his job as he is not bothered by a cramping belly."

"You spend money on two cook's helpers you would not need if you weren't so worried about your worker's bellies." Dr. Miller shook his head, his opinion on the subject easy to discern.

Ignoring the gibe, Henry looked toward Frankie. "Are you finished?"

"Young Mr. Clarke needn't follow your antisocial behavior of retiring to your tent directly after dinner," Dr. Miller chided, before Frankie could answer.

Henry paid him no heed, his attention fixed firmly on Frankie.

"Almost." Reveling again in her freedom to exhibit masculine manners, Frankie wiped her stew plate with the last of her bread and popped it in her mouth as she stood.

She waved a goodnight to the other archeologists and Joey. The young man seemed to be getting along just fine with his tentmate Professor Adams, who seemed as inclined as Henry to share his knowledge of his passion. The two were discussing Viking history as Henry and Frankie walked away.

By silent agreement, she and Henry went about their nightly ablutions, including a trip to the outhouse. When Frankie got back to the tent, Henry wore his trousers and undershirt and nothing else.

But he was sitting at the table, a map of the dig spread out before him.

"I thought..." She let her voice trail off.

"We have to wait until the camp have all gone to bed. Until then, there is always the risk we could be interrupted."

The food had revived Frankie, but she wasn't going to be able to stay awake much longer, just waiting and told Henry so.

"Get your sleep, Frankie. I'll wake you."

"Promise?" Because as tired as she was, Frankie wanted the fulfillment of the promise his heated stare had made earlier.

The look he gave her now was so filled with sexual assurance, heat washed over her in a sensual wave.

Frankie woke with the most amazing sense of wellbeing, soft lips brushing over her own, a hand caressing down her arm. She knew immediately where she was and who was kissing her. She knew those lips, the tickle of that mustache and beard.

She kissed back, her hands reaching for his body in the dark.

Henry was naked.

He'd said he slept that way. The past two nights she'd been asleep before he found his own cot, so she had not been able to confirm his claim.

Though she had not doubted him.

Henry was not a man to lie.

He pulled the sheet down she slept under, tugging her from the cot into the dark. No light cast even the faintest shadow inside their tent. How could the dark be so absolute?

She found herself settled onto a pad on the floor. In the back of her mind, she realized he must have pulled the thin mattress from his own cot and laid it on the floor of the tent.

They made love, the darkness enhancing every touch, every gasp, both of them careful to keep their voices to the lowest of whispers.

It felt more intimate, more private than anything they had done before. Not illicit. For they were doing nothing wrong, whatever society might say. But this was just for them. This touching and joining of their bodies.

She had never felt so natural with another human being, so completely connected.

He held her after, for long moments, while his hand softly rubbed up and down the side of her body, as if to remind them both that they were still connected. Eventually, when she had nearly fallen back asleep, he got her up and into her cot again, her pajamas back on her body, the sheet and bug netting back in place.

She could hear him moving his own bedding into position as she fell back asleep, a smile creasing her lips, her heart warmed in a way she had no desire to examine.

The next couple of weeks were much the same. Frankie spent her days digging, taking an afternoon break for about an hour, like all the workers, but also digging until Henry and the others finished for the day.

She hadn't found anything of note, and it was still new enough, she did not mind. She was in Egypt. She got to share in the wonder when someone, anyone, found something on the dig. And they did find things. Henry had chosen his digging site well and one grave, holding what seemed like a family of bodies had been found.

So far, no artifacts had been found however.

She was surprised that the other workers continue to work on their designated areas, while Henry and Dr. Miller took over the gravesite. She'd find herself stopping to watch Henry work, entranced by his focus, his meticulous care with the grave.

The desert mummified bodies made their way to the exam tables while Henry and Dr. Miller made sure nothing had been overlooked in the grave.

Dinner was a convivial meal with even Dr. Miller expressing satisfaction with the find. Excited chatter came from the workers, who ate in small groups around the camp.

"Those bodies don't look like the mummies in the papers," Joey said.

"That is because they were mummified from being buried in the sand in the dry heat of the desert climate, rather than the ritualistic mummifications one sees in other tombs and graves."

"Why aren't they just bones then?"

Henry explained the current school of thought that led to the many ancient gravesites found with mummified bodies in the Wadjet Provence while Frankie found herself wishing she could take notes.

The next day, they'd been digging for about an hour after breakfast when there was a great whomping sound and then lots of yelling. Frankie went running like everyone else to discover that the support structure in the deepest pit had collapsed.

Workmen were buried under rubble and broken scaffolding.

She stood in dumbfounded amazement for several seconds.

Henry was militant about safety measures and Mr. Ibrahim insisted all the workmen follow them every single time, every single day.

"How could this happen?" Joey sounded as shocked as Frankie felt.

She just shook her head. "It shouldn't have."

While she didn't understand a lot of the mutterings among the workmen, she'd learned the words for the Mummy's Curse and heard them from several different directions now. Thankfully, none of them was Professor Adams.

Frankie liked the man and didn't want to see him sent home to California in ignominy, but she had no doubt that was exactly what would happen if he fed the superstitious talk.

Henry was right there, barking out orders and directing the rescue efforts, even as he joined in to dig the workmen out. Her archeologist didn't give into hand wringing and male vapors.

Dr. Miller on the other hand was one of the people still demanding how this could have happened, rather than attempting to do any sort of damage control.

Frankie ignored him and joined in the bucket brigade removing dirt and debris from the hole. It seemed like it took forever, but probably had only been a matter of minutes when the first man was freed. He was out cold, but was still breathing, though shallowly. His body and face were covered in dirt and Henry used his fingers to clear the man's mouth of sand and dirt and his handkerchief to clean out the man's nostrils so he could breathe better.

One of the boards that was used as a table top in the excavation examining area was turned into a makeshift stretcher to move him as the digging continued.

The next man was awake and crying out in pain. He'd broken his arm and that was really worrying, even in this modern age. They were nowhere near a hospital and depending how bad the break, infection could set in too easily.

Frankie had read the stories.

The last man to be pulled from the debris was neither awake, nor breathing. Somber grief replaced the shock around the camp.

They had lost one of their own.

Lines of stress were hewn into Henry's handsome features and Frankie wanted to hug him in support, but knew she could not do that.

She settled for a *manly* hand on his shoulder. "We will find out how this happened and make sure it does not happen again."

He jerked his head in acknowledgement of her words.

Henry and Mr. Ibrahim would be seeing to the two living men's medical treatment and transport of the body of the third man to be back to his family.

Henry instructed Dr. Miller and Professor Adams to shut down the rest of the dig for the remainder of the day, and to do their best to allay the other workmen's concerns. He told her to stay with Peter, the assistant foreman and assure nothing in the rubble or the dig section was disturbed.

The authorities would want answers and would no doubt send someone out to inspect the site of the accident.

For her own part, Frankie wasn't entirely comfortable with the assumption it *had* been an accident. Not after the deliberate sabotage before the dig ever began.

Peter and Frankie took a few moments to agree how far away they wanted to keep everyone from the collapse.

For the first hour, it was a steady stream of curious workmen coming up and asking questions, wanting to get right up to the spot where the collapse had happened.

Frankie found herself channeling her father rather than her brother, demanding everyone keep their distance. From the look of approval the assistant foreman gave her, she figured she'd made the right choice.

Joey came up, his hands, face and clothes still covered in dirt. "Jeepers, Cousin Henry is going to be livid when he gets back."

Henry had taken the two wounded men to the nearest hospital in the Studebaker, while Mr. Ibrahim had taken the Model T to return the dead body to his family. The workman had been local, so Frankie expected both Henry and Mr. Ibrahim's return that night.

Frankie could only nod. The adrenalin was wearing off and she was drooping.

"Everyone is talking about the Mummy's Curse. I've been asking questions, trying to find out who brought it up first, but..." Joey let his voice trail off and shrugged.

"Gossip runs like an ant colony's death spiral," Frankie agreed. "It just runs in circles until it the conversation dies of exhaustion. Finding that lead ant is a real pickle."

"You study entomology too?" Joey asked, his voice laced with awe.

Frankie shrugged. While ancient history was her favorite area of study, she had other interests. Mostly those her father thought unsuitable for women.

But it wasn't just about spiting her father in silent defiance. "A certain understanding of insects and how they function makes comprehending some of the conclusions drawn by archeologists easier."

"Sometimes you sound just like Cousin Henry. Does that come from getting old, or going to university?"

Frankie almost blurted that she wouldn't know, she'd never gone to university. Just in time, she remembered she was playing the role of her brother and shrugged. "Could be both."

Or simply the more one studied, the more like an academic one began to sound. If she said that, Joey would think she *really* sounded like Henry. Frankie almost laughed out loud at her own thoughts.

"You look like you just told yourself a joke."

"I think I did."

Joey shook his head as if to say *older people, who could understand them?* "Do you want to take a break here? I'll watch to make sure no one gets close."

"How about you go wash up and get something to eat, then come relieve me?" Joey had shown himself to be a level headed teen and his attempt to figure out who was spreading the gossip showed that he was on the same page as Frankie in regard to this accident potentially being something else.

"You don't have to tell me twice. I'll be back in a jiffy."

Frankie gave him a tired smile and waved him off.

She turned to face Peter. "Excuse me."

"Yes, Mr. Clarke?"

"There is no telling when Dr. Thomas and Mr. Ibrahim will return." Though she expected them sometime before dawn, she could not guess when exactly that might be. "I believe we will need to set a rotation of guards over this site through the night."

She didn't like handing over her responsibility, but Frankie knew she wasn't up to the task of staying up and alert all night. Setting a rotation of men would mean no one had to.

The Egyptian man nodded. "Yes, yes, you are right. I will choose my most trustworthy Qifti."

Short of them staying up through the night, that was the best they could do. Unfortunately, there was no way of knowing if the saboteur (and Frankie was almost entirely convinced there was one) was from among the Qifti, or not.

Frankie woke later from sleep to the sound a motorcar engine. Someone was returning. If she wasn't mistaken, that was the Studebaker.

Henry.

She jumped from her bed and got dressed as quickly as possible, foregoing her usual wrapping to squash her breasts flat and tugging on a jacket. She left off her tie as well, but still had to chase Henry down at the site of the collapse.

He was talking to the guards posted.

She waited in silence while he conversed in Arabic with the two men.

Peter came rushing up, talking rapidly to Henry in his native tongue, gesturing with his arms and asking questions.

She only knew that because he would pause for a second, or two, waiting for an answer.

The assistant foreman's face creased with renewed grief and Frankie caught her breath.

Henry turned to her, his face haggard with strain. "The man who was knocked out never woke up."

"He died?" she asked, her own heart squeezing, her mind trying to take it in.

Henry nodded.

"I am so sorry."

"It's a loss for all of us." He sagged, like he just didn't have anything left.

She grabbed his arm, hopefully in the way her brother would do, but in that moment she couldn't be too concerned about how well her male persona was playing. "Come, you need rest. Tomorrow morning is soon enough to tackle the investigation into this incident."

For long moments, Henry didn't answer, but then he jerked his head in a nod, said something to the assistant foreman and the other workmen, and then turned and started walking toward their tent.

For once, Frankie had no trouble keeping up with his longer strides. Henry was moving like an old man.

Knowing that they would cast shadows onto the walls of the tent lit from within, Frankie forced herself not to take Henry into her arms.

She had to settle for words. For now. "We will figure this out, Henry."

"That won't bring two good men back from the grave."

"No, I know." After The Great War and the so called Spanish Influenza, their countrymen had all learned to grieve and the truth that nothing brought back those lost to death. "But we can stop it happening again."

"I thought my safety measures were enough to do that to begin with."

"You can't account for sabotage."

"You think that is a possibility?" he asked, sounding more tired than she'd ever heard him.

"I do." And she was convinced the potential had already crossed his mind as well. Henry was far too intelligent not to have considered it. "Tomorrow, we will examine the scaffolding, but if the sabotage was in the site itself, spots dug out to weaken the dirt wall itself won't show after the collapse."

There was too much probability they would not be able to prove it one way or the other and that bothered her.

"You are right." Henry sighed, his expression grim. "The how is not as important to me right now as the what. Two men are dead, and one is injured and unable to work for two months."

"Get undressed so I can turn out the light." So, she could reach for him in the dark and hold him as she ached to do.

Frankie was careful how she stood when she took off her clothes, making sure she didn't cast a side shadow on the wall, revealing her modest feminine curves.

She didn't bother with pajamas as she usually did, intuiting that skin to skin contact would be the most comforting.

As soon as they were both naked, she blew out that single lantern she'd lit on waking and then simply stepped into Henry and wrapped her arms around him.

He stood stiff for a long moment, but then his arms came around her too and he rested his head against hers. Neither spoke a word, but stood there just holding each other for a couple of minutes.

Finally, Frankie started moving them toward his cot, intending to press him down and tuck him in. "Come on, you are falling asleep on your feet."

"Can we..." He let his voice trail off, then she felt him shaking his head. "Never mind."

"What? Whatever you need, Henry," she whispered against his ear. "I am here for you."

"The cots are sturdy."

"Yes." Where was this going?

"They will hold both of us, if we don't attempt gymnastics."

Or sex. "I'm sure you are right."

"Sleep with me. I don't know if I'll sleep otherwise."

"Of course." She would have to wake early, but she wasn't worried about being caught with him.

Henry established strict rules for his privacy. While anyone was welcome to come to his tent during the day, from after dinner until he reemerged the following morning, no one who had an iota of self-preservation broke the sanctity of his space.

Excluding emergencies, of course, but she was fairly certain they'd had their quota of those today.

Somehow, they managed to squeeze together onto his cot, a single sheet and blanket over both of them. They were pressed together from her head against his neck right down to her toes touching the top of his feet.

She felt his chest heave and knew he was crying silently in the dark. Frankie held him and gave the only comfort she could, her presence.

It felt even more intimate than sex, this moment of utter vulnerability in such a private, self-contained man.

17

It was still dark when Henry woke. The woman pressed against him the only reason he'd gotten any sleep at all.

Yesterday had been a nightmare. He had never had a death on one of his digs. They did not have earth collapses. They were very careful to dig layer by layer, no matter how empty each strata of earth.

He'd heard about digs where the workers caused such mishaps sneaking in to excavate during breaks and digging into the lower strata for the more lucrative ones. Getting paid bonuses for each usable artifact found led to that sort of thing, but it was a widespread practice.

Henry was lucky to have Anum as his foreman. The Egyptian man had thus far prevented such dangerous practices from among his men.

Henry only wished he knew if the collapse had been caused by greed, sabotage or true random happenstance.

They would examine the rubble and scaffolding today, when it was light out. There would have to be an inspection of all of the pits currently being worked in the grid as well, especially those deep enough to be dangerous if the safety measures had not been adhered to.

They were excavating ancient history, well beyond the Roman and Macedonian layers from those occupations.

Frankie made a soft, feminine sound in her sleep.

There was probably something wrong with him, but Henry found he really liked knowing that he was the only person in Egypt who knew she was a woman. The only one to hear such sounds and see her lovely curves before she flattened them with her gauze wrappings.

Funnily enough, as sexually irresistible as he found her, right now, Henry had no desire to wake her to make love. Her presence was all he needed.

He could not remember the last time he cried, but he had last night. In the dark, where no one could see. But Frankie had felt it. He knew she had. The way she'd held him in silence, her whole being soft and soothing, had told him as much. She didn't utter platitudes or shush him.

She'd simply held him as he let his grief and stress go.

It was not that he had known the workers well. Only one had been Qifti and a return from past years' digs.

It was that those two deaths and the broken arm had happened on *his* dig. Henry hadn't engineered the collapse, but he felt responsible for it.

He would provide a gift to the men's family in gratitude for their work, but nothing could bring the two dead men back.

Memories of his own father's death had plagued him all day. Flashes of blood on the wall and floors, his mother's tears, his grandfather's grim façade.

Those men had both left behind families.

It was that truth that made Henry doubt the work of a saboteur. Undermining his workmen, shorting his supplies...those were relatively harmless endeavors, if annoying. And yes, ultimately, if the campaign to bedevil his dig persisted, could eventually lead to an end to his excavation.

But murder?

He could not believe that of any decent human being.

Surely there were none so depraved as that related to the archeology department. Realistically, where else could any saboteur come from?

Who else would benefit enough from the cancellation of his dig?

Even then, Henry felt it was a stretch.

So, he was looking for unfollowed, or inadequate, safety protocols, today with little expectation of finding anything else.

Frankie stirred against him and his arm tightened around her so she didn't tumble off the small cot.

"I need to get up." Her lack of movement did not match her words.

"Just a moment more." He leaned down, inhaling her scent, loving how she smelled like herself and no one else.

She wore no perfume, of course, and washed with a masculine sandalwood soap, but her skin had a subtle feminine musk that Henry enjoyed more than he would have thought possible.

Everything about her was perfect for him. "Thank you for your kindness, last night."

"You are such a strong, self-contained man, Henry. I am glad you allowed me to share your grief." Frankie placed a soft, chaste kiss against his cheek.

"Yes, well, I don't make a habit of tears."

"No more do I."

Of that he had no doubt. Talk about self contained. Frankie was a vault.

Henry thought that her time in the sanitorium had something to do with that. She did not trust others, but last night she had accepted his trust and that was something all on its own.

"Today will be busy."

"You'll want to examine the rubble for the cause of the collapse and inspect the other dig spots," she said.

"Exactly what I was thinking." They spoke in low tones that would not carry beyond the tent walls.

"Do you think it was sabotage?"

"No. Murder is too far a leap from trying to delay my dig's start."

"Maybe the saboteur didn't expect anyone to be seriously hurt. He could have miscalculated."

There could be no she. Frankie was the only woman on the dig and no one besides Henry knew she was female.

"I just don't understand why the sabotage in the first place," he admitted in a frustrated whisper.

"No more I, but one can never underestimate the dark layers of human nature, especially jealousy and greed."

"But jealous of what? Greed for what? I am no Howard Carter. I've had moderate success finding graves, but so have several other archeologists in the area. None of us are getting written up in the papers. We aren't finding golden artifacts and royal mummery."

"Dr. Miller is clearly jealous you have your own dig. Professor Adams makes no pains to hide his jealousy of your family's wealth and support, of your contacts in that echelon of society."

"I suppose, but Frankie, why now?"

"Perhaps Dr. Miller is tired of waiting for his chance to dig in Macedonia. Professor Adams is young, impatient. *Now* is always the right time for the young and impatient."

"You said greed as well." He didn't see how it applied any more than the jealousy, but she'd made a good point for the latter.

"While you are not excavating royal tombs, your position as lead archeologist allows you to be the one to publish journals, to write articles and books. Though you probably don't even consider it with your family's wealth and impending trust fund, but the fact you have seniority status means your yearly professor stipend is bigger."

"Hardly worth all this effort to get a bigger paycheck."

"For a man with your resources, no, but I nearly didn't come on this journey because I was afraid to leave my job that pays a pittance in comparison to your professor's salary. The difference between your stipend and Dr. Miller's may not matter to you, but I bet it does to Dr. Miller."

Henry had never considered such a thing. "I don't think about money."

He had a budget for his yearly excavations, but that budget was generous and staying within its parameters was only mildly challenging.

"You don't need to. You have it." She patted his chest. "I never thought much about it either. When I didn't have to worry about routinely securing enough to pay monthly expenses. Before money was the one thing standing between my independence and living once again in my father's house."

He thought her strong will had as much to do with it as the money. After all, Frankie could have given up on her dream of independence when she saw how hard she would have to work to maintain it. She hadn't. The incredible woman in his arms had insisted on working and providing for herself.

However, he thought he understood what she meant about the money.

No question, Henry had the luxury of never having to worry about rent, much less a mortgage, like Dr. Miller. And Professor Adams had no hope of pursuing his dreams of Viking excavations without an Angel backer or changing universities, which is frankly what Henry had always expected him to do when the opportunity came.

It was something to think about, but Henry hoped very much yesterday's collapse had been an accident. Even if death had not been intended, he could not imagine living with the knowledge he had caused the death of another.

And he could not wish that pain on another.

He did not know who had blackmailed his father all those years ago and forced the gentle man into ending his own life to protect his family's reputation. Yet as much as Henry despised that man, he had always thought the blackmailer living with the knowledge he had precipitated the death of another was in a way its own punishment.

Surprising himself, he said as much to Frankie as they dressed.

She stopped buttoning her shirt and came over to him, laying her hand on his cheek. "Your heart is so pure, Dr. Thomas. I am in awe of you."

"Nonsense," he gruffly denied, but he could feel the heat of embarrassment climbing the back of his neck. "Anyone would think the same."

"You assume a conscience."

"Don't you?"

"I suppose, but not all hearts are pure, even those who have regret for doing ill to others. There is a certain type of person, that if they believe they were doing right, they do not feel remorse for the ill their actions caused."

"You don't think your father regrets leaving you in the Sanitorium?" he asked, assuming she was talking about George Clarke.

But Henry supposed his courageous Frankie could be talking about her deceased husband as well, the man who had locked her there in the first place.

Frankie's hand dropped as she shrugged. "He has certainly never admitted to such feelings."

"Have you ever told him how terrible it was for you?"

"I have never shared the horrors I faced in that place with anyone, but in the letters I sent, I begged him to intervene, to get me out. He knew how trapped I felt, how out of control of my own life."

And in Frankie's mind, that should have been enough to convince her father to intervene. Henry had to agree.

Clearly George Clarke had not.

"Perhaps one day, you will share those awful memories with me." Henry felt certain doing so would help her.

"Lancing the wound to let the infection out?" she asked, her tone managing to convey both wry intellect and vulnerability.

He wrapped his arms around her, holding her in comfort for her or him, he was not sure. "Yes."

"Perhaps, Henry." She turned in his arms so she faced him and pressed her forehead into his chest. "I think you might be the one person I could relive those memories with."

Her trust in him took Henry's breath away. She had not even trusted her beloved twin brother with the details of her time in the Sanitorium.

Frankie was thoroughly exhausted by the time they sat down to lunch the day after the pit collapse.

No doubt partly due to how little sleep she'd gotten the night before, waiting up as she had for Henry's arrival, only to give into sleep shortly before he got back, when she'd woken again.

It wasn't only that though. It was the emotional toll on everyone from the loss of the workers' lives and the third man's broken bone.

Anum Ibrahim, the most patient and positive thinking man, had argued vehemently with Henry's decision not to continue digging until after the pits were examined for safety. The foreman took it as a personal affront that Henry might question if protocols had been followed.

Dr. Miller didn't help as he'd all but accused Mr. Ibrahim of not supervising his workers well enough.

The Egyptian had offered his resignation, which Henry had of course declined, but it had taken a lot of finessing on Frankie's part and that of her unexpected ally, Professor Adams, to smooth over wounded pride and hurt feelings.

Henry respected and trusted his foreman implicitly and threatened to sock Dr. Miller in the mouth if he didn't apologize.

Unfortunately, Henry was cranky at the best of times, and reacted with short temper when Dr. Miller's grudgingly given apology was not immediately accepted by the foreman.

"Don't get your panties in a twist, Anum. You've got more sense than that."

At the look of extreme umbrage on the usually smiling countenance of the foreman, Frankie knew she had to step in, or what Dr. Miller had not succeeded doing, Henry would. And Mr. Ibrahim's departure from the excavation was the last thing her lover wanted.

"Please, Mr. Ibrahim, you must know how much Dr. Thomas values you," Frankie slotted in hastily, grateful the foreman spoke English and that the conversation was happening in that tongue. "He's not himself or he never would have mentioned a woman's undergarments to you. However, you must remember that he made the journey all the way to Qift to find you and ask you to reconsider being his foreman."

She gave Henry a pointed look and by the expression of consternation on his own face, she hoped he'd realized how inappropriate Mr. Ibrahim would have found that particular slang expression.

Frankie herself wasn't thrilled by it as the expression implied a certain lack of control over emotions in the female sex. As men did not wear panties, a relatively new fashion offering for women replacing the pantalette and bloomers popular in decades past.

"I beg your pardon, Anum. Meant nothing by it," Henry offered readily enough with a lot more sincerity than Dr. Miller's apology.

"If my oversight of the workers is not to be trusted, of what use am I here in this camp?" Mr. Ibrahim demanded, his expression not lightening.

He was clearly as offended by Henry's desire to continue the halt to digging as he was by Dr. Miller's implications.

"It is not that at all," Frankie promised. "It is simply—"

"If it was sabotage, we can't be sure only one pit was targeted," Henry said, interrupting her.

"Oh, really, sabotage? That is grasping at straws, if I do say so." Dr. Miller couldn't make his disdain for the possibility any clearer.

"Dr. Miller." That was all Professor Adams said, but his tone was filled with censure.

The older man looked at his colleague, his demeanor less than impressed. "Is there something you feel you can add to this discussion, Daniel?"

"Daniel has more sense than you, Rudolph." There was an air of leashed violence about Henry and the look he was giving Dr. Miller said it might be directed at his colleague.

Dr. Miller seemed to notice and took a step back. "It is not my intention to offend, but sabotage, really?"

"It would be irresponsible for Henry to ignore any avenue of inquiry." The look Professor Adams gave the head archeologist wasn't one of unadulterated approval, however.

Frankie remembered that Daniel Adams had himself thought the Mummy's Curse could be plaguing their expedition this year.

Henry ignored the implied criticism and humbly apologized again for the inappropriate comment to his foreman. He then asked for Mr. Ibrahim's help in confirming no sabotage had taken place.

This finally seemed to settle the foreman's sense of dignity.

Nevertheless, Frankie spent most of the morning playing peacemaker and buffer between a growly Henry and the rest of camp, while Professor Adams did the same for his colleague Dr. Miller. The younger man's patience was impressive, though it was clear at times it waned.

Frankie would have been happy to smack Dr. Miller in the kisser herself, more than once, as the day wore on.

The examination of the scaffolding had shown no obvious tampering, but that didn't mean a saboteur had not undermined the structural integrity of the walls of the pit with under-digging.

There had been an air of fear and even resentment around the dig that morning. The Mummy's Curse kept coming up, no matter how many times everyone was reminded that it had nothing to do with their dig.

While the young Professor Adams did not join in the speculation in that regard, he cast enough looks filled with resentment toward Henry that Frankie worried. Even Joey was subdued today, though he joined in conversations around the camp as he had the day before, his spoken French even better than hers.

A few of the workmen spoke English, but more spoke French in addition to their native tongue of Arabic.

"This talk of the Mummy's Curse is not dying down," Joey said to the table at large now. "I'm ready to give the Bronx cheer to whoever started it, that's for sure."

The image of Joey blowing a raspberry toward some poor worker brought a slight smile to Frankie's face.

Henry's tired eyes warmed as well. "You and me both, cousin. One of the workers is leaving because of it. He told Anum he is afraid for his soul."

"Oh, for crying out loud," Frankie said, her own frustration boiling over.

Dr. Miller frowned. "We can only hope others do not follow suit."

"Do you hope that?" Frankie asked. Her tact had been used up and now she wanted some straight answers.

Someone was feeding these rumors and she wanted to know if it was one of the other archeologists.

"Whatever do you mean, Mr. Clarke?"

Frankie didn't pull a single punch, answering honestly. "I mean that if this excavation gets shut down, you have a much better chance getting your university's support for a dig in Greece."

"How dare you impugn my honor? I suppose you are the one who has filled Dr. Thomas' head with the idea of saboteurs. Bringing amateurs on digs like this never turns out well," he grumbled.

What a bunch of hooey. Amateurs were often brought on digs for reasons like donations (as her father had done) or simply for free labor. Acting as if she was some kind of unwelcome anomaly really made her sore.

"Frankie hasn't filled my head with anything." Henry glowered at his colleague. "And sh... sheesh, he's right. You have more to gain by this dig going under than anyone else."

Henry's near slip of her gender was a strong indicator of how upset he was under all the gruffness.

"There is no saboteur!" Dr. Miller's vehemence was pretty convincing, unless he was as good an actor as she was. "If this dig closes under a cloud of suspicion, getting any sort of backing from the university or its patrons in future is unlikely for *any* of us in the short term."

Henry harrumphed, but he didn't disagree.

"Dr. Miller is right," Professor Adams said, his tone as weary as Frankie felt and without her simmering annoyance. "None of us is likely to try to undermine the expedition, our futures are brighter if we succeed here, not if we fail."

"Only if you believe there is a chance of getting your university to support a dig in your discipline while Dr. Thomas is still with the history department." Frankie was beyond treading lightly on the boards this day.

"I will most likely move onto another institution at some point, ideally one that supports Viking research," Professor Adams said, his tone showing no rancor at her words.

She had a hard time finding fault with the assertion, especially as it coincided with something Henry had said to her about the younger professor.

Regardless, she asked, "Then why were you so upset about the fact Dr. Thomas hasn't introduced you to potential benefactors?"

"Because wherever I go, I'll need connections and thus far, none of my colleagues in the history department have been willing to make those meetings possible."

"It is our department's responsibility, not ours," Dr. Miller said repressively.

But Henry was looking like he'd had some kind of awakening. Her professor was a bit oblivious when it came to others, but he was not a mean man.

Professor Adams shrugged. "If you say so."

"Regardless, all this talk is making it seem like a saboteur is unquestionably at work and that is simply not true," Dr. Miller insisted. "There is no evidence the collapse was caused by anything other than unlucky circumstance."

"And all this talk of the Mummy's Curse?" Joey asked challengingly.

Frankie admired his youthful brashness. She wasn't sure even Edwin was that self-possessed at sixteen.

"Gossip," Dr. Miller dismissed.

Frankie couldn't help adding, "Persistent gossip."

"Gossip often is." Dr. Miller sounded unconcerned with that possibility.

Henry pushed his now empty plate way, his expression grim. "We are down four workers, and more could decide to leave because of that gossip."

"How likely is that, really?" Dr. Miller asked. "There is always gossip on a dig. Howard Carter's excavation is the reason for all this Mummy's Curse business, and he has no trouble keeping workers."

"His dig is famous," Joey said, showing perspicacity beyond his years. "And it's closer to Cairo."

"Anum has sent his assistant foreman to recruit more workers, but until then, we are going to have to prioritize the digging."

"You may end up working on a more productive spot," Professor Adams said to Frankie encouragingly.

"I won't say no to that," she said in her best imitation of Edwin's enthusiasm, but feeling the sentiment entirely.

She would feel even better if she could stay close to Henry. She was worried about him. He took everything on his shoulders and Frankie couldn't get past the feeling that someone wanted to do him, or his reputation, harm.

Though the other two archeologists had made a good case for that someone not being them.

But then who?

And honestly, Frankie wasn't ruling anyone out at this point, even them.

After the discussion over lunch, Frankie was surprised at how feelings seemed to have shifted to a more positive demeanor during the afternoon's dig. It helped that Dr. Miller discovered another grave.

A sense of excitement and anticipation pervaded the workers as a couple of those previously on bucket brigade were brought into the actual digging while they concentrated on the area around Dr. Miller's discovery.

Frankie found a scarab. It wasn't a very nice one, but something more crudely done than the ones she'd seen pictures of from royal and priestly tombs. Henry was thrilled as the lack of gold leafing and fine work indicated a lesser official, or even working class grave goods.

That night he joined her on her cot.

Neither said a word, but they kissed until they fell asleep.

The following days and nights fell into a similar pattern. Neither mentioned how important it had become to them both to sleep together, but they were very, very, *very* careful not to get caught doing so.

The assistant foreman returned with three rather rough looking men to replace the four workers.

He and Mr. Ibrahim had a heated discussion with wildly gesticulating arms when the foreman got a look at his new workers.

"Is Mr. Ibrahim upset about who his assistant hired?" Frankie asked, pretty sure that was the case.

"Yes. The men are not at all trained in excavating, but Peter insists they were the only men he could find. We'll have to put them on bucket brigade and even with three more bodies, I don't think we can go back to the extensive digging we planned for this season."

"Still, you've already made some solid discoveries."

"Yes, we have." Henry didn't sound convinced though.

"Are you alright?" she asked, wishing for something like the hundredth time in the last few days that she could reach out and touch him.

She could probably have gotten away with patting his shoulder without drawing comment, but tended to err on the side of caution.

Her feelings for the archeologist were growing, and while she had no intention of admitting that to him, she worried they would be evident by her demeanor to others if she allowed herself even the most casual of touches in public.

The improved mood of the camp was probably down to the fact that they were digging again, now that the morning had been spent inspecting the pits. There were no breeches of safety protocols found, which left Anum in a much better frame of mind. The workmen were back to earning their bonuses.

Everyone was pleased.

Except Henry.

He spent a lot more time overseeing the dig than examining the finds. That wasn't going to go over well with Mr. Ibrahim if it continued. For now, though, the foreman seemed to be doing his own zealous oversight, accompanied by a great deal more instructions in Arabic than Frankie was accustomed to hearing from him.

For her part, Frankie enjoyed having her hands back in the dirt and sand. She had known she wanted to come to Egypt, to see a real dig in action.

She'd never realized how much she would actually enjoy the work itself.

It was more than learning; it was *discovering* and it fed her soul as nothing else had since that first course on history.

It took a few days, but things settled back into a routine and Henry finally went back to spending his days examining artifacts in situ and then more closely on the tables. He and Dr. Miller argued over potential interpretations, both taking copious notes.

Frankie had taken to spending her afternoon hours drawing the finds. She'd seen the drawings done by the other archeologists and her heart simply could not stand for the beautiful shards of history they found to be memorialized in such simple and inaccurate to size drawings.

When she told Henry so, she expected him to be offended, but he looked at her like she'd said something profound.

"You can *draw*?" he demanded, like she'd been keeping a secret from him.

"Well, yes. To be honest, I really wish I had my paints. I'll try to paint from memory when we return to California, but it will not be the same," she lamented.

"You can paint?" he barked, sounding almost angry.

"Isn't that what I just said?" she teased. "It was one of the few pursuits both my father and husband approved of for me."

Though neither man had been thrilled by her subject matter.

She hadn't been content to paint Egypt inspired pictures but had spent weeks researching her subjects before painting them. She had some of the most accurate paintings of Egyptian finds and imagined pharaonic images outside of a museum hanging on her walls.

"Why didn't you tell me?" he demanded.

"Why would I?" she asked.

"You must know how important it is to accurately document our finds."

"You have a photographer." That was actually Dr. Adams' official position on the dig. Though the assistant professor spent more time digging than he did taking pictures.

"Daniel knows how to use a camera," Henry grumbled. "Getting him to do so is an exercise in patience."

"Not something either you or Dr. Miller have in abundant supply."

"Have you seen the pictures he takes?"

"Well, yes." She hadn't wanted to say anything, but the pictures Professor Adams took were a bit more artistic than documentary.

"Do *you* know how to use a camera?" Henry asked with accusation.

Like she'd been hiding things from him.

Perhaps Frankie should have been offended, but she was more amused than anything. "Actually, no. Not that I would be averse to learning," she admitted. Frankie loved learning new things.

"Daniel!" Henry bellowed.

"Henry," Frankie chided. "You don't have to shout like that. I'm sure I could find Professor Adams if you need him."

"You are going nowhere, Frankie."

"I'm not?" she asked, trying hard to suppress the laughter that wanted to burble out of her.

Why did she find this man's crankiness so darn amusing?

"Are you laughing at me?" he asked grumpily.

"Maybe, a little."

"You are a minx."

She gave him a cheeky grin, but didn't reply because Professor Adams galloped up, moving more like young Joey than a staid teacher of young minds. "What is it? What happened?" he asked, looking around wildly, his concern evident.

"You need to teach Frankie how to use the camera."

"I do?" Professor Adams gave Frankie a considering look. "Do you have a yen for photography?"

"I wouldn't mind learning to do it."

"Would he be taking over my role as photographer?" the assistant professor asked, not sounding terribly worried.

In fact, his tone implied he liked the idea.

"Frankie can take the pictures and you can develop them."

"Fine by me." Professor Adams smiled. "You know I'd rather be digging than documenting."

"I know you learned to take pictures to be included on my dig rather another of the professors in our department." Oh, Henry sounded really annoyed.

But the younger man just shrugged. "Can you blame me?"

"Only if you do not do your job."

"If you were better at sketching for your journal, I might feel more guilty."

"It is precisely because I have no artistic talent to speak of that I requested a photographer be part of our team."

Professor Adams glanced down at the sketch Frankie had been working on. "I'd say Mr. Clarke has enough ability in that area to make up for both of us."

"Agreed." Henry gave her another accusing look. "Frankie has been hiding his light under a bushel."

It was only as Henry used the pronoun *his* that Frankie realized how carefully he avoided referring to her by Mr. Clarke, or a male pronoun. He was equally careful not to give away her secret, but he did it by maintaining his own integrity as much as possible.

Just as she had done.

Her admiration for the man who had become her only lover since her marriage filled her heart to bursting.

"Sheesh," Professor Adams said, sounding very much like Joey. "Don't look at Dr. Thomas like that or everyone is going to know your secret."

18

Henry went still. So did Frankie, her body washing hot and cold in horror.

Daniel Adams knew her secret?

The blond man just rolled his eyes at them both. "Don't look like that either. You think I would tell? Being a member of the Lavender Club myself, I'm not about to put either of you in harm's way."

Neither Frankie nor Henry responded. For her part, she was standing in stupefied silence. Perhaps Henry was similarly affected.

"Funny, isn't it, though? I was certain you didn't swing that way, Professor Thomas. But then you bring young Mr. Clarke on the dig. At first, I thought I was imagining things, but that look he just gave you? That's a look I'd give my eyeteeth to get form another man. It's not just sex, you know." Now the young professor was just rambling.

Like he'd had all these words trapped inside him and finally an opportunity to let them out.

"They say it's about sex and not love, but that's not how it feels to me. You guys either, it looks like."

Frankie felt like a fraud and suddenly her own secret felt too substantial to bear.

It was like Henry knew because he put a heavy hand on her shoulder. "Stop, Frankie." Then he looked at Professor Adams, compassion and concern in his usually grumpy expression. "Whatever you think you know, Daniel, you just took a terrible risk admitting that to us."

Professor Adam's eyes grew suspiciously bright with moisture. "I just feel so alone. Even back in California, it's too risky to go to the Pansy clubs. Not worth it either. The couple of times I went, I just met men, most of them married, who only wanted one thing."

Frankie wanted to hug Professor Adams.

Henry put his hand on the younger man's shoulder and squeezed. "I know you feel alone, but you aren't. I never thought to have someone in my life like Frankie."

Frankie made a choking sound, but she couldn't help it. *Someone like her?* What was Henry saying?

What did she want him to be saying?

"But you're *old*. I don't want to be lonely most of my life."

Frankie stifled her laugh at the *old* bit. Professor Adams was too sincerely upset.

"You don't have to be lonely, but you do have to be circumspect," Henry said earnestly, but still gently, none of his usual crankiness in evidence. "Listen to me Daniel, if you tell the wrong person, if you are *with* the wrong person, you're ripe for blackmail."

The younger man laughed. "What would a blackmailer try to get from me? I don't have any money."

"Do not think that will save you," Henry warned, his tone urgent. "Please, Daniel, have a care."

The assistant professor nodded. "I'll teach you how to use the camera, Mr. Clarke," he said to her. "But I think you should keep sketching. You're really talented."

"Thank you. I will." Frankie wanted to tell Daniel Adams the truth so badly, she ached with it.

Was this how her brother felt? This terrible loneliness and sense of isolation, despite the love of his family.

"Do your family know?" she couldn't help asking.

Daniel Adams' expression twisted into a look too bitter for his age. "I moved across country so they would never find out. My father is a minister. My mother prays for the loose women of today, what do you think she would do if she found out about me? Why? Does your family know about you?"

"They do." That was truth at least.

"And they still love you?" he asked, sounding like he could not imagine it.

"Yes." Of that she had no doubts. Even their prig of an eldest brother still loved Edwin.

"Then you are very lucky."

Frankie thought about that in relation to her own experience with her family and thought maybe the young professor was right. Edwin was lucky, but so was Frankie. Maybe not so lucky she could trust her father with her secrets as her brother had done, but lucky to have a father who had given her freedom even when he had not approved.

He could have tried to control her life as so many fathers did their daughters in this age, forcing Frankie to move far away to maintain her independence, as Daniel Adams had done.

Later that night Henry joined Frankie on her cot, pulling her close. She'd been lying down for an hour, but she wasn't asleep yet.

"I hate deceiving Professor Adams."

"I know you do, sweetheart, but if it comes between his feelings and your safety, you win."

"No. I don't think that's right." But she couldn't reveal her own secret without putting Henry at risk and she wasn't willing to do that.

Which is what she told him.

"You're a woman of deep honor, Frankie."

"Like minds and all that," she said gruffly, hiding emotion she still wasn't ready to face. "Edwin never talks about wanting to settle down with another man."

"Perhaps he is not ready to settle down as you say, but for his own sake I hope when he is, he can find a likeminded man who knows how to be discreet."

"Me too."

"Maybe you should introduce him to Daniel."

"They'd make great friends, but like you said, I don't think my brother is ready to settle down. I would hate to see that young man more hurt than he already is."

"Young man. You talk like you are years older than him when in fact Daniel is only a couple of years younger than you."

She shrugged. "I feel older than him. He reminds me of Joey sometimes."

Henry's laugh was silent but shook his body against hers. "Me too. I think he has spent a lot of his adult years hiding in academia."

"At least he's safer that way." She would never forget Henry's story about his father, who had no doubt thought marriage and fathering a child had made him safe as well.

"My father thought he was safe, married to my mother," Henry said pensively, proving his mind was traveling along the same track as hers. "He should have been. Whoever betrayed him had to have been close enough to know his deepest secrets."

"Or knew the secrets of his lover."

Henry made a strange noise. "You are right. All my adult life, I've tried to determine if any member of our family could have been the blackmailer, but he could have had the connection to father's *amore*."

"He could have been a she. Women are not exempt from the evil of greed."

"No doubt you are right."

Nothing out of order happened over the next days and the camp settled back into a productive rhythm. Henry's tension didn't dissipate however and a couple of weeks after the collapse, Frankie suggested a walk after dinner rather than retiring immediately to work on his journal in his tent.

Henry described the different elements of the desert to her, talking about his first years on a dig in Egypt, his time excavating with his father, and what he enjoyed about being a professor as well as an archeologist. She wasn't surprised to discover that despite his cantankerous demeanor, Henry enjoyed most of his students.

"Their desire to understand the past speaks well of our future."

"Do you think so?" she asked. " The recent rise of the Klan does not. And there is still such inequality between men and women."

Henry nodded. "Of course, you are right, but the more people in our society that understand the cost of those very societal ills in history, the better chance we will make decent decisions in the future."

Frankie said nothing, but she could not help thinking that the death of so many in the War to End All Wars did not speak of educated, rational minds making good political decisions.

"I am a bit of an optimist, I suppose," Henry said, like he was admitting a great failing.

Frankie smiled at him, her heart just full of his goodness. "I think that is a good thing. We need optimists."

Henry stopped and turned to face her, the sun setting behind him casting a soft glow on the sand. "You are an optimist as well, you know."

"You think so? I feel I've become very much a cynic."

"And yet you chose to risk a great deal by pretending to be your brother so you could live out your dream of coming to Egypt on a dig."

"You think that was optimistic?"

"I know it is. If you were genuinely cynical, you would never have believed it could work."

"I guess you are right. I just knew that not trying would be the same as locking myself up behind fear." What was the point of independence, when she made her own prison to live in?

"You're a courageous lady, Frankie."

Warmth spread through her at his obvious approval. "You're pretty courageous yourself. You chose the same path of study your father took despite knowing there would be those who remembered his death and would look askance at you because of it."

Henry's startled look told her he hadn't expected her, or anyone, to realize that. "I could not let the blackmailer win. He took my father from me; I would not let him take the love of archeology."

"Did you love it so much? Even then, when you were young?"

"I did. The smallest find was cause for rejoicing and my father would spend hours wondering aloud what it could mean."

And that had sparked his son's curiosity. "He sounds like a truly unique man."

"I think he was. He was charming. Everyone liked him. Not like me."

"I like you very much." She thought the word might be love, but no way was Frankie going there. Not right now.

Maybe not ever.

Love came with too high a cost, or so she had believed since her failed marriage.

"You do." Henry sounded just a little surprised by that. "I have never had a long term lover, never thought I would find a woman who meshed so well with me."

"We will be friends when we return to California." She didn't make it a question because she did not doubt it.

She could no more imagine her life without him in it than she could imagine one without Edwin, or her female adventurer society.

"Maybe more than friends," he said, his own expression no less certain.

Frankie did not reply, not sure what she wanted to say. To agree would be to admit that what they had was more than simply sexual compatibility, but to deny it would feel like a lie.

And not a lie Frankie was willing to utter out loud, or even to tell herself.

"Did you hear?" Joey came rushing up while Frankie did her best to follow Professor Adams' instructions on the use of the camera.

She was documenting the most recent finds with photographs. Henry was pleased with the results once the assistant professor developed the plates.

Professor Adams seemed equally happy not to have the actual photography be his responsibility any longer, leaving him more time to work the dig as well as pursue his own studies.

Frankie could not imagine being interested in anything more than the excavation at hand, but then she was fascinated by Ancient Egypt.

"Did I hear what?" she asked Joey after taking her last shot of a funerary scarab.

"Cousin Henry has been invited to view the Tomb of Tutankhamun!"

That brought Frankie's head up in a hurry. She stared at the teenager. "He has?"

"Yes! The invitation just arrived. He's allowed to bring one guest. Dr. Miller thinks he's going, being the second-ranking archeologist on this dig."

"Was Dr. Miller named in the invitation?"

"He wasn't and he's in a snit about that. How did you know?"

"I didn't. That's why I asked."

Joey laughed, as if what she'd said had been funny rather than just the truth. "How are the pictures coming? I sure would like to learn how to use a camera."

"I'll ask Henry if it is all right, but if he agrees, I'm happy to show you." She could not offer to teach another neophyte on the use of the expensive and necessary equipment without doing so.

"That would be the Bees Knees!"

Her smile was indulgent, but Joey reminded her so much of Edwin as a teen, so full of vitality and joy. Frankie had been that way too. Her marriage had aged her.

Lately, she'd been feeling a renewed enthusiasm in life, waking every morning with a sense of anticipation for what the day might bring.

"I see Joey made it before me." Henry's deep tones went through Frankie like a caress.

Stifling her atavistic reaction to her lover, she turned with what she hoped was a casual smile. "I hear you are going to the Valley of the Kings."

"We are going."

"Really?" Joey demanded. "You're taking Mr. Clarke? Dr. Miller is going to have kittens."

"That would be a newsworthy feat," Henry replied drolly. "However, I already informed Rudolph that since Mr. Clarke has a sincere and deep, abiding interest in Ancient Egypt, I am taking him as my guest to view Carter's find."

"But..." Frankie could barely breathe with the excitement. "Surely, as the second most senior archeologist, Dr. Miller should be your guest."

"His name was not on the invitation and that is what I told him. I know you want to go, Frankie. Do not allow societal conventions to stand in your way. The only reason Rudolph wants to go is to say he has been. He has no interest in Ancient Egypt and three years on this excavation has not changed that."

Frankie couldn't argue the point. Despite them having already made an important discovery, the Professor of Macedonian Studies had put the barest effort into documenting it and made no effort to research or determine what the burial grouping had signified, or even what era it was from.

He put only the minimum hours into actual work on the dig, spending the rest of his time studying and writing in his own discipline.

Frankie thought it was a waste of resources on behalf of the university to be honest. Surely there were other aspiring archeologists that would bring more enthusiasm and investigative insights to the dig.

Even Professor Adams made more effort to interpret the finds and discuss what each day's revelations meant with Henry.

"If you really want me to come along, of course I would be over the moon to do so." Frankie couldn't hide the grin splitting her face and didn't try to. "It is an opportunity I could not have even dreamed of having."

"That's settled then."

That evening they went for their now habitual walk after dinner.

"I cannot believe I will be able to visit the Tomb of Tutankhamun." Frankie had to forcibly refrain from reaching out to take Henry's hand in enthusiastic happiness.

"I was surprised by the invitation myself. We are not one of the major universities and my dig is really rather small in comparison to many."

"And yet, you seek to do so much with your smaller workforce."

"Not that it has done me much good. We've had to stop work on two of the pits."

"Through no fault to your planning or acumen."

"You are a very stalwart supporter, Frankie." Henry's voice was laced with unusual humor, and something else she didn't want to try to define.

"It is easy to offer support to someone so impressive in their field."

"Few would consider me as impressive as you imply."

"You are being too modest, I'm sure."

He turned from their normal route to walk around an outcropping she had always wanted to explore, but they usually got to talking so enthusiastically she didn't mention it.

Suddenly, it was Henry who grabbed her hand and then pulled her to him, kissing her with knee melting passion. Trusting him to have made sure they were out of the sight of camp, Frankie returned his kiss with unfettered delight.

She was breathless when he lifted his head and smiled down at her. "You are an incredible woman, Frances Edwina Somers."

"I am so glad you know I am me," she said, knowing he would understand her meaning.

"I too find it a pleasure to know that I alone know you are not in fact your brother, but a resourceful and very attractive woman."

"It usually bothers me when men focus on my looks, but I like knowing you are attracted to me."

"As it has led to some of the most satisfying intimacy of my life, I would say so."

"For me too," she said happily.

He shook his head, smiling down at her. "As much as I want to see Carter's find, I am not sure I would have taken the time to go to the viewing if you were not here."

"Oh, I am sorry. Did you want to refuse the invitation? You should not go on my account." Though her heart plummeted at the thought of missing out on the opportunity.

"No. I consider it yet another thing for which to be grateful to you for."

"You are grateful to me?" she asked, a little shocked he felt thankful toward her. She had, after all, inserted herself into his dig under false pretenses.

"Very much so. You have brought joy into my life, Frankie."

"Oh, what a lovely thing to say."

"It is nothing but the truth."

"I suppose we had better start back before anyone wonders why our evening walk took us out of sight of camp for so long."

"One day, I would like to take you into the desert and make love under the stars."

She gasped, the image in her mind immediate and visceral. "I would like that very much."

Though she could not imagine how they were to make such a thing happen.

Henry wished he were still holding Frankie's hand as they came back into the camp. A subversive thought of what might make that possible flitted through his mind. An idea he'd never thought to entertain.

Marriage.

Looking at his lover, he frowned. Frankie had no desire to ever marry again.

It made a man wonder what he could do to change the mind of a very strong-minded woman.

He was puzzling over the problem as they entered their tent. The moment the tent flap closed behind them, he reached for her hand, the need for physical connection too great to deny.

"I like holding hands." Frankie sounded confused by the admission.

However, it made Henry very happy to hear. "I do too."

"John and I did not hold hands like this."

She rarely mentioned her dead husband. Henry stopped and turned to face her, but Frankie's gaze wasn't on him, but on something behind him and her complexion had paled. "Do not move, Henry."

"What?" But he obeyed, staying still. Had one of the larger scorpions found its way into their tent?

"It's an Asp." Her lips barely moved as she spoke, Frankie's attention never swerving from what she saw behind him. "I do not like snakes, Henry."

The coldness of her hand in his told him it was more than not liking the reptiles. Frankie's reaction was more like a phobia.

"Is it awake, or coiled?" he asked.

"It's coiled," she replied, sounding not at all comforted by that fact.

"I am going to turn around slowly," he told her.

"No." Her tone was emphatic, her grip on his hand tightening. "Perhaps he will find his own way out."

"I cannot allow a poisonous snake to wander the camp." Nor could they stand there motionless all night as the snake slept.

"But Henry, if it strikes, it could kill you."

"Yes, but if we let it simply go, it could bite someone else." He squeezed her hand. "Trust me, sweetheart. I know what to do."

Finally, her eyes lifted to meet his. "You do?"

"I do." He tried to put all the confidence he felt and wished he felt into his expression and tone.

The truth was, the Egyptian Asp was one of the most deadly and fastest striking snakes known. In theory, he *did* know what to do, but whether it would work or not, was in question.

He wanted Frankie out of there, but if she moved, she would draw the snake's attention. Soon their body heat would do that regardless of their stillness.

"Okay, I trust you," she said.

Henry took that admission for the gift it was and gently released her hand. "I need you to stay perfectly still, Frankie. Promise me. No matter what."

She gulped but gave a tiny nod. "I promise."

He then turned slowly and carefully, doing his best to make no disturbance in the air.

The Asp lay coiled near the foot of his cot. It could be sleeping, but even the slightest disturbance detected by its enhanced senses would wake it. While most snakes were shy and not likely to attack, this one could easily feel threatened in this unknown environment.

With great care, Henry shrugged out of his coat, glad he'd donned it for their walk as the evening air had grown cool. He walked toward the snake, taking one even step at a time. He knew he could not afford to hesitate.

Throwing his coat over the snake, he jumped toward the bed and ripped a pillowcase off the bed. He then put the case over the now wiggling Asp and carefully scooped it and his coat into the bag. "Quick get me something to tie it."

Frankie leaped out of her paralysis to get him one of her bowties.

Henry tied off the top of the pillowcase as quickly as possible before dropping it to the ground. The pillowcase wiggled and the snake could be heard hissing, but the knot in the bowtie held.

Frankie threw herself at him. "Oh, Henry, that was magnificent." His usually unflappable lover was shaking.

He held her close for a moment but reluctantly stepped back. "Sweetheart, I have to check to see if there are any others."

"You don't think it was alone?" she asked, clearly rattled at the thought.

"I hope so, but we need to be sure. You go out and get Anum, would you? I'll start poking any possible hiding spots with a stick."

"Absolutely not." She drew herself up. "I'm not leaving you alone. What if you do find another one? You'll need my help."

She was so strong. Her fear was there, but so was her determination.

"It is my sincere hope that is not a likely scenario."

"Nevertheless. Let me get a bathing sheet and another pillowcase."

They spent a tense few minutes searching every nook and crevice, shadow and hidden space for other reptile intruders. They found a harmless lizard, but no more asps.

Then it was simply a matter of finding something long enough to pick the bag up with and taking the snake out of the tent. The stick he'd been using to prod dark spaces would do.

It had been sheer luck the now angry snake had not gotten a fang close to where he'd held the pillowcase together.

Henry bellowed Anum's name loud enough to be heard throughout the camp.

The foreman came running, his eyes on the wiggling bag at the end of pole Henry used to measure the depth of the pits.

"It was in your tent?" he asked, sounding horrified.

"Yes. It's now wearing my favorite coat." Now the danger was past, Henry felt more than a little disgruntled at that knowledge.

Amun insisted on disposing of the snake himself. Henry was not surprised. The foreman took personally anything that went amiss in the camp.

Henry should have taken this into more account when he had been issuing orders after the collapse. He'd had no intention of offending his old friend and colleague, but Henry was the first to admit that he was no glad hand when dealing with people.

Frankie was naturally good at it, though she was as frank as her name.

And no one even knew she was a woman, so he could not credit it to politeness shown toward the fairer sex. Frankie was simply better with people than a crusty old professor.

She was showing that right now as she soothed both Anum and Joey while subtly encouraging a full search of the camp for any more potential intruders. Not that Anum needed much encouragement.

The Egyptian insisted on the involvement of every worker, his harangue over such an occurrence after their usual measures taken not for tender ears.

An hour later, no more snakes had been found, but an empty gunny sack used to dispose of dirt had been discovered behind Henry and Frankie's tent.

It could simply have been dropped there.

However, Henry had his suspicions about how it had gotten there and what it had been carrying.

"Cousin Henry, could I have a word?" Joey asked after Anum had declared the camp asp free and finally dismissed the workers to their beds.

"Certainly."

Having heard their words, Frankie stopped in her course toward him and turned to go the other direction.

"Frankie, stop." Henry wasn't holding anything back from her and did not care if his cousin thought Mr. Clarke had become Henry's closest confidant.

He would be right, in essence if not identity.

She turned and gave him a look like her leaving should be obvious. "Your cousin wants a private moment."

"Oh, your thoughts on the matter are welcome, Mr. Clarke," Joey hastily assured.

"Nonsense," Henry declared at the same time.

Joey and Frankie shared a look that Henry ignored.

"Come on then." He waived his hand toward the tent. He did not have all night to stand outside chit chatting.

19

Frankie had to smile despite her upset over the discovery of the asp. As much as she hated admitting it, she was more than a little afraid of snakes.

She was terrified of them.

Her throat was still tight from seeing the coiled asp over Henry's shoulder, her hands still clammy, her heart finally back to a normal beat. Insisting on staying with Henry while he searched their tent and then participating in the search of the rest of the camp had taken a toll on her she was loathe to admit to.

Yet, Henry was as impatient and pragmatic as always and that was both charming and comforting.

He was not upset and seemed ready to go back to life as usual.

All three of them entered the tent after Joey made a bit of a show of looking around to make sure no one else was in hearing distance. It was dramatic and just a little humorous, helping Frankie's fear of snakes to ratchet back even more.

Joey gave Henry an earnest look. "I saw one of those new workmen lurking around your tent earlier."

Surprisingly, Henry frowned, his eyes narrowing, his body tensing. "Did you?"

Joey nodded fast. "I thought he wanted to talk to you and had forgotten you and Mr. Clarke always take an evening constitutional."

The teen made it sound like he thought something differently now, but Frankie could not imagine what.

"Was he carrying anything?" Henry asked.

Frankie went cold inside with sudden comprehension. "You think someone planted the asp?"

"Snakes are shy by nature and almost never come into an active camp." Henry's tone was serious, but still comfortingly pragmatic. "If I were a single archeologist, working on my own? I would have to watch for this sort of thing."

"But Anum does regular sweeps with his men," she said with comprehension.

He nodded. "That an asp ended up sleeping in our tent is highly suspect."

Because even if the snake had gotten inside the tent, it would have been more likely to leave again than to stay until she and Henry had returned from their evening walk.

"I didn't see him carrying anything," Joey offered morosely. "But I agree that snake should never have made it into your tent. A scorpion in your shoe would have been more likely."

Even knowing she took measures to prevent just that, Frankie shivered. "But you say the workman wasn't carrying a bag?"

"He wasn't."

"He could have left it behind the tent earlier," Henry said dismissively.

"Wouldn't someone have seen it?" Frankie asked.

Both Henry and Joey looked skeptical.

"You think this is part of the sabotage?" Frankie asked Henry.

"It sounds farfetched," Henry acknowledged, emotion leaking into his tone. "But damn it, Frankie, you could have been killed."

"So could you, cousin," Joey said with the candor of youth. "Your grumpy demeanor wasn't going to save you from an asp's strike even if it does keep most people from bothering you."

Frankie smiled at Joey's words but frowned again immediately. "Perhaps we should forego the visit to the Tutankhamun tomb."

Frankie did her best to hide her disappointment at the logical step to take.

"No," Henry denied immediately. "This asp business was personal and potentially deadly. We will both be safer away from the camp. I will speak to the ministry office and request an armed guard for the camp to accompany us on our return."

Frankie just knew that was about her. That if she were not staying in his tent, Henry would be trusting that grumpy demeanor to protect him.

Before Frankie had an opportunity to respond to that, Henry was frowning again, his gaze fixed on Joey. "You'll have to accompany us to Cairo."

"What? Why?"

"I believe because you are his cousin and he feels responsible for your safety," Frankie said when it was clear Henry had no intention of answering.

"So?" Joey asked, sounding for the first time since Frankie had met him like a petulant teenager.

"If the camp is not secure, Dr. Thomas cannot leave you here," Frankie explained further when Henry didn't show any inclination to do so.

"I'm still taking Mr. Clarke with me to Carter's find."

"Of course!" Joey looked shocked the matter would even be in question. "Everybody knows he's a keen Egyptologist. He spends more hours on the dig and photographing the finds than anyone except you."

Henry nodded like it was settled.

Frankie had been looking forward to not watching her every word for the drive to and from the Valley of the Kings. Now they had to add a trip to Cairo and a passenger for most of the journey.

Joey left for his own tent and Henry insisted on doing a second sweep of theirs before either began disrobing for bed.

After the lamps had been extinguished, Henry joined Frankie on her cot.

He spent several moments simply holding her close and not speaking. Needing the closeness, Frankie let her body relax into his.

"Would you be willing to share your secret with Joey?"

Frankie thought about it from every angle, but everything she had witnessed about the boy said he was trustworthy and not mean spirited. "Yes."

"Good." Henry's sigh of relief shifted his chest up and down. "I wanted you to be able to attend the viewing as yourself."

Shock rendered her mute for several long seconds. "But what will we tell people?"

"Nothing."

"They will assume I am your fiancé if I am traveling with you."

Henry's shrug said he did not care.

"There may be people there you know."

"Highly unlikely."

"There may be people there I know."

"Again unlikely."

"It is risky."

"But you deserve to go as yourself."

"I..." It suddenly hit Frankie just how much she wanted that.

How much it cost her to play the part of her brother while doing what *she* loved. Every insight and every discovery she made was in her brother's name.

"I want that," she said.

"I know."

And the fact he did? Said so much about how he thought about her and how in tune with her needs Professor Henry Thomas was.

The next morning, Anum made things easier for Henry by bringing up the poor performance of the two men his assistant foreman had hired over breakfast.

"We have been digging for three hours and I have had to remind them to get back to their work several times. They are most disrespectful."

"Do you want to fire them?" Henry asked with his usual directness and then cursed inside his head.

Anum was far more likely to take an indirect route to the same place. And it would take longer to get there if the foreman felt Henry had not considered all the angles carefully enough.

"Yes."

Henry was so shocked by the immediate agreement that he took a moment to react. "Yes? I mean yes. Good."

Anum nodded, his expression serious. "I do not think they are good for the camp. That snake...it is not good that it should find its way into your tent."

Henry had to agree, but he suddenly wondered if Anum suspected foul play as well. He would not ask in front of the others though.

"I have to say I'm glad." Rudolph frowned. "I found the older one going through my papers. What he expected to find, I have no idea."

Certainly nothing of import about Egyptology, that was for certain. Rudolph had grown increasingly disinterested in the dig as the years had gone by and he had realized participating in it would not be an immediate springboard to diving into his own adventure in Mesopotamia.

"You never said anything about finding him in your tent," Henry replied, wondering if his papers had been the worker's target when Joey had seen him loitering outside Henry and Frankie's tent the evening before.

"I dealt with the matter." Rudolph drew himself up, giving Henry a superior look. "You are the head archeologist on this dig, but you are not the only one with authority. I am five years your senior, if you will remember."

Rudolph was chafing at his position of under archeologist far more than Henry had realized.

Frankie made a sound suspiciously like a smothered laugh and Joey had his face turned away, as if hiding his own mirth.

Even Adam looked amused.

Henry felt no humor, but more doubt as he considered his colleague's attitude and remembered things Frankie had said. If Rudolph were unhappy enough, ambition might lead him to unexpected measures.

Rudolph glared at them all before turning his focus back on his breakfast with an air of having dismissed them.

"I think between the two of them, they create more work than they do," Frankie said. "They are both prone to *accidental* spills and the like more than the other workers."

Her emphasis on the word *accidental* implied she didn't believe the dropped buckets, etc., had been accidental at all.

Henry had just thought they were poor workers, but now he wondered.

Was this more sabotage?

Anum wasted no time giving the two workers the heave ho after breakfast, counting out their wages and instructing them to gather their belongings.

"I will drive them back to town," the assistant foreman offered. "It will allow me to find new workers to replace them."

"That will not be necessary," Anum said, his expression immovable. "I will see to the matter myself."

Surprisingly, or maybe not so surprisingly considering how much Anum and Peter enjoyed a good debate after dinner, the assistant foreman tried to argue. However, Anum was having none of it.

It was clear the Egyptian man blamed his assistant for choosing unwisely the first time.

Peter clearly saw that as well, as he argued beyond what Henry would have expected before giving in with bad grace. Which was not like him, but then his own reputation was at stake, and he was being offered no opportunity to rectify his earlier bad choices.

After a long, and most likely unnecessary, harangue of his workers to do their best while he was gone, Anum took off in one of the cars with the two workmen.

Henry had insisted he take another of the workmen with him, ostensibly to gather supplies while Anum sought out new workers.

"I am glad you sent another man with Mr. Ibrahim." Frankie said, after they had gone, her gaze fixed on the Model T growing smaller in the distance.

"It seemed safest."

"If they are part of the sabotage, we can hope that will prevent them hurting Mr. Ibrahim and stealing the car." Still, she worried.

"You have an active imagination, Frankie."

"Perhaps, but I'm still glad Mr. Ibrahim will be safe. If they are involved with the sabotage, he would be too good a target to pass up."

"And risk prison?"

Frankie shrugged. "I don't know, but you cannot deny that losing your foreman and a valuable automobile at this juncture would certainly cause your dig major problems. Perhaps even to be shut down."

"That is true." Henry turned back toward their tent. "However, Anum is an old campaigner and the man I sent with him is his nephew. He will be all right."

"So, there's no chance he would betray Anum for a few pounds. That's good." She let her hand brush his and then stepped away, so it looked accidental and unwelcome.

He knew the truth though and it warmed him.

"Still, I will feel better when he is safe, back in camp," she said as they entered their tent. "Are you sure we should go to the viewing?"

He admired so many things about Frankie, not least of which was her willingness to put her own desires aside for the good of the dig and the potential safety of others.

In this case, it was unnecessary. "Remember, we must go to Cairo regardless."

"To petition for an armed guard from the government? You think that is still necessary with the workers being dismissed and removed from camp?"

"The collapse happened before they came," Henry grimly reminded her.

"Yes, but we found no evidence that was anything other than an accident."

"I am taking no more chances."

"Because of the asp?" She stood so close but did not touch him. They did not touch before turning out the lamps in their tent.

He felt that stricture irritate him as it never had before. "Yes. It could have killed you."

"Or you." Her eyes were green pools of worry.

For him.

"We will go to Cairo and then the Valley of the Kings as planned."

"I hope the government grants your petition. Have you ever had to have guards before?"

"No. But other sites have. Some archeologists prefer to hire private soldiers, but I will see what the ministry office says before going that route."

Her eyes widened. "You are prepared to do that?"

"Everyone's safety is my responsibility." And he would not let any of them down. Not his workmen, not his fellow archeologists, not his cousin and most assuredly, not Frankie.

She stepped close and brushed her hand along his, squeezing his fingers before stepping back. "You are a good man, Henry."

"I am glad you think so."

Anum returned two days later with three new workers, all of them having worked on digs before.

He took Henry aside, his expression grave. "Faisal is a Qifti, who has been visiting the family of his wife in this region. He says he approached Peter for a job when he learned he was in town seeking new workers after the collapse. Faisal was told there was no place for him."

Henry frowned in surprise. "Do you believe him?"

"For what reason would he have to lie?" Anum shrugged, but his expression was not so sanguine. "I believed him."

That meant that Peter had lied.

"Did you find the pool of laborers as barren as your assistant claimed?" Henry asked, not getting a good feeling about this.

"No. There were many men with skills and understanding of the gravity of our work." Anum looked unhappy. "I believe my assistant accepted a bribe to hire the two workmen."

It was not an unknown practice. Workmen would promise part of their wages, or something else an assistant foreman or foreman wanted in order to get taken on. Sometimes, it worked out fine. Sometimes, like this one, it did not.

The question was, had the assistant foreman accepted bribes to do anything else?

"I will talk to him," Anum added after a moment of morose silence.

Henry nodded. "Come and find me after you have done so."

Anum agreed and left.

Frankie's outrage when Henry repeated the conversation to her delighted him, though he did not show it. Her instant loyalty to him and protectiveness were beyond even that of his closest family.

Though he had to admit he felt as protective toward her.

"Anum was only speculating, Frankie. We do not know yet if his assistant took a bribe."

"Anum wasn't speculating about there being a better pool of workers to draw from and that means that Peter lied."

Henry could only agree. "If Peter did not take a bribe, what other reason could he have for lying?" Both to them and to Faisal when the Qufti had asked for a job.

"Exactly." Frankie paced from one side of the work room in their tent to the other. "And if he took a bribe, what else is he willing to do if someone pays him enough?"

"He has worked on the dig since the second year." Henry could not believe the man so proud of his role as assistant foreman would betray them all and participate in the sabotage.

Frankie stopped her pacing and turned to look at Henry. "You think he took the bribe to hire them without knowing they had nefarious plans?"

"*We* don't know they had nefarious plans."

"Someone put that snake in here."

It was likely, but... "We don't know that for certain."

Frankie just shook her head.

"You are jumping to conclusions," he chided.

"Someone is trying to harm you." Her eyes grew glossy, and his heart skipped a beat.

Frankie was not a woman to cry at the drop of a hat. "We do not know that," he said, trying to comfort.

Even if he secretly thought that was likely. If not him personally, his reputation.

"I would rather jump to a conclusion that will keep you from harm than show caution in believing something," she replied fiercely.

Humbled and strangely turned on, Henry merely said, "Thank you."

"No need for gratitude." She brushed under her eyes with impatient fingers and her skin took on a rosy hue. "You would do the same."

He *had* leapt to the conclusion that the snake had been placed in their tent at first because of its potential danger to her. He had also erred on the side of caution in determining that Joey would have to travel with them to Cairo.

"We are very alike."

"I'm not nearly as grumpy," she said with a sniff.

He felt a smile curving his lips. "No. And you are much more lovely."

"Well, I think you are a fine specimen of a man." Her pretty green eyes filled the admiration he wanted to see there always.

"Waiting until night to touch you is becoming more difficult each day," he admitted.

"Yes."

Neither spoke again. For Henry, because that difficulty had become acute.

He could only guess it was the same for Frankie.

That evening at dinner, Anum asked to speak to Henry with his assistant foreman afterward.

They went to Henry and Frankie's tent, but Frankie did not join them. She asked Professor Adams and Joey to come with her on her evening constitutional instead.

Missing his time alone with her on their nightly walk made Henry even more impatient than usual. It annoyed him that she could not be there for this discussion without giving rise to speculation either.

He ushered the two men into the tent with bad grace and felt no guilt for his lack of welcome.

Anum would not have asked to speak to him unless his assistant had admitted to taking the bribe.

"Peter has something he wishes to tell you," Anum said, like a father leading a child to an apology.

The assistant foreman gave Anum a resentful glance, but nodded. "I am very sorry, *sahib*. I hired two men who were poor choices."

"And took a bribe to do so." Henry wasn't about to waste time beating around the bush about it.

They would not be having this discussion in this way, if that were not the case.

"There was no harm in it." The words claimed innocence, but the way Peter eyes shifted to his left implied a lie.

"There was harm. That asp could have killed Mr. Clarke or myself." Henry's choler was rising with each word.

"The asp was an unlucky happenstance, surely," Anum said, his tone disbelieving.

But the assistant foreman would not meet Henry's eyes.

"You knew they were set on sabotage," Henry accused the other man.

"You should have fired Anum back in Cairo, when the supplies came up short." Peter's tone was filled with accusation. "He is too old to be foreman of such an important dig."

Henry's archeological dig wasn't nearly as important as others going on, at least in the eyes of most. Was Peter trying to flatter Henry into looking more favorably on his out-of-control ambition?

It would not work. The idea Anum was too old to be foreman was ludicrous.

Anum gasped. "You would say such a thing, when I brought you on and made you my assistant foreman? Others would not have done such a thing."

"I should have been the foreman. I had worked on Howard Carter's dig and the Harvard expedition." Left unsaid, but felt heavily in the air around them, was his clear belief that as an ex-pat Englishman, Peter believed he should have been given preference.

Unimpressed, Henry promised, "Once news of your actions gets out, you won't be working on any digs in future."

Peter paled. "But I have done nothing wrong."

"We lost valuable time because you hired those men. That asp could have killed someone." Henry glared. "Two men died in that collapse!"

"I had nothing to do with the collapse!" he declared loudly. "You have no proof that snake was placed in your tent by the workmen, either. Only speculation. You are as useless as Anum."

"Anum is far from useless. He is my right-hand man," Henry assured both men, seeing how shaken his foreman was. "You are fired, and I expect all of your things along with you off my site in the morning. In the meantime, Anum, he is to be watched."

Anum bowed and nodded, glaring at the other man. "It will be done."

"If you want a ride back to the town, you will tell me who hired you."

"No one hired me," Peter declared furiously. "I wanted Anum's position and set out to get it. These other things are just bad luck, but maybe they wouldn't have happened if you'd made *me* your foreman instead of an old Egyptian."

"Anum is an excellent foreman. You, however, are a man with delusions and I will make sure other dig sites are aware of that assessment."

"You would not. You do not worry yourself about other sites."

"I will make an exception in this case."

No matter what pressure Henry or Anum put on the man, Peter stuck to his story of having no one else responsible for his plans. He also maintained his innocence in regard to the collapse and knowledge of the asp.

He did not outright deny that the three workers could have been responsible, only that he knew nothing about it.

Could all of this have been one man's ambition gone amok? Peter was right. They had no proof the collapse had been engineered, much less that the asp had been planted in Henry's tent.

20

Frankie said good evening to Professor Adams and Joey before finding her own tent upon her return from their walk.

Henry sat at the table he used to take his notes, staring down at the blank page of his journal with a frown. The pencil in his hand was still.

"Henry." Frankie stepped forward and laid her hand on his shoulder. "Are you alright?"

Henry startled, like he had not heard her enter the tent. Then he blustered. "Yes, of course. Why wouldn't I be?"

"You seemed deep in thought."

Her archeologist sighed and leaned toward her just a bit. "Peter took a bribe to hire those two workers, but that is not all."

"What else?"

Henry stood up and strode into their sleeping quarters. Frankie followed, knowing he wasn't trying to get away from her.

He started undressing. "He admitted to sending me the message saying Anum would not be returning to the dig."

"And the telegram to Mr. Ibrahim?"

"That too."

"But I thought that came from America?"

"He could have falsified it."

"That is a great deal of work. Why would he do such a thing?"

"He wanted Anum's job."

"But..." Frankie's voice trailed off as Henry's naked body came into view.

He didn't seem to notice but moved toward her. "He claimed the collapse was an accident and denied any knowledge of the asp."

"The collapse could have been an accident." Frankie preferred to believe it had been.

Henry doused the lamp and then started undressing Frankie, tugging at her bowtie with purposeful intent. "Yes. And the asp could have just found its way into our tent."

"Bad luck, I guess," Frankie said with a breathless catch in her voice as he made quick work of the buttons on her shirt.

"Mmm hmm." Henry's focus was clearly on disrobing her, not their conversation.

"Is this safe?" she asked, even as she got rid of her trousers.

"I do not care."

Frankie found she did not either. She wanted Henry. Desire whooshed through her like a wildfire.

They ended up in his cot, Frankie on top, riding him.

She bit her hand as she came, keeping the scream blocked. Somehow, he managed to stay silent while his body went rigid with ecstasy under her.

It was only later that she realized they'd forgotten any sort of birth control. For the first time in ten years, the prospect of pregnancy held no terror for her.

Why that was she kept tucked into her heart as she slid into sleep.

The days after Peter had been exiled from the camp were uneventful, leading Henry to believe that he had indeed been both the instigator and the culprit of the sabotage.

Regardless of what his or Frankie's instincts might have leant toward, the collapse and asp must have been unfortunate events. Not engineered.

Without Peter there, the whispers about the Mummy's Curse died down as well. Henry was not sure if the assistant foreman had been feeding the gossip against expectation, or if the knowledge he had been undermining things had taken the legs out from under the gossip regardless.

Either way, Henry felt much better about leaving the camp under his fellow archeologist's supervision and Anum's watchful eye.

Anum had promoted his nephew to assistant foreman, with no sign of grumbling. It seemed it was a given that after being betrayed by his ex-assistant, Anum would want family to rely on, regardless of how much younger the nephew was than some of the other Qifti.

The workmen had taken their typical *Inshallah* approach to life and gotten on with the excavating. Which Henry admired very much.

Despite being almost certain nothing else would happen while he was away, Henry still wanted to take Joey with him and Frankie. They would make the journey to Cairo and he would request an armed guard, this time because of the potential for retaliation.

Peter had been willing to mess with supplies and practice elaborate deceptions in the hope of being promoted to Excavation Foreman. There could be no telling what he might do in reaction to having his hopes of not only being promoted dashed, but those of working on other notable digs in the future.

Henry had made good his promise and written letters to the ministry and several lead archeologists for major digs already. Frankie, furious at Peter's deceptions, had helped. Gossip would ensure that Peter's behavior would be known in the entire Egyptian archeological community soon enough.

Nevertheless, Peter had lived in Egypt since his teens and been working in the archeological community nearly as long. He had made many connections and despite his lack of education and so called breeding, he had resources.

Henry wasn't taking any more chances with his workmen, or his work.

Frankie packed carefully for the excursion to Cairo and the Valley of the Kings. They would be gone for five days.

Despite modern motorcars being able to travel at regular speeds as high as thirty miles an hour on the uneven roads, it would take the better of a day going and coming. While significantly shorter than the leisurely pace of the river cruise she and Henry had taken initially, travel time would still account for two days of the trip.

Frankie included one of the two dresses she had brought hidden beneath her male clothes and a wide brimmed hat that could be rolled up to tuck into her valise. She also brought her usual "Edwin" clothes of course because other than their trip to the Valley of the Kings, it would be too risky for Frankie to drop her male persona.

Dressing as herself to visit the Pharoah's tomb was risky enough. Some might say even ridiculously dangerous.

But Henry had been right. Frankie had a deep-seated need to make that visit as herself.

Pretending to be something she was not was exhausting. She'd told Edwin in her last letter to him how much she admired his strength and ability to do that very thing for so many years.

A wave of missing her family washed over Frankie. Edwin's last letter had been filled with the moving picture he was working on. An *avante garde* endeavor that would send their father apoplectic if he knew about it.

However, Edwin wasn't playing a role in front of the cameras but was working production behind the scenes. So, that was highly unlikely.

Edwin had made friends who understood not only his double life, but his need to create art "that mattered" as he termed it. Of course, he hadn't mentioned the double life of a homosexual keeping up the pretense of heterosexuality blatantly in his letter to her, but he'd alluded to it and Frankie had known what her brother meant.

One particular friend got a lot of mention. A veteran of the Great War, Edwin described the Frenchman, Michel, as taciturn and closed off, but brilliant.

Brilliant at what, Edwin had not actually spelled out. Perhaps the former soldier was simply one of those highly intelligent people who were knowledgeable about so many things.

Like Henry.

Frankie was beginning to suspect that she and her brother had the same taste in men. Unsociable, but very smart and passionate about their interests.

She only hoped Michel was as honorable as her Henry.

Listen to her. Even in her own thoughts, it was dangerous to think of Henry as *hers*. That way lay a path she'd vowed never to tread again.

Not to mention, one Henry had made plain in the beginning, he had no desire to go down either.

"What has you wool gathering?" Henry's voice brought Frankie's head round.

He stood there, dusty from the dig, a big smile on his face.

She jumped up. "What's happened? Another discovery?"

She loved Henry's smiles, but they were not a common occurrence and this one had to bode some sort of major finding.

"A grave filled with goods as well as a coffin. There's a very good chance it is part of a larger burial plot."

"Oh, that is amazing!" Frankie abandoned her valise. "I want to see."

"I thought you might."

Everyone was standing around one of the two pits that were still being worked. "Why are they all just standing there?"

"I am doing the excavating at this point," Henry said.

"You won't want to leave it," Frankie said, no worry at her own loss of opportunity finding room in the joy she felt on his behalf.

"I will excavate what I can today and then it will be left for my return while another pit is opened and the second pit's crew continue their work."

Frankie was barely listening as she strained to see inside the pit. They were down several feet and she could see the lumps that indicated goods and a partially excavated coffin.

"It is amazing," she breathed.

"Yes." His simple one-word agreement was filled with a wealth of satisfaction. "Would you like to help me?"

"You trust me to?" she asked with unfettered anticipation, fully aware that Anum would have been in the pit with him if she was not there.

Henry's gorgeous grey eyes shone with affection. "Yes."

She hoped she was the only one who recognized that look as warm regard toward her, but reveled in how good it made her feel regardless. Still, she took a surreptitious look around, but no one seemed to see anything amiss.

Dr. Miller wasn't even there. No doubt he was in his tent working on his Mesopotamia research. Professor Adams gave them a knowing, but benevolent look while Joey simply bounced in place, eagerly waiting to see what would be revealed in the pit.

Anum was smiling in approval, so Frankie's concern he might be offended at being supplanted was put to rest quickly while the other workmen stood around chatting and pointing. Finding a coffin was a big deal.

Mummies were aplenty in this part of Egypt and several digs had successfully unearthed dozens if not hundreds, but a coffin? Those were rare finds indeed.

Frankie took her tools and climbed down into the pit with Henry. He began brushing more sand, dirt and rubble away from the fragile wood and she could not believe she was going to be doing this with him.

And yet, it felt right. This partnership felt more natural than anything had in her adult life. Like she was meant to be right here, with this man.

And not just in this moment.

She couldn't afford to mull on that revelation as she needed all her focus to be on what she was doing. So, emulating his movements with brush and small trowel, she began work on fully unearthing the coffin as well.

Back breaking hours later, when it had been uncovered completely and could be moved, they both stood. Stretching tired and cramped muscles, they looked at each and then went still, and simply looked at the coffin in silence for several long moments.

It was not that they hadn't found mummies before. Several had been found, examined, drawn, and photographed before being reburied as was Henry's way.

He took meticulous notes on location and any items found nearby.

This coffin was special. For one thing, it *was* a coffin.

For another, the quantity of funerary goods indicated by the number of potential lumps and those already unearthed, suggested some level of wealth as well. So, perhaps a landowner?

She could only speculate, but perhaps once all the buried objects were unearthed, they would shed light on ancient history long forgotten.

Frankie drove most of the way to Cairo, though after a great deal of pestering, she agreed to teach Joey how to drive on one of the long stretches in the desert. He was a natural with the clutch, which was a good thing because Henry wasn't the most patient backseat driver.

Though he'd been fine when he'd been in the passenger seat beside Frankie.

She'd been shocked he didn't insist on driving, but he was happy to let her. She supposed it seemed more natural to those in camp, that she the younger "man" in a lesser position, should do the chauffeuring.

Henry made it clear he was willing to take his turn driving but showed no interest in taking over teaching his younger cousin to drive. They stopped for a midday meal and petrol in one of the towns along the road that ran parallel to the Nile.

They were carrying two extra gas cans for those times there were no places to buy petrol, but luckily, they hadn't needed to use them yet.

Frankie and Henry agreed it was a good time to tell Joey about the subterfuge. He took it much better than Frankie expected.

"You're a real livewire, aren't you Frankie?" Joey asked with clear admiration in his voice. "Imagine pretending to be a man so you could come to Egypt. Is Frankie your real name?"

"I am called Frances Edwina Summers, but my friends call me Frankie." And she'd instructed Joey to call her by that name when they were alone after telling him the truth.

"I'll be careful not to slip in front of anyone at the dig, but we *are* friends, aren't we?"

"We certainly are," Frankie agreed. "Only a friend would teach you to drive."

She and Joey both laughed, but Henry didn't crack a smile. "She's got more patience than I do."

"Most people do, Cousin Henry, if you don't mind me saying so." Joey didn't look, or sound, offended.

Henry smiled then. "No, Joey. The truth is not an insult."

"It can be," Frankie said, disagreeing. "But not in this case. You may not be the most patient man with the rest of humanity, but you are a good man. Your friends and family can rely on you."

Joey nodded. "I was sure you were going to send me packing, but Pops said you never would."

"He was right," Henry agreed, not sounding particularly pleased by that.

Joey smiled anyway. "He likes to think he always is."

"His plan to give you a chance to explore your interests wasn't a bad one," Henry replied. "I would have preferred more notice than you abruptly showing up in Cairo though."

"Pops thought that would bug you."

"It sounds like your father knows Henry pretty well," Frankie mused. And if that were the case, why had the man resorted to blackmail to get Henry to agree to take Joey on the dig?

"Yeah. Maybe." Joey gave Henry a serious look. "He says your dad was a good man, no matter what I hear otherwise."

"He implied otherwise," Henry said with a frown.

"Nah, that's just pops. He likes to get his own way, but he told me he thought spending the summer with you would be good for me. He said that you are your own man in a way a lot of our family aren't."

Henry got that look that said he was actually a little embarrassed. "That is good to hear. My father *was* a good man."

"He was like Professor Adams."

"What do you mean?" Frankie asked.

"The way he and one of the Qiftis look at each other. It's like how my mom and pops do when they're going out for an evening. I don't think they'll do anything though because they could get in trouble."

"Do you think anyone else has noticed?" Frankie asked, worried for the young professor she'd come to think of as a friend.

"Nah. I watch everyone. It's how I am and no one minds because I'm still a kid in their eyes."

"You're sixteen. You're doing a man's job."

"But still..."

"Others see you as a teenager. And that allows you some leeway in the nosiness department," Henry said with an almost there smile. "You're a clever young man, Joey."

Joey turned bright red and looked away. "Thanks, Cousin Henry."

Frankie thought others wouldn't notice the way Professor Adams and the Qifti worker looked at each other because it simply would not occur to them. For whatever reason, Joey was more in tune with the concept of homosexuality. Probably because of the family gossip about Henry's father.

The fact he did not condemn Professor Adams, or Henry's father, spoke well of the young man's moral compass, in Frankie's opinion. Though she was sure there were some who might disagree with her.

Just as there were many whose opinion differed strongly with hers on the role of women in society. Those people were why she'd been forced to resort to subterfuge to follow one of her dearest dreams.

The busyness of Cairo was a shock after the relative silence of the dig in the desert. Streetcars and automobiles vied for room on the narrow streets, while sellers hawked their wares from storefronts or market stalls.

Frankie did not mind that Henry was driving on this leg of the journey, as it allowed her to gawp to her heart's content. She could spend months in Cairo and never grow bored of all there was to see and experience.

As much as she wished it could be otherwise, they booked three rooms at the hotel again. Joey could have stayed with Henry without comment, but Frankie was well aware how easy it was to look at her professor a certain way. Which could lead to speculation, neither could afford.

There was always the risk she would be recognized as a woman as well, no matter how remote that risk was.

So, they got three rooms on the same floor, near each other.

She was certain Henry would come visiting when the coast was clear.

They ate a late dinner together in the hotel dining room before returning to their rooms.

Frankie was not at all surprised by the quiet knock on her door sometime later.

She opened it and stood back so Henry could slip inside.

Already out of her clothes, she had left her undergarments and drawstring pajama bottoms off. Frankie stood there, wearing nothing but her pajama top that barely brushed the top of her thighs.

The flare of heat in Henry's gaze said he appreciated her choice. "You are so sensual, Frankie."

"With you, I am a lot of things I have never been." Stepping toward him, she smiled, anticipation drumming through her veins

He didn't reply, but stood there waiting, like he knew she wanted to undress him. Which is what she did. Removing his vest and then his tie, before doing the same to his braces.

Neither spoke while Frankie methodically went about the task she'd set for herself. She did not touch him other than what was necessary to get his clothes off, and yet with each undone button and article of clothing removed, her desire grew.

She wanted this man in her body and her life in a way she had never craved another and knew she never would.

"You are special," she told him as she pulled away the last piece of clothing, revealing his robust, naked body to her gaze. "To me, but I think even more to the world. You are a unique man."

"I am only me, Frankie," he said, like a warning. "Human like any other man."

"I wonder if the wives of the pharaohs thought they were human like any other," she mused.

Henry's laughter surprised her. "I am hardly a god-king."

"No. And I am glad, because I do not want a man who is beyond my reach."

"No man could be. Anyone would be lucky beyond measure to gain your notice as a lover, as a companion."

Those words hit her like sweet arrows directed at her heart. They hurt in a way, but they felt good too and she treasured them.

Henry was not a man to flatter for the sake of flattery. If he said a thing, he meant it.

He followed his words up with a sensual kiss that brought their bodies into contact. When it was over, her pajama top was gone and Frankie's nipples were hardened peaks from sexual need.

His tumescent sex rubbed against her stomach, even as his arms held her close. She reached down to touch it, but he stilled her hand. "Tonight, we will take things slow and savor every moment. We have only four nights in the hotel, where we can share a bed."

They would spend the next day in Cairo, and Henry hoped to get an appointment with the ministry office as well as contacting his university via telegraph. The following day they would rise before dawn to make their viewing of Howard Carter's excavation site.

They planned to spend one more day in Cairo after that, in case they needed to for Henry's meeting with the ministry office.

He was right that their more private time in a hotel with a real bed and the ability to touch each other with the lights on was limited.

"I like seeing you when we touch," she told him as she brushed her hands over his furry chest.

She loved the feel of his masculine chest hair and muscles under her hands. He was solid and real, his movement from youth to adult male complete and established.

He stepped back. "Look all you like, Frankie. I will be doing the same."

Which indeed he was, his eyes roaming over her body with clear pleasure, and eliciting a reaction that should have been reserved for touch.

But every nerve ending lit like the lamps in her parlor, electric current buzzing through Frankie's body, increasing her need for physical touch. The temptation to simply step back into him, to let their bodies press together was great, but he was right.

This opportunity might not come again until after the dig was over for the season. She drank in the sight of his man's body. Tree trunk thighs, hair on his chest and belly, strong limbs that held her with a comfort she'd never known in her dead husband's embrace.

The fact that actually seeing Henry was so fulfilling and *important* scared her a little. These feelings she had for him could not be described as *just sex*, if they ever could have been.

"I find more satisfaction simply looking at you than I have in the embrace of other women." Henry sounded both confused and slightly worried.

Just like her.

"We are well matched," she said.

"From our first kiss," he agreed.

Frankie stepped forward. Henry moved at the same time. They reached out and touched, and then they were kissing again, this kiss feeling like something more than a prelude to sex.

Somehow, they made it to her bed, and settled on the crisp sheet together. She'd pulled back the bedding already, in anticipation of what was to come.

Suddenly Henry cursed and jumped from the bed.

"What?" Frankie asked, her body on fire with need for him.

"The rubber condom." He looked chagrined. "I almost forgot it. Again."

"Would that be the end of the world?" Frankie could imagine a little boy frowning in concentration like Henry.

It was so sweet a picture she didn't take in Henry's response to her words at first, but then she did and her heart plummeted.

"An unmitigated disaster, I would say," he'd said grimly. Like her having his child would be the worst thing he could imagine.

Frankie did not know how to respond to that, and thankfully she did not have to. Henry donned the contraception and returned to her bed.

She still wanted him, but her bruised heart retreated from the proceedings. Unwilling to lose her sense of autonomy, even to her own emotions, Frankie took control of their lovemaking, riding him to a physically satisfying conclusion, if not an emotional one.

Henry's words should not hurt so much. They had both agreed from the beginning that this thing between them was without strings. They were not committing to a lifetime together and what could be more binding than a child?

Frankie should never have even asked if it would be so bad. Of course, it would. She didn't live in a world where she could get away with an unwed pregnancy. Her father would insist on marriage and if she categorically refused, he would send her into seclusion and make sure she gave her baby up.

Frankie remembered one of the women who had been at the sanitorium with her had been there for exactly that reason. To give birth to a baby that she was then forced to relinquish.

The woman's screams and tears had been heart wrenching. She'd been much quieter giving birth than after, when her baby was removed from the room without her ever being able to hold it.

The only way to avoid such an outcome for herself would be to either marry Henry, which he'd made clear he had no desire for, or to run away from her family and build a new life pretending to be something she wasn't.

A *recent* widow.

Henry finished his morning ablutions, irritated and still thinking about the night before.

Frankie had made him return to his own room as soon as they were done making love. Disgruntled, he'd asked why he could not stay the night and she'd told him it was too risky.

Too risky. From the woman who had asked if making love without the condom would be so bad.

Too Risky. From the woman who had spent the last several weeks living in the guise of her brother.

Too Risky. From the woman who had traveled by herself from England to Egypt.

Frances Edwina Summers was a woman who lived her life taking risks.

And she had kicked him out of her bed. He didn't like sleeping without her. He'd gotten used to having her body next to his in the narrow cots they used in their tent.

He supposed when they returned to Wadjet she was going to decide *that* was too risky. Pretty soon, she would be telling him that it was too risky to make love at all.

Henry's bad mood stuck with him as he made his way to the hotel dining room for breakfast.

Frankie was strangely silent over breakfast, like she was thinking about something. Though she answered whenever Henry or Joey engaged her in conversation. She and Joey made plans to explore Cairo while Henry went to the ministry office to request an audience.

His jealousy of his younger cousin spending that time with Frankie was ridiculous and so he told himself several times throughout the day as he worked his way through the runaround that inevitably came with any government interaction.

By the time he had engaged in a series of unsatisfying wires back and forth with his university, receiving their refusal to fund security for the dig along with an oblique reference to the possibility his excavation might well not be funded the following season, even Henry could admit his mood was vile.

Further disgruntled that Frankie and Joey were still out and about, Henry retreated to his room to brood.

He spent time writing the day's events in his diary, composing a blistering letter to the head of his department and finally, another to his cousin telling him what a cracking archeologist Joey would make.

The financier, who no doubt expected his son to come back to

America having placed archeology firmly in the hobbyist slot of his life, could take that and put it in his pipe and smoke it.

Which might not actually be fair to the man who Henry was fairly certain actually *would* accept it, if his son chose the path of the academic rather than the financier.

That same man had not been above taking a pot shot at Henry though, and using his dead father to do it, so Henry didn't feel too badly for his uncharitable thoughts.

There had been a time when he and his cousin had been as close as brothers. Randall was only a few years older than Henry and after Henry's father had killed himself, Randall's father had made a point of spending time with Henry. No doubt he'd felt sorry for his sister's only child, but Henry had never been made to feel like the object of pity.

And Randall had become his closest confidant.

For a time.

Randall's interest in finance and business had been firmly entrenched by the time he went away to university. As Henry's own interests had gone in the direction of academia and archeology, they spent less and less time together.

Randall's marriage and subsequent fatherhood had widened the gap between them, so they saw each other mostly during the holidays.

Still, nothing Henry was writing was untrue. Joey would make an excellent academic and archeologist. The two were not always mutual, but in the teen's case, they were.

Even if he had monopolized Frankie's company the entire day and kept her away from the hotel far longer than Henry had expected.

21

The two showed up in time for dinner, but Frankie's demeanor was odd and Henry intended to find out what was wrong.

He didn't get the chance that night, however. She told him obliquely, but unmistakably, that she did not expect him to come to her room that evening. She couched it in terms of them both needing an early night since they would be leaving for the Valley of the Kings so early the next morning.

Henry might have argued, or even simply asked if they could please have a word, but Frankie had looked as tired as she claimed to be. With dark circles under her eyes and her usual energetic posture drooping, he could only hope she got enough sleep that night so tomorrow she would get the most out of the experience at Carter's excavation site.

Henry had little hope of the same for himself. Without Frankie next to him, his sleep was fitful.

Frankie focused on navigating the streets of Cairo toward the road that would take them into the desert and ultimately to the Valley of the Kings. Like other large cities, Cairo had streetlamps on the main thoroughfares. Despite the superior illumination provided by the Studebaker's headlamps, she stayed on those lit by the tall lamp posts.

They were approaching the outskirts of the city when she pressed the brake to slow down for a turn, but the Studebaker did not slow. She pumped the brake harder, again and again, to no effect.

She swore, adrenaline surging through her, making her heart race.

"What is the matter?" Henry demanded.

But Frankie could not spare the time to answer. She focused entirely on slowing the heavy automobile. Shifting down one gear, she let the engine decrease their speed, before swiftly down shifting a second time and then pulling the emergency brake at the last possible moment.

The Studebaker slid to a sideways stop not six inches from the stone wall of a building.

Frankie gasped, her entire body shuddering with relief.

"You did it again!" Henry proclaimed.

Turning to stare at him dazedly, Frankie asked, "What?"

"Saved us. You did the same with your stellar driving in Los Angeles. What happened?"

"The brakes failed." Frankie could hardly believe it. "Lucky for us, we were still in the city and I don't drive like my brother."

"You mean with the gas pedal to the floor?" Henry asked with a strained laugh.

"Yes."

"I know brakes aren't the most reliable system in a motorcar, but we bought this Studebaker because their design was supposed to be superior."

"I checked the brake lines when we arrived in Cairo, made sure they were tight," Frankie said, trying to understand how the brakes could have failed so completely.

For them to lose that much fluid between the hotel and here with the few stops she'd made, the brake line had to have been barely attached. That *could* happen driving over bumpy roads for a long period of time, but sitting in the hotel's parking area?

"You think the automobile was tampered with?" Henry asked grimly.

"Yes." No point pretending otherwise.

"We will have to get the car repaired, but if we hurry, we can still make it to the viewing in the Valley of the Kings."

"You still want to go, even knowing someone is trying to harm you?"

"We do not *know* that—"

"Believe me, Henry," Frankie interrupted. "Someone tampered with the brake line. They had to have."

His expression was unreadable, cast in shadows as it was. "You did a visual inspection of the line?"

"Yes." Hadn't she just said so?

"And the seal was tight?"

"Yes. This Studebaker, it's got a better braking system than the Model T, though I know some would disagree, but these are sturdy cars."

"That is why Anum and I chose this one, but it is a year old, Frankie."

"That is practically new. Honestly, I'm surprised you found one for sale in such good condition."

"The man who had it wanted a flashier European automobile."

"Sounds like Edwin, though he's all about the speed."

"Whether someone tampered with the lines, or not, we still have to get the car repaired if we are going to make it to the Valley of the Kings in time for the viewing."

"But—"

"Whoever tampered with the brakes cannot follow us there. The number of armed soldiers guarding the tomb would be enough deterrent."

Frankie had to agree. They were lucky enough to wave down another motorist and get a lift to a local garage. It took some doing, but the Studebaker's brake line was reattached and tightened, and the brake fluid refilled. It was an easy fix, even if it took precious time to accomplish.

When Henry offered to drive, Frankie accepted. She'd had enough excitement for one trip and was happy to let him take over the wheel.

Henry's attention was firmly on the pale dawn illuminated distance in front of them, his concentration on his driving absolute.

Grateful for the confidence that gave her and in no mood to talk, Frankie did nothing to break that concentration.

Who had sabotaged their car? Peter was the first face that came to her mind, but she hadn't seen him around the hotel at all. Not that he would have wanted to be seen.

Still. He was from Qift, not Cairo. Perhaps the hotel staff had noticed him? She could ask when they returned from the Valley of the

Kings. Joey had remarked the day before on seeing the pushy man, who had wanted to be hired on by Henry for the dig, driving a taxi.

Thinking it unlikely, Frankie had been amused nonetheless and said, "Well, it looks like he hasn't gotten the foreman position he was looking for."

Now, she couldn't help wondering, had it been the same man? And if he was a taxi driver, how had he thought he could get hired on as a *rais*?

Yawning, she turned in the seat and leaned her head against the squabs. She'd had a hard time sleeping the night before. Sometime before the cock crowed, Frankie had realized she was craving Henry's presence.

She'd grown used to the sound of his breath in the dark and the heat of his body beside hers. So used to it, that she'd started wondering if they could have the future she'd promised herself she would never willingly embrace again.

Marriage.

Only, Henry had made it clear that he was no more interested in that kind of future with her than he had been in the beginning.

Frankie would have sworn *both* their feelings had changed though. He was protective of her and jealous of her time with others without being ridiculous about it.

So, why would her getting pregnant with his child be an *unmitigated disaster*?

Because he didn't want to marry. It was the only answer she could come up with.

It hurt more than she ever would have thought to know that his feelings had not changed like hers had.

Frankie had a lot more to lose in the married state than Henry did, and yet she'd begun to believe that marriage to him could be different. That she would not lose her independence, or ability to make her own choices within the bonds of marriage.

To one particular man. Henry.

Perhaps she had been fooling herself.

If not about his future behavior, at least about his intentions.

For some reason, Henry was no more interested in a long term commitment with her than he had been in the beginning. Maybe he wanted to continue having sex with different women, no complications or strings attached.

Nausea roiled in Frankie's stomach at the thought of Henry sharing his body in that way with someone else.

Only she'd agreed to those terms at the outset. She could not try to change them now, not and maintain her own sense of personal integrity.

She'd spent the last night wrestling with the question of whether it would hurt more to break things off now, or to let them run their course to a natural break later, when they both returned to America.

A tiny flame of hope that he might realize he was no more prepared to live without her than she was him refused to be extinguished.

He'd made it clear he did not like sleeping alone. He was also flatteringly keen on the sexual side, when he'd told her that he didn't take many lovers, so had to be okay with long bouts of celibacy.

Only, he had instigated sex at the dig, even when they both had agreed it was terribly risky.

Frankie had been no more able to maintain her physical distance and somehow, she'd convinced herself that meant they were feeling the same things, thinking the same things about the future.

This lingering hope made her feel the fool, something she promised herself she would never be. Still, she could not quench it.

"You have been very quiet," Henry said, his voice bursting into the silence between them.

"You are concentrating on the road. I do not wish to distract you." Which was the truth, if not all of the truth.

"Understandable, but I believe we can converse without risking me running us into a ditch."

"It's not you I'm worried about."

"You and I both checked the car over and it is fine."

"That's what we thought when we got into it this morning."

"Yes, but this time there was no chance for someone to have tampered with so much as a door handle."

She sighed. "True. I'm just tired."

"Did you sleep well last night?" he asked bluntly, his tone clearly disgruntled.

"No." She could have lied, but that was not Frankie's way. "Did you?"

"No. I missed you."

Did he hear himself? If he'd missed her last night, how did he think he was going to feel when they got back to California?

"There are only a few weeks left on the dig," she pointed out obliquely.

He did not answer, but his frown was ferocious.

"What?" she demanded after a few more miles of silence.

"There is nothing preventing us from seeing each other when we return to California. We live in the same city."

"I thought you didn't do relationships." If her tone had a sting to it, he had only himself to thank.

His body filled with tension she could feel, even if she hadn't been able to see the straightening of his shoulders in the shadowy interior of the car.

"I am not ready to let you go," he said baldly.

That bothersome little flame of hope burned brighter and she had no chance of squashing it. "So, you want to what? Date?"

"Yes." Well, that was unequivocal.

"You know if we do, my family and yours will assume we are courting." Unless they dated secretly and Frankie refused to even consider that was what he was suggesting.

"They can assume what they like." Which implied there would be no hidden assignations but did not suggest he considered dating a precursor to anything more.

Not for a man who spent his life living by his own rules and cared very little what others thought.

So, not an answer to the question she did not want to ask. Would he consider marriage?

Would she? In something more than the abstract?

Could she risk giving someone that kind of legal power over her again? Her time the sanitorium had been a reminder that no matter how far they had come in this new modern era, there was still a long road ahead before women enjoyed the same freedoms and privileges as men.

If that day would ever come.

Frankie was no innocent. She fully understood that wealth went hand in hand with power. If women from rich families like her own could be treated as basely as they had been in the sanitorium, what chance did women who had no powerful family behind them have?

Which was why, as much as her attachment to Henry grew day by day, night by night, the prospect of signing over her freedom with a wedding band still terrified her.

Even with a man as honorable as Professor Henry Thomson, Archeologist with a Conscience

"Were you able to set up a meeting with the ministry office for tomorrow?" she asked, changing the subject.

"No. I met with them yesterday."

"Oh. You did not say."

"You did not wish to talk last evening."

She couldn't deny that she'd shut down his conversational overtures and gone back to her room straight after dinner. She'd needed time to come to terms with how she felt about his comment the night before.

She wasn't sure if she'd managed that entirely, but she was feeling a little less vulnerable, and that was a good thing.

"What happened at the meeting?" she asked him when he didn't continue.

"They've refused to offer any sort of security or protections." Frustration rang in Henry's voice. "The minister had the damn nerve to say that my dig does not produce enough artifacts to justify the expense of seconding a unit of soldiers."

"But that's monstrous. Because you are respectful of the artifacts you dig up and don't just send everything on, they're going to punish you?"

She knew Henry's approach to excavation was not the norm, but she'd naively thought others, especially Egyptian officials, would appreciate it like she did.

"They've been pushing me since the beginning to change the way I excavate. Both the Egyptian officials and our own American government types."

"That just doesn't make sense to me."

"It's all about prestige. The more artifacts accumulated, the more prestige bestowed on the Ministry Office."

"I suppose, but your university has stood beside you. That's good."

His harsh bark of laughter said she was mistaken. "My university is furious that they aren't getting the same kind of loot as Harvard."

"They keep funding your expeditions though."

"Because it takes very few university dollars to do so."

"Because your grandfather does most of the funding."

"Yes. If they tried to shut down my dig, they risk losing his other donations as well."

Money controlled so many decisions, including academic ones that should be based on knowledge and bringing more of it to the world. When she said so, he just laughed in that jaded way again.

"Does that mean your university won't pay for private security?" she asked, concerned.

"They have denied my request, yes. One of their wires alluded to the possibility that there might not even be a dig next year."

"But your grandfather, you said he donates too much for them to do that."

"I found it very confusing myself." And frustrating, by his tone.

"And your grandfather? Would he provide funds to hire security?"

"Probably, but I do not want to ask for more money from him."

"Why?" she asked, before she could stop herself.

Then she worried he would dismiss her question as none of her business.

"My uncle and my grandfather argue enough already about the money Grandfather donates to my excavations every year," Henry offered without hesitation though. "Uncle Louis is furious that I don't bring back more lucrative artifacts and that grandfather's money is an investment that sees a return in historical revelation rather than money."

"Your uncle doesn't want your grandfather funding your digs?"

"No. He was the same about my father's work, but even more vitriolic about mine, according to my mother."

"Louis is your father's brother?" She thought he had to be, considering which grandfather funded the digs.

Besides, Henry's maternal grandfather was deceased.

"Yes."

"Randall is your mother's brother?" Frankie confirmed, wanting to keep things straight.

It was strange how hungry she was for details of Henry's life, her interest in every aspect he was willing to share too keen to ignore.

"No, he's my cousin, the son of my mother's brother."

"Oh." Considering the small age difference, that made a lot more sense. "So, there will be no armed guard to return with us?"

"No." Henry's anger was potent. "At least not from the ministry, or my university. I can use money I had set aside for a research trip during the spring."

"You would do that?"

"To protect my workers? Yes."

"You're a good man, Henry." She was also glad on his behalf. Someone had loosened the brake line and she didn't want Henry returning to the excavation without armed protection.

Not that he didn't already have that in her, though she'd never mentioned the fact she carried a gun in her valise. Frankie was a crack shot, but she'd certainly made no showing with that asp.

Men, unlike snakes, did not scare her into immobility.

"I am glad you think so." Henry didn't sound happy though.

"What is wrong?"

"What is right?" he asked with a level of cynical sarcasm she rarely saw from him.

Impatience? Yes. Cranky disregard for the opinions of others? Yes. Even good natured sarcasm.

But this kind of negative cynicism was not like him.

"We are on our way to view the tomb of a Pharoah that lived thousands of years ago. I'd say that was pretty right," she informed him. Despite their less than auspicious start, today promised to be one of the most illuminating of her life. "You found a coffin burial that looks like it could be part of a plot. That's amazingly right."

His lips twitched in an almost smile. "You have a point." Then he frowned again. "I did not like sleeping without you the past two nights."

She hadn't either, but they both had to get used to it. "We won't be able to share a bed when we return to Los Angeles."

"I know." And he didn't sound happy about that either.

To tell the truth, she wasn't any more enamored with that truth than he was. "I suppose we should enjoy it while we can."

"That is not the impression I have gotten from you the past two nights."

"I had some things to think about."

"Things you want to share?"

She was tempted, but still not certain enough in her own mind to open that particular Pandora's box. Besides, now was not the time. "To-day is for seeing Howard Carter's discovery. There is time enough when we return to Cairo to share confidences."

Whether she would be any more prepared to share them, she had no idea.

They were on a deserted stretch of roadway when Henry pulled the automobile off to the side.

Assuming they were stopping so he could relieve himself, Frankie did not comment.

However, once they were stopped, he turned to face her. "Now is probably the best time for you to make your transition back to yourself."

"Oh...I..." Frankie stumbled on her words like she so rarely did. "I've decided not to do that."

"Why?" he asked, his dark brows furrowed.

"It's too risky."

He stared at her. "You did not think it was too risky yesterday, or the day before that. You brought a dress and stockings with you. I saw them."

"Yes, well, if someone is there that knows either of us, the cat will be out of the bag, won't it?" And she'd been fooling herself to think otherwise.

"That is highly unlikely."

"But not impossible," she said with mild exasperation. "Especially for you."

"This is a once in a lifetime opportunity, Frankie."

"I know." She really, really did.

She also knew that if they were sussed and word got back to her father, marriage would be on their horizon, regardless of what either of them wanted. Giving serious consideration to the possibility had brought Frankie's fear of that state back to roost.

Even if she were less wary of marriage, Frankie would not allow Henry to be forced into something he didn't want simply so she could have a memory of visiting the Pharoah's Tomb as herself.

"What has increased the risk in your mind?"

"If either of us is recognized, word will get back to my father somehow and then we would be forced into something neither of us wants."

Whether or not she could overcome her fear of so called wedded bliss enough to make a legal commitment to Henry, Frankie was certain she didn't want that event to come to pass as the result of being forced into by her father.

If she lost certain freedoms again, it would be because she voluntarily gave them up, not because someone took them from her.

She would never allow that to happen again.

"And that would be bad?" Henry asked, his tone noncommittal.

His words were so like hers of the evening before that Frankie's hurt driven temper got the better of her. "An unmitigated disaster, I believe you said."

"That is not what I said."

"It is."

"Frankie—"

"No. It is not worth the risk." She said it with a finality she hoped he would respect.

Because Frankie was feeling the urge to cry and that would mortify her.

His jaw taut, Henry nodded and then resumed the drive.

Tense silence reigned for several miles, but eventually they began talking about the Valley of the Kings and the many archeological discoveries made there. Their stilted conversation grew more natural, and Frankie was grateful.

The crush of people visiting the tomb surprised Frankie. How obvious it was that Howard Carter had little interest in interacting with the plethora of guests to his dig site did not.

His reputation as unsociable and sometimes short tempered was well established.

Frankie could barely believe what she was seeing, from the lintel of the tomb to the grave goods on display (though most had been removed from the camp already), to the outer coffins, it was all too incredible.

Who would have thought such a discovery would be possible in the 20th century? A nearly intact tomb from a millennia dead Pharoah.

They spent the drive back to Cairo talking about everything they had seen, as well as the few words Henry and Howard Carter had managed to exchange.

Carter's respect for Henry was clear in his willingness to converse with the professor from California, when he'd made his reticence to speak to other archeologists in the viewing group clear.

But the conversation was by necessity short and Henry said he planned to write the other archeologist with follow up questions. To be on those kind of terms with such a famous man in the field boggled Frankie's mind.

Frankie did most of the driving on the return trip to Cairo, but she and Henry kept up a steady stream of conversation about what they had seen, what it might mean, and the possibility there were as yet more undiscovered tombs in the land other archeologists, before Howard Carter, had determined tapped out.

By the time they reached the hotel, Frankie was pleasantly exhausted and half tempted to skip dinner. Only she knew Joey was waiting with keen enthusiasm to hear about their visit to Tutankhamun's Tomb.

They were heading toward the stairs when she heard a voice that froze her in her tracks.

"Edwin!" Her father's shout carried across the lobby, gaining the attention of everyone in its radius. "Come here!"

22

The fury in her father's tone could not be mistaken. He thought she was Edwin, but he was still angry about *something*.

Frankie could only guess what that might be. Perhaps he was unhappy to find Edwin in Cairo when their father expected her brother to be in the desert on a dig.

What her father himself was doing in Cairo, Frankie could not begin to imagine.

Her grip on her driving goggles tightened and she wished she'd left them on. Then there might have been some chance of fooling her father into thinking she was Edwin. However, with the best will in the world, Frankie didn't think she could do that without them.

Her father might be autocratic and terribly old fashioned about some things, but he knew his children. There was a reason she and Edwin had been careful never to let their father see her dressed as her brother to attend lectures with the history tutor.

Suddenly Henry was standing between Frankie and her father. "Mr. Clarke, we did not expect to see you here in Cairo."

No, they definitely had not.

"I'm sure my son had no expectation that I would come, but how he thought he would get away with the masquerade, I have no idea."

"Masquerade?" Henry asked, his tone carefully neutral.

"I will speak to my son privately," her father announced with finality. "He will not be returning to your excavation with you. I apologize if that puts you in a bind, but it cannot be helped."

That pronouncement finally unstuck Frankie's limbs and she spun around to face her father. "No, please, Father."

Charles Clarke jerked like he'd been landed a punch to his kisser, staring at Frankie like he'd never seen her before. And in that moment, she realized the masquerade he referred to was *not* her pretense at being Edwin.

"Frances?" he asked, his tone so shocked it registered as a whisper.

Then the expression on his face went from utter bewilderment to narrowed eyed fury in the space of a single breath. He opened his mouth to say something, probably to shout it.

But Frankie shook her head with desperate vehemence. "Don't, Father, please!"

"Mr. Clarke," Henry snapped, his tone cracking like a whip. "Consider your surroundings."

Her father's mouth closed instantly, but his expression did not lighten in the least. The glare he was giving her was sulfuric.

"I believe we should request a private dining room for our dinner," Henry said with quiet authority.

"We will meet in my suite," her father countered, his tone brooking no argument. "Come."

"We must check in with my younger cousin," Henry countered. "F—"

"Stop," Frankie instructed Henry before he could give away the truth that he knew of the subterfuge. So far, her lover had said nothing that could not be explained away. "I will speak to my father. Alone."

Her father *might* forgive her and her siblings, eventually. He would *not* forgive Henry. Just as important, if her father knew that Henry was aware of Frankie's status as a woman, her autocratic and powerful parent would insist on marriage to protect her reputation.

Even if George Clarke never discovered the two had become lovers, he would consider them sharing a tent compromising enough for such drastic action.

Frankie's stomach twisted in knots. She was certain that regardless of who the hapless man might be her father would bully into it, the railroad and mining tycoon would see marriage as the solution to his woes with his willful eldest daughter regardless.

While she had no intention of giving in to anything of the sort, she was under no illusions that refusing to do so might not cost Frankie her place in her family.

Before either Henry, or her father could reply, Joey arrived. "Cousin Henry! I cannot wait to hear what you and Frankie saw in the Valley of the Kings."

And with that simple use of her first name, Joey had revealed that not only did he know who she really was, but that Henry did as well.

"Who are you young man?" Her father asked, his choler residing somewhat in the face of the need for proper behavior in front of strangers, showing that he had not recognized what calling her Frankie had meant.

The hope she could still protect Henry from her father's wrath burned brightly inside her.

Joey startled, like in his haste to reach her and Henry he hadn't noticed the other man.

Rallying quickly though, he put his hand out. "Joseph Kingston at your service."

"This is my father, Mr. George Clarke," Frankie said, hoping Joey would realize he needed to curtail his tongue.

"It is a pleasure to meet you, Mr. Clarke," Joey said, his hand still extended, his expression friendly and open.

Frankie's father stared at the hand presented to him like he didn't know what to do with it.

However, good manners won out and he shook the youth's hand. "Hello, young man."

"My father is Randall Kingston; you may know him?" Joey withdrew his hand, smiling.

Her father deigned to crack the barest of smiles. "He is well known in my circles, as is his father."

Frankie couldn't believe it was the sixteen-year-old boy diffusing the tense situation. She was impressed and grateful.

However, she was no fool. And no amount of teenage charm was going to diffuse the explosion coming when her father put two and two together.

Henry still stood with his body an immovable barrier between her and her furious father.

Although Frankie was perfectly capable of standing up for herself, she still appreciated Henry's attitude. Few men, especially one who stood to lose so much, would have stood up to George Clarke.

Unfortunately, it would most likely fan her father's already crackling flames of wrath once he realized that Henry knew Frankie was a woman.

Sure enough, her father's eyes narrowed, his expression that of a man who had just realized something important. "You called *him* Frankie," her father said to Joey. Then he glared at Henry. "You knew."

"Isn't that his name?" Joey asked guilelessly, showing he'd cottoned on quickly and was doing his best to undo his gaffe.

But Henry said firmly at the same time, "I did."

Frankie wanted to scream. Now was not the time for Henry's chivalry to surface.

"Not before time," she interjected quickly. "By the time he realized, he had little choice but to go along with my plan."

"I always had a choice," Henry contradicted her.

"Would you please..." She wanted to tell him to clam his trap, but it wasn't Henry's fault this situation had come to pass.

It was hers. And while she could not regret it for herself, neither could she allow him to pay the price for her decisions.

"Please what? Lie?" Henry demanded.

Frankie was reminded of Henry's initial disgust upon recognizing her plan to take her brother's place. He'd said then that he would not lie for her.

But couldn't he bend enough to lie for his own sake?

Joey was looking like he knew he'd put his foot in it and was trying to figure out how to extract said appendage, but then his expression turned earnest.

"Stop trying to cover for me, Cousin Henry." The teen turned to her father with a beseeching look. "I knew about Frankie, but Cousin Henry had no idea. Do you think he would have let her stay in his tent if he had done?"

Frankie's heart sank into her toes. That clinched it, she just knew it did.

The shift from fury to calculation in her father's expression happened so fast it was startling, even though she was expecting it.

In his effort to protect his cousin, Joey had just landed Henry squarely in it. Darn it. And Henry looked like he had no intention of saying anything to get himself out of *it*.

It was her turn to glare and Frankie would be surprised if her expression wasn't more ferocious than her father's. "No. Just no. I know what you are thinking and it is *not* going to happen. Do you hear me? More importantly, not one more word of this discussion is happening here. I have had the most amazing day of my life and I will not allow you to ruin it."

"I am not the one ruining anything, young l—"

"You're doing your best to," she said, interrupting him before he could even warm up to his rant, much less call her *lady*. "I'm not going to let you. Besides, I am exhausted." She looked apologetically at Joey. "I'm having a tray in my room for dinner."

She turned her gaze back to her father, letting it chill several degrees before saying, "I will come to your suite tomorrow morning, and we will talk then."

Expecting her father to argue and come over furious again, she was shocked when he looked almost hurt and then gave a curt nod. "Very well. But I expect Dr. Thomas to be there as well."

"No," Frankie said vehemently.

At the same time that Henry uttered a very calm, "Fine."

"*I* will see you in the morning," she told her father, her tone every bit as intransigent as his ever was.

Frankie would deal with Henry later.

"I expect to see you in your own clothes," her father said, his disdain for her current attire obvious.

"These are my clothes." And she was done with her father and his attitudes.

Frankie had spent several weeks living as a man and the freedoms she'd enjoyed had brought home just how much of her life she had to live with limits Edwin did not. She had no more patience for the men like her father who imposed those limits and put so much effort into maintaining them.

Spinning on her heel, Frankie headed toward the staircase.

She made no pretense at polite niceties. She was so angry with her father, she could barely see straight. His arrival had ruined everything. Her time on the dig. Her time with Henry.

It could very well ruin her reputation. And if George Clarke had his way, she was certain it would result in her loss of freedom as well.

He might not incarcerate her in a sanitorium as John had done, but her father would do his best to see Frankie wed to someone he considered suitable.

That was not going to happen, but regardless, Frankie was not ready to go back to California. She was not ready to give up her friendship, much less her sexual relationship with Henry.

Only she had no choice. Not if she was going to protect *the grumpy professor's* freedom as well.

Henry was right beside her by the time she'd turned the first corner on the grand staircase. Joey's rushed footsteps right behind them.

No one said anything until they had exited the stairway and turned into the relative safety of the corridor.

"I'm sorry. I went and bungled it by calling you *Frankie*," Joey said in a rush. "I shouldn't have done that. And I was going to be so careful on the dig, too."

Frankie almost agreed, but she knew she could not take her bad mood out on the earnest young man. Joey had been her friend and she liked the teen. His mistake had been an honest one and he'd realized it immediately, doing his best not to let her father know the truth.

It was Henry's stubborn insistence on full disclosure that had given her father the real ammunition.

Honestly though? The fact she hadn't been sussed out to this point had been something of a miracle.

Or testament to how determined both she and Henry had been to perpetrating the masquerade.

Digging deep, she found a smile for the youth. "I understand, Joey. You didn't see my father at first and had no way of knowing it wasn't safe to use my first name. I'm the one who told you to, after all."

"Yes, but..." Joey let his voice trail off, like he wasn't sure what he was supposed to say.

"Besides, I think with your cousin's need to be so utterly *honest*, the truth would have come out anyway."

She couldn't help shooting Henry a frown. The man did not need to lie, but neither did he have to *offer* information that could be of harm to himself.

Frankie would do her best to undo the damage done and protect both Joey and Henry from becoming targets of her father's wrath.

"Your dad is a real Father Time with the old-fashioned attitude to go with it," Joey said with casual disregard for any concept of respect for his elders. "You could just see him planning the wedding between you and Cousin Henry in his head."

Frankie was in no mood to admonish the teen. Her father did have *old-fashioned* ideals, but worse, he was always sure he was right.

Frankie shot Henry a sidelong glance. Thus far, he had said nothing. His expression was even more enigmatic than usual.

So, no help there.

Frankie stopped at the door to her room, surprisingly relieved when Henry stopped as well. She'd thought she wanted to be alone, but realized now all she wanted was to spend whatever time she had left to do so with Henry.

Understandably, Joey stopped as well. Even if his own wellbeing wasn't at stake, the teen's curiosity was burning so brightly, the corridor should have been lit like a ballroom with electric chandeliers.

Frankie unlocked her door and stepped inside, quickly moving so the others could follow her. Both men did.

Her shoulders slumped just a little in relief, but then she wasted no time in peeling out of her now stifling coat. "I need to see a man about a dog."

It had been a long drive and her body's basic needs hadn't gone on hiatus just because of the stress of the situation.

Joey guffawed. "You're pretty good at pretending to be your brother."

Frankie gave the young man a tight smile. Her use of male slang probably was funny to the teen. For Frankie, she'd grown accustomed to speaking like Edwin. She resented the knowledge that what was acceptable for men to say to each other would be at best cause for humor like Joey's, but more likely frowned upon, if a woman said it.

Henry remained silent, his expression grim.

Her basic needs too urgent to be put off, Frankie left without even trying to figure out what was going on with Henry.

He was alone in her room when she returned.

"Where is your cousin?"

"I sent him to bed. He's had a long day."

"Even so, I would have expected him to stay so we could develop a cohesive strategy for dealing with my father." Not to mention to satisfy the teen's curiosity.

"My cousin will have no more interactions with George Clarke." The finality of that statement left no room for discussion.

Nevertheless, Frankie asked, "Does he know that?"

Henry gave a short nod of acknowledgment.

She hoped Joey was as certain of that as Henry seemed to be. She didn't think they could afford another disastrous encounter between her father and the youth. She might be able to gloss over the shared tent by telling her father truthfully it had two rooms.

That she and Henry shared one for sleeping did not need to come out. Though she couldn't be certain it wouldn't if *either* Joey or Henry were part of the conversation.

"Did you need the necessary?" she asked.

"I used the bathroom at the other end of the corridor."

While Frankie would have preferred rooms with en suites, it was nice to have shared bathrooms at either end of the hotel's corridors on the floors.

Frankie plopped into the armchair across from the bed. "I cannot believe my father is here in Cairo. What are the chances?"

"I would say after discovering your friend masquerading as you in England, pretty high." Henry walked to the window and pulled back the heavy curtain to stare out at the night sky.

"What? You think he knows about Winnie?" Frankie hadn't even considered that possibility, which only went to show how discombobulated she was by her father's arrival.

Joey had caught onto situational nuances faster than she had!

"Mr. Clarke mentioned the masquerade before he recognized you."

Frankie had forgotten that comment until just this minute.

She jumped up from the bed, grabbing her coat again. "Oh, no. I must speak to Winnie. And Edwin. I've got to wire him."

"I do not know how you will manage to contact your friend as we don't know if your father sent her back on the first ship to America, but tell me what you want to write and I'll get the wire sent," Henry offered.

"No need. I'll see to the wire." How she was going to contact Winnie, Frankie had no idea.

Henry turned back to face her, a frown drawing his brows together. "Frankie, you cannot go to the telegraph office this time of night alone."

"What?" she demanded. "Now that my father knows the truth, you are going to start treating me like I'm just a helpless little woman?"

"You will never be helpless," Henry said, his expression unreadable. "However, I would not send Joey alone either."

"There was a time when I was as helpless as I could ever imagine being. I will never return there, but I am no sixteen-year-old child."

"No, you will not." Henry spoke like he was making a vow. "And I know you are not a child." The look he gave her said that his sexual interest in her was far from dead.

"Then what?"

"Cairo, like any other large city, has its underbelly and after everything that has happened, I would not feel you were safe wondering the streets alone at night."

About to argue, she considered his words. Honestly? She didn't want to leave Henry alone right now either. Someone was trying to harm him and he should not be left unprotected.

"You may accompany me, if you like," she offered, planning to tuck her pistol into her pocket.

She had no intention of leaving Henry unprotected or going anywhere without it somewhere on her person for the foreseeable future. Which meant she simply could *not* return to California.

His lips twitched, like he found something amusing, but he nodded. "I would like that, yes."

"Fine." She yawned and then shook herself. Sleep was a long way off.

They still had yet to discuss how she was going to handle her father and the fact that Henry needed to steer clear of the other man until Frankie had done so.

"What do you think made my father follow his children to England?" She was sure he'd had no inkling of the subterfuges she and Edwin had planned.

"The desire to spend time with his daughters?" Henry suggested. "His wish to vet the men you and your sister were meeting? An inclination to reconnect with his British relatives...it could be anything."

"You know my father rather well for having met him so recently." Because every one of those scenario's sounded far too feasible.

Henry shrugged. "You talk about your family."

And Henry listened, filing away the information in his big brain just like she filed receipts in the wall to ceiling cabinets of her old bookkeeping office.

Frankie and Henry headed back downstairs. The telegraph office had an operator on duty throughout the day and night, but they would have to go there themselves rather than using the hotel service to send the telegram if they wanted it to go out immediately.

Which Frankie did.

After sending her brother a message apprising him that the jig was up and paying the surcharge for emergency delivery, she waited impatiently for an answer. It came within the hour.

Arrive tom. STOP

"He's coming tomorrow," Frankie said to Henry.

Henry tensed. "You want to go back to California then?"

"What? No, of course not."

"If Edwin comes to Cairo..." Henry looked around them significantly, like he didn't want to continue.

However, the only other person in the office was the telegraph operator and he had gone back to his desk, leaving her and Henry alone in the lobby area.

"I cannot be Edwin if he is here being himself."

"Precisely."

For a moment, she hesitated. She'd thought maybe she could put off the confrontation with her father until Edwin arrived.

She did not look forward to facing her father alone, but knew it had to be done, especially if she wanted to stay in Egypt. Which she did. If not for her own sake, for Henry's.

She rushed to the counter and sent a new telegram.

Do not come. Will msg you tom. STOP

Her brother's reply showed his absolute trust in her judgement in its brevity.

OK Love You. STOP

Tears burned Frankie's eyes, but she blinked them away. Her brother's love had never been in question. She wasn't going to come over emotional simply because he'd told her so.

She and Henry returned to the hotel.

Where she'd been exhausted and ready for bed before, Frankie was now keyed up and restless.

Henry was still in his strangely silent mode.

When they reached her room, he acted like he wasn't going to join her. Even knowing he would and should inevitably distance himself for her plan to protect him to work, it hurt.

She laid a hand on his arm, to stop him going on to his room. "We need to talk."

He gave a jerk of his head in acknowledgement and followed her into her room.

Once the door was shut, Frankie sat, this time on the edge of the bed. "You cannot come tomorrow morning when I speak to my father. If there is any hope of convincing him you were an unwitting player in this farce, you cannot be there."

"I was not unwitting," he reminded her, like she might have forgotten. "I made my decision to support your masquerade and I do not regret doing so."

Those words carried so much relief for her, Frankie's body slumped with it. Knowing he did not regret letting her come on the excavation meant the world to Frankie, but she couldn't let him pay a price for what was ultimately her choice.

She laid her hand on his arm. "I appreciate that. I really do. I will never forget my time in the desert with you, for so many reasons."

"You make it sound like we will not be friends in the future, but we agreed we would continue seeing each other."

"Surely you realize that is impossible now."

"Why?"

"My father is going to demand I marry and it is going to take a lot of persuasion on my part to convince him that you are not the sacrificial lamb meant for that endeavor."

Her thoughts of returning to the dig went up in a puff of smoke as she said those words aloud. She would have to see to Henry's protection, but perhaps she could leverage her return to California with her father in exchange for him paying for armed security for the dig and a bodyguard for Henry.

"Why?" Henry asked.

"Why what?" Heart sore and tired again, Frankie could not think what Henry wanted to know.

The thought of losing Henry *now* was shredding her heart.

"Why can't I be that sacrificial lamb?"

"No, Henry. I won't allow you to sacrifice your freedom for me."

"But you would marry some stranger?"

"I won't be marrying at all." She swiped at her wet cheeks. "Even if it means being disowned by my family."

"I thought you were more worried about your father having you committed again."

"He could, but I still won't give in. I survived the sanitorium once. I will survive it again."

"You are not going to a sanitorium," Henry said unequivocally. "He has no grounds to commit you."

"He's wealthy and powerful, those are all the grounds he needs." But Frankie would run before she let it happen again, whatever brave words she spoke about surviving the ordeal.

"Damn it to hell, Frankie, you could be carrying my child. Do you think I would allow that to happen to you?" Henry demanded, anger lacing his tone.

"Oh, I hope not." She no longer had rosy dreams of what that could mean. All Frankie could see in that regard was a nightmare outcome she could not stomach. "If I'm pregnant, will you help me run away?"

"What are you talking about? If you are pregnant, we'll get married, damn it." He sighed and dry washed his face. "Look, Frankie, I know you don't want to marry again, but even you must realize that would be the safest outcome for you and our child."

"I never said it wasn't. You're the one that said it would be an unmitigated disaster."

"From your viewpoint, not mine."

"I never said that. You did," she pointed out again.

"Because you don't want your freedom curtailed. I am doing my best to respect the life you wish to lead."

"What does that mean?"

"It means that if it were up to me, we would never sleep in separate beds again."

23

"We could have that without marriage."

"Certainly, we could, but it would scandalize my family and yours. I promised myself that I would never bring scandal to my mother or grandfather. My own father took his own life to protect them, I cannot dishonor that memory with my own actions."

She nodded, understanding in a way she wouldn't have before coming to Egypt and getting to know this amazingly honorable man.

Frankie reached for Henry. "Can we please not spend our last night together arguing?"

"You want to make love?" he asked, like that surprised him.

She leaned up and kissed him in answer.

But he held her shoulders, not letting her press against him. "You are exhausted."

"I want you," she said baldly.

"Heaven help me, I always want you."

Then they were kissing again, their bodies pressed together as close as they could get with their clothes on.

There was a desperate tinge to their lovemaking, a frenzy that could only be soothed with naked bodies writhing together in the bed.

Later, as she lay curled into his body, Frankie realized that there had been a tenderness too. A sense of intimacy deeper than anything they had ever shared.

Henry was gone when she woke, the narrow bed feeling empty

without his presence. Frankie got up, going through her morning ablutions quickly.

Wanting to send the message that she would not fall in with his plans without a fight (or at all in certain terms), she dressed in her *Edwin* clothes in defiance of her father's edict.

But it wasn't her father who opened the door when she knocked, it was Doris.

"Oh, Frankie, I'm so sorry! Dad insisted on coming to Egypt to speak to Edwin when we refused to tell him where you were." Doris threw herself into Frankie's arms, hugging her tightly.

Frankie returned the embrace, surprised at her younger sister's vehemence.

"Stop choking your sister," their father admonished from behind Doris. "She and Professor Thomas have some explaining to do."

Frankie patted Doris bracingly and stepped back. "It is all right, Doris. There is nothing you could have done."

"Winnie is just gutted."

"Where is she?"

"She stayed with Cousin Bernice. When Dad came over all gloom and doom, threatening us and denouncing Winnie as a charlatan, Bernie got her back up and threw him right out of the house. It was magnificent!"

"That will be enough out of you, Doris!" their father barked.

But Frankie's younger sister paid him no heed. "She offered me sanctuary if I wanted it too, but I didn't know what he was likely to do. Whatever it was, it would be better if I was there to support you and Edwin."

"You are a cracker, Doris and a wonderful sister."

Doris blushed, but grinned. "It took you long enough to figure that out."

"I am sorry."

"Don't be. You were never mean, but you just stopped trusting everyone after you went away."

"I'll explain why another day."

"You will?" Doris' eyes grew round. "You always refuse to talk about it and Edwin and Dad say it's your business, not mine."

"Well, Father wouldn't want you to know just how little he's actually willing to do to protect his daughters."

"That is entirely unfair." Her father gave her a reproachful look. "You were under the care of your husband and a doctor."

"I was incarcerated in a sanitorium against my will." Which told her sister where Frankie had gone a bit more bluntly than she'd been intending.

"The doctor had to agree with your husband's assessment, or you would not have been admitted."

That reasoning carried no truck with Frankie at all. "The doctor can go to the devil!"

Her father rocked back on his heels like Frankie had actually punched him in the kisser. "Frances! That is not how a lady speaks."

"I am an adult woman, not a pampered *lady*, and I can speak how I like."

"Your mother would be appalled," he said, like passing the greatest indictment on her behavior.

"Mother would *never* have left me in that place and she would have been ashamed to know you did, so don't bother casting stones when your house is made of glass."

His face blanched and her father seemed to shrink in on himself.

Frankie could not pity him. She had only spoken the truth.

"You may be right at that," he said in a subdued tone. "However, I will not fail you again."

"Whatever do you mean by that?"

"Once word of this escapade gets out, your reputation will be in tatters."

"That might matter if I ever wanted to marry again, but as I do not, it is of little importance to me."

"That is not what your fiancée has told me."

"My what?"

"I did not claim to be her fiancée." That was not a voice she expected to hear in her father's suite this morning.

Frankie had told him to stay away, but when she turned it was in fact Henry standing there.

"I told you not to come."

"Yes."

"So, what are you doing here?" And telling her father she wanted to marry?

"You said you planned to marry my daughter, what exactly do you call that?" her father blustered before Henry could answer her.

"The truth," Henry said succinctly.

"You don't want to marry me."

"Do you want to return to California with your father?" Henry asked her, giving nothing away with his expression.

Frankie opened her mouth to answer, but then snapped it shut. No, she did *not* want to go back to California.

"I will not have you forced into a marriage you do not want," she told him with all the certainty she felt in her heart on the matter.

"That will not happen."

What did that mean?

"Frances, for once in your adult life, be reasonable." Her father just had to put his oar in. "If word gets out about you being here in Egypt, pretending to be your brother, you'll be ruined."

"I am not a Victorian maiden."

"Neither are you a high-flying flapper."

"I could be if I wanted."

"But you do not want that. You want to study history."

"You're about a decade too late with that observation."

"You do not think I knew before? If I had realized at the time what I thought was an innocent subterfuge of you pretending to be your brother to attend lectures, I would have—"

"You knew?"

"Of course I knew. It was not Edwin who could hold a conversation about ancient culture at the dinner table."

"He was always more interested in theater."

"My indulging you both has led to all of this," her father said, sounding weary and appearing old for the first time.

"Allowing your children to follow their own path is a good thing." If she was sure of anything, it was that truth.

"That is what your oldest brother always said."

"Chuck?" Frankie and Doris asked in shocked unison. "But he's always such a stick in the mud," Doris added.

"Charles may not share a taste for adventure with his siblings, but he has always supported yours." The censure was clearly there.

If Chuck didn't judge them, they should not be judging their older brother.

Considering some of the ludicrous views he had about female autonomy, Frankie wasn't sure she could be that magnanimous.

Henry cleared his throat. "Frankie and I need to see about hiring armed security before we return to the dig."

"I am far from done talking to my daughter," her father replied.

"What more is there to say?" Frankie wanted to know.

Her father had indulged her love of history but now regretted it. He believed allowing Edwin the freedom to explore his love for the theater was also a mistake.

Basically, who they were was not good enough for him.

"You have not agreed to marry Professor Thomas."

"That is my problem, surely." Henry's words were polite enough, but his tone was steely.

"Yes, well, I suppose it is at that." Her father indicated an already laid table. "Come, join us for breakfast and you can explain why you need an armed guard for your dig."

Not wanting her father to determine the return to Upper Egypt was too dangerous, Frankie was about to refuse when Henry moved to the table and held a chair out for her.

She considered simply leaving, rather than falling in with their plans, but then it occurred to her that Henry might be hoping her father would increase his monetary support of the dig to cover the cost of the armed guard. Frankie could deal with another unpleasant meal with her father for the sake of Henry's safety and the continuation of the excavation.

Frankie sat down and Doris followed suit, showing she intended to follow Frankie's lead. The gesture was not lost on either man. Her father frowned, but Henry's lips tilted up on one side in a nearly there smile.

Breakfast wasn't so bad, despite all the underlying tension. Frankie's voice held a distinct chill whenever she was forced to address her father, but for his part, the older man seemed to be trying to mend fences.

He said several things that could be taken as compliments toward Frankie, but she refused to acknowledge any of them.

Henry laid out the sabotage and other anomalous events in his usual unembellished factual fashion, which nevertheless seemed to entertain her sister and father. Until he mentioned the asp.

"A snake? In your tent?" Doris demanded, goggle eyed.

Just as Frankie had worried would happen, her father started looking upset again.

"Is this a usual occurrence?" her father asked. "I never considered such a thing when I arranged for Edwin to join your dig."

"It has never happened to me before."

"I think it was planted," Frankie offered.

"Why?"

"Someone has it in for Henry," Frankie said, realizing she wanted to be sure he had security more than she wanted to return to the dig without argument from her father.

"Why would you think such a thing?" her father asked.

"Really?" Doris asked at the same time.

Frankie nodded to her sister before telling her father about the failing brakes the day before.

"But surely that could happen with any car. Brake systems are notoriously unreliable."

"Which is why I checked it the night before."

"And it was all in order?" her father asked without remarking on the fact that she'd been the one to check it.

"Yes."

His lips pursed and released in that way he had when he was thinking. "Did you know your uncle is in Cairo?" he asked Henry.

"My uncle?" Henry asked. "Do you mean my cousin Randall? Perhaps he has decided to collect his son early."

"I may be in my fifties but my eyesight is just fine. I know the difference between Louis Thomas and Randall Kingston."

"Uncle Louis is here in Cairo?"

"Yes. I saw him yesterday, when we were checking in. He was talking to a local man."

Henry appeared shocked. "That surprises me. Uncle Louis always refused to do business with anyone not of Western European descent."

"He's not a member of that awful group the KKK, is he?" Doris asked.

The resurgence of the Klan had been a topic of grave concern to the women in Frankie's adventure society, but she hadn't realized Doris knew about it. Perhaps the time had come to extend an invitation for Doris to join *Et Audaces in Mulieriebus.*

"As to that, I would not be surprised," Henry said grimly.

"Oh, you must be so embarrassed to have to call him family," Doris said with blatant pity.

Their father laid his cutlery down, his expression severe. "The only person who should feel embarrassment for such idiotic thinking is Louis Thomas."

Frankie wanted to ask if that meant her father would not be embarrassed if she was sussed out in her guise as Edwin, but she was more focused on the fact Mr. Thomas was in Cairo.

"Your uncle is here," she said to Henry. "For all we know, he's been here all along."

"You think he could be behind the sabotage?" Henry asked.

"Let's not forget the attempts on your life."

"Pretty pathetic attempts," Doris said with youthful dismissal.

"They would not have been if Henry had not known what to do with the asp."

"And your sister's excellent driving prevented an accident when our brakes went."

"You two are rather sweet," Doris said, smiling.

Frankie gave her sister a quelling look. "You think you are funny."

"No, in fact, I was being serious, sister mine."

Frankie felt heat rise into her face, but her father was actually smiling.

Henry didn't seem perturbed by Doris's observation, so Frankie let it go.

"Professor Thomas had convinced me that your return to the dig in your guise as Edwin had much to recommend it, but now..." He shook his head. "How can either of you be safe under the circumstances?"

Frankie was pleased her father didn't make it about her being a woman, but regardless she would not be deterred returning. "That is why he was trying to get troops seconded. The ministry department refused."

"We'll see about that," her father said in a way that usually annoyed Frankie.

Right now, she was grateful for it. If she knew her father, they would have a compliment of soldiers returning with them to Upper Egypt.

After breakfast, her father left to harangue government officials. Doris wanted to go shopping at the Bazaar, but Frankie wanted to find that taxi driver and speak to him.

The man had pretended to be a dig foreman and she just knew he could answer some burning questions she had.

Henry suggested Joey take Doris shopping.

"I thought you didn't want your cousin anywhere near my father," Frankie remarked.

Henry shrugged. "Now that Mr. Clarke and I have an understanding, Joey is in no danger from him."

"From his wrath, you mean."

"Yes."

"You told my father you intend to marry me." Frankie frowned. How had that fit in with his near pathological need for honesty?

"I did."

"I thought you never lied."

"I try very hard not to."

"But..." She let her voice trail off, not really wanting to take Henry to task for managing the impossible.

Her father.

"Engagements can be long standing," he said obliquely.

"How long would ours last?" she asked. Until he was ready to move on? She wondered.

"As long as you need it to."

"You would allow it to go on indefinitely to protect my reputation?"

"Among other reasons, yes."

"What other reasons?"

"I like your company and wish to continue keeping it."

"Yes, you said." In and out of bed, he'd made that clear.

"You two are pulling a fast one on Dad?" Doris asked, admiration lacing her tone.

"In a manner of speaking," Frankie admitted.

"Oh, that's delicious. Only..." Her face fell. "I really like you as a couple."

"We are a couple," Henry said with certainty.

"Only you don't plan to actually marry."

"We will do whatever makes your sister happiest," he said, before Frankie could even open her mouth to reply.

Since she would be happiest never to have to say goodbye to him, this engagement was looking to last much longer than she was sure he was bargaining for.

Henry arranged for a driver and car for Joey and Doris, while Frankie and her sister had a chat. Frankie wanted to know if Winnie was okay, so she asked first thing when the two women were alone in Doris's room, while her sister got ready to go out.

"She's fine. She and Bernie hit it off first thing when we arrived at the manor."

"Bernie is Aunt Bernice?"

"She's not actually our aunt, but our cousin."

"Oh."

"Father." They said in unison and then both women smiled.

"Winnie really is the Bee's Knees." Doris sounded admiring.

"I agree," Frankie offered because it was true. "We've been friends since finishing school."

"But her father lost his fortune." There could be no doubt the horror Doris felt at such a circumstance.

"Yes."

"She's had to work to support her family ever since."

Frankie just nodded. She knew all this, what she wanted to know was if Winnie was okay right now and said so.

Doris waved her hand airily. "She's the cat's pajamas. Winnie told me to tell you she'll be on the ship returning home as planned."

"Oh, that's good." Relief washed over Frankie. "I'm so glad our cousin wasn't angry when she learned of the deception."

"She thought we were all very clever girls to have come up with it. That's how she put it." Doris grinned. "She's got some very modern ideas, but anyone younger than her is a *girl*."

"I think I would have liked to have met her."

"She said the same about you and hopes you'll come to visit."

"Maybe, I will." A *woman* could dream.

Frankie and Henry saw Joey and Doris off on their shopping expedition. Henry gave the driver explicit instructions to keep an eye on the two young people.

Doris might be older than Joey by a few years, but Frankie still thought her sister was naïve to the ways of the world. Even if Doris saw herself as a Flapper.

Neither heard Henry give his instructions though and for that Frankie was grateful. She didn't need a lecture from her sister on how Doris was a twenty-one-year-old adult woman. Frankie was aware, but could not help feeling protective and probably always would.

The thought gave her pause in regard to Henry's attitude the previous night and her father's pretty much all of the time.

If only George Clarke had protected her the one time she'd needed it most. Frankie would find it so much easier to trust his motives now.

"*Sahib*, Mr. Clarke!" A familiar voice sounded from behind them.

Frankie and Henry turned and beheld the dig's former assistant foreman, Peter. He was dressed more formally than he had been on the dig, wearing a suit jacket and tie, both quite rumpled, however.

"Peter," Henry acknowledged the other man. "What are you doing here?" Frankie asked. "You know Dr. Thomas isn't going to hire you back."

"No one else will either, not now that you've put out the word I'm not to be trusted." The man sounded more disbelieving than accusing. "It is as if all my years of experience mean nothing."

Since she found his disbelief hard to swallow, Frankie did not respond.

Neither did Henry, though he was not glowering, as Frankie would have expected, but looking at Peter speculatively.

Frankie had to admit to her own racing speculations. No longer even willing to entertain the possibility that Peter had been working alone, she wondered if he would be more forthcoming now.

If not, why bother approaching Henry?

Unless Peter thought Henry might be persuaded to give him a letter of recommendation? Peter was the arrogant sort of man to believe that his betrayal could be easily dismissed like that.

"If you could spare a few moments of your time, *sahib*, I think you would be glad to hear what I have to say."

Henry nodded with a slight jerk of his head and then turned back toward the hotel. He said nothing as he led the way to the front desk, where he requested a private room for a meeting.

As always, the manager was very accommodating, providing a small, private sitting room and an offer of refreshments.

She was surprised when Henry accepted, requesting a coffee tray.

"Very civilized. Yes, I knew I was right to approach you, *sahib*," Peter said.

"Dr. Thomas," Henry corrected. "I am not your employer."

Peter winced, but nodded his head up and down several times. "As you wish."

Once the coffee tray had been delivered and everyone had a demitasse cup in front of them, Henry fixed a gimlet stare on Peter. "Speak."

"The information I have for you is worth something, I think."

"Do you?" Henry asked, his tone only mildly interested.

"I do. I should like to come to terms before I offer up valuable details you could not possibly come by otherwise."

Frankie had no patience for this. This man knew who had been doing their best to not only undermine Henry's dig, but do him harm and probably even kill him.

She pulled her gun from her jacket pocket, pointed it with a steady hand at Peter and cocked it.

The sound of the hammer clicking back was unnaturally loud in the room and caused Peter to jump.

"What the hell, Frankie?" Henry demanded, showing more emotion now than he had in response to Peter's claims.

"I have a steady hand and I am a crack shot. Start talking, Peter."

Sweat popped onto the would be paid informant's forehead. "You can't point a gun at me, I am a British citizen."

"And yet, here I am with my pistol pointed at your head. I keep it in good repair. There will be no misfire if I pull the trigger," she informed him.

"You carry a gun?" Henry asked, his tone shocked.

"I do."

"Since when?"

"I have had my pistol with me since my arrival in Egypt. I started carrying it in my jacket after the incident with the asp." She gave Peter a baleful stare. "You have only yourself to blame."

"I had nothing to do with the snake. I told you!"

"Henry may believe you. I do not."

"It was them, the workers he paid me to hire. I would never have harmed you, *sah*- Dr. Thomas!"

"Who paid you?"

"The same man who paid me to sabotage your dig."

"You engineered the accident?" Henry asked, his voice shaking with fury. "Two men died."

"That wasn't supposed to happen. It was supposed to collapse in the night."

"And yet, it didn't."

"I couldn't cut too deeply into the support timbers. It would have been obvious what happened."

"You killed two men," Frankie repeated.

"No, he did! He paid me to do it. It's his fault."

"Whose fault?" Henry asked, ice in his eyes and his tone.

"You don't understand! I need to be paid for this. I cannot get another position on a dig because of your letters sent far and sundry. I need money."

Frankie dropped the muzzle of the gun downward. "I can shoot you in the leg. You may survive, you may not, but you'll live long enough to tell us what we want to know."

"You wouldn't! You're no ruffian. I know all about you, Edwin Francis Clarke."

"Whatever you think you know, you had better understand this, I would and will do exactly that. You may not value the lives of the men you took, but I do."

"I didn't take them, I tell you. It was him."

Suddenly Henry grabbed Peter by the lapels of his jacket and shook him. "Who, damn it?"

"Your uncle, Louis Thomas. He approached me after the dig last year and said he knew of a way for me to get the foreman position. I asked him what was in it for him, you can't trust a man who hasn't got a stake in something," Peter babbled. "He said money."

Henry dropped Peter back into his seat and Frankie carefully brought the hammer back to a safety position on her pistol.

"I've told you what I know. Will you pay me now?" Peter asked.

"I'll give you exactly what you have coming to you," Henry said.

Peter must have thought that sounded as ominous as Frankie did because he paled. He jumped to his feet, like he meant to run from the room, but Henry grabbed him. "Put your pistol away, Frankie."

Frankie did so without asking why.

Then Henry called out and the door opened, two Cairo police officers coming into the room.

Peter was arrested amidst voluble protests.

"You gave instructions for the manager send for them while you were requesting the room?"

"I did. We could not allow Peter to get away with killing two men, no matter who he blamed for it."

"I thought you believed him about not sabotaging the scaffolding."

"I changed my mind."

Frankie nodded. "You saw him and you knew he was up to no good. I thought he was going to ask for his job back, or a recommendation, despite everything."

Henry frowned. "I'm sure he thought I owed him that."

"But you set him straight."

"I did."

"Do you think he'll testify against your cousin in court?"

"Whether he does, or he doesn't, I want to find that taxi driver."

Frankie agreed. "But even with both their testimony, what are the chances your grandfather will believe them, much less a man of your uncle's status being found guilty?"

"I do not know." Henry's tone left no doubt he shared her concerns, however.

"If only we could get him to admit his villainous behavior in front of witnesses."

"I believe that only happens in dime store novels, Frankie."

She wasn't so sure though. "We could confront him. I'd make a pretty good witness."

"No."

"What? Why not?"

"You have not been revealed as yourself because no one looks too closely at you."

"But he'll look very closely indeed if I am the witness against him. Only I could get Edwin to testify."

"And perjure himself?" Henry sounded genuinely shocked.

Frankie sighed. "I know you are right, but we cannot let your uncle get away with what he has done."

Not least of which was because Henry would not be safe otherwise. She could not stand the thought of him in danger because of his uncle's greed and machinations.

24

They spent a rather fruitless day trying to find the taxi driver, returning to the hotel after sending another wire to Edwin.

Frankie told him to stay in Germany, that things were handled with her father.

She knew Edwin would think their father had decided to be reasonable, not that a fake engagement had saved all their bacon.

As much as she hated the thought of leaving Egypt, Frankie couldn't help looking forward to the ocean voyage home. She wanted to hear about Winnie's adventures and Edwin's, for that matter.

She couldn't help wondering if another man would be joining them on the crossing. Edwin had managed to mention Michel in one of his Telegrams despite the need for shortened speech.

The veteran of the Great War had made an immense impact on her brother.

Frankie readied herself for dinner, wishing she could drop her impersonation of Edwin if only for the evening, but knowing that if she wanted to return to Upper Egypt with Henry, she could not risk it.

Her father had left a message that he wanted to meet in his suite before dinner. He had news he did not want to share in a public place.

She went to her father's suite, knowing that Henry would meet her there soon. Her father was still dressing for dinner when she arrived and Doris let Frankie in.

Looking relaxed, Joey was lounging on one of the armchairs in the suite's sitting room. Frankie took that as a good sign that her father was in a pleasant mood at least.

"Did you find the taxi driver?" Doris wanted to know.

"No. And because we don't have a name, there's little chance of his compatriots pointing us in the right direction."

Doris patted Frankie's arm consolingly. "Tomorrow, we can help you look."

"It would be better than another day spent shopping." Joey yawned pointedly.

Doris pretended to hit him. "Why you!"

Joey laughed and the rest joined in.

Frankie was still smiling when there was a knock on the door. Once again, Doris answered, but their father came out of his private bedroom at the same time.

"That will be Professor Thomas, I expect."

It *was* Henry, looking dashing in a formal suit for dinner. Frankie wondered if he kept some luggage here at the hotel as he'd worn the suit on the ship, but she hadn't seen it in his things at the dig.

Her father stepped forward, his hand extended. "Professor Thomas, good evening."

Henry shook her father's hand, responding in kind.

"Oh, you look like the cat's pajamas," Doris exclaimed to Henry before turning to Frankie. "If you've got to get shackled to someone, it might as well be him."

"Marriage is not a shackle," her father admonished censoriously.

"Not for a man, certainly," Frankie agreed.

Doris rolled her eyes at their father. "Trust a man not to realize the inequality of the married state for men and women."

"It would have been nearly impossible for me to have John committed as he had done to me, not least of which because had it been your son and not your daughter sent against his will to a sanitorium, you never would have stood for it. John's parents would most certainly have prevented it." Chagrined, Frankie snapped her mouth shut.

She wasn't sure what had prompted her to say such a thing.

Until recently, she *never* spoke of that time in her life, but particularly not with her father.

Several emotions crossed George Clarke's features.

If Frankie didn't know better, she would think he'd had an epiphany quickly followed by remorse and grief. However, he was back to looking like his usual self so quickly, she doubted her own perceptions.

"Frances, I would like a private word, if I might have it," he said to her unexpectedly.

Frankie looked at Doris to see if her sister knew what their father wanted, but Doris was giving her a look that said, "I don't know, but I hope you'll tell me later."

Frankie bit back a smile at her sister's patent curiosity, and said to her father, "I thought you wanted to speak to Henry about your visit to the ministry office."

"I will in due course, but this is more urgent."

"Okay."

"Modern slang," her father shook his head. "A *yes* would have done."

This time Frankie made no effort to stifle the short laugh that bubbled up. She used very little of the modern vernacular in her speech compared to either Edwin or Doris. In fact, Frankie had no doubt that her younger sister would comment on their father's attitude.

"Don't be such an old stick in the mud," Doris said, not disappointing.

Before their father could take umbrage, Frankie headed toward his personal room. "Let's talk in here, it will be private enough."

Surprisingly, her father followed.

When they got to his room, he went to shut the door, but they both heard a peremptory knock from the other room. Frankie stayed her father from shutting the door completely with a hand on his arm. "Did you invite someone else to join us before dinner?"

"No."

Frankie had a feeling, like tingles in her gut. She refused to ignore it. "Stay here," she instructed her father. When he looked to argue, she said, "Please."

He opened his mouth, shut it and then nodded.

She slipped out and heard the tones of an older man conversing with Doris at the door. Frankie's sister had her body and the door positioned so the man could not see into the room.

"I will have to ask if he wants to see you," she was saying to the man.

"He damn well will see me. He's my nephew."

Frankie looked to Henry. *Uncle Louis?* she mouthed silently in question.

He nodded.

She grabbed Joey and jerked her head toward her father's bedroom. The teen didn't ask what she was about, but followed her silently, a sense of anticipation buzzing in the air.

They got into the room just in time as Louis Thomas pushed his way into the suite over Doris' voluble protests. Frankie cracked the door so she could see the room beyond and hear what was being said. She waved her father over and he came, though his expression showed his disdain for eavesdropping.

"This is how you spend Father's money, shacked up with some floozy in the best suite the hotel has to offer!" Louis shouted at Henry.

Looking superbly unaffected, Henry apologized for his uncle's deplorable manners and suggested Doris leave them to their privacy.

With a smile and a nod for Henry and a glare toward his uncle, Doris flounced off to her own room.

"Grandfather is never going to fund another of your money draining schemes once he hears of this." The satisfaction in the older man's voice could not be missed. "You and that tart."

Frankie's father stiffened beside her, like he was going to go out and defend Doris' honor. Frankie jerked her head in the negative, imploring him with her eyes not to ruin their one chance at the impossible. Witnesses to overhear a confession.

If Henry could guide the conversation in the direction they needed it to go.

Frankie had no doubts about her archeologist's ability to unearth the truth.

Now, if her father would just cooperate.

Surprisingly, he subsided with a silent nod of acceptance.

"That is exactly what you wanted though, isn't it?" Henry asked, his tone scathing.

Louis sniffed. "I do not know what you mean."

"You've been doing your best to discredit and sabotage my dig, not to mention have me killed."

"What are you on about? I would never do such a thing."

"Drop the pretense of honorability, Uncle Louis. It's just the two of us here and we both know you hate that Grandfather spends his money on my excavations, just as he did my father's."

"Your father," Louis Thomas said with pure dislike. "That pansy!"

"His homosexuality bothered you, but I can't think why. It did not impact you."

"It was an abomination. He was an embarrassment to the family." The older man was growing increasingly agitated.

Henry's expression could have been carved from granite. "A respected scholar in his field, an eminent archeologist, married to my mother, father to a son. He was no embarrassment."

"Father should never have funded his fantasies of discovering lost civilizations."

"My father wasn't looking for lost civilizations, he was searching for artifacts from those we already knew about."

"Don't correct me. I am not stupid!" Spittle flew from the older man's mouth.

Frankie thought he was becoming distinctly unhinged.

"To think your grandfather favored his defective son. *Isn't he clever? He is going to do great things while all we will ever do is make money,"* Louis ranted. "My brother was a pansy who never added a single penny to the family fortunes, but Father was prouder of him than me. I worked long hours, but did Father ever thank me? No. But he thanked your father for *seeking the truth of history* every single year he went out on a dig."

"My father is no longer here to compete for Grandfather's affection," Henry said coldly, clearly not moved by his uncle's jealousy and feelings of being placed second best.

"No, he is not. He did us all a favor offing himself, didn't he?"

Frankie wanted to storm out there and smack the smug look off that man's face. She knew his remark had hurt Henry. Though you wouldn't tell it by his blank expression. But she knew.

Her father's hand on her shoulder reminded her that they had a purpose to this eavesdropping. A purpose Henry seemed totally focused on, because he had refrained from punching his uncle in the kisser.

But honestly? Frankie wasn't sure how long that steely self-control was going to last.

"My father's death was a loss to our family and to society as a whole. I wonder, Uncle Louis, who will grieve when you die? If anyone does."

"And who will grieve when you do?" Louis asked snidely. "That fancy piece in the other room?"

"I'm not going to die any time soon, so we won't be finding out." Henry's tone was nothing short of taunting.

Frankie pulled her gun from where she had it tucked in the back of her trouser waistband. She didn't cock the trigger, but she was ready.

The tension in the other room was thickening second by second.

Louis's face had gone beet red. "You think just because you've survived a couple of near misses in motorcars and a poisonous snake in your tent that you'll survive your next mishap?"

Only a slight flaring of Henry's grey eyes showed his surprise at his uncle's words. But the mention of two near accidents with motorcars implied he knew about the dangerous driver in Los Angeles, which in turn, implied that hadn't just been negligence after all.

"How did you know about those *mishaps* as you call them, if you didn't engineer them?" Henry asked mildly.

"Word gets around."

"However, I never told anyone else about the car that almost ran us off the road back home."

"The other car passengers talked."

"No, they didn't."

"Fine! They didn't. What good does it do you to know I hired inept men to shorten your life? It won't stop me doing it again."

This man was more mentally disturbed than any of the patients who had been at the sanitorium with Frankie.

"When you go to jail, it will."

"I'm not going to jail." Louis laughed. "No one is going to believe a man of my standing would do such a thing."

"I think you will find they will."

"Nonsense. On your word? The son of a man so unstable he took his own life."

"The son of a good man."

"Your father was not *good*! He refused to give into the blackmailer's demands at first, did you know that? He was going to let your mother and you suffer the brunt of his shame."

"How do you know that?" There was a dangerous quality to Henry's tone.

Louis didn't seem to notice, as he answered blithely, "Who do you think was behind the blackmail? Your father was better at discretion than he was at being a man."

"My father was a much better man than you." Henry said it flatly, like there could be no question he spoke the truth.

That seemed to enrage Louis further. "He was *not* better than me! He was a drain on the family coffers, just like you are! Father is going to stop funding your pie in the sky digs once he knows how you're really spending his money, what you are doing over here in Egypt."

There was so much satisfaction in Louis's tone, it was sickening.

"You are wrong on all counts. Are you aware that Peter was arrested this morning after he confessed to being hired by you to sabotage my dig? Two men died from the sabotage."

"Egyptians! What do I care about them?"

"I care about them, very much. As do the authorities."

"So? You only have his word for it that I hired him. I know he told you initially it was all his idea. I will say he was trying to blackmail me for money and when I didn't pay, he made the story up."

"You can try that certainly, though how you will explain the fact he knew you at all, I do not know," Henry said, like he didn't care either way. "However, how do you propose to get out of an incitement to murder charge now you've confessed to me?"

"I'll say you are unhinged and I never said any such thing."

"You are so sure you have all the answers." Henry shook his head. "But you are wrong. Do you believe I will allow you to continue as you are? Edwin Clarke could have died on all three of the occasions which you engineered accidents for me."

"So? He's a pansy just like your father was. Everyone knows it. His father would probably thank me."

That was too much for Frankie's father. In a strangely gentle but adamant gesture, he moved her aside and then stormed into the other room. "Thank you for killing my child?"

Louis spun around. "Mr. Clarke, what are you doing here?"

"This is my suite, you puling coward! That girl you called a tart is *my* daughter and the younger sister to the daughter who is engaged to marry Henry!"

Oh, crap. Frankie would have to be very careful.

"What? No, that's impossible! Henry is not engaged!"

"Put my child's life at risk, will you?" Her father stormed forward and gave Louis the punch he so richly deserved.

Only Frankie knew it was on her behalf and not only Edward's. Something that had been tight and constricted for too many years loosened in her heart.

Henry's uncle fell backward, laying there dazed for a moment.

"You think that authorities won't believe your nephew, you'd better damn well be certain they will believe me. As will your grandfather. I'll see you disinherited, destitute and in jail by the time I'm done with you."

Louis rolled over and then onto his knees, standing slowly. There was a gun in his hand when he came upright though. And it was pointed at Henry. "You! You lured me here and tricked me into saying things to incriminate myself!"

He sounded like he'd gone round the bend, but the look in his eyes said he had enough clarity to pull that trigger to devastating effect.

Henry took a step toward his uncle. "What are you going to do? Shoot me? You? A man who hires other men to do your dirty work?"

She could see it in Henry's tense posture. He was going to use his Judo to disarm his uncle.

Frankie could not let that happen. There was too much risk of Louis's gun going off. Raising her own pistol, she shouted, "Step back."

She hoped they would all listen to her, but she could not spare a glance to make sure. Raising her hand, she cocked the pistol at the same time and then she took aim and fired.

The sound of the pistol shot cracked through the room. The gun flew from Louis's hand, banging against a wall. He screamed, cradling his hand against his chest. Then he glared at her. "You shot me, you tried to kill me."

"I shot your gun and I always hit what I'm aiming at," Frankie apprised him.

Henry barked out, "Joey, go downstairs and fetch the manager, have him call for the authorities."

"I'm not going to jail!" Louis ran toward the door and right into Henry's fist.

He crumpled to the floor in an unconscious heap.

"That felt very satisfying, I must say," Henry said with one of his almost there smiles directed toward Frankie.

"I could not agree more," she said.

"Frances! When did you learn to shoot?" her father demanded.

"When John's things were returned after his death." One of her fellow members of her female adventurer's club, *Et Audaces in Mulieriebus*, had taught her.

Frankie found she enjoyed it and practiced until she could hit both a moving and stationary target with absolute accuracy.

"That was cracking!" Joey exclaimed.

"Wasn't it just!" Doris agreed. "I can't believe you shot the gun right out of his hand."

"Better than having to shoot him," Frankie said. She'd never shot a living thing and was glad that hadn't had to change this evening.

The authorities came and took Louis Thomas away. Her father arranged for them all to give their statements the following day as he saw no reason to have his dinner ruined by the actions of a villainous coward.

Doris and Joey were buzzing with excitement over dinner, but both Frankie and Henry were more subdued. She wanted to be alone with him, to ask how he was feeling, to hold him. It had to be awful to find out that his uncle's actions had driven his father to suicide.

Her own father was also more silent than usual, though he did inform them, in a rather subdued manner, that he had arranged for armed guards to be provided by the ministry for the dig.

Frankie was relieved and said so, thanking him. Henry seconded her thanks, but it was clear he was still annoyed with the ministry not listening to him in the first place.

Doris and Joey wanted to rehash what had happened with Louis Thomas and everyone else at the table let them, adding very little to the conversation.

After dinner, her father asked again to speak privately to Frankie and she nodded, inviting him up to her room. Henry followed silently behind.

Neither she, nor her father, said anything when Henry joined them in the hotel room. Whatever her father wanted to talk about could be discussed in front of Henry, as far as she was concerned.

An urgent need to spend some time with Henry tightened her chest and she didn't want him out of her sight until they had at least had a chance to talk, but she would prefer he stayed the night in her room.

Once her father was seated in the armchair and she and Henry were sitting on the side of the bed, she asked, "What did you want to discuss?"

"I wanted to apologize, for not pressing John to get your release from the sanitorium. I did not believe it was my place to come between a husband and his wife."

This was nothing new. "You said so at the time."

"You did not accept it then and I can see you do not accept it now."

"You are my father. My husband had me incarcerated against my will and you had the power to get me out, but you left me there."

"It would have been a scandal if I had preempted his rights."

At least her father didn't deny that with his money and influence, he could have affected her release.

"Better to leave me trapped and in danger for six months."

"In danger? Nonsense," her father dismissed.

And the damn broke, sending fissures through her heart with the power of the pain crashing through her.

"The first night I was there, I woke to the sound of a woman screaming," Frankie informed her father. "She was begging them to stop."

"Who?" her father asked, sounding appalled. "It was a rest sanitorium, for goodness' sake. They weren't supposed to have seriously disturbed patients there."

Frankie ignored him and continued, "She was a long-term resident, a woman who had been committed by her family. I do not know what she was like when she arrived at the sanitorium." Frankie gave her father a look. "I doubt she was *seriously disturbed*, but by the time I arrived she barely spoke."

Henry took Frankie's hand in his, but said nothing, waiting for her to say whatever she needed to.

"Moira never washed her own hair or changed out of her nightclothes without forced assistance." Memories of the woman, who had been less than ten years older than Frankie still haunted her.

The wild hair, the unkempt clothing, but it was the look of despair in her eyes that Frankie would never forget.

"It took me several days to fully realize what was happening," she added, her voice catching and she could not help it. She despised crying for herself, but that woman deserved her grief. "Two orderlies were visiting her at night. They hurt her. *They raped her.*" Frankie made herself say the horror laden words.

"Surely you told John," her father said forcefully.

Oh, she'd told John all right. "Yes."

"What happened?" Henry asked, shifting closer to her, like he wanted to share his body heat and comfort with her.

She looked up at him gratefully. "He told her family, and she was removed from the sanitorium." Probably to be moved to another one, because she was *not fit for polite company*. "One of the orderlies was fired. I never knew the name of the other one and apparently she didn't name him either."

Fury burned in Henry's eyes. "And John left you there?"

"Yes, John left me there. I lay in bed every night, terrified someone would come into my room. I barely slept, which only fed John's belief I needed more *enforced rest*. He would not listen when I begged him to get me out. He said I'd become hysterical."

"But surely..." her father let his voice trail off, like he didn't know what he wanted to say.

"I was angry, I was frightened, I was *not* hysterical. There were women in there who had hysterectomies, not because they wanted them, but because the doctors said it would improve their disposition. There was a girl, not even twenty, whose father had brought her in because she had sex with her boyfriends. She was such a lively, sweet thing."

"What happened?" Henry asked gently.

"They were talking about doing the hysterectomy on her, but another doctor came and suggested something else. Some kind of surgery on her brain."

Henry stiffened at that. Her father gasped.

She glared at her father. "I'd been there three months when she came. I couldn't let them hurt her like that."

"What did you do?"

"I staged a riot as a distraction while one of the other inmates helped her escape." Frankie had given the young woman the name of one of Frankie's contacts in *Et Audaces in Mulieriebus*, who she knew would help the younger woman get away and build a new life.

They'd succeeded, but not without a price.

"I was *treated* with ice baths for a week after that, and pills that made the entire world go fuzzy for another month after that."

Her father was pale as parchment. "That was when you stopped writing me."

"There was no point. You were not going to help me."

Henry slipped his arm around her, his body a solid presence beside her, his silent support unmistakable.

"I didn't know. You did not tell me." Her father sounded anguished, not accusatory.

So, she did not take umbrage, but she did give him a level look. "I begged for you to get me out of there. You refused."

"Even if she had told you, what are the chances that letter ever would have been mailed?" Henry asked cynically.

Frankie had thought the same at the time. Her doctors said that her treatment was a private medical matter, between her, her husband and her doctors. She'd been forbidden from telling Edwin anything when he came to visit and fearful of what they would do to her if she disobeyed, Frankie had remained silent.

John must have believed the doctors when they told him that she needed the medication and the ice baths. Not that she was ever privy to those conversations. Everything was decided for her, without her input during those six months.

Once they'd taken her off the medication, because John said she could not return to society acting like a Zombie, her brain had started working again and Frankie had soon realized the only way out was to act like she was *better*.

She'd pretended an improvement of spirits and a desire for John's company, when she would have been happiest never to see her husband again. She had even lied and said she wanted to try for another child.

Edwin had been lobbying John, all along, to bring her home as well.

It worked. John said he thought she was much improved, and the doctors had pronounced her cured. She'd returned to their modest bungalow in Los Angeles with John. That first night, he'd had sex with her. Unable to help herself, she'd cried silently the entire time, though she never once demurred.

When John turned on the light to wash up, he'd seen her tear-stained face and red rimmed eyes. He'd never tried to touch her intimately again.

Frankie had maintained a distant, but pleasant demeanor with him after that, but he'd realized that she no longer loved or trusted him. Quite how he had done, she'd never figured out, but he had.

And rather than put her back in the Sanitorium, he'd gone off to war.

And died.

She'd been a widow, but the only thing she'd felt had been relief and guilt for that relief. No grief. She'd left that to those who still shared a bond of love with the man whom she'd grown to despise.

"I didn't know," her father repeated, his shoulders slumped.

"Now you do." Though she'd never intended to tell him.

"And I understand why you doubt me." He swallowed and stood, his eyes suspiciously shiny. "For what it is worth, I deeply regret not helping you. John was not the man I believed him to be."

She had no trouble believing that. Frankie could not imagine any circumstances under which her father would have allowed her mother to suffer or be put at risk as John had done with Frankie.

"I will not interfere in your life any further, but I promise you that if you ever need me to act on your behalf again, I will."

Frankie nodded, her throat too thick with emotion to get any words out.

She accepted that her father was sorry, but it did not change the past and it would take time for her to forgive him. Only now, she knew that someday she could.

25

"Thank you for letting me be here while you spoke to him about all of that," Henry said to Frankie, his arm still around her.

She looked up at him, his beloved features such a comfort to her. And he was beloved. Reliving the end of her marriage with John had put many things into perspective, the most important of which was her feelings for Henry.

Because she knew deep in her soul that he would never behave as John had done.

"I am glad you know, but even so, that was all a long time ago. How are you doing with your uncle's revelations?"

"As you say, my father's death was a long time ago. It is reprehensible that one brother could do that to another, but Uncle Louis is a truly disgusting human being."

She had to agree. "His trying to have you killed and undermining your life's work is pretty recent though."

"True, but in doing so, he will go to prison where he belongs."

"Do you think your grandfather will disinherit him?"

"Even without your father's threats if he doesn't, yes, I think he will."

"You think my father will threaten him?" she asked askance.

"Oh, yes. You and your brother, could have been killed by his machinations against me. He'll ruin Uncle Louis no question."

"Edwin wasn't really here in Egypt," Frankie pointed out.

Henry shook his head. "But you were, my dear. And Edwin was in the car in Los Angeles."

"You are right."

"Your father is very protective of all of you, but I think going forward his need to protect you will grow even stronger as he wants to make up for his lack ten years ago."

"He said he won't interfere in my life."

"He did not promise to refrain from interfering on your behalf."

"It's the same thing."

"If you say so."

"You might be right," she had to admit. "But I don't want to talk about my father, or the past, unless you want to?"

"No, I don't want to talk at all."

So, they didn't.

He did spend the night in her room, and they even spent some of it sleeping.

The next day was taken up with giving statements and discussion with the authorities on how best to proceed with charges against Peter and Louis. When it became clear that neither George Clarke, nor Henry Thomas were going to argue against the two men being tried in Egyptian courts, things became much more friendly.

As far as Frankie was concerned, both men deserved to face local justice for their crimes. They were both directly responsible for the deaths of two men and that could not go unanswered.

When they returned to the hotel, her father offered to return to the States immediately to break the news to Henry's grandfather.

Frankie waited to see what Henry wanted before saying anything herself. The only thing she knew was that no matter what he decided, stay in Egypt, or return to America, she would be with him.

Henry looked at her. "What are your plans, Frankie?"

"If you are staying in Egypt, I am staying. If you are returning to the States, I will accompany you." He might not admit it, or even realize it, but finding out that his uncle had wanted him dead and was, for all intents and purposes, responsible for the death of Henry's father, would impact him.

He needed someone who would be there when grief overwhelmed him. Frankie was determined to be that someone.

Henry reached out and would have taken her hand, but stopped himself at the last second just as she stepped back.

Such an action while she was masquerading as Edwin could have dire consequences.

Her father chuckled. "I do not know how you two have managed this pretense so far. Your affection for one another is as obvious as the nose on my face."

Heat climbed into Frankie's face, but she wasn't about to deny it.

"We are more careful usually," Henry said mildly, but he didn't seem offended in the least by her father's observation.

"Have you considered returning to the dig as yourself, Frances?"

"How could I do that?"

"For one thing, you would have to bring your sister with you to be proper, an engagement notwithstanding."

"But what if someone recognizes me?"

"Not likely to, are they?" he asked. "They might remark on how alike you and your twin brother look, but there will Doris be, calling you Frances."

Frankie could think of one person who would certainly recognize the truth, but she wasn't worried that Professor Adams would blab their secret.

"Doris refers to her sister as Frankie, just as I do," Henry said.

"So, pass it off as a joke between you. That you called her brother by your name. They are going to suspect, but then they would next season when you came as Henry's wife. They won't *know* though, will they?"

Frankie looked to Henry. "What do you think?"

"I think that your father is right. If you are coming back with me next season, we may as well handle the speculation now."

"How will we explain Edwin's absence?" Frankie asked.

Henry shrugged. "We'll simply say that your father wanted him to return home, which is true."

"Though I'm under no impression that you are actually going to tell me where your brother is," her father said dryly to her.

There was humor, not anger in his eyes.

Frankie breathed a silent sigh of relief. She'd been waiting for him to start haranguing her for the information. "You are right, I won't, but I appreciate you understanding that."

Her father nodded. "Yes, well, I suppose it is time I acknowledge you and your brother are old enough to make your own decisions."

"If you truly mean that, I'm very happy."

"I do."

"Thank you. I know Edwin will be glad to hear it as well."

"He is probably off somewhere making a movie."

Frankie shrugged noncommittally.

"Perhaps it is time I looked into investment in the film industry. If your brother wants to make moving pictures, we might as well keep it in the family."

Frankie couldn't help it; she threw her arms around her father. "He will be so pleased."

After only a second's hesitation, her father hugged her back, his arms tight around her, like he never wanted to let go.

"I love you, Frances. Both you and your brother."

Frankie's throat was too tight with emotion to answer, but she nodded against his chest.

It was a reconciliation she had never expected, but if her father's new perspective was a genuine one, and he had never lied to her, then maybe she would not have to hold him at such arm's length in the future.

Henry had some things he said he wanted to take care of that afternoon, now that they planned to travel back to Upper Egypt the next day. Doris wanted Frankie to shop with her for things she might need on the Excavation site.

Frankie's younger sister was positively thrilled to be going on another adventure and not have to return to California with their father. Frankie, herself, had a few things to buy since she would be returning to the dig site as herself.

After a whirlwind afternoon of shopping, the two women returned to the hotel in time for dinner with the men.

Joey had spent the day relaxing in his room and reading, so he was the liveliest person at their table.

"What a lark!" he said about Frankie's return to the dig site. "You're a real corker, Frankie."

"She's as strong and bright as her mother ever was." Her father's voice was filled with warm approval.

Something Frankie had heard very little of since becoming an adult and getting married.

Doris gasped, "Oh!"

Only she and Frankie could truly understand what a ringing endorsement that was coming from their father.

"Thank you, Father." Frankie smiled at him.

He cleared his throat, tugging at his collar. "Yes, well. It is only the truth."

Doris jumped out of her chair and rushed around the table to hug their father. "There's hope for you yet."

Frankie stifled laughter at her sister's backhanded compliment.

Her father was looking pleased though, when Doris sat down. "I suppose I'm doing something right if I've gotten hugs from both of my daughters in one day."

And that was important to him, Frankie realized. She'd always thought he didn't really care how she felt about him, but he did.

"Treat us with the same respect you do Chuck and Edwin and you're likely to get a lot more of them," Doris said.

Frankie grinned. "What she said."

Her father's nod had no humor in it. He was making a promise, even if he wasn't saying it out loud.

Later, in her room, Frankie had done her nighttime ablutions and waited for Henry's arrival. She wore a pale pink silky night slip Doris had given her with a knowing smile.

Perhaps her sister was not the babe in the woods Frankie had always assumed.

Certainly, Frankie had never owned anything like this herself before.

When the soft knock sounded on her door, she jumped up and opened it quickly.

Henry stepped inside and she shut the door, locking it firmly behind him.

He stopped when he saw her, his expression going dark and hungry. "I like that."

"I do too."

She went to reach for him, but he stepped back and shoved a sheaf of papers toward her.

"What is that?" she asked.

"Your assurance that I respect your right to make your own choices for your life."

"I don't understand." But Frankie took the papers.

They looked like a legal document. At the top it said, *Enduring Power of Attorney*.

"What is this?" she asked again.

"It is a power of attorney." Henry cleared his throat, his expression as serious as she'd ever seen it. "They give you the power to make any decisions in and for my life that you wish to."

"I don't understand."

"You could have me committed. You could buy a car in my name. You could take all of the money from my accounts."

"You...you're...why would you sign such a thing?"

"So that you know things between us will always be equal. I don't expect you to marry me right away, but someday, if you are ever ready bind our lives legally, you will know that you go into that binding with the same rights and powers over me as I would have over you."

"This is more than that," she said, the hand holding the papers trembling.

"It is my promise to you."

"That you would never have me committed?"

"That I will never make a choice for you, that I will never demand my way, that your voice has as much volume in our life together as mine does."

"That's...that's..." Frankie couldn't get the words out. She was crying and for once she did not feel weakened doing so.

This man was saying he did not see her as the *weaker sex* or *chattel*, or anything less than equal.

The papers dropped from her hands as she surged forward and threw herself into his arms. "I'll marry you."

The kiss those words warranted ended up with them naked and writhing together on the floor.

Afterward, she sat beside him, running her hands appreciatively over his hairy, naked body. "I meant it. I want to marry you."

He sat up and cupped her face. "I love you, Frankie, with everything inside me. I would give up archeology for you."

"Not necessary." She swallowed back emotion. "I know you love me and I know it's real, not some shallow emotion pretending to be love." His love was not conditional on her being anything other than who and what she truly was. "You would never have had those papers drawn up and signed them otherwise."

He nodded, acknowledging the level of trust signing those papers had taken. "My grandfather is going to adore you. He enjoys women unafraid to show their intelligence. My mother is one of his favorite people."

"What will she think of me, do you think?" Frankie asked, settling into his arms as they leaned against the bed.

She'd never felt the *freedom* she did in this moment, to simply be herself completely with another person. Naked in every way.

"As long as you love me, she will think you are the *cat's pajamas*." Henry's expression turned serious. "You do love me?" he asked bluntly.

"How can you doubt it? I have to love you more than I fear giving up my freedom to want to marry you. And I do want to. Even without that *Power of Attorney* thing, I was coming to the conclusion that marriage to you would be nothing like marriage to John was, that it was something I could want."

"I'm glad. When your father showed up, I was so damn angry. I thought you were coming around to seeing me as someone you could trust, but if you'd been forced into marriage? You never would have trusted me."

"No one was going to force me into anything." Of that Frankie was certain. She would have argued, put her foot down and refused. If her father had gotten too draconian, she would have run.

"You would have run," he said. "I would have followed you."

She laughed, the sound free and full of all the joy she was feeling.

"That's why you said if I got pregnant, it would be an unmitigated disaster. You didn't want me to agree to marry you because I had no other option."

"You will always have choices. You are too resourceful not to, but yes. I was terrified of the idea that you would feel pressured to agree to something you would always resent."

"You? Terrified?" she scoffed. "The man who stared down a venomous asp?"

"I did not stare that snake down. I took it by surprise and that is the only reason my uncle's plans didn't come to fruition."

"Imagine it falling asleep like that."

"The snake might have been drugged to keep it in the tent. Perhaps they misjudged how much depressant to give it."

Frankie nodded and shivered. "I do not like snakes."

"I do not like them either."

"But you aren't terrified of them like I am."

His shrug shifted his body against hers, a delicious reminder of their skin against skin circumstances. "So? You are not a snake charmer, but an archeologist."

"You think I really could be one?" she asked, visions of years of adventures digging during the season.

"You already are."

"I really do love you, Henry."

"Because I believe you are an archeologist?"

"Because you believe I can be anything I want to be."

"I do."

And she knew that, to the very core of her being. "I believe in you too."

"We are perfectly matched then."

"For a lifetime."

"For a lifetime, and if the Pharoah's were right, our souls will join even after death."

She thought the Pharaohs probably were.

A Note from Lucy

Dear Reader,

I've been fascinated by the ancient history of Egypt for over a decade and for me that meant researching the history of archeology in Egypt as well. That history is rich with human drama and wit.

While Harold Carter and Lord Carnarvon's discovery of the Tomb of King Tut is what most people think of when the subject of early twentieth century archeology in Egypt comes up, there were so many working in the field at that time and making fascinating discoveries.

While I was researching for this story specifically, I came across two stories that impacted me deeply. The first was Jane Dieulafoy (1851 - 1916), an archeologist who dressed as a man to fight in the Franco-Prussian War with her husband, and later continued the masquerade when needed so they could excavate together in more dangerous, or socially limiting parts of the world.

The second was a biography of the life of Katharine Woolley (née Menke; June 1888 – 8 November 1945). Although she was a widow in her 30s when she joined Sir Charles Leonard Woolley's excavation in Ur, gossip about a single woman living with so many men reached the excavation's sponsors and she was forced to marry Sir Woolley, or leave the excavation.

During a time when women were enjoying more freedoms than ever before, and indeed when the British Museum instructed them to be paid and treated equally with men of the same education and experience, she still had to be married to continue archeology in the field.

The other major inspiration for my story came from my own ancestry research. When I came across not one, but three direct or adjacent female ancestors who had been incarcerated in sanitoriums by their husbands during the 1920s, it really struck a chord. The 1920s are a century behind us and yet we are facing so many of the same societal issues and human experience as the Roaring 20s did.

And Frankie's story was born. She's not a flapper (not all 1920s women were), but she *is* independent and determined to stay that way after what she considers a disastrous first marriage.

It was inevitable that Frankie and Henry's story would evolve from such rich inspiration. Frankie has faced some of the harshest realities of the life of a woman in the 20s. Henry's own family experienced tragedy born of the norms from the time in which they lived. Yet both are intrepid, unwilling to be oppressed or suppress their dreams, whatever the cost of pursuing them.

I hope the journey you take with them is the *cat's pajamas* for you, like it was for me.

Hugs and happy reading,
Lucy

About the Author

With more than 8 million copies of her books in print worldwide, award winning and *USA Today* and international bestseller Lucy Monroe has published over 80 books and had her stories translated for sale all over the world. While she writes multiple subgenres of romance, all of her books are passionate, deeply emotional and adhere to the concept that love wins. A true devotee of romance, she adores sharing her love for the genre with her readers.

Sign up for her newsletter: https://www.lucymonroe.com/newsletter/

Lucy's website: https://lucymonroe.com

Follow Lucy Monroe on social media:

Facebook: LucyMonroe.Romance

Instagram: lucymonroeromance

Pinterest: lucymonroebooks

goodreads: Lucy Monroe

YouTube: @LucyMonroeBooks

TikTok: lucymonroeauthor

More Books by Lucy Monroe

Historical Romance

ANNABELLE'S COURTSHIP

The Langley Family Trilogy
TOUCH ME
TEMPT ME
TAKE ME

MASQUERADE IN EGYPT

Single Title Contemporary Romance
CHANGE THE GAME
WIN THE GAME
THE REAL DEAL
WILD HEAT
HOT ALASKA NIGHTS

Syndicate Rules
URGENT VOWS (Jul 2023)
DEMANDING MOB BOSS (Sep 2023)
RUTHLESS ENFORCER (Nov 2023)

Mercenaries & Spies
READY
WILLING
AND ABLE
SATISFACTION GUARANTEED
DEAL WITH THIS
THE SPY WHO WANTS ME
WATCH OVER ME

CLOSE QUARTERS
HEAT SEEKER

Anthologies & Novellas
SILVER BELLA
RAND (3 Brides for 3 Bad Boys Trilogy)
COLTON (3 Brides for 3 Bad Boys Trilogy)
CARTER (3 Brides for 3 Bad Boys Trilogy)
DELICIOUS: Moon Magnetism
by Lori Foster, et. al.
HE'S THE ONE: Seducing Tabby
by Linda Lael Miller, et. al.
THE POWER OF LOVE: No Angel
by Lori Foster, et. al.
BODYGUARDS IN BED:
Whose Been Sleeping in my Brother's Bed?
by Lucy Monroe et. al.

Classic Romance
THE GREEK TYCOONS ULTIMATUM
THE ITALIAN'S SUITABLE WIFE
THE BILLIONAIRE'S PREGNANT MISTRESS
THE SHEIKH'S BARTERED BRIDE
THE GREEK'S INNOCENT VIRGIN
BLACKMAILED INTO MARRIAGE
THE GREEK'S CHRISTMAS BABY
WEDDING VOW OF REVENGE
THE PRINCE'S VIRGIN WIFE
HIS ROYAL LOVE-CHILD
THE SCORSOLINI MARRIAGE BARGAIN
THE PLAYBOY'S SEDUCTION
PREGNANCY OF PASSION
THE SICILIAN'S MARRIAGE ARRANGEMENT
BOUGHT: THE GREEK'S BRIDE
TAKEN: THE SPANIARD'S VIRGIN
HOT DESERT NIGHTS
THE RANCHER'S RULES
FORBIDDEN: THE BILLIONAIRE'S VIRGIN PRINCESS
HOUSEKEEPER TO THE MILLIONAIRE
HIRED: THE SHEIKH'S SECRETARY MISTRESS
VALENTINO'S LOVE-CHILD
THE LATIN LOVER 2-IN-1 HARLEQUIN PRESENTS

(WITH THE GREEK TYCOON'S INHERITED BRIDE)
THE SHY BRIDE
THE GREEK'S PREGNANT LOVER
FOR DUTY'S SAKE
HEART OF A DESERT WARRIOR
NOT JUST THE GREEK'S WIFE
SCORSOLINI BABY SCANDAL
ONE NIGHT HEIR
PRINCE OF SECRETS
MILLION DOLLAR CHRISTMAS PROPOSAL
SHEIKH'S SCANDAL
AN HEIRESS FOR HIS EMPIRE
A VIRGIN FOR HIS PRIZE
2017 CHRISTMAS CODA: The Greek Tycoons
KOSTA'S CONVENIENT BRIDE
THE SPANIARD'S PLEASURABLE VENGEANCE
THE MAHARAJAH'S BILLIONAIRE HEIR
AFTER THE BILLIONAIRE'S WEDDING VOWS
QUEEN BY ROYAL APPOINTMENT
HIS MAJESTY'S HIDDEN HEIR
THE COST OF THEIR ROYAL FLING
BLACKMAILED BY THE BILLIONAIRE
HER OFF LIMITS PRINCE
CINDERELLA'S JILTED BILLIONAIRE
HER GREEK BILLIONAIRE (Aug 2023)

Historical Paranormal Romance
Children of the Moon Novels
MOON AWAKENING
MOON CRAVING
MOON BURNING
DRAGON'S MOON
ENTHRALLED anthology: Ecstasy Under the Moon
WARRIOR'S MOON
VIKING'S MOON
DESERT MOON
HIGHLANDER'S MOON (Sep 2022)

Contemporary Paranormal Romance
Montana Wolves
COME MOONRISE
MONTANA MOON

CPSIA information can be obtained
at www.ICGtesting.com
Printed in the USA
LVHW052344280623
751055LV00002B/108